The Tapestry of Love

ALSO BY ROSY THORNTON
FROM CLIPPER LARGE PRINT

More Than Love Letters
Hearts and Minds
Crossed Wires

The Tapestry of Love

Rosy Thornton

W F HOWES LTD

This large print edition published in 2010 by
W F Howes Ltd
Unit 4, Rearsby Business Park, Gaddesby Lane,
Rearsby, Leicester LE7 4YH

1 3 5 7 9 10 8 6 4 2

First published in the United Kingdom in 2010
by Headline Review

A CIP catalogue record for this book is available
from the British Library

ISBN 978 1 40746 128 1

Typeset by Palimpsest Book Production Limited,
Falkirk, Stirlingshire
Printed and bound in Great Britain
by MPG Books Ltd, Bodmin, Cornwall

FSC
Mixed Sources
Product group from well-managed
forests, controlled sources and
recycled wood or fiber
SA-COC-1565
www.fsc.org
© 1996 Forest Stewardship Council

For Mum and Dad, who have also gone native.

'It was perhaps the wildest view of all my journey. Peak upon peak, chain upon chain of hills ran surging southward, channelled and sculptured by the winter streams, feathered from head to foot with chestnuts . . .'

Robert Louis Stevenson, *Travels with a Donkey in the Cévennes*

PART I

CHAPTER 1

THE AUTUMN TRANSHUMANCE

Never in her life had Catherine Parkstone imagined so many sheep.

Applying the handbrake, she sat back and watched the passing tide. They were streaming down the hillside to the right, above the road, a bobbing phalanx maybe twenty or thirty animals wide, before slowing and spreading wider as they reached the brief plateau of tarmac, the way water pools below a flight of rapids. A few stragglers circled off on to the grass verges and began to graze. But the central current continued its course and began to pick up momentum again as it narrowed to siphon through a gateway gap in the drystone wall on the left.

Aground in the centre of the flood, Catherine's car split the sheep the way rocks split flowing river water. For a dizzying moment she entertained the illusion that the car might dislodge and be swept downstream with the sheep.

Caffeine, she thought, and closed her eyes. She had had none since the last of the coffee from her thermos when she'd stopped to picnic at an *aire* near Montluçon. What she did have, wedged in the glove compartment, was a chocolate bar from the terminal at Le Shuttle. Dairy Milk: family size. Catherine smiled at the name. When Tom was at home, he and his family-size friends would descend on the kitchen cupboard and bear off a bar this big, exulting like seagulls over a crust. Lexie was different; she would peck at it guiltily when nobody was looking, just one square gone at a time, chipped from a corner and the foil tucked back.

Catherine opened the car window. The first thing to assail her was the scent: unexpectedly sharp and clean, somehow, the heated tang of herbs and lanolin and manure. Then the sound struck her. The register was high, a sort of hectoring monotone – a bit like Prime Minister's questions in the House of Commons. The thought almost made her laugh out loud.

Would she be able to get Radio Four at La Grelaudière? she wondered. *Yesterday in Parliament.* Reception had been difficult up here when they were kids. Her mother would twiddle at the knobs on the old Phillips portable they brought with them; she'd think she had it but then it would waver to a whistle and be driven out by French voices or the sound of marching bands. But these days it would be different, wouldn't it? Things were digital now.

Still immobilised in the flow of animals, Catherine cut the engine. She glanced at her watch – the habit of an organised lifetime – before reminding herself that there was no longer any reason to hurry. The removal van wouldn't be there until tomorrow morning at the earliest, and more likely the afternoon. She had all the essentials here with her in the car – including her old sleeping bag and the carpet bag with her tapestry silks – and no one to please but herself. The back seat was folded down and most of the space behind her was filled with tomato plants. It was foolishness, really. The Grobags were already splitting as she'd lifted them in and would have been spilling compost all the way, and goodness knows what a bashing the tender vines had taken on those first wide sweeping hairpins up from Alès. But it was not yet the end of September and when the time had come she found she couldn't bear to leave them there on the patio, still laden with fruit.

A figure appeared up to the right, moving with the stream. She watched his approach. As he drew nearer she saw that he was in fact a she, not much older than herself, maybe fifty or fifty-five. Abruptly, the woman stopped by the side of the road and spun round to face the current. Like Canute, thought Catherine, fancifully – though Moses would be closer to the mark. The herd parted: those that had passed the shepherd continued impassively on their way, while those before her halted raggedly and raised their heads to stare, until the closest few set the pattern for the rest by losing interest and starting to graze. Catherine fired the ignition and put the car in gear, smiling her thanks at the woman. She received no answering smile, only a short nod of acknowledgement. Just as she was pulling away, though, she heard the woman call out to her: two short, gruff syllables which she either didn't catch or couldn't understand, perhaps a cévenol dialect word – or maybe the woman was only calling to her sheep.

As Catherine drove on, a new turn of the hill swung into view, and above her she saw further tributary streams of white moving down the mountain to join the confluence. It was strange, she had always defined the Cévennes by its emptiness – the space, the desolate beauty – so there was something disorientating about this teeming of life, the hillside as busy as the slope of an anthill. Yet if anything is out of place here, she told herself, it's me and not the sheep.

It wasn't that Catherine was ignorant of what she was witnessing. She had read about the transhumance: the twice-yearly movement of livestock which was once common throughout all the mountain regions of France. She'd seen it depicted on postcards, outside village grocery stores and *bartabacs*, displayed along with scenes of tumbledown sheep sheds, mountain waterfalls and old men in clogs. The spring transhumance saw flocks driven on foot from their winter pastures in the valleys up to their summer home on the high grasslands above the tree line; the autumn transhumance saw the reversal of the process.

It was hot now in the late summer sunshine at

the end of the afternoon. The metal of the car door seared her skin if she shifted her elbow where she rested it out of the window as she drove. But the return of the flocks to the valley heralded the coming of winter. It was impossible to avoid the observation that she was travelling the other way, leaving behind the comfort and security of home and heading up the mountain; maybe she should take it as an omen. But Catherine was not a woman to believe in any such nonsense. She pulled in her arm, wound up the window and focused on the road ahead.

CHAPTER 2

THE HAYLOFTS

She woke to the noise of traffic. For a moment, in the fuddlement of ebbing sleep, all was perfectly in place: it was the sound to which she had awakened on thousands of other mornings, the sound of the village high street in Long Hartslow, Buckinghamshire. But when she tried to shift her legs to find a cooler patch of duvet she found movement impeded, and became aware of an aching hardness in her hip. The darkness, too, was more complete than it ought to have been. That's when it came back to her – the memory of pulling closed the heavy wooden shutters the night before. She was in her sleeping bag; she was on the floor; she was at Les Fenils.

All of which meant that there absolutely should not be any traffic noise outside the window. Catherine wriggled out of her nylon cocoon, and felt her way across the bare boards to the bedroom window. It took her a moment to find the unfamiliar catch, and another to work out how to release it; then she pushed back one shutter and let in the day. The sun had yet to climb its way above the crest of mountain over the house to the

8

east, and the light was thin and pearly grey; by its pallid gleam Catherine could make out the hands of her watch showing a quarter to seven. Her eyes readjusted blurrily to the outside world. A hundred yards away, across the narrow gorge, lay a sheer wedge of grey-black, chrystalline rock and a tumble of vertiginously clinging trees.

Where was the noise coming from? She let her gaze drop to the small, stony terrace below, which served as driveway and yard of Les Fenils. Almost directly beneath her, close to the wall, idled a tiny tractor, half hidden and completely dwarfed by an overladen trailer. Its owner was standing on the stone step of her front door. The chain bell pull was connected to nothing and if he had knocked she hadn't heard him.

'Hello,' she called – in English – then, '*Allo.*' What was wrong with her? They only ever said that on the telephone. In her best French, she resumed, 'Hold on, sorry, I'm just coming down.'

Stopping only to pluck her fleece from the floor, she hurried to the door, and then down the stairs at a trot; they were wooden and rustically proportioned, too serious to be attempted two at a time on a first acquaintance. She had locked the door when she went to bed, and now she cursed herself for her dithering as she struggled with the key.

'I'm coming,' she called again through three inches of oak.

The key lodged in place with a clunk; it turned, and she pushed wide the door.

'Good day, Madame,' said the man on the step. A drooping grey moustache concealed all evidence of amusement or disdain. He held out a hand, which she duly shook. 'Bouschet.' If she were in any doubt that this word was his surname, he dispelled it by adding with quaint courtesy, 'At your service.'

'Good day, Monsieur,' said Catherine. 'Parkstone – Catherine Parkstone.' It seemed polite to fall in with his formality, but she offered her Christian name on top as a gesture of friendship. 'I've just moved in.'

He nodded gravely.

'I got here last night. The lorry will come later, I hope. Furniture, you know . . .' She waved a vague hand behind her towards the interior of the house.

'Of course.' Another solemn inclination of the head.

There followed a short silence, after which Monsieur Bouschet coughed. 'I've brought up your hay.'

'My . . . ?'

Foin, she repeated to herself, thoughts skating in all directions. It did mean hay, didn't it? His glance slid across to the trailer, which, she now properly noticed, was piled with a toppling mass of yellowing vegetation.

It was difficult to know exactly what to say.

'I cut it in June, and then again at the start of September.' Monsieur Bouschet was talking slowly, and she couldn't be sure if this was his habitual manner of delivery or if it was intended for her benefit. 'This is the first load. I can bring the rest up later.'

Catherine collected her tattered wits. 'Thank you,' she said. 'Thank you so much, Monsieur. It's extremely kind of you.'

It had been dark by the time she arrived last night and she had paid very little heed to the outside of the property. Old Madame Sauzet, her predecessor as châtelaine of Les Fenils, had passed away in the New Year, according to the seven grandchildren who had assembled in the solicitor's office in St Julien to sign the deeds of conveyance; the grassy terraces below the house should have been several feet high in weeds by now. That the neighbourly farmer should have taken it upon himself to keep the small piece of ground tidy touched Catherine profoundly.

'Really, it's very good of you to have taken the trouble. Perhaps I could make you a cup of coffee?' She had only one mug but would drink hers out of her cereal bowl if she had to.

The moustache gave a twitch. Was he smiling underneath it? His eyes, certainly, held a soft gleam.

'Where would you like me to put your hay, Madame?'

Ah, yes. Her hay. She cast her eyes round the yard as if seeking inspiration.

'You cannot lack for a place, surely. Not at this house.'

11

She looked at him helplessly for a moment, before she remembered. *Les Fenils* – the haylofts. It was an excuse to laugh, and although he didn't join her she could see that he was pleased, and her embarrassment ebbed a little.

'Well, where did Madame Sauzet keep her hay?' she asked, surprising herself with her cunning.

His satisfaction swelled. 'In the old cattle byre,' he answered at once, indicating the entrance to the first of the three outhouses which tagged on to the western end of Catherine's new home.

'Good, then. We can put it in there.'

Already he had turned and was back at his tractor. Retreating into the hallway, she found her boots where she had discarded them last night and pulled them on, hopping as she did so, and wondering whether it would be ruder to leave him to his task alone or to join him still clad as she was in Tom's old checked pyjamas beneath her fleece. She had asked and asked her son to clear out the remains of his belongings from his old room; at the last minute she had pilfered a few sentimental oddments for herself and bagged up the rest for Oxfam or the tip. The pyjamas were good – really, perfectly decent – and her eagerness to show her gratitude won out over social convention.

By the time she was back out in the yard, boots laced, he had backed the trailer up to the arched double doors of the cattle byre and let down the tailgate. He had brought his own pitchfork but there were two others, wreathed in cobwebs, leaning up against the wall in a corner. Catherine selected the less heavy-looking of the pair and set to work beside him. It wasn't difficult to load the fork with hay and then deposit it on the growing heap on the rough-flagged floor. She soon worked up a rhythm and with it a sweat. If it hadn't been for Tom's pyjamas she would have taken off her fleece. Monsieur Bouschet kept his jacket on; he didn't even look warm. The load on the trailer was reduced by little more than half when her arms began to tire; pride, however, forbade her to pause in her work while a man who must be twenty years her senior never missed a measure. By the time her fork was striking the wooden floor of the trailer at each thrust, a small angry knot had formed between her lumbar vertebrae and her throat was clogged and dry. She was very glad when Monsieur Bouschet extended a hand to help her up on to the trailer to scrape together the last of the stalks, which he tossed on top of her neat, new hayrick.

She jumped down without assistance, straightened her spine carefully and offered him another smile.

'Coffee, now?'

Unspeaking, he followed her out into the yard and then in through the house door. She kicked off her boots in the hallway but he kept his on as she led the way into the large farmhouse kitchen which formed the main downstairs room of Les Fenils.

'There's nowhere to sit, I'm afraid,' she said.

He nodded. 'The furniture lorry.'

'Yes.' His habit of few words was easy to slide into; smiles were simpler, anyway.

She filled her kettle at the low ceramic sink and plugged it in, using one of the two-pin converters she had brought with her. She pushed in the button – and no light came on. Nonplussed, she tried jiggling the pins in the socket, but there was no response. Strange, because it had worked all right last night. Her guest, who had not moved more than a step inside the door, reached over and threw the light switch. Nothing.

'Oh, no.' Catherine turned to him with an apologetic shrug, which she hoped he didn't take as a Gallic caricature; she just found she used her body and hands more in French. 'It must have blown the circuit.' The solicitor, Maître Dujol, had said something about not overloading the circuits with all her foreign appliances. Now, where on earth were the trip switches?

But Monsieur Bouschet was shaking his head. 'Power cut,' was his pronouncement. 'We get them a lot at this time of year. It's the thunderstorms.'

Catherine's eyes were drawn unbidden to the window, beyond which, in the triangle above the cliff edge opposite, the sky showed serenely blue.

'Thunderstorms?'

14

Now it was his turn to shrug. 'Not just here, perhaps. But somewhere.' He drew up his arms and folded them decisively. 'It will be October next week.'

'Right,' said Catherine. 'Yes.'

She had only her English electric kettle, no more traditional version she might boil on the hob – and besides, the Calor gas had run out halfway through cooking last night's omelette.

'Look, I'm afraid . . .' What a shame she hadn't any bottled beer among her supplies. Except that would hardly have done either, would it, at just past 8 a.m.? 'Can I offer you a glass of water?' she finished lamely, and he stepped forward to take the proffered mug with every show of grateful good manners.

There seemed nothing more to be done, then, than to thank her neighbour once more for his kindness in cutting her grass, and to take the empty mug which he handed back to her. Another nod, and he was gone, leaving her alone in her empty kitchen, with no coffee and no means of heating the water for a shower.

At least her hay was in and stacked. Pity she hadn't been able to tell Monsieur Bouschet that she had no earthly use for the stuff.

An hour later, washed in cold water and dressed in jeans and jumper, Catherine was sitting in the sunshine on the stone front doorstep eating bread and strawberry jam. The door behind her was the more imposing of two doors that opened on to the terrace courtyard at the front of Les Fenils. They stood at right angles to each other, one leading into each arm of the long, low, L-shaped house. There was no back door, because the north wall of the house – the back of the longer of the two arms – was solid and windowless, built to fit snugly against the wall of grey-black cévenol granite which rose steeply above it, house and gorge chiselled from the same rock. The east wall, to the rear of the shorter arm, was also solid, and painted to four feet above the ground in tarry black pitch. That's where you'll have to look out for water getting in, the surveyor had said.

From where she sat on the step, Catherine saw the tops of the small orchard which sloped away below the house in front of her and to the right; built in terraced steps, it was shored up on dry-stone walls and held together by the roots of apple, greengage and Mirabelle, as well as the tenacious old turfs which Monsieur Bouschet had mown for her. Further up into the crease of the hill to her left, beyond the short south wing of the house, stood a cluster of sweet chestnut trees, traditional providers of flour for mountain bread, and at their feet a row of empty beehives. That was the limit of her land, and from her lowly vantage point she could see no further in any direction – except for straight ahead of her, south across the little valley to the ridge of wooded hillside opposite.

This, she knew, was only a narrow side gully, a

pleat in the skirts of the greater mountain range leading up to the peak of Mont Lozère. The main length of Les Fenils faced south across the gorge, but the shorter southern arm faced west down the valley, and away to distant hills. If she had taken her breakfast upstairs and looked from the window of the little side bedroom she could have seen it now, that breathtaking view which had sold her the property back in June. On a morning like this one, she was sure, it would appear much as it had done then: the unimaginable space and distance of it, layer upon layer of blue mountain silhouettes, fading into bluer skies. For the moment, however, she was content to sit on the sun-warmed stone of her own step and learn the face of her own small valley.

The silence was deep and cocooning. It made her jump, therefore, when the jaunty double toot of a car horn multiplied off the rocks in the gorge as it rose to meet her. It was impossible to tell how far away the vehicle was, or even if it was in her own valley at all. She sat still and waited. Just as she was dismissing the possibility of its approach, the car's horn sounded again and this time behind its echo she could make out distinctly the whine of an engine in a low gear. Catherine stood and walked to the edge of the terrace. From there it was possible to see, half hidden in the woods below, the final twist taken by the road before it turned towards the hamlet of La Grelaudière; she was in time to catch a flash of sunlight on bonnet or windscreen through the canopy of trees. Then silence again; it was disconcerting how completely the folds of the mountain could blot out sound. And then quite suddenly the engine was loud and close at hand, and with a final tootle-toot the vehicle appeared, bouncing into her courtyard. A small yellow van: it was the postman.

She stepped forward, smiling, as the uniformed driver swung open the van door and laid one polished boot on the gravel.

'Madame,' he said, placing in her hands a postcard and a long, brown envelope.

As she reached out and took them, he caught and held her eye. 'Engleesh.' The word not quite a question.

Mutely, she nodded.

'Have a nice day,' said the postman in flawless hamburger-joint American and swung his leg back inside the van. He was already backing up as he pulled the door to; then he revved the engine and sent pebbles scattering as he roared away in first gear, saluting her with his horn from the first tight turn where her terrace dropped down to become the road.

Catherine sat back down on the step with her mail. She turned first to the official-looking envelope and tore it open. It contained a single folded sheet of A4, bearing the crest of the Direction Départemental des Affaires Sanitaires et Sociales and dispatched from its administrative offices at

Mende. What could the local sanitary authorities want with her? she wondered. The answer, it appeared, was her water supply. She was enjoined in the most emphatic of terms not to drink any of it until she had sent a sample for analysis. To drink it, she was informed, could constitute a serious danger to health. The contact details of several private laboratories were supplied, where at a cost of around 120 euros she could assure herself that her water source contained no more than safe levels of nitrates, lead, mercury, cadmium, atrazine and several other, unfamiliar words, one of which she had a strong hunch meant radioactivity.

It had been another selling point for Catherine: the water for her taps sprang straight from the hillside a few metres above the roof of Les Fenils. Her very own spring water – the joy of having for free what others paid to carry home in super-market bottles. It was so clean up here. There couldn't, surely, be a farmer sending poisons leeching into the soil at this altitude; above her there was nothing but forestry and sheep. She stared with incredulity at the granite of her wall. Could it really be harbouring dangerous concentrations of heavy metals? It had to be nonsense, a piece of French bureaucratic of-ficiousness, some standard formality for any new householder not on the mains. It had nothing to do with her mountain and her rock. But the morning was taking on a certain ironic complexion, nevertheless. No electricity, and now no drinking water, either.

The postcard was from Walton-on-the-Naze. The picture dealt her a guilty lurch: Walton was an awfully long way away from here. It couldn't be from her mother, of course; it was over a year since Mum had been able to hold a pen, even if she'd had any words to write. Catherine turned the card over, and smiled. Her daughter, Lexie. So sweet of her – and indicative of uncharacteristic forethought. She must have posted it a week ago for it to arrive on time.

> Hi, Mum. I know you said there was a wait for a landline – and I'd text you but I know there'll be no reception up there in the wilds. Hope you're alive. Get yourself to civilisation, call me and tell all.

It wasn't only the postcard that decided her. There were chores to be done and as most of the day was hers, she might as well go down to St Julien.

She had left her tomato plants in the car overnight, so now she unloaded them carefully and lined them up beside the wall where Monsieur Bouschet's tractor had stood. In their stead, she hauled from the kitchen the two empty Calor containers. She locked the front door and pushed the outsize key into the pocket of her jeans, where it lay across her hip like a sword.

There were two hairpins, one swinging each way,

before the road brought her down to the rest of La Grelaudière. It was scarcely a hamlet, consisting, besides her own house, of no more than a straggle of four inhabited dwellings and a few animal sheds. The farm closest to hers must be *chez* Bouschet; the tractor and empty trailer were out in the yard. All four chimneys wore plumes of woodsmoke, sending its resinous aroma through her open window as she drove past. The scent stung Catherine's lungs with jealousy. There was a woodburner in her kitchen but it was not connected to a boiler, nor to a range for cooking, so until the weather turned colder the chimney of Les Fenils would remain empty of breath.

As Catherine's small car regotiated a series of tight zigzags, she worried about how the removal van would fare. Maybe they would unload every-thing here at the roadside and she'd have to take it up piece by piece in the car – or if it wouldn't fit, then in Monsieur Bouschet's trailer. The notion had a curious appeal.

The long sequence of hairpins gave her no time to take in the view, so that when she reached the next straight, sloping stretch it was a shock to see how much closer the valley floor had come: the sensation was very much like emerging from cloud on descent to an airport. The church belfry of St Julien, which had been a glimpse of distant triangle among the trees, now appeared not far below her; she felt she could have leaned over and tossed pebbles on the little church and its surrounding patchwork of rooftops. The proximity was deceptive, however; a turn led the road away again and it was fully ten minutes later before she finally entered the village.

The little square with its stone market cross was busier than it had been when she came through last night but she had no trouble finding a spot to park. She switched off her engine right opposite the ironmongers, with its Calor sign out front. Taking her mobile phone from the glove compartment where the chocolate bar from yesterday still lay, she pressed Lexie's number, and slit back the foil and broke off a corner.

'Hello, Mum.' Her daughter's voice answered almost at once, sounding so near that Catherine's smile broke like a wave.

'Hello, love,' she said, the words smudged in Dairy Milk.

'Listen, Mum, I'm really glad you rang. Something's just come up. Might be the sniff of a new job.'

'Oh, yes?' Catherine tried to inject in her voice a hopefulness to match her daughter's.

'Yes. Some contact of Ella's, a friend of a friend, says there's something going on another magazine. Actually not trade press, for once. It's one of these hobbyist publications, and apparently they have a circulation to kill for. They're carried in Smith's and everything.'

'Well, that does sound promising.'

Since dropping out of her English degree after

one year to go to journalism college, Lexie had been in pursuit of a dream. Not for her the world of the newspaper hack, covering flower festivals, cats up trees and two-car pile-ups on the local bypass. Magazines, she was adamant, were the way to go. One day – she remained convinced despite her mother's gentle nudges towards realism – she would be writing a witty 800-word opinion piece for the *Observer* colour supplement at her kitchen table every Monday morning and taking the next six and a half days off. The journey towards that goal had become stalled somewhat during the last eighteen months, which Lexie had spent as a junior in features at *Air Cargo Monthly*.

'They're paying a bit less than what I'm on now, but there's flexitime and a car allowance. And this person of Ella's says everyone there is really friendly. Lots of women, apparently, which would make a change.'

The average age of the staff at her present workplace, at least as presented by Lexie, was somewhere approaching sixty – and practically all of them men.

'So, what's the title? Will I have heard of it?'

A short, quick laugh, unaltered since her daughter was nine or ten, made Catherine's heart contract.

'Doubt it, Mum. Not your thing – nothing to do with needlework or gardening. It's called *Fondant Magazine*. Apparently, it's essential fortnightly reading for frosters and cake decorators everywhere. Everything you ever wanted to know about sugarcraft in one accessible publication.'

She could tell that Lexie was giggling, which made it all right to join in.

'Lots of pictures of cakes?'

'Oh, cakes are just the start of it. You'd be amazed what people will make out of icing sugar and glycerine.'

Catherine's eye drifted round the old, stone square. Sugarcraft magazines seemed a world away from the life of St Julien de Valvert.

'Would the job be in features again?'

'Worse luck, yes. Bottom of the heap, pretty much. But it's a smaller staff than at *Air Cargo*, so there might be a chance of doing my own subbing now and again.'

'Well, I really hope they want you for it.' It seemed strange to Catherine that knowledge of cake decorating should not be a qualification for the post – Lexie had never been known to cook anything fancier than a poached egg. But that was apparently how it worked; eighteen months ago she'd known nothing about international air freight, either.

'Thanks, Mum. Honestly, I feel so badly in need of a change of scene. I'm not kidding, if I have to go out and do another crappy story about some new refrigerated container, or big up some piddling little airline that's expanded its capacity by half a per cent, I swear my head will explode. I'll rip all my clothes off and run round Gatwick Airport naked and screaming. At least icing is real. I'd be writing stuff that's going to be read by real people, who might actually care. As in, at least get some pleasure out of it.'

Catherine was grinning but pressed her voice into serious sympathy. 'I can imagine . . . By the way, thank you for the postcard. It arrived this morning to greet me – perfectly timed. It was a really nice thought.'

'Oh, that.' She could picture Lexie's negligent hand gesture.

'Did you go and see Gram at the weekend, then?'

'No. Not for a few weeks, actually.' Lexie sounded apologetic, puzzled. Then she said, 'Oh, the postcard – of Walton, yes. I bought a whole bunch last time I was there.'

'Maybe Aunty Bryony will go. She said she was planning to visit last time we spoke.' Catherine's sister was always full of good intentions, until work spiralled up to fill the weekend yet again.

'I'll go next week. Or it might have to be the week after.'

Lexie was good, and went pretty regularly, perhaps once a month. Tom would have gone too, if he could, but his post-doc was in St Andrew's, which might as well have been the Cévennes. It was Catherine who had driven over to the nursing home once a fortnight on a Sunday morning, without fail, for more than three years. It couldn't help but leave a gap.

'Look, Mum, don't beat yourself up.' Lexie

could be alarmingly perceptive sometimes. 'Half the time Gram doesn't even know it's us when we go, does she? She has no idea if you've been or not. I mean, she can't remember whether she hasn't seen you for six months or you've just come back from the loo.'

But Catherine hated the idea that inside her confusion her mother might still be lonely.

'You've only got one life,' her daughter was saying. 'This is what you want to do, so you need to do it.'

And of course she was right. What was the use of putting her life on hold? Waiting two years – or five years or ten years – for Mum to die? If she wanted Les Fenils, it had to be now, while she was still young.

'Now,' said Lexie, 'before you're too old.'

On the pavement outside the car window, two women had stopped to talk; one of them held, dangling from her fingers by their legs, a pair of white chickens. As Catherine watched, one of the birds flapped a half-hearted wing.

'But hey, Mum, you still haven't told me how you're getting on. Is it totally wild and idyllic and wonderful?'

'It's fine. I'm starting to sort myself out.'

'You don't sound too ecstatic,' said Lexie blithely. 'I bet the drains smell, don't they? And you can't get proper Cheddar cheese. And what of the indigenous population? What are they like? Not too bellicose, I hope.'

'Actually, I've met one neighbour already. He was perfectly charming and—'

'I know what the trouble is,' her daughter interrupted. 'Completely understandable, you poor thing. All very scenic over there and everything but naturally you're missing me.'

CHAPTER 3

NEXT DOOR

It was on her third morning at La Grelaudière that Catherine went to call on Monsieur Bouschet. To leave it longer might have appeared unneighbourly – and she needed to head off any further consignments of hay.

There was no need to follow the road down to the lower part of the hamlet; a footpath, meandering between rocks and overhanging ferns, offered a route both more direct and more precipitous. The path brought her out at a point on the road only yards from the gateway she took to be Monsieur Bouschet's. *Next door*: she savoured the incongruity of the phrase. Stone posts which could have done service as megaliths stood sentinel at either side of the farmyard entrance, but no name was displayed, any more than there was at Les Fenils. An unnecessary measure, no doubt, in these parts.

The property was built to the same L-shaped plan as her own and offered a variety of doors. She chose the most likely looking and knocked. There were no vehicles visible in the cobbled yard and she was on the point of leaving when the door was opened by Monsieur Bouschet.

'Ah, good day, Monsieur. I thought I'd come by and thank you again . . .'

When she reached the word 'thank', he puffed out his lips with a soft plosive sound; he motioned gratitude away, and Catherine inside, with a chop of the hand.

The kitchen was ample but low-ceilinged and darker than her own, and it took her eyes a moment to adjust, even though the day outside was far from bright.

'Come in, Madame. Sit down. I'll go and fetch my wife.'

The master of the house effaced himself at once through a door at the far end of the room, leaving Catherine to take a seat at the kitchen table. Over half its length, it was covered with tools, jars, bottles and wooden trays of apples and pears; the other end, where Catherine sat, was clear but for a basket of walnuts, a sheet of newspaper and a white ceramic bowl. Somebody had been cracking open the nuts, scattering the shells on the paper and depositing the kernels in the bowl.

The far door reopened and in bustled Madame Bouschet. She was small and slight, with a sleek bob of hair which was either dyed to that star-tling black or else it was a wig; the impression it gave, combined with Madame Bouschet's diminutive stature and light step, was of a little girl, so that when you looked into her face, the deep lines came almost as a shock. Her movements were quick and birdlike where her husband's were deliberate and slow, but she was certainly of an age with him. Catherine put them both in their early seventies.

Monsieur Bouschet effected the formal introduction. 'My wife, Marie-Josèphe Bouschet. Madame Parkstone.' He pronounced it *Park-e-ston*, lubricating with vowels the difficult, clustered English consonants to soften them into manageability. It was one of the things she had loved, coming here on holiday as a child: the loose, liquid syllables of the south. Here the people embraced their words lovingly; here, they seemed to say, there is time.

Catherine rose to shake hands, and then Madame Bouschet offered her coffee or a *syrop*. The bottle she produced wasn't lemon or orange but the bright vermilion of grenadine; it hardly looked like something three adults would drink.

'Nothing for me, really, thank you,' said Catherine, before remembering her manners and asking meekly for a glass of water.

Madame Bouschet poured three glasses – mineral water, Catherine noted, from a bottle in the fridge – and sat down next to Catherine. Her husband took a chair opposite.

'Your furniture arrived all right, then,' said Madame Bouschet equably. Nobody in La Grelaudière could have missed the passage of the

Pickfords lorry, which had negotiated the sharp final bends only with extreme difficulty, much shouting and waving of arms by the driver's mate and the spinning of wheels in loose gravel at the side of the road.

'Yes, thank you, though it was a bit of a squeeze getting the van up to the house. Everything's in, and I've made a start on the unpacking.'

The French couple both nodded their sympathy and understanding, and Madame Bouschet surprised her by volunteering, 'If you need an extra pair of hands, you have only to ask. I'm thinking of the polishing. I know how filthy china can get when it's been wrapped.'

'That's very kind of you.' Catherine pictured the old crockery she had unfolded from its newspaper the day before; much of it had been hers since she was in digs, the year before she was married. None of it exactly merited the name of china. It occurred to her that she should have brought something to give them, some small gift. Something from England, maybe, like a jar of Oxford marmalade, if she'd had such a thing. Perhaps later in the week she might bring them some of her tomatoes, or a basin of the sweet, golden Mirabelles from the orchard at Les Fenils. Except they must have trees of their own, at the back of the house; maybe she would get a chance to check on her way out.

'Tomatoes,' said Monsieur Bouschet, as if reading her mind. She looked at him inquiringly, and saw that his lower lip was pushed slightly forward beyond the lower reaches of his moustache, and that his eyes were sorrowful. 'It's not obvious.' *C'est pas évident.* There was no translation for it, really. Generally it meant that you couldn't tell, that it wasn't a done deal. But what wasn't obvious about tomatoes?

'He's right,' said his wife, eyeing Catherine kindly. 'Maybe if you had a greenhouse. But without it . . .' An eloquent forward thrust of the lips, the exact mirror of her husband's expression.

'Ah, yes – a greenhouse,' agreed Monsieur Bouschet. Of course, he would have seen the tomato plants in the back of the car the first morning.

'Down in St Julien, perhaps you'd have a chance,' continued Madame. 'But up here? *Pas évident.*'

The descent to St Julien by road might take twenty-five minutes but Madame Bouschet said the name as if it were half a world away.

'You're gardeners?' Catherine asked, thinking of the tomatoes, but then realised how foolish it must sound. 'I mean, of course, you're farmers.'

Her neighbours exchanged a look, which might have held laughter – though not, she sensed, at her.

'Retired,' said Monsieur Bouschet crisply.

'So he says. He's been saying it for five years now, but we still have a few goats, and the chickens and geese, of course, and a pig every spring. So he's out of bed every morning at six doing the feeds, come winter come summer, the same as

32

the forty years previous, and there's hardly a night when I call him into supper but he's got a bit of fence to mend or some other little job wants doing out in the barn. When did we last get away at the weekend to spend some time with the grand-children? How can we, when the chicken coop always just needs fox-proofing or one of the nanny goats is ailing? Retirement, he calls it!'

Catherine grinned. It was by far the longest speech either of the couple had yet made, and she imagined she wasn't the first to have heard it.

'Grandchildren, you say. So you have a family?'

Madame Bouschet stood and went over to a tall oak dresser at one side of the room. She returned with a photograph in a gilt frame.

'Jean-Marc,' she said, pointing to a dark-haired young man of about thirty with his arms round two younger women. 'Claudine. Isabelle. But this must be ten years ago now.'

'And the grandchildren?'

'Five. Four boys and one little girl.'

'Cécile,' added the fond grandfather.

'And you, Madame?'

Catherine wished she had a photo of her own, but she had never been in the habit of carrying one with her. She also wished she weren't still 'Madame' but didn't know quite what to do about it.

'I have two. A daughter, Lexie – Alexia – and a son, Tom. Lexie is twenty-seven and a journalist. Tom is twenty-five; he's a biochemist.'

'Journalist,' repeated Madame Bouschet with some reverence, while her husband murmured, 'Scientist.'

Regretting her small surrender to maternal pride, Catherine plunged on quickly. 'No grandchildren yet, though,' she said, enabling her neighbours to offer their condolences and hopes for better fortune to come.

As they spoke, Monsieur Bouschet had begun picking up walnuts. There was no nutcracker on the table; he simply took them one at a time, laid them in his palm and crushed them with a sharp contraction of the hand. They were 'green' – fresh walnuts – their shells mottled and trailing strands of black beard. She watched his hands in fascination as he worked. His fingers were stained to an inky brown.

'And your son and daughter, they're back in England?' inquired his wife.

'Yes. Or rather, Lexie is. Tom lives in Scotland.'

'It's very far.'

'Yes.' Catherine gave the brave smile expected of her and tried not to think just how far. 'And your family? Where are they?'

'Jean-Marc is in Paris, and the girls are both in town.'

'In town?' Catherine assumed she meant Mende or Alès, or maybe even Montpellier.

Madame Bouschet nodded. 'In St Julien, yes.'

The notion of the village with its single market square and half-dozen shops as being the bright lights of town made Catherine want to laugh; but she merely smiled and said, 'It's lovely for you that they have stayed so close.'

This produced a grunt from Monsieur Bouschet. 'True. Not many youngsters stay.' He cracked another walnut, prising from the halves of shell the buttery yellow kernel. 'Not since the park.'

'Sorry?' Catherine was at a loss.

'The Parc National des Cévennes. What is there for young people to do if they stay? How are they to earn their living? No development, no new housing, no new industry.' His hands kept working, with no change of rhythm but with markedly more emphasis. 'It's either farming, or tourism.'

The last word was spoken with some animosity, but then he seemed to recollect himself; both of them regarded Catherine almost anxiously.

'Oh, I'm not a tourist.' It came out in a rush, her voice sounding higher than she'd intended.

He couldn't really have thought she was a tourist, could he? What would a tourist be wanting with a byre full of hay?

'I'm going to set up a business here.'

Monsieur Bouschet put down his walnut. He and his wife both stared.

'I'm a needlewoman.' It seemed the best place to start, a credential they would understand.

'A dressmaker?' asked Madame Bouschet. Her own floral print housecoat was not homemade; it had the look of the market stall or the mail-order catalogue.

'No. Soft furnishings. I'm hoping to make curtains and cushions, you know. And upholstery, too. I cover chairs and couches.'

Madame nodded, but offered no firmer opinion than, 'I see.'

'I thought I would go round to the farms, and the houses in the village, and see if anybody needs things making. Up here,' she wafted a hand towards the window, 'I thought it might not be so easy to buy cushions and chair covers. Getting to shops – I mean to Alès or a big town – well, *c'est pas évident.*'

From a drawer in the table, Madame Bouschet had drawn a pair of nutcrackers and, as Catherine spoke, began to share her husband's task. She nodded again.

'People never used to have curtains, not when I was a girl. We just closed the shutters at night. Now most women make their own. There's a stall comes once a month to the market in St Julien, every fourth Thursday. Madame Gariépy, from Mende. She sells fabric off the roll.'

Catherine had imagined as much. 'But I could offer more choice. I could drive down to Nîmes or Montpellier every so often and pick up a good range of material, or show people catalogues and fetch particular prints to order. My idea is that people might like a service to their door. I could do everything: measure for curtains, advise about colour schemes.'

Catherine tried not to notice the farmhouse

kitchen in which they sat, its wood and tiles and stone unrelieved by fabric of any kind, apart from faded, blue-and-white checked curtains at the two small windows. She wished she had a nutcracker too, to keep her hands occupied.

'Actually, tapestry is what I enjoy most. My own designs. I like to make chair covers out of tapestry, or cushion covers. I thought people might have ideas about patterns or motifs they wanted, and I could come up with a design to fit their ideas.'

The two walnut shellers had no comment to make about this. But Madame Bouschet's hands paused and she looked up from her work.

'It's slow, a tapestry.'

Catherine smiled. 'Yes. But I'm not short of patience. There are the evenings, you know.'

'Ah, yes.' The Frenchwoman returned her smile. 'The evenings in the mountains in winter. You won't lack for time.'

'The thing is . . .' Catherine wanted Madame Bouschet to understand why she had come here, what it was that drove her. 'The tapestry and the needlework, it's always been just a hobby for me. I had my children young, and have only ever been a wife and mother – apart from a part-time job in a bookshop. I've never had a *métier*. Not like you.'

'And your husband?' It might have been an inquiry about his profession, but Catherine thought not.

'Divorced,' she said succinctly.

They both stopped shelling nuts for a moment and murmured the customary commiseration; less heartfelt than you would receive for widowhood, she always imagined, but less embarrassed, too.

She answered as she usually did. 'Oh, it's a long while ago now.' Seven years, in fact, very nearly. 'With the children grown and gone, it seemed the time to sell the house, to give my ex-husband his share of the capital and find something smaller for myself, and use the money left over to start up my own business.'

She wondered if she were creating awkwardness, relating her life story to strangers this way, but Madame Bouschet nodded again over her nutshells, before glancing up and asking, 'Why here?'

Because of the low cost of housing. Because of a flight of crazy nostalgia. Because. Because.

'It's beautiful,' was all she said in the end.

Did they see its wild, desolate beauty, when it had always been the daily backdrop to their life? Would her reason sound trivial, naive or, worse, patronising? It seemed not. Monsieur Bouschet grunted, and his wife wasn't smiling but she did look more than satisfied.

Madame Bouschet began to gather the fragments of walnut shell on the newspaper into a tidy heap and said, 'Right, lunchtime, I believe. Madame, will you stay and break a crust with us? I made a fresh loaf this morning.'

Catherine wavered. She had made her visit early

with the express object of avoiding a mealtime, but she supposed a man would be hungry before noon if he had been up feeding livestock at six. She hated to offend, but more than anything she hated to impose.

'It's extremely kind of you, Madame. Really. But if you don't mind, there are so many things I ought to be doing at home.'

She saw at once that she had chosen wrongly. Madame Bouschet continued to the dresser and reached down heavy china plates – two only – and something about her demeanour suggested a retreat into formality.

But at the door, Monsieur Bouschet, who showed her out, held her hand a moment longer after they had shaken goodbye.

'So, you won't be needing the rest of your hay?' he said. And this time, beneath his moustache, she was certain he was laughing.

CHAPTER 4

THE BLACK BEAST

The rain held off that day. The sky above the gorge shifted through slate and petrol to a surreal midnight blue but continued to hold its moisture. The next morning, though, when Catherine awoke it was to a heavy drumbeat on the shale roof tiles. It rained all that day and throughout the next two without stopping or even really easing off. She had thought herself used to wet weather at home, but English rain was an apologetic, half-hearted affair compared with this obdurate downpour. It wasn't torrential but it was unremitting. Catherine stayed indoors, donned an extra sweater and unpacked the remainder of her cardboard boxes.

Every morning when she opened the shutters in the side bedroom, she saw the view – that beautiful view from the summer – only in memory. The reality at best was a shroud of thinly falling grey, half masking even the nearest trees, and behind it, in all directions, only looming shapes of denser grey. At worst there was nothing but bars of rain.

On the fourth morning she thought she detected

a marginal lightening to the south over the main valley, and the steady rhythm seemed slightly less intense. By lunchtime it was unmistakable; the rain was slowing, and by early afternoon it had faded to a fine, soft mizzle. Seizing her chance, Catherine laced her boots, pulled on her raincoat and headed out to the car.

She stopped at the farm gate to exchange greetings with Monsieur Bouschet, who was also taking advantage of the respite. Wearing an empty plastic fertiliser sack like a tabard over his working overalls, he was clearing the clogged guttering of his goat shed with a trowel. He nodded his good day and then indicated the sky with a jut of the chin.

'*C'est triste*,' he said: sad, the weather. '*Mais c'est normal.*'

Catherine leaned her elbow out of the car window. 'Oh, yes?' Her attempted cheerfulness, she feared, sounded rather brittle.

'Yes. It's October, after all. We generally expect a good soak before Toussaint.'

She nodded, trying to remember exactly when All Saints' Day fell, and watched as he dislodged a clod of mud and chestnut leaves.

'It's a good test for the roofs, anyway,' he said, shifting along a yard or so. 'How are you, up there?'

'Watertight so far.'

He nodded. 'Good roofs at Les Fenils.'

Down in St Julien, the shingled river bed had disappeared under a swilling torrent. Catherine

41

parked her car in the square and walked back to the stone bridge to take a closer look. Leaning on the parapet, she felt a chill rise off the water below and breathed in a cocktail of earth and iron filings. The scent matched the colour of the water, which was that of rust, flecked here and there with pinkish spume. How did it achieve that pigmentation, when the rocks hereabouts were greyish-black? It must be the soil, she told herself, averting her mind from the admonishments of the Direction des Affaires Sanitaires. It was too noisy by the river to speak on the mobile; she returned to her car to make her calls to Tom (out), Bryony (out) and Lexie (just dashing out).

She replenished her provisions at the grocery store. Madame Peysasse, the owner, packed Catherine's jars of *rillettes* and tins of anchovies and tomato puree into a cardboard tray which had once held peaches, then piled her fresh vegetables on top with the bread.

'The river seems rather full,' ventured Catherine as she took her change.

'The rain,' said Madame Peysasse, with barely a shrug. Reaching round, she separated a clump of flat-leaved parsley from the mass in a tall jug behind the counter, shook the water from the severed stems and brought them to her nose, inhaling deeply. 'You like? With garlic, and your anchovies, you can make a *persillade*.'

When Catherine gave her mute assent, the

42

shopkeeper twisted the herbs in a scrap of paper and tucked them into the side of the tray.

'That's very kind of you,' said Catherine, finding herself disproportionately pleased with the small gift. Madame Peysasse dismissed her thanks and moved across the shop to hold open the door.

On the threshold the elderly Frenchwoman squinted up at the sky, which was lowering again. '*C'est triste,*' she said.

As Catherine left the village and took the turning towards La Grelaudière, she heard the first grumble of thunder, a muted warning from behind the protective bulk of the surrounding hills. As she mounted the slow hairpins, its volume increased but she couldn't tell whether the storm was coming nearer or its sound was merely amplified and distorted the way the post van's horn had been. There was no sign of any lightning.

The storm broke when she was still a few bends short of La Grelaudière. One moment the rain wasn't there and the next it was, falling in sheets as if thrown by a hose. Visibility was poor. As she swung round the turn immediately below the hamlet, the teeming grey beyond the windscreen thickened and changed shape. A figure loomed out of the rain. It was a man, but not Monsieur Bouschet; in spite of the rain and his lumpy coat, she could see that this man was taller and thinner. As he lurched to the side of the road, she slowed to a halt, thinking to offer him a lift. She wound down the passenger window so that water splashed and fizzed on the plastic trim and ran down the inside of the door. The man bent and a face came into view: younger than she had thought, maybe thirty or thirty-five, colourless in the damped-down light and swaying slightly. 'You're not from here.' He spoke in the thick, slow accent of the country. Then he straightened and moved away, clutching his coat more closely about him.

Cathering let in the clutch and drove on. You're not from here. You don't belong.

At Les Fenils the electricity was out again. The flash storm appeared to be over and the rain had ceased as quickly as it had begun, so that she reached her hallway without getting wet, but it had taken its toll; she leaned on the wall with her box of groceries under one arm and clicked the ineffective switch off and on again. Candles, that was the other thing she had meant to buy. Four of the half-dozen she had brought with her from England were already burned to stubs; if the power didn't come on again before tonight she would have to light her last pair. It was already gloomy in the old stone kitchen, though it was barely half past four. Why, she wondered as she stared at the sombre granite, did the Cévenols not plaster and whitewash their walls?

The recessed larder cupboard was wide and deep. Did Madame Sauzet, on her own here in her later years, fit her few necessities on a quarter of a shelf the way Catherine did, or had she been one of those women who hoarded things, oblivious to sell-by date, with a squirelling instinct born in wartime austerity? For the first time it occurred to Catherine how much she regretted not having met the previous occupant of this kitchen. Kneeling on the floor to stow her tins and packets, Catherine felt a dampness in the granite flagstones. Then the daylight in the room suddenly dimmed further and she became aware of the silence only as it ended. She sat back on her heels and closed her eyes. Overhead and all around – on the roof and sills and the terrace outside – the timpani had resumed.

She felt suddenly chilled. Maybe it was the lack of electricity; if she could have thrown a switch and created a cheerful glow, light might have passed for warmth. She decided the time had come to light the woodburner in the kitchen. There was a whole wall of logs chopped and stacked in the woodshed, next to the byre. She pulled on her raincoat and made the short dash to the shed. The lock on the door was awkward and by the time she had wrestled it open, water was dripping down the back of her collar.

She found a sack and picked up one of the roughly chopped logs. She was surprised by its lack of weight. The wood wasn't just seasoned, it was old, its insides decayed to powder and air. Can this really have been the fuel Madame Sauzet was burning last winter, before her death in the New Year? As she worked along the stack, lifting logs at random, Catherine found them all to be similarly insubstantial. What looked like a winter's supply of wood would blaze away to nothing in a month.

At least it would light easily. But by the time she had manoeuvred her haul out of the shed and into her hallway, the hessian sack was soaked through. For kindling she was limited to a copy of the *Guardian*, which burned away almost before the logs began to take. There was no breath of wind outside to draw the smoke, which drifted out to sting her nose and eyes rather than find its way up the flue. After several attempts, the wood at last began to burn – with smoke and no heat. She didn't dare close the glazed door of the woodburner for fear of snuffing the fire completely.

At least she had gas, a kettle, milk and tea. With the last two candles lit and the woodburner giving off at least a semblance of life, the room was smokily comfortable.

If only she could rid herself of the feeling that she was a squatter here, or camping, in this house which seemed as organic as the outdoors – its timbers the trunks of chestnut trees, its floor and walls carved from the mountain against whose flank it crouched. It was to banish the feeling of impermanence, of making shift, that she went to fetch her sewing box and the carpet bag which contained her yarns. She should work. A whole week she had been here and she hadn't sewn a stitch; needlework was what she had come here to do, and it would be good to feel she had begun.

She had a canvas stretched ready on the frame from before she left England. For Catherine, the genesis of any new design lay not with the canvas or even with a paper sketch but invariably in the yarn. It was among the silks that she would find the colour and the texture she was seeking. She didn't pull the frame towards her now, therefore, but reached for the bag of silks, delving in and pulling out skeins at random, laying them across her lap, reds and blacks and browns. Her preference had always been for organic dyes, and in this place it seemed all the more appropriate that these were natural pigments: the colours of plants, of the rocks and of the earth.

Vegetable, mineral . . . and animal. She turned over in her hand a skein of fawnish-grey, fine textured and with a haze of soft fuzz surrounding the strands of silk, bringing to mind the hidden places of an animal's underside: the belly or the pit of a forelimb. Black – a glossy, rich blue-black – had the sheen of wet dog. And a pale moon yellow would pick out eyes: watchful eyes in the dusk.

She had her idea already, from a story in a book Lexie had given her as a late Christmas present, picked up in a second-hand shop when the notion of the Cévennes began to harden from daydream into practical plan-making. *Legends and Folklore of the Auvergne*, the book was called, although in fact its tales were drawn from the whole Massif Central, down into Lozère and over as far as Albi. The story was '*La Bête du Gévaudan*' – 'The Beast of Gévaudan'. The myth was supposed to be founded in truth: the gruesome reality of almost one hundred Cévenols slain in quiet places across the mountains in the middle years of the eighteenth century. Many were children. One young girl was taken, it was said, and only her bonnet and clogs left behind; another went missing at Christmas and what was eventually found of her was insufficient for burial – not enough, according to lurid local lore, to fill even a small stocking. These events of comparatively recent times had melded with more ancient and tenacious fears: the were-wolf in half-human form; the hell hound; the bogey man.

The mouth – that was the place to begin. That terrible maw, with its slash of crimson and the glitter of wet, white teeth. The rain dulled the daylight, and Catherine had to peer close to thread her needle. As she started to stitch, the mouth took on concrete shape in her mind, and above it the long muzzle and angry brows, the broad, heavy skull. And the eyes, the blankly vigilant, liquid eyes. She saw it all clearly, translated into the colours of silk. It was funny how, even as a child, she had been able to visualise a picture or pattern as soon as she began to sew; she had only to begin and the image would emerge, a template for her to follow, like the outline that forms on closed lids after staring at something too long. It was never quite the same with a drawing on paper. She'd loved her paints and crayons, but it was fabric and yarn which were her true medium. The tactility of it – the slide of the thread through her fingers and the snap as she pulled it tight. In contrast, Lexie had never wanted to sew. Nor did she sit and draw or colour as a girl. She was always writing, even then: poems, or tiny books stapled together from scraps of paper. Tom, meanwhile, would be taking things to pieces, or else – unusually for a boy – buried deep in a book.

The streak of red mouth on the canvas was finished and the curl of an inky lip was taking form when the light defeated Catherine. She pulled a candle close to examine what she had done, and found herself satisfied. She should stop and make tea, and perhaps something to eat. And after that, if the power cut persisted, she might read, provided the candlelight didn't strain her eyes. Or she could try to find an English station on the radio, plugged in upstairs beside her bed. It hadn't been used on the batteries for a long time; she hoped they wouldn't be dead. Maybe she should tune to *France Inter* instead, and try to follow the news. The practice would be good for her. It was still more of a struggle than it should be to keep track of what was being said.

You're not from here.

With a jerk she pushed away the tapestry frame, averting her eyes from the sneering mouth. What in heaven's name was she doing here, all on her own in this godforsaken place? Why had she come? But there was nowhere to go back to now, no bolt-hole to run to, with her pride and her finances in tatters. The house in Long Hartslow was packed up and sold. Her house: the family home. The house where Lexie had taken her first steps on the little half-landing, while Graeme was in the bath one Sunday morning. It belonged now to methodical Mr Finch who'd moved from room to room taking forensic stock of his impending purchase, and Mrs Finch, who exclaimed in delight and held her daughter's hand while ten-year-old Charlie ran straight out into the garden. It was theirs now. Les Fenils was all there was.

Five o'clock. By the time she had cooked and eaten and washed up, it would be six or six thirty. Was that too outrageously early, she wondered, just to go to bed?

CHAPTER 5

AN AXE FALLING

One morning towards the end of that week Catherine determined to get outside, rain or no rain. Her tapestry was progressing well but there were only so many hours a person could be indoors on her own without going stir crazy.

There was nothing she could usefully do in the garden; her tomato plants, taking their chances by the woodshed wall, had rotted, root and stem. What she needed was a proper walk. The day before, she had walked down to the hamlet and back during a slight lull in the weather, but nobody had been outside at the Bouschets in the fine, stubborn drizzle, and she had not yet had the courage to knock and introduce herself at the other three dwellings. Today she decided to walk the other way, up instead of down, to the ruined house which stood on a rocky promontory a hundred yards or so up the gulley and into the chestnut woods beyond. She hadn't had time to investigate beyond the promontory on her two visits as prospective purchaser. There had been so much to discuss with the estate agent about the house

51

and outbuildings and services – including, she recalled, a long disquisition on the septic tank. If the path did not peter out in the woods but continued up beyond the tree line, she would be able to try for mobile reception. The PTT's confident promise of a landline up and running in a week had become the hopeful suggestion of two weeks, maybe three. There was no signal at the promontory, she already knew, and St Julien was a long way to drive to speak to another human being.

At around mid-morning the rain seemed to have stopped; there had been a perceptible rallentando outside, until the tempo was the slower and heavier one of water dripping from eaves and nearby branches. Pocketing her phone, she waterproofed herself in raincoat, headscarf and wellingtons and set off up the hill. She had forgotten how beautiful it was beyond her walls, even thus blanketed in grey. It was good to be out.

Once among the trees, the path ceased to be stony; the peaty earth was almost silent beneath her rubber soles and there was little sound at all except for dripping water and the swish of her sleeves as she walked. Presently, though, some fifty yards past the promontory, where the woods grew denser again, she thought she heard the gurgle of running water. No real surprise, of course, that with all this rain some should find its way into the bottom of the gorge; there was nothing that could be called a stream further down, at La

Grelaudière, but perhaps its course took it underground somewhere between here and the hamlet. To her right the trees sloped away steeply, and here and there she caught glimpses of the opposite flank of the gorge, much closer than she had expected. A final rightward turn of the path and she stopped in mid-stride. In front of her was a bridge. It was narrow and wooden and not entirely reassuring-looking, and she saw as she moved on towards it that it crossed the brook at a height of some twenty feet. There was a single handrail on the downstream side only.

The planks felt slippery in the wet and she wished she had on her walking boots, which offered better grip. She crossed quickly without looking down. On the opposite bank, a short, hard climb took her away from the water, but she was frustrated to find that the path then doubled back the way she had come. She was wondering whether she ought to turn back and look for some other way to get to the top of the gorge when the narrow path met a broad, flat track. On a tree trunk opposite she saw a double stripe of paint marked on the bark: red and white. So this must be one of the *grandes randonnées* – the mountain footpath equivalent of a motorway. She'd had no idea it was here, running along the other side of her own small valley. She added a decent walking map to her mental to-buy list.

Catherine was about to turn left and take the track up the gully when a sound from down the hill caught her attention: an axe falling, the thud of wood being chopped. It could have been a forester but somehow she thought it sounded more domestic. That meant there was a house close by.

She was right. After less than twenty yards the downhill path curved round to the left and off it forked another track. This one was rocky and rutted and led down a steep slope from which the trees had been partially cleared. Through the remaining branches she glimpsed a swatch of grass and behind it a section of wall. She must be almost on a level here with Les Fenils. This property must be more or less straight across the valley from her own house, perhaps as little as a few hundred yards away. It was strange to think of having a neighbour so close, and so well hidden. She had never noticed lights from this direction, nor seen smoke above the trees, and in this resonant, damp stillness it was amazing she hadn't been able to stand on her terrace and hear each strike of the axe.

She set off down the track towards the house. The man was splitting logs on a stump set aside for the purpose close to his orchard wall. He was intent on his work and did not appear to notice her approach. She put him at her own age or a little older; his hair was streaked more to grey than black, but his arms below the rolled-up shirt sleeves were lean and closely muscled.

She waited, hesitating, a few yards away. It wouldn't do, she supposed, to hail someone unexpectedly when they were wielding an axe. But it seemed he had been aware of her presence from the start; without turning, he laid down the axe and spoke in immaculate English.

'Good morning.'

Only then did he face her and hold out a hand. She accepted it, smiling. His hand was damp with sweat.

'*Pardon*,' he said, registering the same thing. 'My apologies, Madame.' He withdrew his hand, took a scarlet handkerchief from his trouser pocket, and wiped both hands fastidiously. His smile was guarded; private and ironic. 'So you are the Englishwoman.'

When he first spoke she had taken him for a compatriot, but his French was equally flawless and unaccented. Catherine chose French for her reply.

'That's right. Over at Les Fenils. I didn't realise your house was so close – that is, I hadn't realised it was here at all, until just now. But how did you know? About me, I mean?'

The smile widened, deepening the lines which bracketed the sides of his mouth. 'Ah, well. Here, you are in the mountains. Things are known.'

It was something she could have imagined Monsieur Bouschet saying with a slow nodding of the head. From this man, though, the words had a quite different feel. Almost mocking.

'Patrick,' he introduced himself. 'Patrick Castagnol' – the first person she had met here to volunteer a Christian name.

55

'Catherine,' she reciprocated. 'Catherine Parkstone.'

'Well, I fear the heavens are about to send us further bounty, and it's a serious walk back to Les Fenils in the rain.'

It was true; the light had shifted in a way that Catherine in little more than a week had already learned to gauge.

'So perhaps, Catherine Parkstone, I can offer you a small glass of something?'

She resisted the urge to glance at her watch. It couldn't even be midday. There was also a small shock of familiarity in hearing her name pronounced the English way.

'That is very kind,' she said. 'Thank you.'

Patrick – he was quite impossible to think of as Monsieur Castagnol – gathered together his fire-wood into a large woven basket, then picked it up in one hand and his axe in the other. She followed him through a door into a kind of corridor room where he stowed the log basket by a wall, between a short row of boots – all in a man's size – and an impressively proportioned wine rack.

The kitchen into which he led her was no less austere than the Bouschets' though substantially less cluttered. Its focus was the traditional one of a central refectory table surrounded by upright wood and wicker chairs. (You couldn't say these people were not in need of some soft furnishings.) Drying herbs and onions adorned the walls and beams, farmhouse-style, but there were none of the trappings of a daily agricultural existence: no tools, or rolls of wire, or stock magazines. The main addition was books. Stacks of recipe books stood by the range, and a double shelf housed rows of *livres de poche* and, among them, she noticed, some English paperbacks.

'An *eau de vie*, perhaps?' He had taken a half-empty, unlabelled bottle from a cupboard and was holding it to the light. His hands caught her attention; their backs had the weathered tan and toughened knuckles of a life out of doors but his nails were trimmed and polished. What *montagnard* had manicured hands – even a Frenchman? 'It's homemade,' he explained, as he twisted out the cork. 'From my own damsons.'

'Isn't that illegal?' she asked without thinking.

He laughed. 'When a police officer passes, I close the shutters.'

She touched the liquid to her lips and felt its burn. There was a faint aroma of fruit but the taste – if you could call it a taste – was nothing but heat. 'Yes, I should imagine you're not disturbed very often, up here.'

'I could be doing anything I wish.' He said it neither flirtatiously nor dangerously but with straightforward seriousness. Then he smiled. 'Besides, in this weather . . .' A very French shrug. 'In a mountain winter, one needs something to keep out the cold.'

'Does it get very cold?' It wasn't entirely a stupid question. Before her removal she had studied

57

statistics of rainfall and temperature, but data were recorded no closer than Mende, and that was in the valley.

'Not cold so much, not Alpine weather. We have frosts at night for much of the year, but rarely any serious weight of snow. Not like on Mont Lozère, or in exposed places above the tree line. And in autumn, of course, it rains.'

'So I see.'

He took a swallow of *eau de vie*. 'But perhaps wet weather does not concern you so very much. *It's only a bit of rain.*'

He had been speaking French, but he delivered this final phrase in English, the model of dogged British stoicism.

Catherine laughed and replied with something her mother used to say. 'A drop of water never hurt anybody, said the drowned man.'

She had begun in French out of politeness. But to continue with the exercise was foolish; his easy, idiomatic English was so much better than her competent, unpolished French.

'Have you lived here long?' she wanted to know. His surname, Castagnol, had impeccable cévenol credentials, yet somehow he had a Parisian feel about him.

'All my life,' he said simply. Perhaps her surprise registered with him, because he went on to expand. 'I was born here in this house, in my bed upstairs. Both my parents died in the same bed.'

'But you've been away?' she persisted. His accent

in French was of the region, but modulated: softer and at the same time more precise.

He shrugged again. 'University, city life. I came back.'

She nodded and left it at that, taking another sip of the fiery plum brandy, feeling it scorch its way to her stomach. She wished she could decently have asked him for a piece of bread. When she glanced up again, she saw that he was still looking at her, his eyes unreadable.

'This place exerts a kind of pull,' he said. 'Maybe you will learn to feel it too.'

'Maybe. Is that one of the *grandes randonnées* back there, that runs past the end of your track?'

'Yes. It heads south from here, crosses the ridge and strikes the road halfway up the next valley, near Le Crouzet. The other way it continues upwards, heading for Mont Lozère.'

'Do you walk there much?'

He shrugged. 'Not as often as I should, perhaps. Shooting, sometimes, or mushrooming in the woods, but rarely far from home. Besides,' he smiled suddenly, 'I could walk a long way and get nowhere. The footpath doesn't connect me to the world. My access is from below the house – a track that comes in at La Grelaudière.'

Catherine stood up and walked to the window, still with her drink in her hand. The rain was starting to fulfill its threat, but through the descending curtain of grey she could make out at the end of his yard a gate and the opening of a

59

lane just wide enough to take a vehicle. 'Of course,' she said. 'The track that joins at the last hairpin, just before the hamlet.'

'That's the one.'

She turned towards him, standing with her back to the rain-filtered daylight, leaning against the sill. 'But it must be well used in summer. The footpath, I mean. Do you get a lot of hikers?'

'This isn't Haute Savoie, nor even the Gorges du Tarn. But there are some passers-by, yes.' He swirled the liquid in his glass and didn't look up as he added, 'Donkeys, in particular.'

'Sorry?'

'Donkeys.' He raised his eyes then, one brow slightly elevated. 'A train of latter-day Modestines. Your fellow countryman has much to answer for.'

Light dawned, and Catherine slid back into her seat at the table, laughing. *Travels With a Donkey*.' Lexie had bought her a copy of that, too: a battered edition from the 1930s, with stylised pen-and-ink illustrations.

'I understand there's a place in Le Monastier where you can hire the animals,' he said. 'Retrace the steps of Robert Louis Stevenson through the villages and high passes of the Cévennes. No doubt they have a website, by which means they attract this straggling caravan of devotees. Elementary school teachers, for the most part, from the Paris suburbs, with earnest wives and pale, freckled children.'

'Clutching the volume before them like a

guidebook?' It was a glorious image, and the alcohol was making her mind dance. 'And what happens when they get to the other end? Presumably the firm sends a lorry for the donkeys, the way they do with canoes on the Tarn, to get them back upstream.'

'Presumably.'

'Or maybe they just turn them loose and they find their own way back.' Homing donkeys. This stuff of his was lethal; maybe she should ask for that bread.

'So he actually came this way?' she asked, getting a grip. 'Stevenson?'

'It's possible.'

'Only possible?'

Patrick put down his glass. 'The narrative is precise about the places he passed through – the towns and village, the major landmarks. But as for which path exactly he took to cross the mountain spaces in between,' the shrug again, 'it's not very clear.'

'So they're everywhere?' What would he think of her if she descended completely into giggles, like a schoolgirl with her first rum and Coke? 'All over the hillside in the summer, on every path and sheep trail, literary pilgrims with rented donkeys?'

'Not quite that, perhaps,' he said, but his eyes joined in her laughter.

He drained his drink and she was obliged to continue to sip gingerly at hers under a steady scrutiny she found unsettling. She wasn't used to being looked at; women her age weren't. 'And you?' he asked at length.

'Am I a pilgrim, you mean?' She tried for lightness. 'Well, not a literary one, at any rate. My mission is far more mundane. I have come to start a business here.'

'*Ah, bon?*' His tone was warm; he seemed pleased that she had surprised him.

'Yes. Nothing grand, just a home furnishings business. Curtains and cushions and upholstering.'

'A needlewoman.' When he said it, it seemed something admirable, something worthwhile. 'You have come to soften and civilise us with your silks and velvets, perhaps.'

'Not quite that.'

'And what would you do for me, Catherine Parkstone, if I hired you to improve my living quarters here?' He cast his glance round the farmhouse kitchen and hers followed it, slightly embarrassed – although she knew at once where she would have started: a long, cushioned runner on the oak settle which stood against the far wall, curtains at the bare, shuttered windows and another across the recess which led to the stairs. His gaze had returned to her, soft but penetrating. 'You think my house is in need of a woman's touch?'

'Curtains cut out draughts,' she replied briskly, her cheeks hot. When he laughed, she regretted her defensiveness, and was obliged to watch him enjoying the response he had provoked.

'You are quite right. Male or female, we all feel the bite of a cold wind.'

She swallowed the rest of her *eau de vie* and said, 'I would love to make some suggestions for you, if you're really interested. I could do some sketches or maybe show you some samples of fabric. The settle there, that would look great with a cushioned seat, and maybe these dining chairs could be upholstered to match.'

His original detached and mildly ironic manner resumed as he inclined his head gravely. 'That would be most kind. I should receive your ideas with very great interest.'

The light which fell across the table between them had modulated again. Things appeared brighter and less blurred; the rain was lifting.

'Maybe I ought to go while there's a break in the weather,' she said, rising. 'I don't suppose it will hold off for long.'

'Undoubtedly not.'

'Thank you.' She hoped he wouldn't feel she was running away – even if she partly was. 'For the drink,' she added, 'and for the shelter.'

He rose and came round the table, leading the way back to the corridor room through which they had entered. From a shelf near the door he reached down another unlabelled bottle. This one, she saw through the gloom, was a rich, deep purple in colour.

'Damsons again, but a liqueur, this time.' He held it out to her. 'It may be more to your taste.'

63

'Oh, goodness, thank you.' She took it and smiled up at him, gratitude driving out awkwardness. 'That's really terribly kind of you.'

'For friendship,' he said. 'And to keep the damp at bay.'

'For friendship,' she repeated obediently.

'And you must call again, when you are over this way, taking your British constitutional. Besides which, I hope you will soon be bringing me your plans for the transformation of my house to feminine comforts. Or should I say, simply, to comforts.'

'I'll do that,' she said. 'And if you like what I come up with, you will be my very first client.'

CHAPTER 6

TELECOMMUNICATIONS

'Iaced it, Mum. The interview – I wiped the floor with them. The job is mine.'

Catherine's telephone line at Les Fenils had been in operation for an hour, and she was talking to her daughter.

'I am the new queen of royal icing,' said Lexie. 'The doyenne of whipped frosting, the hottest voice of *Fondant Magazine*.'

'That's fantastic.' Her daughter's enthusiasm had always been irrepressible – and completely irresistible. Catherine was grinning like an ape. 'I'm so pleased for you, love. When do you start?'

'I already have.'

'Gosh, that was quick.'

'Oh, well, they had a space for me straight away, and I had holiday owing at *Air Cargo*. Besides, I couldn't have stood it another minute. Seriously, I'd have been in some padded cell right now, bashing my head and mumbling about lower deck pallet sizes. But blimey, Mum, what's that noise? Is it on the line?'

'That? Oh no, it's rain,' said Catherine, after

65

taking a moment to focus. She barely noticed the drumming any more.

'Really? It's quite nice here. In a boring, grey, English October sort of way.'

'So, tell me everything,' Catherine said. 'Are they nice people at the new place?'

'Cake people are the loveliest people. It's practically our masthead slogan.'

'And mainly women, I think you said.'

'Exclusively – except a bloke or two in commercial. You've never seen so many pink cardigans.'

Catherine couldn't recall Lexie owning a cardigan since first year juniors. 'Not many other young people in the office, then?'

'You'd be surprised, Mum. At *Fondant Magazine* even seventeen-year-old temps seem to favour pastel knitwear. You won't recognise me at Christmas. I'll be the one in the mint-green twinset.'

Christmas. Was she going to be able to persuade Lexie over for Christmas, then? She hadn't presumed, of course, and wasn't going to raise it now, not with the new job to bed itself down.

'And they're a sociable lot, are they?'

'Frightfully. Pub every Friday after work. Lunchtimes, too – anyone who's around and not dashing off somewhere. They've even got a pub quiz team.' She began to giggle. 'Apparently they're unbeatable when questions come up on crystallised fruit.'

'A bunch of journalists?' said Catherine.

'They're usually demons for trivia, aren't they? I bet it's not only cakes they know about.'

'True. I, for example, could field almost anything on air freight container specifications. They'll have to put me straight in the team.'

'And what about the work – the writing? Is it going to be interesting, from what you've seen so far?'

'It's a blast. I mean, of course it's not all inter-viewing Jane Asher, but I've met some crazy people. There was this woman on Tuesday who's made over eight thousand wedding cakes, in an oven that looks as if she had it for a wedding present herself in about nineteen fifty-four.'

Lexie loved talking to people. And she was good at it. But after the initial steep learning curve, would cake decorating get boring, the way air transport had? Catherine hoped not – or at least that the fun would take longer to wear off.

'And then yesterday I was in Clacton,' her daughter continued, 'covering the Essex Sugarcraft Fair. I managed to sneak off for a bit, to nip over to Walton and look in on Gram.'

'Oh, thanks, sweetheart. That's really good of you.'

'I was going to snaffle her out some cake, but I seriously wonder what's underneath some of those icing extravaganzas. Square of foam rubber, I shouldn't wonder, or else a sponge that's three months old and has already been round fourteen previous sugarcraft exhibitions.'

Mum used to make excellent cakes. A buttered slice of her Irish tea brack in their packed lunches bought her and Bryony the top of the trade in crisps and chocolate bars. But that was a long while ago.

'How was Gram?'

She ought to have been the next phone call – should probably have been the first one, in fact. Catherine hadn't called at all yet since her arrival. But Mum on the phone was very hard work. Her words were few, and those few were painful and uncertain. Dementia had begun to scramble her thoughts five years ago, well before the stroke which had brought down a curtain on her ability to express them. It was tough enough when you were there in person and could at least watch TV with her, or sit and hold her hand.

'She wasn't too bad, actually,' said Lexie. 'Not upset, anyway, or getting agitated about things.' That was always the worst: when whatever logic there was to her inner universe ran into conflict with things you said. That's when she got angry – or cried. 'I mainly told her about the new job, and she just listened.'

At least Catherine could raise a smile at that. 'I can well imagine.'

'Yeah, yeah, I know. Poor Gram. An unresisting audience – powerless to fight back.'

'Oh, I think she still knows how to make her feeling known, all right, when she wants someone to shut up.'

Mum had always had time for Lexie and her passions.

'Did she say anything much at all?'

'Not a lot. She wasn't really wanting to. She knew who I was, though, and what I was talking about, I'm fairly sure. When she doesn't try to speak, sometimes I think it means she's feeling happier. Calmer. Wouldn't you say? Mind you, she did call me Bryony at one point.'

'She always muddled names, even before,' said Catherine, wondering why this error irked her so particularly. So few words, and Mum had to choose to use Bryony's name. Why did she never mistake Lexie for Catherine?

'I saw Dad at the weekend, too.'

'Oh? How was he?'

'OK. Asking after you.'

Graeme was another person she ought to ring. They were grown-ups; relations were amicable between them even if they never quite managed comfortable. They shouldn't be needing their daughter to ferry messages to and fro.

'I told him you were living like a nomad up there, with no mains services. Or a survivalist, maybe – one of those nutcases who hole up in the woods in the American Midwest, with piles of armaments and corned beef and five years' supply of bottled water.'

Her mother laughed. 'I'm drinking the tap water now, actually. It's fine.' She had dutifully sent off her sample for analysis but wasn't waiting for the results. Madame Bouschet, when consulted, had been summarily dismissive of the sanitary authority's letter. And Catherine refused to imagine toxicity lurking behind her water's crisp, mineral bite. It tasted as clean as winter.

'Right,' said Lexie. 'And, I know, don't tell me – you can't get corned beef over there in any case.'

'Certainly not. Do survivalists eat wild boar pâté, I wonder?' Actually, she supposed they might. 'Or pasta with fresh truffles? Or marrons glacés? They sell wonderful homemade ones in the *confiserie* in St Julien.'

'Shut up, Mum. You're making me jealous. Is there really a *confiserie*? I didn't realise it was that civilised.'

'Well, it's a bit of everything. *Boulangerie, pâtisserie* . . . but they do sell sweets. And everything's made at the shop.'

'Maybe I need to come over and interview the *pâtissier* for *Fondant Magazine*. Way to wangle an expenses-paid trip.'

'I think the owner would enjoy that.' Monsieur Folcher, the widower who ran the bakery, had an eye for young women. She'd seen him selecting those toddlers with the prettiest mums for the favour of his free lollipops. 'So what else did Dad have to say?' she asked.

'He wanted to know if you'd found any likely soulmates.'

It was an easy line to laugh away, but not entirely funny. Graeme used to talk a lot about being soulmates during the first ten years of their marriage; for the second ten, not nearly so much. The Bouschets ran through her mind, and Patrick Castagnol, and loneliness.

'Give me time,' she said. 'It's barely been four weeks.'

'Oh, and Mum, I nearly forgot. The other thing is Gram's house.'

Catherine's chest closed off to breath. 'What about it?' Mum's house, she thought; *our house.*

'Oh, nothing dreadful, don't worry.' Lexie must have caught the edge of her reaction. 'It's just that one of the tenants has moved out. Had to drop out of his course, so he's leaving the area. Going home to bum off his parents, I'd imagine. Save himself the rent.'

'Right. I see.' Breathing returned, carefully regulated. 'So we'll need to advertise, try to re-let the room.'

'All sorted,' declared her daughter blithely. 'The others knew someone. Another student friend, who was unhappy in halls and wanted to move out to a shared house.'

'So I'll just need to sort out a new tenancy agreement for them to sign, then. With this new person's name on it as well. The original is on the computer. It won't take a minute to amend and I can get it in the post to them. What's the new tenant's name? Do you know, or shall I give them a call and ask?'

Thank goodness she had the phone line working

71

now. It would have been tricky to arrange things from the village square in St Julien.

'He's called Dan and he seems very nice. Very tidy habits, I'm certain. Clean vet's certificate and banker's reference.'

Puzzled, Catherine said, 'You've met him?'

'Yes. Me and Dad went over on Sunday afternoon. And it's OK about the tenancy agreement, too. Dad sorted that out. Took the old one and got it altered and photocopied. It's all signed, sealed and delivered, or whatever it is the lawyers say.'

'You and . . . *Dad*?' What on earth had this to do with Graeme? 'Why?'

'Aunty Bryony was all tied up, she had some big client meeting on Saturday and it ended up being Sunday as well. And we couldn't call you, could we? And Tom's in Scotland, which is pretty useless. So Dad said, would I like him to help? He drove us over there, and we had a pub supper on the way home.'

On the way home? Mum's house was in Colchester, Lexie lived in Stockwell and Graeme in High Wycombe. He'd driven halfway round the home counties.

'Well, that was terribly kind of him. He really didn't need to . . .' But who else was there to do it, with her in France? Uncontactable, abdicating her responsibilities. It really was kind of Graeme and she was grateful, but frustrated at the same time. This was her job. Which bedroom, she wondered, had been re-let? Her old one? Bryony's?

72

'It's fine, Mum, honestly. And if this new boy burns the place down, you can blame us, all right?'

'Well . . .' There should be more to say, but she couldn't think what. 'Thanks,' she finished.

'So, anyway, you're back in the twenty-first century now – you've rejoined the world of global telecoms.'

Catherine smiled and relaxed a little. Her glance rose from the stone floor to where her camping kettle stood on Madame Sauzet's Calor gas stove. 'The twentieth, maybe. Perhaps even the second half of the twentieth, at a pinch. I still can't get the internet working.'

'Seriously?' For Lexie, it went without saying, a life entirely offline would be simply unthinkable.

'They're supposed to have sorted it out, along with the phone. Not broadband, but at least a basic connection.'

'Not broadband?'

The horror in her daughter's voice had Catherine's smile widening. Worlds apart, she thought. The very idea of accessing the web at La Grelaudière seemed almost preposterous. She hadn't noticed an iMac amongst the walnuts on the kitchen table *chez* Bouschet. Though Patrick Castagnol . . . She'd bet he had a laptop somewhere.

'Oh, I can make do without a fast connection, that shouldn't be a problem. But I could do with access, at least.'

'Course you bloody could. So I can email you

73

when I need to, for a start. Send you photos of cakes I've been writing about.'

'I can hardly wait. But what I was also thinking was, I need the internet so I can get started properly with the business.'

Apart from beginning a tapestry and promising Patrick Castagnol some sketches for his kitchen, she had done nothing at all. Much longer, and she would begin to suspect herself of putting it off. She had a card ready to put up in Madame Peysasse's shop window, and details to supply for listing at the Chambre de Commerce in Mende. But there had been no point in doing these things before now; she'd needed the phone and internet first. And there was her website, too. A university friend of Tom's had kindly designed the rudiments for her already for a nominal sum, and she just needed to arrange a domain name and hosting – once she'd found out what that meant.

'Right, yes, the business,' said Lexie. 'How's it going, by the way?'

'As I say, I need to get going on it properly now. But it's been raining.' What a limp excuse that sounded; she laughed to show that she recognised it as such. 'You've heard it, even down the phone. When it rains up here, love, it rains as if it means it. Really not the best weather for going round knocking on doors to drum up trade. It isn't easy to try and interest people in new curtains while you stand dripping on their doorstep.'

Lexie was robust. 'Rubbish, it's absolutely the

best weather. Means they have to invite you in, doesn't it? Can't stand chatting in the wet. And if you look half drowned, they'll need to make you a hot chocolate, too. And by then you're in, you're well away. You've done a full recce of their interior décor, and off you go on your sales patter.'

'Funny you should say that. I've already found one prospective client by almost exactly that route.' Except that it hadn't been hot chocolate.

'Great. What's she ordered?'

Catherine let the pronoun pass. 'We haven't worked out the details yet. I'm doing some drawings.'

'Great,' said her daughter again. 'Look, Mum, I've got to go. Work calls. I have to round up a photographer and go out to a factory unit in Gravesend. We're doing a feature on marzipan fruit.'

'Have fun, then.'

'You, too. And email me as soon as you reach the nineteen nineties.'

When she'd replaced the receiver, Catherine walked over to the table where her computer stood, connected to the modem and its stubbornly unflashing light. She picked up the PTT booklet with the imperious French instructions and then laid it down again.

She moved across to the larder cupboard and opened the door, running her eye over her stock of dry goods. Had she enough raisins? The old exercise book of recipes, stiff-covered and cloth-bound, was in the top drawer of the dresser – the same place it had been since the dresser was bought to stand in her newlywed's kitchen at Long Hartslow. She thumbed through to find the page she wanted. Here it was: a sheet of paper glued in, the words tidily transcribed in the handwriting her mother would never use again. The recipe for Irish tea brack.

CHAPTER 7

A MAN OF AFFAIRS

By a week into November Catherine had met all the inhabitants of La Grelaudière. It was not a large community, even by cévenol standards: eight souls in total, if you counted the two outlying *propriétaires*, herself and Patrick Castagnol.

Besides the Bouschets there was another solid farmer couple in their sixties, who lived in a broad, low, single-storey house set a short way back from the road behind a cobbled yard. The Mériels were mainly in goats. The animals – eighty-seven of them, as Monsieur Mériel informed her proudly within minutes of their first meeting – had the run of two steeply sloping paddocks to the side of the house or, when it was wet, were packed in a complaining mass under an open, tin-roofed shed near the road. Since it was still raining as often as it wasn't, Catherine had generally approached the house past a sea of bony, white, staring faces, haloed with steam and bemoaning their confinement in quavering trebles. Madame Mériel made goat's cheese in a room which was half cellar, built into the hillside to the rear of her

77

kitchen. Everything about the Mériels was rich with the aroma of goat, from their untidy, muggy kitchen to their scrubbed skin. The only modern feature of their farm was the milking parlour. A gleaming construction of concrete and aluminium and steel, quite out of proportion to the squat, granite farmhouse and the rest of the outbuildings, it looked like something air-lifted in by NASA. Built to comply with new European Union regulations, explained Madame Mériel. There had been some subsidy, she added, in confidential tones – and evidently a loophole in the planning strictures of the Parc National. Monsieur Mériel wore spotless white overalls and hat whenever he went into it. He would have given Madame Park-e-ston a tour, he said, if only he'd possessed a second set of overalls.

Two square cottages on either side of the road completed the hamlet. The one on the left as you went down the hill was occupied by an elderly widow by the name of Volpilière – elderly even by local standards. She must have been well into her eighties, if not in her nineties. Catherine was almost afraid of crushing her fingers when she offered her hand. But no doubt the brittleness was an illusion. She said it was seventeen winters since she'd buried her husband; Catherine had no doubt she would see out a good few more.

The cottage opposite, on the right, was everything Madame Volpilière's was not. From the smeary windows and unpolished step to the weeds which snagged the path and overspilled the patch of ground by the side door where abandoned cold frames still stood, the whole place shouted neglect. Here lived the only resident whom Catherine had not formally met. They had not spoken since the first week when he had loomed at her out of the rain, though she had once or twice seen him standing watching her from behind a half-closed shutter. His name, she learned, was Guillaume – nobody mentioned any surname – and he drank. They all told her the same, in voices of hushed pity or disapproval, accompanied in every case by an identical hand gesture: a fist twisted in front of the nose, like a lemon on a squeezer. Madame Bouschet claimed that Guillaume was some kind of second cousin of Madame Mériel's; if this was true, the Mériels never mentioned it. Although the man was rarely seen outside his house, the same was not true of his dogs. He kept three or four, an ill-kempt and assorted gang, which would set up a barking whenever they heard the approach of footsteps or a car. They learned to recognise Catherine's and fall silent as she drew close; all but one were fearful and hung near the house door but that one, a yellowish hound more smooth-coated than the rest, would trot towards Catherine with a lopsided gait, eyes cast off to the side, as if expecting a sharp word or a blow. The animal's desire to ingratiate, however, never quite overcame its caution; she could speak to it but could not touch.

And as for Patrick Castagnol, he kept himself to himself. She never encountered him walking down to the hamlet as she regularly did, to pass the time of day with the closest dwelling human beings. She suspected they might think him aloof, with his shelves of books and his university education. But if that was the case, they gave no hint of it.

Madame Bouschet had found a small armchair, upstairs in a bedroom, which she had commissioned Catherine to re-cover. The existing upholstery, worn to a shine on the seat and arms, was a traditional, floral print in cotton calico, sprigged cornflower blue on beige. Catherine had something richer and heavier in mind for it – perhaps a toile de Jouy – and had brought round a sample book to show her customer.

'This one would be warmer,' she said, fingering an interlocking leaf pattern in russets and browns. 'And it would be very . . .' Good-tempered, she would have said in English. She struggled for a French equivalent. A fabric couldn't exactly be *gentil*, could it – or *aimable*? 'It would be hard-wearing,' she ended limply, 'and wouldn't show the dirt.'

Madame Bouschet poured hot water from the kettle over tea bags in three plastic-handled glasses. 'It's not too dark? I do like cheerful things.'

'This one then, maybe?'

Seating herself and sliding the sugar bowl close to Catherine's elbow, she took a look at the swatch: leaves again, in reds and golds.

'Perhaps.'

Catherine smiled; she could recognise polite indifference. She pulled her glass of tea towards her and pushed the sample book across.

'See if there's anything you like.'

Monsieur Bouschet, who had been sharpening a penknife at the end of the table, rose and walked over, standing behind his wife as she turned through the squares of cloth. She did so one-handed, stirring spoons of sugar into the remaining two glasses with the other.

'There,' said her husband, reaching over her shoulder to touch one of the samples. 'That one.'

It was pictorial: a woodland scene, though it wasn't possible to make it out in full from the five-inch swatch. Probably it had a hunting theme; Monsieur Bouschet's thumb was resting on a running dog, its rear half severed at the pinked edge of the material.

'Oh, yes.' Madame Bouschet smoothed her finger across the forest canopy above the dog's head. 'That's nice.'

'All right, then.' Catherine flipped the cloth square over to check on the yarns and see the price. 'It won't work out too dear, and it should sponge clean without too much trouble.'

'He looks like Flambard,' said Monsieur Bouschet, sitting down with his tea and still looking at the woven hound.

'Nonsense, *chéri*. Flambard is chestnut.'

Catherine stifled a giggle: the dog in the fabric,

like its surroundings, was a handsome shade of Lincoln green. She had met Flambard: he appeared to spend his life in a mesh-fronted enclosure to the side of the house. Slim, long-legged and spaniel-eared, he always stood with his front paws on the wire to watch her approach, frantically wagging the small round knot where his tail should have been. A farm dog, she understood, was kept to round up stock and trot to heel when out with the guns. But this wasn't an outdoor dog the way Guillaume's pack were outdoor dogs. She would lay money that his master paid frequent visits to chuck him beneath the chin under the guise of taking him scraps.

Catherine's tea had a bitter edge which furred her teeth; she wasn't used to drinking it without milk. She lifted the paper fob that Madame Bouschet had draped over the side of the glass and squeezed the tea bag with the back of her spoon. She had no saucer in which to deposit it, and her hosts were drinking their tea with the bags still in, giving her no clue. She settled for laying the spoon on the table with the tea bag balanced on top. They all sipped in silence for a while, and then her hostess inquired, 'So, Madame, are you finding many clients for your enterprise?'

'I haven't really got going yet, but I'm sure it will take off once I've had a chance to do some advertising.' Word of mouth, too, she wanted to add, but it might have sounded presumptuous. 'I'm doing some work for Monsieur Castagnol,' she ventured instead. 'Cushioning, and perhaps some curtains.'

'Ah.' Both the Bouschets nodded their heads but volunteered no further opinion.

Seized with curiosity, Catherine pressed on at random. 'It's a lonely place he has up there.' Stupid: it was no lonelier than Les Fenils, and besides, might not mountain people consider lone-liness a virtue?

Madame Bouschet pecked at her tea and nodded again. It was her husband who was moved to comment. 'His father kept three hundred head of sheep at one time, up on the high pastures.'

Unsure quite how to respond to this intelligence, Catherine settled for raising her eyebrows, hoping to look impressed. When nothing further was forth-coming, she said, 'But the son is not a farmer?'

Monsieur Bouschet shook his head. '*Un homme d'affaires*,' he said. A businessman. 'Like you, Madame.' It was said with perfect graciousness and she decided that she had imagined the edge of irony.

Madame Bouschet provided further elucidation. 'Tourism,' she said. 'He owns four or five cottages over near Florac. Left to him by an uncle. He lets them as *gîtes ruraux*.'

'Tourism,' repeated her husband, the disapproval now undisguised – though not, it seemed, directed at their neighbour. 'Something still permitted to us blessed Cévenols by those pen-pushers at the Parc National.'

Madame Bouschet smiled at Catherine. 'He's a good boy, though.'

Catherine returned the smile. It amused her to hear a man of fifty referred to in this way – particularly a man like Patrick.

'He came home for more than a month when his mother died. It wasn't quick – a tumour, you know. But he came and stayed until the end. The same when his father went, too – though that was far more sudden.'

'I'll give him that,' agreed her husband with a sigh. 'He did what a son should do.'

'And the sheep?' Catherine couldn't help wondering aloud.

'Sold,' said Monsieur Bouschet.

'*Bien oui,*' said his wife. 'Things change, I suppose. Madame, can I offer you another cup of tea?

The following week – now almost halfway through November – the rain stopped and the weather grew colder. There was a thermometer on the dashboard of Catherine's car, indicating the outside temperature. She had never known why the manufacturer had chosen to supply it, but now she watched it in fascination as the temperative dropped steadily while she negotiated the tortuous climb back from St Julien. It began to make sense to her about the tomatoes: they wouldn't have stood a chance up here.

As autumn took its course, the *tramontane* rose up in the north and swept down the valleys from the Haute-Auvergne, howling in the chimney day and night. A line of Victor Hugo repeated itself in Catherine's head as she stitched her tapestry by the woodburner. *Le vent qui vient à travers la montagne me rendra fou*: the wind which comes across the mountains will drive me mad. The skies were still pewter, but swirled now with high, wild, wind-chased clouds in shades of angry orange. The view across the valley re-emerged in all its desolate splendour.

Even though no rain fell, a penetrating wetness persisted. It seemed to rise up from the sodden earth or even from the ancient rock itself. The massive oak doorframes of Les Fenils were so swollen with damp that the doors ceased to close without a struggle. Mushrooms sprouted in the sloping cellar beneath the kitchen which Catherine had been clearing for wine. She peered, intrigued, at the tiny, sprouting forms and decided to buy a field guide to the fungi of France on her next expedition to the village. There was one in the pharmacy window.

Her house, like every other in the region, was constructed of mortarless stone walls almost a metre thick. Rain water penetrated the gaps and crevices to a depth of no more than half a metre, so the walls kept the rain out, but it occurred to Catherine that she was going to be spending her winter encased in saturated granite. Perhaps this was the reason why the walls were not rendered and painted inside. She pictured plaster dropping away in waterlogged lumps. Even with her wood-burners stoked and lit for sixteen hours a day, the air in the house was heavy with humidity. No wonder the Bouschets and the Mériels hung their dried hams and *saucissons durs* inside the kitchen fireplace; anywhere else in the house and they would soon have been fleecy with mould.

One fine Saturday evening, taking her best torch, Catherine walked through the woods and across the footbridge to dine with Patrick Castagnol. She might remain mistrustful of his polished fingernails, but it would be good to talk about something other than grandchildren, horticulture and the sadness of the weather. Besides which, the man could undeniably cook. The lunch he had given her when she took him her promised drawings had been an experience she was more than willing to repeat.

Tonight, as he showed her into the smoke-warmed kitchen and gallantly helped her off with her coat, a rich, gamey aroma assailed her: a slow reduction of herbs and wood fire and autumn.

'Something smells good,' she said, walking over to the range and laying her hands on the warm, enamelled metal.

'Wild boar.' He opened the oven door an inch or two and squinted through the escaping billow of savoury steam. His mouth formed the shape of satisfaction. 'I shot it twelve days ago,' he said as he straightened. 'A happy stroke – they rarely stray close to the path. He was a young male, this season's litter or the season's before, no more than that. I've had him hanging in an outhouse.'

Catherine stared at him; she had a horror of killing in the raw. She was no vegetarian, but she preferred her meat without its claws. She swallowed. 'So . . . there are boar here in the woods, then?'

'Boar are shy creatures. It is most unlikely you will be disembowelled on your walk home.'

She managed a laugh and put from her head the sound of animal screams. She did have to admit it smelt absolutely delicious.

'How do you cook it, then, wild boar meat?' she asked, curious in spite of herself.

'Ah, how to answer that question?' Patrick motioned her over to the table where she sat down and he poured her a large glass of red wine. 'You might as well ask how to cook a pig. There are as many ways as there are parts of the beast. At Christmas I shall have boar chitterlings, no doubt, to roast beside my partridge. I have already made *boudins noirs*, when I bled the carcass. I shall give you one to take home with you.'

Catherine smiled queasily and hoped he would forget. 'But tonight?' she prompted.

'Tonight I have made you a casserole. A species of *potée auvergnate*, I suppose you might say, except that I am a Lozérien and so I use not cabbage but wild greens. And naturally I have to add chestnuts.'

'Of course.' If the fruit of the surrounding

chestnut woods could be ground to flour for bread, then why not stewed in a *potée*?

The wine was good, and already going to her head. At least this time bread was to hand. He fetched from the small side oven a battered baking tray on which were arrayed slices of toast topped with mushrooms. Except that mushrooms on toast did not begin to do justice to what she bit into. The cèpes were small and smooth as cream, and tasted of loam and leaf mould. The bread underneath was not so much toasted as dried to a crisp uniformity of texture, and had been rubbed with garlic and criss-crossed with dark green olive oil.

'Good?' said Patrick, but with a smile that suggested he was in no doubt as to the answer.

'Are these from the woods too?' she asked.

He nodded. 'You have to know where to look. But I will share a small secret for a beginner. They are not fond of chestnut trees; they favour areas of holm oak or pine.'

'You aren't afraid that I shall trespass on to your side of the stream and poach your fungi?'

'As I say, you are a beginner. You may know your English mushrooms but you do not know these woods. I don't think I need view you as a threat.' His eyes held an uncomfortable challenge, and she allowed hers to fall away.

'Oh no, certainly not.' He was quite right about her ignorance. 'I'd have no idea where to look. Do they grow on tree trunks, or rotten logs?'

'No, merely on the forest floor. And they do have another advantage for the novice.'

Catherine took a sip of wine and looked up inquiringly.

'They bear little similarity to any of the poisonous varieties. You are unlikely to make an unfortunate mistake.'

She grinned and took another bite. Disembowelment, death by poisoning – what cautionary tale next for the unwary stranger in woods? The *Bête du Gévaudan*?

After the *cèpes*, Patrick lifted from the oven a heavy brown ceramic dish, round and high-sided with a matching lid, which must surely have stood service in this kitchen since his grandmother's time. He placed it on a folded tea towel in the centre of the table and fetched plates from the side oven. When he lifted the lid, the outdoors was suddenly inside the room, except warmer and more familiar, like favourite restaurants and childhood suppers.

'It smells delicious,' was her inadequate comment.

And the taste was as good as the promise.

'How on earth does a chestnut end up like this?' she pondered as she swallowed a buttery mouthful. 'A chestnut is . . . well, it's a nut. It's supposed to be hard. It starts off hard, at least. I've had chestnuts in things before and they've always been chewy. These are like biting into marshmallows.'

'It is a dish to cook slowly. For when one is

unhurried.' Over his wine glass, his gaze matched the words.

'You'll have to give me the recipe,' she said. 'If you don't mind parting with another secret, that is. I'm very rarely in a hurry these days.'

There was something liberating about talking her own language for an evening. It was funny how, for all her competence, she never felt entirely her real self when conversing in French with the Bouschets, the Mériels or Madame Volpilière. It wasn't the search for words – or not always or only that. It was more a feeling of everything being filtered, somehow, like communicating through gauze. She almost felt she was speaking a part. But here, in English, it was all so much more direct. What of Patrick, though – was he quite himself, in this language which was not his own?

They ate for a short while in silence. Then she took a swallow of wine and said, 'My sister, Bryony, is coming to stay for Thanksgiving.'

Patrick raised an eyebrow. 'I didn't know the English observed Thanksgiving.'

'We don't. Not as a rule. It's just Bryony being Bryony. She can't come at Christmas, and she used to have an American boyfriend who infected her with foreign ideas about yams and pumpkin pie.' More than one American boyfriend, in fact, but it seemed disloyal to be precise about the matter.

'So you are going to celebrate with her your survival of the first few months in this new world of yours,' he said, smiling. 'And how has your early harvest been?'

She thought of her order book, the first page slowly starting to fill. 'Well, I'm not sure I can claim much in the way of produce yet, but I think I've at least sown some good seed.'

He nodded. 'And what of the natives? Will you be able to tell your sister that we are safely quelled?'

'Actually,' the opening was too perfect to let pass, 'didn't the New England settlers invite the indigenous people to join them at that first Thanksgiving feast?'

'Are you sure that isn't just the colonist's version of history?'

She was not to be deflected from her purpose. 'We'd like to carry on the pilgrim tradition – invented or otherwise. I'd be delighted if you would come to supper with us while she's here.'

'That's most kind,' he said, but nothing more, so she pressed on without much direction.

'Not that I'm terribly good at cooking, not in the French manner, anyway – I certainly can't compete with a meal like this. And I doubt I'll be serving anything I've gathered myself, or grown or shot. It will all be from Madame Peysasse's shelves in St Julien. Oh, except for the Mirabelles. I picked them when I arrived and laid them out on trays in the woodshed. They're past eating, but I still have enough left for a tart.'

'I'm sure you are too modest. And I love a good Mirabelle tart.'

That almost made things worse: an expectation to live up to. So she flung in at random, 'You'll like Bryony.'

It was the kind of thing you could normally just say, without people taking you up on it. But not Patrick Castagnol.

'I shall?' he said. 'And why is that?'

His directness surprised her into answering with the truth. 'Because everybody does.' Ever since Brownies, when Catherine's friends had shown no interest in the little sister who was to start in September – until she turned up and they fell under her spell. 'She's the outgoing one.' Catherine was so accustomed to the fact of it that there remained no trace of resentment, if indeed it had ever been present. Even for an overshadowed, older teenaged sister, Bryony had been impossible not to love.

'And can she cook?' he asked.

'Ah, no. The kitchen is certainly not where Bryony shines.' Much like Lexie; she'd have trouble baking a potato.

He shook his head. 'Then she cannot be a woman of true feeling.'

For a second, Catherine was stung to defensive irritation at this remark, but then she giggled. 'What nonsense,' she said. 'She has a feeling for food, all right. She appreciates fine cuisine. She just prefers other people to cook it for her. And judging by tonight, I think she may well have the right idea.'

Suddenly emboldened, she found herself asking him, 'Have you ever been married?'

The starkness of her own question surprised her, but her curiosity outweighed discretion. If it also surprised him, he gave no sign of it.

'Yes. For a time. But I think I need not ask you the same thing.'

That disconcerted her. 'Why not? What do you mean?'

'A woman like you,' he said. 'It is impossible that you should not have been married.'

From most men she would have accepted it as a simple compliment, almost a banality. But coming from him, it made her feel oddly exposed.

'Well, you're right, for what it's worth. I was married for almost twenty years. I have two children – both grown now, of course.'

'Well,' he said, with a return to detachment, 'perhaps I will meet them too one day when they come to visit their mother. But for now I shall be honoured and delighted to meet your sister. What may I bring with me as my contribution to the feast? I believe the native Americans brought roebucks they had killed.'

'Don't you dare. If you turn up with a side of vension, or even so much as a stray mushroom, I shan't let you in the house. This is to be my turn to repay your hospitality. And you'll just have to put up with whatever you're offered.'

'Whether it's buttered squash and cranberry sauce or old English suet dumplings, I am certain

I shall very much enjoy my venture into New England.'

'Oh no, I didn't mean—' she began, before she saw that he was teasing her. She flushed, and smiled, but spoke seriously nonetheless. 'Believe me, I am very happy with my corner of this foreign field, exactly as I find it. I have no desire to turn it into something it's not.'

There was cheese to follow the *potée*, and then a handful each of late autumn raspberries which he served in a wine glass, splashed with his own liqueur. It might have been tempting to accept his offer of the spare bed rather than face the dark walk home, but it was many years since Catherine had slept easily without first cleaning her teeth with her own toothbrush. He walked with her as far as the footbridge and saw her safely across, and then she made the rest of the way home on her own.

The night sky was still unclouded and there was a sliver of moon, so that as the path took her out from the woods, past the end of her house and down into the open space of the terrace, she found she could switch off the torch.

As she approached her door, she thought she saw something there: something unexpected, a blacker stain against the wood. She drew closer. Something was definitely hanging from the latch. She reached out a hand – and instantly recoiled. Animal fur. Soft, cold, dead animal fur. She could make it out now: a rabbit, hanging by its bound back paws, the pelt soaked darker at the nape, the jaw slackened in a lifeless gape. For a second she stood and stared in horror, and then her glance fell to the doorstep, where there was something else. A glass jar. She flashed her torch and received a glimpse of tiny, pale, clustered forms in frozen suspension, like some monstrous laboratory specimen. Bending, she picked up the jar and turned it round in her hands. There was a label, handwritten in old-fashioned French copperplate. *Noix au miel.*

Her laugh, sudden and over-loud, did nothing to steady her racing pulse. Walnuts in honey, and a rabbit for the pot. It was neither a gruesome threat nor eerie, black cévenol sorcery – just neighbourly largesse from Monsieur and Madame Bouschet.

CHAPTER 8

BRYONY

Thursday was market day in St Julien de Valvert. Catherine found it an irresistible pleasure; it drew her to the old, stone marketplace the way it drew women and men from farmhouses and hamlets scattered up and down all the surrounding hills. There were rarely more than twenty stalls. They stood in three tidy lines in the square itself and continued in single file a short distance along the street towards the bridge. The outlying vendors sold the usual array of cheap clothes and household goods. A dark-haired lad from Florac came once a month with a trestle table of CDs; they were mainly cheap imports and compilations, but his own taste ran to Breton folk, so that every fourth Thursday the river end of the square rang with piped accordions and stamping clogs.

The centre of the market was reserved for produce. Monsieur Folcher set up a canopied stall outside the *boulangerie*, to compete with the organic baker who came up from Alès with walnut bread, and wholemeal loaves the size of millstones which he cut into wedges and sold by the kilo.

There were usually two butchers and sometimes a fishmonger with an open-sided Citroën van. Another vendor sold only *saucissons durs*. Most were pure pork, some with the addition of chestnuts, walnuts or dried *cèpes*, or else rolled in dried herbs. The stallholders were not so much merchants as producers: farmers who brought their own fruit and vegetables here to sell. In September, when Catherine had first arrived, there had still been apricots and late peaches, but now there were apples and golden yellow William pears. Figs, too, almost too soft to lift without splitting. One stall had nothing but wild mushrooms – at least eight species of freshly picked ones, as well as plastic tubs full of dried varieties '*pour vos casseroles*'. There were long, crinkly black cabbages such as Catherine had previously seen only in Italy, and beetroot, and bunches of spinach, and fat, blanched leeks; there were butter beans for drying, their creamy pods stippled with purple.

'Oh, dear,' said Bryony, casting her eyes round the marketplace. 'Will we be able to find anything to buy, do you think?'

At her side, Catherine squared the bag on her shoulder. 'It's nearly the end of November,' she said. 'What did you expect? Strawberries?'

'Well, maybe root ginger, at any rate, and fresh coriander. I've been going to this little Thai place round the corner from work. In Leadenhall Street. Thai restaurants used to be so eighties but they're right back in now. And I'm sure you could cook Thai – you were always good at curries.'

Catherine eyed her sister and felt a familiar tussle of affection and exasperation. 'I don't think people round here bother much with food fashions. Pacific rim influences are not greatly in evidence.'

'So it would appear.'

Next to where they were standing an elderly man was selling goat's cheeses from an inverted packing case. His stock, which totalled fewer than a dozen items, was laid out neatly on sheets of newspaper.

'Do we need cheese?' asked Bryony in tones which suggested she very much hoped not.

'I like to buy my cheese from Madame Mériel,' replied Catherine, taking her sister by the elbow and shepherding her across the square to where that lady's stall was situated, its plastic counter and refrigeration unit fully EU compliant. 'She lives at La Grelaudière – in the hamlet, you know.'

'Let me guess. The place that bleats as you go past?'

Catherine grinned at the description. 'Shut up,' she muttered.

Madame Mériel looked up at their approach and wiped her hand on her apron before extending it towards Catherine.

'Good day, Madame.'

'Good day. Madame, this is my sister, Bryony, who has come to stay with me for a few days. My neighbour, Madame Mériel.'

The Frenchwoman gave her hand another

precautionary rub. '*Enchantée, Mademoiselle*. I hope you will have an enjoyable visit. Is this your first time in Lozère?'

Bryony shook hands and, to her credit, her nose displayed no trace of a wrinkle. Catherine left her sister to attempt a stumbling account of their family holidays in her rusty O-level French. *Mademoiselle*. At forty-five, Bryony was only three years her junior, and she doubted that Madame Mériel had Patrick Castagnol's professed powers of divining whether a woman had or had not been married. It must be the make-up, she decided. Who but Bryony would wear foundation and blusher to morning market in St Julien? But she did look great.

'And how long are you staying?' Madame Mériel was asking.

'Oh, only until Sunday night. I have to be back at work next week.'

'You work in London?'

That must surely be a lucky stab – Madame Mériel knew Catherine had lived in a village in England but not where it was, nor anything about the location of her family. Or perhaps it was something about the make-up again.

'Yes, in the City. I'm a lawyer.'

'*Ah, bon?*'

Not just any old lawyer either, Catherine wanted to tell her neighbour. A top five firm, and Bryony had made partner before she was thirty; an influential player in the corporate department.

'Bryony works extremely hard,' was what she settled for. 'She rarely takes a holiday. It's a miracle I've managed to get her here at all.'

'Then you must make the most of it,' said Madame Mériel. 'There is nothing like having family around you.'

Catherine chose a pair of medium ripe cheeses, and watched their maker wrap them in waxed paper stamped with the Mériel name and the proud boast *Producteur Artisanal Lozérien*. As they moved on in search of further supplies, she half wished she'd invited the Mériels to supper, and the Bouschets as well. Her sister's presence would have given her the excuse to take this next step with her scrupulously formal new community. They never called at Les Fenils except to leave offerings of produce. Whenever she dropped in on them, they were swift with the offer of refreshment, or even to stay for a meal, but she sensed that a formal invitation would be something of a different character. It would never have worked, though. Nobody in the hamlet spoke more than three words of English, and Bryony's limited French would have left her quickly bored. That's why it had to be Patrick; it could only be Patrick.

At the larger of the butcher's stalls they bought a brace of guineafowl and some home-smoked bacon, and then they browsed for vegetables. Potatoes, carrots, shallots, a black cabbage: keep it simple, decided Catherine. There was no point in trying to compete with a man who could cook the way he did. And wine: Bryony was the wine list expert, let her buy the wine.

'I'm thinking of having a stall here myself, actually.' Catherine threw the information in casually, while selecting six of the plumpest figs to go with Madame Mériel's cheese. 'In fact, I've already applied to the Mairie.'

Bryony hadn't asked about the business since her arrival last night, and Catherine was curious to see her reaction now. It was typically oblique, however. 'The Mairie? You mean this place actually has a mayor?'

'Certainly.' Catherine laughed. 'I'm planning to sell cushions, essentially. There's already a fabric stall once a month: a woman called Gariépy, who comes from Mende. But she only sells material on the roll, and small haberdashery items: zips and ribbons and bias binding. No crafts or anything in that line. I thought I could make up cushions, and sell those along with some of my tapestry work. Mainly, it would be a showcase. I'm going to get some business cards printed and hand them out.'

There was no hint of mockery from Bryony; in fact, she was nodding with some enthusiasm. 'A presence. That's what you need, to get your name known, start to build a customer base. You can get people chatting, tell them what else you could do for them. It makes a lot of sense.'

Touched by this burst of interest, Catherine linked her arm through Bryony's as they set off back towards the car. 'Everybody comes to the village on market day. Women from the outlying farms, people from all the hamlets for miles around. It's a captive audience. I'd have my entire potential clientèle all in one place, filing past my stall.'

Bryony halted and turned, swinging Catherine with her. She scanned the marketplace a final time. 'Right. A prime publicity site.' She wasn't smiling but there was a glitter in her eyes, the same glitter that had lurked there since she was ten. 'In fact, it's almost exactly like having an advert on the escalators in the tube.'

Instead of hitting her, Catherine chose to laugh and it was in harmony of spirit that they set off back up the hairpins to La Grelaudière. Despite the falling thermometer, Bryony wound down the passenger window and breathed deeply.

'What's that smell?' she wanted to know.

Catherine inhaled. It was the smell the valley always had: in snatches, the acridity of wood-smoke, and behind it everywhere the darker, mellower scent of what had been here before the settlement of man. Earth and water and rock, and spent leaves returning to earth.

'That's real life,' she said. 'Not that you'd recognise it. It's what things smell like when you're not in a city.'

Bryony looked across at her and grinned. 'Sure it's not those goat's cheeses on the back seat?'

'No. We're still four kilometres from the Mériels'

place, not quite within range – but it will hit you in a moment, don't worry.'

Closing her eyes, Bryony leaned back against the headrest and sighed. 'You're not wrong about the holiday. It was long overdue.'

'Has it been frantic, then, at work?'

'No more than usual. But that's the thing – it's the unremittingness of it. Hardly a chance to turn round. I was meaning to take a weekend break all summer, and it never quite happened. Had to cancel plans twice.'

Plans on her own or plans with a man? Catherine wondered. But there would be time for those questions later, when they'd opened a bottle with lunch.

'I had those five days in Gran Canaria, back in February, and that's been it this year. Oh, and an afternoon in Madrid in September when my meeting finished early and the flight wasn't until eight o'clock. Two hours looking at Velázquez in the Prado.'

'You work too hard.' Catherine took advantage of a brief stretch of straight road to glance at her sister. Beneath the professionally applied make-up, any lines were undetectable, but powder couldn't hide the tiredness in her eyes. *Don't be old*, thought Catherine irrationally; she couldn't bear her little sister to be old. 'You're a senior partner. Surely you could work more reasonable hours if you wanted to. There must be some perks of the job.'

'Senior or otherwise, it's not our decision. It's the client who dictates. They need something, we jump.'

'Well, it's great that you're here. And I promise there'll be no jumping to be done. I won't even make you peel the potatoes. If you can operate the corkscrew, that'll be your lot.'

'Sounds bloody good.'

Catherine snatched another sideways glance. Her sister's eyes remained closed, strings of tension in her neck seemed to soften a little. It would be good to pamper her these short few days – to see some proper colour in her cheeks which hadn't been applied with a brush.

'Maybe you could have a nap this afternoon, after lunch. We were in pretty late last night.'

'Really? What time was it?'

'After two in the morning by the time we got back.' Half past, before they were actually in bed and even then Catherine had found sleep elusive, the headlit hairpins still swinging back and forth behind her closed lids.

'That's only one o'clock GMT,' said Bryony. 'An early night for me. I'm not like you country types. Made of much sterner stuff.'

'Oh, yes? Is that why you snored practically all the way back from the airport?'

'I don't snore.'

Catherine grinned. She was twelve, and Bryony nine. 'How do you know?'

'I've never had any complaints.'

All right, then, not nine – maybe nineteen.

'Perhaps they've always been too much the gentleman to say.'

'You think?' Bryony opened narrow, panther eyes. She enjoyed being outrageous, but Catherine wasn't giving her the satisfaction of a reaction. Besides, with her working schedule, you could bet her sister's love life was nowhere near as exciting as she liked to paint it.

After some bread and ham Bryony did go up to bed, taking with her a second glass of wine and one of Catherine's old paperbacks from Long Hartslow. The first would detain her no more than five minutes, was Catherine's surmise, the latter even fewer. Since when did Bryony read novels, anyway? By its weight, Catherine was guessing that the suitcase she had helped her inside with last night contained a stack of legal files along with the underwear. She hoped her sister really was snoozing, and hadn't gone upstairs to work.

All was quiet above, however. The construction of Les Fenils made it very unforgiving when it came to travelling sound. It consisted of a single stone shell, separated into floors only by timber. Not only did rain play the house like a drum but mice in the rafters of the woodshed, next door to her bedroom, were amplified to the size of polecats. If things were this silent, Bryony could only be asleep.

The guineafowls were spatchcocked and

studded with rosemary from the bush at the edge of the terraced orchard; there was no need for them to go into the oven yet. The vegetables were peeled and covered with water. The figs lay slit open on their plate and were drinking in the drizzled flavours of honey and thyme. For now, there was nothing left to do. The tiredness of last night – or, rather, this morning – began to drag at her limbs, but Catherine had no desire to take a nap herself and instead she lit the gas beneath the kettle for coffee.

From over on the dresser she fetched the frame with her latest piece of tapestry. She'd chosen a simple mountainscape, cast in a dapple of light and shadow. As always with her, the image had been born in colour and texture. The first thing of all had been the smooth splash of pure white in the middleground where water tumbled over rock, a stream making itself visible for a moment before resuming its hidden channel below the surface of the turf. Then had come the pasture itself, stippled and striated in a surprising pallet of shades, not only of green but of brown and blue and gold. In the foreground, dashes of diagonal motion caught the passage of the *tramontane* where it swept through the toughened grasses, just as it tugged into billows the sky above. Movement: the challenge was to stitch movement into the static yarn.

Then there were the rocks, the ancient grey-black rocks, fixed points in the swaying sea of

106

grass – though even these appeared to be shifting as the sunlight danced across them. Her needle was threaded with a bluish-white silk, and with it she edged the outline of a stone where it trapped the light; but her tired eyes leapt and refused to focus, and she had to lay down her work. As she continued to stare at the fabric, the full picture of her imagination gradually resolved itself over the half-finished stitching. The hillside was a litter of rocks. The grass was cut through with swathes of scree and pocked with larger boulders. There were no drystone walls here, nor any other trace of human hand upon the landscape: the rocks lay where they had fallen. Or, perhaps, where they'd been cast. It was curious, she thought, how deep-seated was the desire to see some evidence of agency in everything about us. Local legend had it that the stones which lay strewn upon the hills were no accident of nature but had been thrown down by giants' fingers. According to Lexie's book, the story was already age-old when Rabelais placed Gargantua here, striding across the Cévennes and pausing to empty his clogs of pebbles now and again as he passed by.

The thud of a bedroom door and Bryony's footsteps on the stairs brought Catherine back to reality.

'Tea?' she suggested as her sister entered the kitchen.

'Thanks. I think I'd prefer coffee. Sleeping in the afternoon is a terrible idea. I feel more knackered than before.'

While Catherine stood up to fill the kettle and relight the gas, Bryony took the chair she had vacated and pulled the tapestry frame towards her.

'Mountains,' she said. 'There's a surprise. You haven't thought about embroidering tropical beaches instead, have you, just for a change of scenery?'

'It's not embroidery.'

'Sorry?'

'Needlepoint, not embroidery. It's different.'

Bryony was gazing down at the emerging image, her finger tracing the curl of water where it gushed from the rock.

'This is actually good, you know. Is this what it really looks like, up there? Maybe we should get out for some walks.'

'We should,' said Catherine, delighted. 'Tomorrow, if it's fine. I'll take you up through the woods to the head of the valley, and you can see the view. I mean, it's good from the window of the bedroom you're in, but it's even better from the top. Did you bring shoes?'

Bryony's feet were a size and a half smaller than her own, so she couldn't lend her anything.

'Trainers will do, I imagine. It's not the Eiger.'

Catherine grinned. Expensive trainers, no doubt. They'd need to go through the washing machine before they'd be fit for the gym again. Or more likely, Bryony would throw them away and buy new ones.

Bryony still held the tapestry frame tilted

towards her. 'What's it for?' she wanted to know. 'A commission – a client?'

'No, actually . . .' Should she say? But what reason was there not to? 'I'm making it for Mum.'

'For Mum?' Bryony didn't look up, but continued to frown down at the canvas and proffered no further comment.

'Yes.' She pitched on. 'It's so difficult on the telephone. I never know, when I ring, what kind of state she's in, and the staff never say anything, they just fetch her anyway. I talk, but you know what it's like. Even when she's in her more lucid moods, she can't say much back. I have no real idea whether she understands what I'm telling her, or even who I am. So I don't ring much. I've been writing letters, and Mrs Aldridge says they read them to her, but it's the same as with the phone calls, isn't it? I don't know if it's getting through.' It sounded like a rush of excuses.

Still Bryony said nothing.

'So, anyway, I thought maybe a tapestry. Something physical she can touch and look at. Her eyesight is OK, according to Dr Kapoor, it's just the interpretation, somehow, with reading. Her brain not always remembering how to decode the symbols. But something visual – she watches TV, after all. I thought something visible, something tangible . . .'

'And mums always like something you've made yourself,' Bryony finished for her drily.

There was a pause, while Catherine gazed at the

tapestry over her sister's shoulder, fighting the prickle of tears. It was so empty, this landscape she was stitching for her mother, so unpeopled. Would Mum find it beautiful and soothing, the way she herself did? Would it be a relief from the clutter and confusion of her illness? Or would it just throw back cruelly an interior desolation?

'You think it's stupid.'

'No.' Bryony's finger fretted at some roughness in the stitching, a place where the yarn was flawed. Then she softened. 'No. I just think you worry too much.'

Too much? Catherine pulled her hands inside the sleeves of her sweater. This was their mother they were talking about. How could she worry too much?

'You have to think, what is there you can do, really? Even if you were there and not half a continent away, up a bloody mountain. Even if it weren't for my job. If I could get away every weekend. What could we actually do?'

'I know.'

'Even on the days when she knows who we are, I'm sure she forgets we've been. I don't call her either, or hardly ever. I don't see a lot of point.'

'I know,' said Catherine again, extracting her hands and laying them on her sister's shoulders. Soothing Bryony was instinctive – and someone else's guilt was so much easier to deal with than her own.

'The thing is,' said Bryony, 'we could never be

there enough, could we? Even if we were always on hand, she might know us when we were talking to her, but then the next moment she wouldn't, and she'd still feel angry and muddled about it, and get just as agitated.'

The world her sister inhabited seemed in general so alien to Catherine that it brought her up short when occasionally their perspectives chimed. 'You're right,' she said, momentarily cheered. 'Though I think I'll still send her the tapestry. If I get on with it, it'll be done in time to post for Christmas.'

'Why not?' agreed Bryony, finally turning round. 'Now, where's that cup of coffee you were meant to be making me?'

CHAPTER 9

L'ENTENTE CORDIALE

Bryony produced champagne. It must have been in one of the bottles she had bought and put in the fridge, rolled up in Madame Peysasse's brown paper.

She untwisted the wire and was loosening the cork with a practised rotation of finger and thumb. 'Let's have the glasses, then. Don't want to waste any of the good stuff.'

Catherine wasn't sure about champagne – whether it had the same ostentatious connotations as back in England, or whether here it was merely good wine. At least it was Patrick Castagnol they were serving it to and not the Bouschets or the Mériels, though Catherine suspected he was the sort of man who preferred to open his own champagne.

'Here you are, we'll have it in these.' Catherine didn't possess any champagne flutes. The good crystal had fallen to Graeme's lot, and she'd never really missed it; one set of all-purpose wine glasses seemed wholly sufficient. 'Is it going to go pop?'

'God knows, after all those hairpin bends. I'm amazed you manage to get anything up here in one piece.'

But Bryony knew what she was about. The cork came out with a soft kiss; a whisper of vapour rose from the mouth of the bottle, but nothing more. As the foam began to well, she was over the first glass and pouring with an expert hand.

'To what do we drink?' asked Patrick from where Catherine had seated him at the other side of the table. 'To Thanksgiving? Or perhaps to *l'Entente Cordiale*?'

Bryony pushed a glass towards him and shook her head. 'To my sister,' she said. 'Health and happiness in her new home.'

'Of course.' His glance swung to Catherine. 'Our esteemed hostess.'

'Catherine,' they said in unison, and she smiled and raised her own glass.

'To Bryony as well. Thank you for coming.'

Her sister, she decided, was looking gratifyingly relaxed. Tonight for the first time the candles were lit not due to a power cut but for their convivial effect; combined with the glow from the wood-burner and a small lamp on the dresser, they cast the room in a warm, low light. *My kitchen*; she felt it really was this evening, and no longer Madame Sauzet's. In the soft chiaroscuro, Bryony's tired-ness was invisible; in fact, she was beautiful. If it had been Lexie looking that way, Catherine would have hugged the knowledge to herself with fierce possessive pride; as it was, she absorbed it with a quiet satisfaction.

They needed something to eat, however, along

113

with their drinks. 'Don't move,' she said, and rose to check the grill.

Something peculiarly English, she had thought to herself beforehand – though usually a savoury to end the meal and not a snack to precede it. And that was calculating without the vagaries of French grocery shopping. Madame Peysasse did stock good Algerian dates, a box of which Catherine had bought a week or two back as a buffer against evening consumption of chocolate by the bar. But fine rashers of bacon were unknown locally; the butchers sold only fat oblongs of *poitrine fumée* for chopping into chunks. And so instead of grilling the dates in a cloak of bacon, she had stoned and grilled them with a melting cube of bacon pressed inside.

'Devils on horseback,' she announced with a mock flourish, as she brought the grill pan to the table. 'Except they're back to front. The bacon should be on the outside.'

'Weird,' said Bryony, staring at the dates.

But Patrick was smiling at Catherine, brows raised. 'Devils on horseback? A colourful picture. But in this case, we are to assume, the horses are not ridden but gallop with devils beneath their heels?'

Catherine took one and bit in. It wasn't bad at all.

'I'm sorry it's not wild boar, though,' she said as she licked her lips. 'Just plain old butcher's bacon.'

114

Patrick took a swallow of champagne and sat back in his chair. 'You ought to get a pig,' he said.

Catherine stared at him and said nothing.

'Since, that is, I find it impossible to imagine your getting a gun. A domestic pig, therefore, would seem to be the answer.'

She wasn't sure if she was being teased. Bryony, beside her, was wide-eyed, too gleeful even to snort.

Patrick spoke with quiet authority. 'The pig has a natural affinity with woodland. In fact, the pig is the only domesticated animal which lives in complete symbiosis with the forest.'

'They don't damage the trees, then?' inquired Catherine, amused but fascinated.

'Not at all. Their foraging will harm no tree of more than one or two years' growth. Instead, they turn over the soil beneath, aerating it and manuring it as they go along. At the same time they plough up the undergrowth, clearing the forest floor of the scrub that can otherwise be a fire hazard.'

'That's brilliant.' Bryony helped herself to another inverted devil. 'You have to buy a pig, Cath, you absolutely must. You can fatten it up, and next time I come you can slaughter it and bring me bacon and eggs in bed. Meanwhile you'll be helping the environment and saving yourself from being barbecued in a forest fire.'

Patrick smiled at her and continued. 'The woodland here is perfect for pigs, being so rich in chestnuts and acorns. Almost every cévenol farmer had three or four pigs in the forest at one time. It was still in practice when I was a boy – Monsieur Volpilière kept pigs in the wood. But the habit died out. A great pity, in my view.'

'How did they get on with the wild boar?' wondered Catherine. She pictured silk-skinned, pink farm pigs. The wild boar were on home ground, and had tusks.

He shrugged. 'Not a problem. They left one another well alone. Domestic and indigenous pigs can readily live side by side. The forest has food enough for both.'

It was an attractive notion, though Catherine treated it with a measure of scepticism. What did he really know of pig-keeping, this man who wasn't a farmer? But Bryony was still grinning in delight. 'A pig,' she said again. 'A pig of your very own.'

That seemed to signal time to serve the guineafowl. With her back to the table as she lifted the roasting tin from the oven, Catherine examined her mild unsettlement. Mockery from her sister was only to be expected, but she'd be happier if it were directed at Patrick too.

Bryony fetched the corkscrew and a bottle of red from the dresser. 'You prefer to shoot your dinner, I understand,' she said to Patrick. 'More of a hunter-gatherer.'

He smiled again, evidently enjoying the jibe. 'I take what the woods have to offer, as men here have always done. Firewood, nuts and wild fruit, mushrooms. Why is game any different? A pigeon, a rabbit, even the occasional boar.'

'Game,' said Catherine, putting down the warmed plates more abruptly than she'd intended. 'Isn't that exactly what it is? Just a game for you. It's not your living, not a necessary source of food.' *Not really yours, this way of life to which you pretend.*

If he took her question as confrontational, he was far too polite to let it show.

'You are right that I have other sources of income. I am in a position,' he cast an amused eye at Bryony, 'to buy my dinner rather than shoot it. But if I live in the forest, why should I not partake of what it provides?'

Catherine felt churlish, then, as well as a little flushed. 'Why not?' she agreed, and slid half a bird on to his plate. 'Help yourself to vegetables.'

The main course was eaten in perfect amity, and with fulsome compliments upon her cooking which Catherine found it hard not to enjoy, however unmerited she felt them to be. They sat for some time finishing the bottle of Burgundy before she brought out the Mériel cheese and her honeyed figs, and it was much later again when she remembered the *tarte aux Mirabelles*.

'Ah, the moment I had anticipated,' said Patrick as she placed it on the table. 'I must admit I had given up hope. I thought you had changed your mind. But I was forgetting the attachment of the

English to their desserts. *Les puddings*. Why, indeed, should one confine oneself to just one?'

'It's a conspiracy, Patrick,' was Bryony's view of the matter. 'My sister is determined to send me home fat, by feeding me two puddings.'

Catherine ignored her. 'They're my own Mirabelles.' Bryony had still been asleep this morning when she had fetched the tray in from the woodshed and selected the best ones for her tart. 'If you can count them as mine when all I did was arrive and pick them. Strictly, I suppose they are Madame Sauzet's Mirabelles.'

But Patrick shook his head. 'Your trees, your fruit, whether you have tended them or not. I don't suppose, in fact, that your predecessor has pruned the trees or applied any fertiliser for many years past. Fruit trees are remarkably forgiving of neglect. They still produce their crop.'

'You're right, they do look very neglected. I thought next year, after the blossom, I'd thin the branches out, on the Mirabelles and the other plums and apples as well. It should make them fruit much better. And it'll give them a chance to get some air circulating, help fight off disease. The greengage is sticky with fungus. Or I'm afraid it might be woolly aphid.' The pests here didn't seem quite to match their Buckinghamshire cousins.

His eyes were warm upon her. 'You are a gardener, then, as well as a businesswoman?'

'As are you.' She had noted on her visits the well-husbanded orchard, the neatly trimmed fruit bushes and beds of winter kale, as well as a tumble of late-blooming roses on an outhouse wall.

He inclined his head graciously as he accepted a slice of tart.

'I'll have to talk to you about what to plant,' she said. 'I imagine the climate up here is rather unforgiving.' This was not entirely ingenuous; she had already taken comprehensive planting advice from Monsieur and Madame Bouschet. But her enthusiasm was real. 'I've already dug over some space on one of the terraces, down beside the orchard. It looks as though Madame Sauzet grew vegetables there at one time.'

'She did. Or rather, it was her husband. He produced the most excellent leeks. It is good soil that you have here, I believe. But that was some time ago, of course.'

Catherine nodded. 'It was a mass of weeds. Thistles as high as my waist. But the soil underneath looks serviceable enough. And I've dug in manure – I asked Monsieur Mériel and he kindly brought up a trailer full of muck from his goats.'

At this, Bryony choked on her pastry. 'God, that explains the farmyard aroma out there on the terrace. I thought it was wafting up from the valley. But you've actually imported your own goat smell.'

'Was it summer manure?' Patrick asked.

'Actually, yes.' Catherine gave him a quizzical look. 'Monsieur Mériel told me it was old manure, stored from the summer. He made quite a point of it, in fact. But why should it matter?'

'Manure from pasture-fed goats is an excellent fertiliser, but winter manure, when they are fed on hay, is too dry, too rich and concentrated. It would need to be composted before you used it.'

Bryony grinned and shook her head, tutting. 'Didn't you even know that, Cath?'

Patrick turned to Bryony gravely and said, 'Do you not have a garden?'

She laughed. 'I live in a flat.'

This did not deflect him. 'There are flats in cities around the world with balconies overflowing with flowers, or turned to useful production. Herbs, chilles, tomatoes, strawberries – all do very well in containers.'

'I don't have a balcony.'

Patrick raised his wine glass and surveyed them both across the rim. 'Two sisters,' he said, 'and so very different.' Catherine felt herself pinken again, and was glad when he went on. 'How long have you lived in this flat of yours, Bryony?'

'Must be just over fifteen years.'

'And does it feel like a home?'

Bryony evaded. 'It's pretty comfortable. I've had it redecorated all through, and a new bathroom put in.'

'But do you belong there? Do you feel connected?' He leaned forward, elbows planted on the table. 'Is it part of your soul?'

Talk of souls was usually liable to send her sister into shafts of sarcasm, so Catherine was amused to see her prodding at her tart and saying nothing.

'Everyone should plant things and watch them grow. It is an impulse as old as man. To plough our furrow, to till our patch of earth, however small it may be – to form a connection with the place that is ours.'

Bryony's tart was still taking a jabbing but at least she was smiling again.

'You will see,' said Patrick. 'Your sister will plant her garden here, and tend it, and when she comes to harvest what she has grown she will begin to feel herself at home.'

'Oh, I've no doubt about it,' said Bryony, finally pushing away plate and spoon, along with an uneaten section of crust. 'Come the spring, Catherine will be practically part of the soil.'

At five o'clock the following afternoon Catherine was climbing into her car, alone. Sunset might not be officially for another half hour, but experience told her that as soon as the range of hills above her to the west blocked out the sinking light, it would be all but night. She had no desire to tackle unfamiliar hairpins in the dark.

The road up to La Grelaudière from St Julien she knew so well by now that even in the beam of her headlights she could judge the line of each bend with relative ease. And familiarity was a necessary aid. The trajectory of car lights was not designed with mountain roads in mind. On the approach to a corner, the headlights would continue to point straight ahead, lighting up a wall of rock face on an inside bend or a patch of empty night sky on an outside one. The driver was obliged to peer from the side window into pitch blackness to try to divine the direction of the road. Catherine had no intention of attempting the exercise on a road she had driven up only once.

Her client, Madame Besson, had pressed her to stay for a glass of crème de cassis, inexplicably served in a tumbler and topped up with water, so that the liqueur was indistinguishable from Ribena, and she had sat at the table for a while and talked. Madame Besson was a cousin by marriage of Madame Peysasse in the grocery store, and she was thinking of new curtains for the bedrooms as well as for the small sitting room whose windows Catherine had come to measure. There was therefore plenty to discuss. But Catherine's eye was on the angle of the sun and the height of the western horizon, and she had risen and made her excuses.

'I ought to be getting back. I'd like to be down to the main road before dark, if I can. These bends, you know, at night. *C'est pas evident.*'

'Oh, yes,' agreed her hostess. 'But of course. You are used to driving on the left.'

Her car was parked in the lane outside. There was no yard, the house fronting directly on to the little road, so she had edged over as far as she'd dared into the rocky shoulder opposite, behind the Bessons' muddy Peugeot, averting her eyes from the adjacent drop. Climbing into the driver's seat now, she wished that she had thought to turn round earlier, in preparation for the descent. She had to pursue the road further uphill for half a kilometre before finding the fork of a track where there was room to back round. It was steep and rocky and she revved the engine as she engaged first gear and released the handbrake. Back on the road and facing the valley, the quality of the light arrested her; forgetting her hurry for a moment, she pulled over and stopped. The sky was a luminous mauve, a colour that would never have seemed credible if she had replicated it in a tapestry. It cast everything round her into sharp definition, giving the illusion that road and rocks and vegetation were illuminated from some hidden source, like ethereal stage lighting. She had a clear view between the trees, down to the valley of St Julien de Valvert, the 'green valley' – although in this light it was etched in shades of grey and pink and silver. And there across from her, on a level with her eyeline and slightly to the east, was the crease of mountain which she supposed must be her own valley. From this angle and distance it took her a while to be certain, and even then the knowledge came from calculation – from the matching of remembered folds and dips and outcrops – and not from any real feeling of recognition. It was disconcerting.

No smoke was visible. Her own burners would have died low by now, unstoked since late morning. As soon as Bryony had emerged and consumed a late breakfast of unaccompanied black coffee, they had set off up the hill. It was a windy day. Catherine had taken a small rucksack with gloves and bread and cheese and fruit, in addition to her water flask. By one o'clock they'd reached the point where the gorge shallowed to nothing and broadened to meet a ridge of grassy rock-strewn pasture. There they'd chosen a flat-tish, lichened stone on which to sit and eat their picnic. Beyond the shelter of the trees and without the exertion of walking, they'd needed the gloves before they'd finished their apples.

'OK, fair enough,' Bryony had said, as she tossed away her core.

'Fair enough what?'

'The view. I can see the attraction. Might be worth becoming a pig farmer to have that to look at.'

'You think so?' said Catherine.

'Oh, definitely. For you, I mean, with the pigs. Not me.'

On the descent they'd followed a smaller path which led down the opposite bank of the stream and brought them out on to the *grande randonnée* not far above Patrick's house. He was not chopping wood this time but in his shirtsleeves stripping ivy from the walls of an outhouse. Was he never indoors doing paperwork for those holiday cottages of his, or reading his books? He had stopped work and taken them inside to drink a tisane, and they had talked away another hour of the afternoon.

An invitation to stay for dinner followed naturally, and Catherine had urged her sister not to decline on her account, simply because she had Madame Besson to visit, and the Bouschets' finished curtains to take round at eight, because they had insisted she come and take a glass of something and see them hung in place.

Catherine consulted her watch: five fifteen already. Somewhere in those darkening hills Patrick and Bryony might already be opening a bottle of wine while he considered what to cook.

It took Catherine longer to renegotiate the twisting road in the gloom, and by the time she was crossing the old stone bridge at St Julien it was after six, getting on for seven by the time she reached Les Fenils. Arriving home in darkness, she found a need to switch on more lights than she strictly needed, and the radio, before she coaxed the kitchen woodburner back to life. Two nights her sister had been here, that was all, so why did the house feel so lonely now it was just herself again? There was cold guinea fowl left on the carcasses, or she could strip them and boil them for soup, but lethargy overtook her. She just made a pot of tea, and pulled an armchair to the woodburner, chewing the end of a baguette from the morning and staring at the reluctant flames. If the Bouschets asked her to stay and eat with them, this time she would not refuse.

She had reckoned without the early hours kept by country people, however. Eight o'clock was evidently not the time for a pre-dinner aperitif as she had rather imagined; as Monsieur Bouschet showed her into the kitchen, a savoury smell still hung in the air but his wife was stacking the last piece of crockery on the drainer.

'You will take coffee with us, Madame Park-e-ston? Or can we offer you a small liqueur?' she offered, wiping suds from her hands on the front of her pinafore.

The curtains Catherine had sewn were for here in the kitchen. She had made them to measure for the two small, deeply recessed windows which had formerly been adorned in faded blue check. She unfolded her handiwork from the brown paper in which she had wrapped it and held it up: Lincoln green with the running dog among the foliage, to match the re-upholstered chair, which had now been moved from upstairs to pride of place beside the range. Monsieur Bouschet poured Catherine a thimbleful of sweet, crimson alcohol into a tumbler, while his wife took the curtains from her and began to thread in the pile of hooks which lay waiting on the table.

'Thirty years we must have had those old things up,' she said. 'I remember making them when I was pregnant with Jean-Marc. We hadn't bothered up till then, but I wasn't much use on the farm the size I was, and I had some blood pressure problems, if you remember, Augustin?' She pushed a yellowing plastic hook through a loop in Catherine's binding. 'You said I should put my feet up, but I couldn't just sit still and do nothing, so I knitted non-stop for the baby and when I wasn't knitting I was hemming curtains.'

Her husband looked at her and his moustache showed a twitch. 'There was never a baby had so many woollen pullovers and booties. You were determined he should not catch cold.'

They laughed together, and Catherine smiled uncertainly until Madame Bouschet took pity and explained, 'His birthday is in June, Madame.'

The new curtains were a good fit. Catherine cast a satisfied eye on their even drape, and the warmer feel they gave to the room than the old, blue cotton.

Monsieur Bouschet nodded his approval. 'I still say he has an air of Flambard.'

After that, it was impossible not to take a seat with them at the table and share the pot of coffee which was popping on the hob. There was more of the sugary, red liqueur – homemade, undoubtedly, but from what summer fruit it was impossible to discern – which nevertheless packed a kick and filled Catherine's chest with a core of warmth. There were old photos of Jean-Marc as a baby, frowning concentratedly from his knitted cocoon, and the girls as well, as toddlers, in matching summer frocks. And from a drawer Monsieur Bouschet produced snaps of Flambard's prede-cessors: two earlier spaniels in the same marbled chestnut, each laughing widely at the camera, tongue lolling, with a dead bird at its feet.

'Duc was Flambard's sire,' he told Catherine, pointing with a blunt forefinger. 'And old Fox was a half-brother to his dam.'

'Our dog had an English name, you see.' Madame Bouschet was smiling.

'He was a good dog, was Fox,' said Monsieur Bouschet, looking at the photograph and nodding slowly. 'A very good dog.'

There was no need to think about hurrying home on Bryony's account; when Catherine had dined with Patrick, he hadn't served dinner much before nine. But it would be good to be back well before her, to ginger up the fire again and get the outside light on. Her sister had no torch – but of course Patrick would lend her one, or even walk her home all the way on the unfamiliar path.

At nine thirty Catherine thanked the Bouschets for their hospitality, receiving thanks and compliments on her needlework in return, and left.

As expected, Les Fenils was in darkness on her arrival, with only the one light by the main door lit as she had left it. Pleased to be in first, she went upstairs to close the curtains in her sister's room against the night outside, absent-mindedly straightening the duvet and smoothing the pillows. Had Madame Sauzet had portable heaters upstairs, she wondered, when winter came? Or was heat in a bedroom a soft habit for valley folk?

Back in the kitchen again, Catherine filled the kettle and put a match to the gas. Bryony might want coffee again – or they both might, if he came too. Patrick might even accept a stiffer drink before his walk back, or they could all have a nightcap together. She took the bottle of Armagnac down from the dresser.

She settled back in the armchair by the wood-burner. It occurred to her that she'd had no dinner to speak of, but it was late and she was tired. Maybe she would eat something when they came. Or maybe she wouldn't bother.

A clench of her neck muscles, stiffening where her head lay tipped on the arm of the chair, jerked Catherine back to wakefulness. The gas – she had fallen asleep with the gas on. The camping kettle was still spilling steam, clouding the room with vapour. Springing across to shut off the flame, she was relieved to find there remained a half-centimetre of water in the bottom, saving the kettle from destruction. She lifted it off the hot ring, only just remembering to use the cloth and protect her fingers. The room spun and she had to close her eyes for a moment, clutching at the front of the old stove; it must be the lack of supper, the low blood sugar – or maybe she was too old to get up that suddenly. Her legs and back felt stiff as well as her neck, which she rolled round tenta-tively, feeling the click as her tendons found their way back into place. She peered at her watch, impatient of the concentration it took to badger her bleary eyes into focus.

The hands formed a narrow V, close to the vertical: it was almost midnight. For such a small kettle, it took a surprising amount of time to boil dry. And they weren't back; Bryony was not back.

They might still be eating, sitting across the table and laughing over cheese or coffee or *eau de vie*. Or they might be on the path up in the woods, making their way here now; it was no darker at midnight than at six, after all, and Bryony would have his arm to hold in the steep places. Or he might have suggested that she stay over in the spare room. Of course, that was the most likely thing; knowing Bryony, she would have drunk more than was entirely sensible and on the whole it was much for the best if she'd accepted the spare bed instead of risking the walk home. The plank bridge would be slippery and those trainers didn't have a lot of grip.

She should go to bed herself; there was no point in waiting up when they weren't going to come. But instead of leaving a light on just in case and going upstairs, Catherine sat back down in the armchair. Why shouldn't Bryony stay the night with Patrick? He'd suggested the same thing to her, she reminded herself. Except it wasn't the same thing. She knew – didn't she? – that it wasn't the same thing at all. She couldn't banish from her mind the thought of Patrick's bed, where he had been born and where both his parents had died. The bed to which, she was suddenly unshakably certain, Patrick Castagnol had taken her sister.

★　　★　　★

After an hour of dozing uncomfortably in the chair, and four more of fitful sleep upstairs in bed, Catherine decided to cut her losses and call it morning. A shower, which by virtue of the idiosyncrasies of the immersion heater was on this occasion scalding hot, purged her of the night's gremlins; a clean shirt and underwear fortified her further, and coffee, bread and jam completed the revival. By seven she was working at her sewing machine in the slanting daylight from the kitchen window, running up the lining for Madame Besson's curtains.

It was soon after nine when they arrived. Engrossed in watching the blurred rise and fall of the needle as she steered its endless progress towards her, she did not hear their footsteps outside, nor the opening of the outside door. It was Bryony's voice in the hall that caught her attention above the whir of the machine: two indistinct words and then a laugh, swift and careless. From her companion, there was only an answering silence.

'Hello,' she called, gathering together the fabric where it had spooled out across the table. 'You're back, then? Would you like some breakfast?'

They appeared in the doorway, Bryony in front and Patrick slightly behind and to the side. Her sister's eyes were bright with tears from the outside air and she still wore Catherine's gloves.

'Fresh out there, this morning? You'll want some coffee, at least.'

'I'll make it.' Bryony peeled off the gloves and tossed them down beside the sewing machine. 'You never put enough in.'

If Catherine expected Patrick to appear awkward, she was confounded. He drew out a chair and sat down at the table, smiling his usual smile.

'The industrious seamstress is already at work, I see,' he observed, 'and putting us idlers to shame.'

Even this last word, which for Catherine hung resonant in the air, was spoken with no hint of self-consciousness. And Bryony, as she lit the gas, was actually humming.

'We saw the wild boar,' she said, breaking off and turning to face Catherine. 'Up in the woods, over on the other side of the gully – on Patrick's side. A whole little troop of them, trotting away from us up the path, and then off into the woods.'

'Really?' The delight on her sister's face was difficult to resist. 'Did you get a good look at them?'

'Oh, yes. They were quite close, no more than ten yards or so. We came round the corner and there they were, just up ahead.'

'How many?'

'Five or six, I suppose.' She glanced at Patrick for confirmation, but he merely inclined his head, leaving her to tell the tale. 'Patrick says it would be a female with this year's young.'

'Oh – were they stripy?' Catherine had seen postcards in the rack by Madame Peysasse's shop door: picture-book piglets, their orange-brown fur dotted and dashed in creamy white.

'Not any more, no. They were pretty well grown.' Bryony's eyes flitted to Patrick again. 'If they're a late litter they stick together through the winter, apparently. Then the males go off on their own in the spring, but the females often stay in larger groups.'

Patrick was smiling, but his eyes were on Catherine as much as on Bryony. 'They do indeed. A lone female with her young is a rare occurrence. Especially in winter.'

Bryony grinned and turned back to her sister. 'Honestly, Cath, they were suddenly right there on the path. You should have seen them.' There was something in her voice that caused Catherine a flash of irritation. Bryony was right: these were her woods; it should have been she who had seen the boar.

Catherine fetched cups and all three of them sat to drink their coffee. It was bitter and thickly black; even in the mornings Bryony made no concession to milk, though Catherine watched Patrick stir in two sugars.

'I am the worst of reprobates,' he said as he lifted out his spoon and the coffee continued to revolve. 'I owe you a profound apology.'

He lifted his head to look at Catherine and from the corner of her eye she saw Bryony's head jerk up as well. His manner was grave, his grey eyes inscrutable.

'Three nights only you have your sister here with you, and I have the unpardonable ill manners to keep her from you for so long.'

'Not at all.' Catherine wasn't quite sure what she was supposed to say; but if he wasn't embarrassed and neither was Bryony, she had no intention of showing she was rattled herself. 'I was just sorry to be working and to have to say no to dinner with you.' Carefully neutral, she turned to her sister. 'I imagine I missed a treat.'

'Definitely. Patrick made *gougères*.'

A discussion of the best method of producing light choux pastry followed, leaving Bryony free to replenish her coffee cup and take it over to the woodburner, where she kicked off her wet trainers and began to steam dry her socks.

After five minutes, Patrick drained his coffee and put down his cup. Without looking across at Bryony, he announced, 'I must be on my way.'

'I can't offer you any breakfast first?'

'Thank you, but no. I have to be in Montpellier by noon. A lunch engagement – I regret that I cannot reschedule. And I'm afraid I shall not be back much before five.' His eyes were still fixed studiedly on Catherine and away from her sister, who kicked her toes against the step of the wood-burner and did not look their way. 'I fear it means I shall not be back before you have left for the airport.'

That this was news to Bryony, Catherine was almost certain. Clumsily, and with a vague thought

134

to sparing her sister's feelings, she said, 'Oh, what a shame. We could all have done something together. When you come again, Bryony . . .'

Patrick stood up. 'That would be delightful,' he said. 'I look forward to that very much.'

Catherine tactfully did not follow him into the hallway, leaving Bryony to see him out, but they were gone barely a moment before the door banged shut and Bryony was back in the kitchen.

'Is there any coffee left? Two cups don't seem to have done the trick, I need another dose if I'm expected to be up at this time on a Sunday. I'm not made for country hours.'

So there was to be no unburdening now that they were alone – and Catherine found she was more relieved than anything.

'Come off it. I bet you're up at seven most weekends at home, working. You'd probably be in the office by now if you weren't here.'

Bryony pulled a face. 'That's different. Work is as good as caffeine for getting the brain going. It's all this sitting about doing nothing I can't handle.'

'Right, then. In that case, make yourself useful. Get those soggy trainers back on and go out and fetch some more logs in from the woodshed. You can take the sack from by the door.'

'Slave-driver,' muttered Bryony as she tugged at her laces. 'We wouldn't need logs if we were still in bed like civilised human beings.'

Still in bed. There was not the least indication of discomfiture from Bryony, any more than there had been from Patrick. Maybe Catherine was old-fashioned to expect it. She had been divorced a long time, after all, and before that had been married still longer. She might even have begun to doubt her own interpretation of the situation, had it not been for the small telltale signs she'd observed when the pair first came home. It was not imagination, she was sure it was not: Bryony's heightened complexion, which was more than just the outdoor walk, and Patrick's outstretched arm, as they stood in the kitchen doorway, his fingers falling lightly away from her sister's waist.

'Well, we're up, and I for one have work to do, so we might as well be warm. Go and get the logs and I'll make us another pot of coffee.'

CHAPTER 10

FRESH AIR AND GOSSIP

December drove out the autumn damp to leave clear skies and bright sunshine. In the early mornings, frost edged the twigs and rimed the stone window sills of Les Fenils, but after lunch it was warm enough for Catherine to take a chair out on to the terrace with a book and a cup of Madame Bouschet's lime flower tea. During the span of the short afternoons, latitude triumphed over altitude. For almost the first time since her arrival, Catherine remembered that this was the south, that she might be above eleven hundred metres here but the compass placed her on a level with Orange and Digne – and indeed Bologna. She kicked off her boots and wiggled her toes at the sun.

The novel she was reading was in French. It was about an American couple touring the Côte d'Azur shortly before the war. She hadn't read anything in French since school. Maybe if she hadn't met Graeme – maybe if she hadn't turned down her place to read French and Spanish at the University of Sussex in favour of marriage and, very shortly afterwards, pregnancy with Lexie – she would have been able to immerse herself in the story. As it was, written French on the page remained a chore.

She had been lent the book by Patrick Castagnol, to whom she'd happened to remark on having exhausted the supply of reading matter she had brought with her from England. Though she hated to admit it even to herself, he was the reason she was persisting with the book, with periodic recourse to the dictionary.

After the awkwardness of that Sunday morning when he walked Bryony home – awkwardness on her own part if not on his – Catherine was surprised by how easily they slipped back into the pattern of tentative friendship which had begun before the visit. She'd accepted an invitation to dinner the following Friday and the week after that he had come for lunch and brought her the book. Every afternoon she had walked in the woods, but seen no sign of a wild boar.

Bryony had phoned the first evening after she was back in London, and talked about work. She had rung again one more time since, but Patrick was mentioned by neither of them.

If Patrick and Bryony had both put that night from their minds, then so should she. Business, in any case, was absorbing her more and more. In fact, she shouldn't be idling away even this much of the winter sunshine sitting reading on her terrace.

Two weeks ago she had received a commission to re-cover a divan for an elderly gentleman in

St Julien. His name was Fraissenet, he had informed her on the telephone in the exaggerated tones of the hearing impaired. He was the father-in-law of Monsieur Folcher the *boulanger* (for some reason her new customers always felt the need for an introduction) and he lived in rue des Quais.

Monsieur Fraissenet's terraced cottage, like all its neighbours on his side of the road, backed directly on to the river. The cottage was narrow and the divan long and broad. On her first visit she had taken her sample books and perched on it beside her client, drinking mint tea while he turned over the flaps of material. She had taken measurements and brought away the two small, cylindrical cushions. These were now ready to return, and the rest of the fabric was folded and waiting on Catherine's spare bed, but there remained the problem of how to move the divan. It had occurred to her briefly that she might do the work in the cottage, but Monsieur Fraissenet's single downstairs room afforded little space for manoeuvre. The floor was dusty and stone-flagged, the air smoky and the table given over more or less entirely to storage. There would have been nowhere to lay out and cut the fabric; with the divan pulled out from the wall, she doubted there would even be room for the two of them to stand up. The only feasible option was to shift the divan up to Les Fenils and work on it there. And for that she would need to borrow a trailer.

The afternoon was golden and there was no particular hurry, so she made her way down to the Bouschets' on foot. Monsieur Bouschet was working in the yard when she reached the stone gateposts, hosing out what looked like an old tin bath. The bath lay tipped on its side and he played the hose into it with one hand while he scrubbed at it with a long handled yardbrush in the other. Behind his heels half a dozen white geese dipped and ducked curiously, receiving a jet of water for their pains if they ventured too near.

Catching sight of Catherine, he straightened and raised the brush in salutation. 'Madame. Just give me a second to shut off the water.'

He laid down the hose, sending a sheet of water across the cobbled yard. The geese picked their feet out of the flood and moved as one towards the upturned bath, where their beaks set up a percussion of tapping on its lower side.

'*Têtes de linotte*,' said Monsieur Bouschet, shaking his head as he returned from the tap. 'It's the tub I put their food out in, you see. They don't seem to see it's empty.'

Catherine smiled. 'Birdbrains – that's what we say in English.'

Catherine continued to watch the geese in silence, until Monsieur Bouschet cleared his throat. 'Are you coming inside?'

'Oh, yes. Thank you. If I'm not interrupting too much.'

'Marie-Josèphe is just doing the accounts.' One

side of his moustache lifted a little. 'She won't be sorry you've come.'

Inside the kitchen, Madame Bouschet was studying bank statements. She removed a pair of wire spectacles from her nose, folding them carefully and laying them next to her pencil before rising to greet her visitor.

'Madame Park-e-ston. Would you care for a glass of something?'

'No, thanks, honestly. I shan't stay a moment. I can see you're busy. I just came to ask something.'

The man of the house was already retreating back outside. His hand was on the door handle when Catherine said, 'Actually, it was you I wanted to speak to, Monsieur. I really don't want to hold up your work, but I need to beg a favour.'

He turned, stepped back into the room and inclined his head formally. 'Anything, Madame. I am at your service.'

His gravity made her want to laugh. 'I was wondering whether I might make use of your trailer. A tractor and trailer, in fact.' She smiled and opened her palms skywards, a gesture she seemed recently to have acquired from somewhere. 'And I shall need a driver, too.'

'Nothing so easy. It will be no trouble at all.'

'There's a piece of furniture I need to fetch, from a house in St Julien.'

'When would you like it done?'

'Oh, any time. There's no great hurry. Whenever you can spare the time.' But then there was the

141

difficult thing. She drew a small breath. 'And you must permit me to pay you.'

The request, as she had expected, produced a chorus of protest, not only from Monsieur Bouschet but from his wife as well. They could not possibly allow it; it was not to be thought of for an instant. But Catherine's resolve was firm, her speech prepared. She held up a hand.

'Please. You are too generous, but please listen to me. If you insist on taking no payment for your trouble, how can I ask you again?'

Madame Bouschet opened her mouth to say something but Catherine forestalled her.

'I am a businesswoman. For my business, I shall need from time to time to move furniture and other items too large for my car. I have no van, no trailer. So I shall need to hire one. I could do so in Mende, no doubt, or perhaps even in St Julien. There must be haulage firms. But it would be so much more convenient for me if I could hire a trailer closer to home. Right here in La Grelaudière, in fact. It is perfect for me.' The upturned palms again. 'You would be rendering me a great kindness, Monsieur, and substantial assistance to my business, if you would agree to be my occasional driver.'

The French couple were both silent. She saw them exchange glances, impenetrable. Then Monsieur Bouschet approached her, and beneath the moustache she was sure that he was smiling.

'Like partners, you mean?'

'Exactly.'

Slowly, he extended a hand, which she took, and he enclosed hers warmly. 'In that case, I shall be very happy to do business with you, Madame.'

It seemed uncivil, after that, not to accept a glass of grenadine to seal the deal. Not that a specific sum of money had been mentioned, and she was sure there would still be some ticklish reverse haggling to go through at some future stage; for now, however, she was satisfied to have gained her point, and happy to be sharing a glass of bright red sugar syrup in the spirit of friendship.

'As it happens, Madame, I had been wondering whether I might ask you a favour too.' Her hostess raised sharp blackbird eyes towards Catherine.

'Of course. What can I do?' It would be nice to be able to repay some part of their kindness. They were always making her small gifts of produce and she could never think of anything appropriate to give them in return.

'We are going away for Christmas this year,' said Madame Bouschet. 'To Paris.'

Her husband, who had seated himself at the table with them to drink his grenadine, laid his hand over hers. 'Jean-Marc and his wife have been asking us to go there every year. Such a bother, getting all that way at this time of year. The trains are so crowded. But this year we could hardly say no.' He coughed, and let his wife spell it out.

'My daughter-in-law is expecting.'

'Ah – congratulations,' said Catherine. 'So, this will be number six, I think you said.'

Their gratified smiles told her she had remembered correctly.

'All that way,' grumbled Monsieur Bouschet, 'with presents to carry. And it's always either too hot or too cold on a train in winter time. We'll probably catch our death. And then there's the métro – it'll be worse than Alès cattle market.'

Madame turned her hand over to take hold of his. 'The journey, he complains about. But really, it's his stomach talking. He doesn't care for his daughter-in-law's cooking.'

He jutted his chin. 'Fancy Parisian ideas. Salads on little dishes, and barely enough of anything to chew on.'

'Maybe not this year.' His wife was smiling. 'Jean-Marc says she's been sick as a dog, poor thing, so she maybe won't feel like all that fiddly carry-on.' The smile stretched to a grin. 'I thought I'd take my pinafore.'

Catherine joined in their laughter. 'So, this favour you wanted me to do . . .' She was fighting down images of herself in wellingtons, clutching a bucket of scraps and surrounded by determined geese. 'Because, you know, I really haven't ever—'

'It's Madame Volpilière.'

'Oh?' Catherine looked at Madame Bouschet in surprise.

'She always goes to her great-niece's house for the Christmas holiday, over beyond Mende.'

'Right.' *And*? This year she couldn't go? It was Madame Volpilière they were asking her to feed? In Long Hartslow it had always just been the neighbours' cat.

'We've always driven her over there on Christmas Eve, you see. Have done ever since her husband died. Seventeen Christmases, it'll be, this year. It's not so very far, not much more than an hour each way.'

'Maybe an hour and a half,' was her husband's more cautious estimate.

'I know it's a lot to ask. I dare say you'll be very busy yourself. Do you have your family coming?'

'No.' It came out a little abruptly, and Catherine was pleased to be able to rush on. 'No, it's just me, so I'll be delighted to help. Really, it's no trouble at all. I imagine it's rather a long way for her to drive, is it, at her age, and with the icy mornings?'

They both stared at her, and she wondered what she had said amiss.

'Mountain driving,' she went on hopefully. 'It's very tiring.'

It was Monsieur Bouschet who stopped her. 'She doesn't drive.'

Of course. 'She – she's had to stop?' Her eyesight, perhaps – because, for all her years, the old lady seemed active enough.

'Stop? Oh, no. Madame Volpilière has never driven a car.'

'Never?' When she thought about it, it was obvious. Her scrubbed front step butted directly on to the road, and there was no yard or driveway to the rear, only the tidy vegetable plot. The rusting, white Citroën van which was always parked at a tilt on the verge below the pair of cottages could only belong to Guillaume; Catherine had never seen him drive it, but the sea of litter on the back seat should have been a clue. And there was never another vehicle.

'Monsieur Volpilière did the driving,' explained Madame Bouschet. 'In that generation, you know, it wasn't so unusual. She never learned.'

'But seventeen years—' began Catherine, then stopped. 'How does she get to the shops?'

'We run her to the market most Thursdays,' said Monsieur Bouschet. 'Or she goes early, with the Mériels, and comes back with us. Not that she ever buys much. You know how it is with you women, she mainly likes to stand and talk.'

'She keeps rabbits,' put in his wife. 'In hutches round the back. As well as her vegetables, of course. I don't think she eats a lot.'

'Like a sparrow.' Monsieur Bouschet pinched his wife's arm. 'These old birds are all the same. Reach a certain age, and they survive on fresh air and gossip.'

Five minutes later, back out on the road holding a jar of damson jam, Catherine turned at first not uphill but in the other direction, to stand and look down on the rest of the hamlet. Only the Mériel farmhouse was properly visible from this corner by the Bouschets' gate; she could see a corner of

Guillaume's roof, with two of the shale ridge tiles dislodged to drunken angles. The right-hand curl of smoke would be his, and that to the left must be Madame Volpilière's. Four houses, with two more up the hill in the woods; a vegetable garden and a few rabbit hutches. That this should be the full compass of a woman's existence for seventeen years was almost beyond imagining – and made Catherine suddenly conscious of how far she was an outsider.

Turning on her heel, she crossed the road and set off back up the loose scree path towards home. Tomorrow she would drop round and make the promised offer of a lift to her elderly neighbour. It was ten days until the twenty-fourth, and on Friday she had to go into Alès to pick up an order of curtain fabric and get herself a haircut. What would Madame Volpilière say, she wondered, to a shampoo and set?

It had been an uncomfortable moment, when Madame Bouschet had asked if the children were coming for Christmas. More uncomfortable than Catherine had anticipated, because she had never really expected them to come – not with their busy jobs, and the difficulties of air travel at holiday season. Tom and Lexie had both apologised long before December and many times over, and she had thought herself resigned to spending the festivities alone. Telling someone the hard truth should not have made it harder, but it did.

It would be the first time she'd ever been on her

own. Even after the divorce, the children had always come home for Christmas. Graeme had left in January, and by eleven months later he already had Suzannah there to make things less like home for Lexie and Tom – or else Catherine had the sympathy vote; either way, there was never any question of their going to their father and not to her. She was grateful for their loyalty.

Lexie often spent Boxing Day with her dad, and Tom had seen the New Year in with him sometimes too, when he was still in Oxford rather than St Andrew's. But at Christmas they had always been hers. When Lexie telephoned a week ago to confirm for the tenth time that she really did have to work and couldn't possibly get away, Catherine had wondered about Graeme and Suzannah but been much too proud to raise it. Lexie had spared her the difficulty.

'Dad's been nagging at me to go over there this year, since I'm not going to be with you. Of course I said no.'

'Why? You should go, sweetheart. Graeme would be so happy to have you.'

'Don't be silly, Mum. I told you, I'm working over the holiday. If I can't come to you I can't go to him either, can I?' said Lexie, as though getting to High Wycombe and getting to the Cévennes were the same proposition.

'You're not working on the twenty-fifth, are you? Just go for the day.'

'Oh, I don't know if I can face it. I'll be knackered.

And good for no kind of conversation, unless it's about butter icing.'

'Still, he'd love to see you.'

'Mum—'

'Go!'

'All right. Oh, and I'm going over to Walton on Boxing Day, to see Gram.'

'Thank you, sweetheart. You're a good girl.'

Catherine had ordered a single wild duck from the butcher's van at the market – leaner than a farmed bird, just enough for one – and picked it up on the Thursday. It was on the Sunday, four days before Christmas, that the call came, quite out of the blue. Tom.

'Mum, is it too late for you to have me?'

'Sorry?'

'If I got a flight. I found out there's a cancellation I can have. Last-minute stuff, I know, but it means it's cheap. And the thing is I just completed one run of tests in the lab, a bit sooner than I'd thought, and there's going to be a hiatus anyway because the next thing will be a new set of cell cultures and it needs the Prof to be there to oversee, and he's going out to Perth to see his family and take in a conference in the New Year. Perth, Australia, I mean, not Perth, Scotland. So it means I can get away after all.'

Catherine had to press her hand over the mouthpiece so he didn't hear her chuckling. Her son was in general a man of few words, and here he was prattling like Lexie. Covering his tracks.

'That's wonderful. Are you coming to Nîmes? When does the flight get in?'

'Actually, that's the thing.'

'What is?'

'The timing's not ideal. That's probably why I managed to get a cancellation. I'm actually flying out on Christmas Day – in the afternoon. I mean, if that's all right with you?'

'Of course it is.' Christmas Day, the middle of the night, what did she care, if Tom was coming? 'We can eat late, or on Boxing Day, however you like to do it.'

She couldn't leave a duck in the oven while she drove to Nîmes and back, but she could roast it earlier and they could have it cold: a meal for one would make a perfect late snack for two. And the next day she would cook whatever she could lay her hands on. It was too late to get hold of anything locally but she'd drive to the butcher in Alès if she had to. A goose, a leg of lamb. *The fatted calf*. Not that Tom could ever be accused of prodigality; Lexie was the expansive one, Tom was always more cautious, more guarded. But Catherine was feeling extravagant: her son was to be home with her after all, and she was over-flowing with bounty enough for both of them.

He looked tired. Probably it was the rush to pack, and the flight, and the late drive back from the airport last night. By the time they had shared their late supper and half a bottle of wine, it had been almost one in the morning. But still, he wasn't Bryony: he was young, he was her little boy. He had no right to look so tired, and it tugged at her heart. She wished she could tell him – without his laughing at her – that he should eat better, work less, sleep more.

At least now she could insist that he stay seated at the table while she cleared the lunch plates and did the washing up. He still spoke little, and she kept up a cheerful monologue as she clattered pots and pans at the sink. Was something on his mind? she wondered. But when she came to think about it, this was the way it always was when it was just the two of them, the slight stiltedness of their relationship being so often masked by the third factor of Lexie's easy banter. Or not even stiltedness, she told herself. Tom simply didn't talk a lot.

'I thought maybe we could have a walk in a while, once I've finished tidying up. If you feel like it?'

'Fine.'

'Only, the view is really good from the top of the valley, once you get up above the tree line, especially on a clear day like today. It's well worth the climb.'

He grinned at her. 'It's OK, Mum. You don't have to convince me. I like walking.'

There was no need, in his case, to ask about footwear. Beneath his jeans he had on, as always, a pair of battered black boots, ankle-length and army-style.

They set off up the path, past the short, south wing of the house and into the woods. At first the path was wide enough to accommodate them side by side, and Tom offered her an arm in a gesture of mock chivalry. But after the first few twists, where the slope grew steeper, it narrowed so that they were forced to separate, and she allowed him to take the lead. She wondered what Patrick and Bryony had done at this point, coming down the other way that morning. Had they, perhaps, had space still to link hands?

'There are wild boar in the forest here, did I tell you? Bryony saw a group of them when she was staying.'

'And you didn't?'

'No. She was – I wasn't with her that day.'

'Aunty Bryony on her own in the woods?' A grunt of laughter.

Catherine said nothing.

'Hard to imagine. There are no cabs up here.'

That allowed her to laugh and protest, 'Bryony did quite a bit of walking, actually, while she was here. You'd be surprised. Ruined a perfectly good pair of designer trainers.'

'Taken with the place, was she?'

It was a hard one to answer. 'Well, she was certainly impressed by the view – as you will be too, I promise. But I think she was quite glad to be going home.'

'Back to civilisation.'

At the next turn the path levelled and widened

for a stretch and he halted to allow her to draw alongside; they were almost at the first rocky promontory, the one with the ruined walls. She was amused to note that he was using the pause to catch his breath; regular walking on the mountain had equipped her with better lungs for the climb. Did he get out of the lab enough? she couldn't help wondering. Did he still ride his bike?

'No shops,' he said, as they set off uphill again. 'No gym. No theatres. No, I can't see Aunty Bryony surviving here long.'

Catherine gave a half smile. 'I don't suppose Bryony ever has time for the theatre.'

'But I'm sure she likes to know she could.'

They walked on together in silence for a short way before he spoke again, plucking back her drifting thoughts. 'How about you?'

'How about me, what?' She knew what he meant but was playing for time.

'It's pretty quiet here.'

A master of understatement, her son. 'No gym, you mean, and no theatre?'

His eyes were scanning the forest away to the side; maybe he was hoping for wild boar.

'No library,' he said. 'No bookshops. Not much company.'

She followed his gaze off into the trees, but could perceive no flicker of movement there. Early morning would be the time to come, not in the afternoon after a long Boxing Day lunch. His flight back wasn't until tomorrow night. Perhaps she

153

would suggest they get up early, when it was getting light. They could even bring a flask of coffee up here and sit and wait. Sitting still and quiet: that might be their best chance.

Lightly, she tucked her hand back inside his arm. 'I'll be OK,' she said.

They climbed in silence as far as the bridge, where Tom stopped for a while, leaning over the rail and staring down at the rush and roar below. The bridge had been built at a natural narrow point of the stream, where steep cliffs closed to compress it into rapids; the rock walls amplified the water's usual murmur into the impression of a much greater torrent. Just yards downstream, in the direction of her son's gaze, the gully opened out and the little river bed grew broader and flatter. There, presently, on a low, horizontal stone, she saw what had caught his eye. A small bird stood with its toes to the water's edge. Brown and nondescript, it was distinctive in no respect except its strange behaviour. Like some diminutive boxer it wove and bobbed in a continuous series of ducking movements, eyes fixed ahead.

'What's it doing?' wondered Catherine. There was no need to whisper for fear of startling the creature; in fact she had to lean close to Tom to make herself heard above the noise of the water. She hadn't expected a reply, so he startled her by saying, 'Just what it does.'

'Sorry?'

'It's a dipper. They do that.'

It ought not to have surprised her that he knew the name of the bird. He was a scientist; he was twenty-five. There were undoubtedly many things he knew and she had no idea he knew.

'What's it doing?' she wanted to know. 'Fishing?'

'More likely getting insect larvae. From the surface of the water.'

After watching a while without speaking, they set off again, up towards the junction with the main footpath, and she resisted the urge to quiz him. Since when was he interested in these things? When did he become a bird-watcher?

Instead, she said, 'Maybe I should buy a book. A field guide, you know – a bird book. I've already bought one about mushrooms.'

'The Collins is the best one.'

Catherine glanced at him sideways, and then away again. 'Right. I'll have a look on Amazon.'

It had been different with Lexie. When she started infant school she had been driven by the same imperative urge as her mother to share everything as soon as she was home: every detail of her day and the new things she had seen and done. And that situation had changed very little in the intervening years. But with Tom, the process of separation – which she fought not to think of as exclusion – had begun on his first day at nursery without her.

'The pocket version would probably be enough. It includes just as many species but without so much explanatory text.'

She could never say he had exactly pushed her away. He was here with her; he had taken her arm again. But still she was unnerved at times by his quiet self-sufficiency. Eyes back on the trees ahead, she found herself, nevertheless, smiling wryly. Not to be needed: it was as alarming for a mother as being needed too much.

By the time they emerged from the woods on to the open pasture above, a liquid sun was fattening and distorting over the far western hills, a reminder that, for all the brightness of the weather, they were less than a week past the shortest day. Catherine had brought a torch as a precaution, but they oughtn't to leave it too long before heading back. Beside her, she became aware of Tom's stillness. Already in a few short months she had forgotten the effect the view could have upon people witnessing it for the first time.

'Bloody hell.'

Actually, it would have been better to come up here in the morning, when the light would have been behind them. Looking now, as they were, almost directly into the sinking sun, it was necessary to squint, so that the successive layered horizons bled one into another in ripples of watery gold.

Away to both sides, out of the direct line of the sun, there was more definition. She could see the contours of the hills, the ridges and hollows, and where the trees began and ended. What she couldn't make out was any sign of habitation. Her eye scanned the whole vista for a roof, a wisp of smoke, an early light flickering on. Nothing. This afternoon, unusually, even here above the shelter of the woods, there was scarcely a breath of wind. It was almost preternaturally silent, and the silence lent depth to the conviction of emptiness. She knew there was life there before her, invisible among the trees and on the far distant slopes: houses and farms, animals being fed and fires stoked, women peeling vegetables for supper. Yet it seemed almost impossible that it should be so, as unreal as staring at the night sky and imagining life in other galaxies.

It had been an odd kind of Christmas. Yesterday, on waking, it had seemed most unlikely that it could be Christmas morning at all. She had called Lexie early, to reach her before she set off to Graeme's, and had misjudged it, catching her gruff and hazy, and their conversation had been brief. After breakfast she had spent an hour hemming curtains, conscious that Tom would be here soon and no work would be done. Then the call to Walton-on-the-Naze. Mrs Aldridge had fetched her mother and she had conveyed her cheery greetings into the void. She had been talking on, filling the silence with brittle chatter about Tom's coming, when Mrs Aldridge was back in her ear, telling her it would be dinner time soon and wishing her a merry Christmas.

'She'll have a lovely time, dear, don't you worry. We're having all the trimmings, and the primary school children are coming in tomorrow to sing carols.'

Her own Christmas dinner had been bread and cheese. She'd had little appetite, in any case. Her good deed the day before, chauffeuring Madame Volpilière to her relations on the other side of Mende, had not gone unrewarded; brooking no opposition, the great-niece had insisted that she stay to a family lunch which lasted until four o'clock, obliging Catherine to undertake the return journey in darkness, her passenger seat laden with preserves and boxes of homemade *langues de chat*. After her solitary Yuletide repast, she had taken a walk up here, as she did most afternoons, before it was time to think about heading off to the airport. Today had seemed more like the real thing, more like her real Christmas, though even this had been strange, without Lexie, and with a leg of lamb in place of turkey. And no parsnips. The French didn't seem to know what a parsnip was, at least not anywhere round here, and the salsify she had roasted instead at Madame Peysasse's suggestion had not been the same thing at all. Tom's present – a sweater in the traditional cévenol pattern, commissioned from Madame Bouschet because Catherine was no knitter – she had posted to Scotland two weeks before, so she had nothing here for him to unwrap except some small, token things: sheepskin gloves and a box of marrons glacés. He had flown light, in any case, with only a small carry-on rucksack.

'There's this girl, Mum.'

Catherine had almost forgotten her son was there beside her, so the unexpectedness of the words was all the greater.

'Oh?' She kept her eyes carefully on the hills.

'Recently, at uni.'

For how long? Is it serious? She cast about for a safe question. 'Does she have a name?'

'Mo,' he said. 'It's short for Morag,' then added, somewhat superfluously, 'She's Scottish.'

'You could have brought her with you. You know that.'

'It's not . . . we're not . . .' But she knew they were, or he wouldn't have mentioned it. He had said nothing about any girl since Jenny in his final undergraduate year. 'Not yet, anyway,' he finished.

The gold at the horizon was blurring to pink, making everything appear molten, insubstantial.

'I'm glad,' she told him quietly.

The sun was beginning to set as they headed for the path back, and the trees quickly curtained them round with twilight. They'd be needing the torch before they reached home; for the moment, though, they were better without its dancing beam, which would only focus their eyes away from the last of the surrounding daylight. They walked abreast, matching stride for stride. Downhill feet fall more heavily than uphill ones, and the rhythm thrummed the resilient forest floor, their boots crunching here and there on fallen chestnuts. Deaf to anything but their own footsteps, and half blinded by the dusk, neither of them noticed the approaching figure until it was almost upon them.

'Good evening.' Patrick's voice.

'Good grief, Patrick. Are you trying to scare us half to death, jumping out at us like that?'

Across two yards' distance she could just make out his smile. 'I don't believe I jumped,' he said, hands upraised in a play of wounded innocence. He turned to Tom. 'Tell me, did you see me jump?'

Tom was solemn. 'I wouldn't have said so.'

Formally, she effected the introduction. 'My son, Tom, come to visit for Christmas. Tom, this is my neighbour, Patrick Castagnol.'

Patrick stepped closer and the two men shook hands; Catherine wished her stomach muscles would relax.

'Where's your place, then?' Tom asked.

Before Patrick could answer the question with an invitation, she stepped in quickly. 'His house is a little further down, on this side of the stream. It's almost directly opposite Les Fenils, in fact, just across the gorge.'

'Right among the woods?'

'Indeed, yes. I cannot deny it, I am a forest dweller. We have an expression here in Lozère, to describe woodsmen such as myself. As rough-hewn, we say, as if cut with his own axe. Not that all who live in the woods,' he continued, 'are necessarily of the woods. Take your mother here, for example.'

Catherine drew instinctively closer to her son and slipped her arm inside his.

'One could never for a moment imagine your mother becoming rough-hewn. However, I have high hopes that I might yet instil in her a little forest lore. Teach her to distinguish a *trompette de la mort* from a *pied de mouton*. Perhaps to recognise the tracks of deer and boar.'

Tom, at her side, was laughing quietly. 'Well, she might learn to trail them but I don't think you'll ever persuade her to shoot them.' His forearm applied invisible pressure to her wrist. 'More likely try to feed them her sandwich.'

'Ah, yes. I fear you are right.' Patrick bowed his head towards her, his expression unreadable in the gloom. 'Your mother is all heart.'

'How was your Christmas?' Catherine asked him, casting around for a change of tack.

He shifted a negligent shoulder. 'Much as always.'

She felt guilty, then, remembering that he had been married too, although he had never mentioned children, and feeling suddenly pleased that Graeme had had Lexie this year.

Turning fractionally, Patrick addressed Tom as well. 'If I cannot persuade you to stop now for a glass of something to ward off the chill, then might I perhaps invite you to share my table before the end of your stay?'

'We should probably be getting back,' said Catherine, hedging; with a mother's jealous desire,

161

she wanted her son to herself for this short space of time.

'I'm off tomorrow night,' said Tom, filling her with sweet gratitude. 'I have to be back in the lab, it's only a flying visit.'

Then Patrick naturally had to ask about Tom's research, and about St Andrew's, and the invitation was tacitly forgotten. They turned their steps downhill together until the place where Patrick's track forked off the main path. Here Patrick halted and shook Tom's hand in both of his, bidding him good health and good luck and declaring himself, in the old-fashioned way, enchanted to have made his acquaintance. When he took her own hand she realised how cold she had grown, standing talking.

'Perhaps, then, if I cannot have both of you, I might at least prevail upon you, Madame, to join me for a meal soon. Maybe Friday evening, if you are free?'

He of all people had never called her 'Madame', and the mock formality of it made her want to laugh, but she kept her reply rigorously sober. 'Friday would be lovely. Thank you.'

Alone again, and over the footbridge to her own side of the valley, it was some time before she or Tom spoke. What did you think of him? she wanted to ask, but could not find a way that wouldn't sound foolish. Finally, where the path narrowed and she stepped ahead with the torch to light the way, Tom solved the difficulty for her.

'What a charming man.'

He spoke drily, as he almost always did, and she couldn't gauge his thinking.

'Funny,' he went on, his voice expanding in the darkness at her back, 'all those tales of the colourful locals and I don't think you ever mentioned him.'

In spite of the cold, Catherine felt heat creep into her cheeks. She said nothing.

'He seems like he might be quite fun. At least he has plenty to say for himself – someone you could talk to. I suppose that's no common commodity up here.' He paused. 'I don't know, though.'

Catherine, still silent, found herself holding her breath as she walked.

Her son's voice sounded suddenly close, just behind her ear. 'I suspect he's a bit too smooth for his own good.'

CHAPTER 11

SAINTS AND SINNERS

Had she been prone to thinking that way, Catherine might have feared that the first winter – the cold, dark weeks after Christmas was over – would be the time when she was most likely to regret the conveniences and companionship of Long Hartslow. But as things worked out she was much too busy during January and February to have leisure for such foolish homesick fancies.

Monsieur Fraissenet's outsize divan had been manoeuvred with some difficulty through his front door and the length of the rue des Quais, which was too narrow to admit Monsieur Bouschet's tractor and trailer. Reclothed in an elegant Prussian blue jacquard, it had made the opposite journey two weeks later, to be met with delighted satisfaction from its owner. His daughter, of course, came round to see the completed article, and then his son-in-law Folcher, from the *boulangerie*. Half of St Julien soon followed – for Monsieur Fraissenet had a large family and many friends – and Catherine's handiwork was universally admired. Orders for upholstery work flowed in apace, and Monsieur Bouschet was called into frequent use as haulier. Her market stall was now open. She had been assigned a pitch just off the main square towards the bridge, beside another newcomer who sold beeswax candles and furniture polish along with his own honey, and had invested in a folding trestle table, made for her by a carpenter nephew of Monsieur Mériel. Her business cards arrived from a firm in Mende, there being no printer in St Julien. (The proprietor was a distant cousin of Maître Dujol, the notary, on his mother's side.)

After chauffeuring Madame Volpilière to her relatives' house and back at Christmas, and their jaunt to the hairdresser at Alès, Catherine had assumed a regular place on the roster for ferrying her elderly neighbour to St Julien. Catherine tended to set off at a slightly less early hour on Thursday mornings to set up shop than did the Mériels with their cheeses; the timing seemed to suit Madame Volpilière, who had no objection to squashing her thin frame into a passenger seat piled high with Catherine's wares for the downhill drive, and then helping her arrange them on the trestle table. The old lady seemed to enjoy spending at least part of her market day morning, once she had completed her own modest shopping, sitting behind the stall on a foldaway canvas stool and holding court to the tide of her passing acquaintance.

In between orders for curtains and the re-covering

of chairs, Catherine was kept busy maintaining a stock of cushions and bolsters for the stall. These bolsters were something of a new discovery. Madame Bouschet had taken her, one day in the New Year, into the bedroom she shared with her husband, to show her the new dressing-mirror her son Jean-Marc had given her for Christmas. Venetian glass, she had announced in reverent tones as she led the way up the stairs, and indeed it was a handsome piece, its intricate ormolu frame somewhat out of kilter with the heavy plainness of the rest of the room. There was plenty of the clutter of life here, just as there was in the kitchen below, but precious little ornamentation.

'My husband complained, of course, because he had to carry it home on the train. It isn't heavy, but I was so scared he would drop and break it.'

'It's beautiful,' said Catherine, and meant it, though the mirror was not greatly to her own taste.

Madame Bouschet swelled. 'It is, isn't it? Jean-Marc is doing very well. Paris, you know – there is always plenty of work for an electrician. Though of course he is saving what he can now, for the baby.'

'Beautiful,' Catherine said again, her glance travelling away to the rest of the room out of professional habit.

'Perhaps we could do with some new curtains.' Madame Bouschet's gaze had followed hers, and Catherine felt herself colouring a little. Her hostess was quite unperturbed, however. 'I've thought so for some time, actually. Just a simple print, nothing too fancy – and maybe have the bolster to match, and a cushion or two.'

The pillows on the bed were not rectangular in the English style but close to square, cased in white cotton and laid on top of the made bed. Beneath them, at the bed's head, was a long, shallow ridge. As she spoke, Madame Bouschet moved to the bed and moved aside the nearest pillow, drawing back the bedspread to reveal the cylindrical bolster, covered in plain grey and white ticking. Catherine joined her and prodded it curiously. It wasn't goose down like the pillows but something with much less give in it; horse hair, perhaps, or even chopped straw by the dry sound it made. She pictured possible effects: curtains and bedspread in a matching print, and the bolster and some small cushions in a complementary colour to lay on top with the pillows.

After she had made the cover for Madame Bouschet's bolster, bolsters and bolster covers became a staple output for the stall, along with her cushions – and a briskly selling line. Tapestry, although her favourite medium, was a slow labour; when worked in wool instead of silk it grew more rapidly, but the time involved still made the end product prohibitively expensive for the local market in most cases. For her cushions and bolsters she therefore worked mainly by combining fabrics, experimenting with texture and colour, discovering a delight in velvet, and adding extravagant flourishes with ribbon and piping. Leaf designs became a signature motif.

Having abandoned the production of tapestry cushions, however, she found she had the time and inclination to go back to a larger work. The *Bête du Gévaudan* had long since been completed and was stretched across a piece of plywood she had found in the woodshed; it leaned against a wall in a downstairs passageway, its yellow eyes gleaming dangerously in the shadows. Her mother's mountain landscape had been gift-wrapped, packed and posted off in early December. Whether she had opened it, or grasped who had sent it and why, Catherine didn't know and hadn't liked to ask. Her new project was on a slightly more ambitious scale: a frieze some six feet long and three feet high. Although she had said nothing to him yet – indeed, the idea might not appeal to him at all, and the tapestry could just as well be for herself – its proportions were exactly those of the back of Patrick Castagnol's oak settle. Ostensibly, her work on his kitchen was finished. Heavy new russet and gold curtaining draped the stair alcove and hung at the windows; the tall, oak dining chairs were upholstered in the same fabric, while a runner now cushioned the settle's wooden seat, its geometric cover hand-worked in thick carpet wool. The upright back was currently unadorned, its plain oak boards slotted simply together, tongue in groove. Years of waxing had lent the wood a pleasant enough patina, and perhaps he liked it the way it was; very probably he did. But in her mind's eye she saw it embellished with her frieze, framed in a simple oak moulding and lightly padded behind.

The weather continued cold, at least at night, but largely bright, so that there was good light by which to work until well into the afternoon. Day by day, Catherine was able to measure the retreat of the dusk as the year waxed towards spring. In the emerging scene before her, however, it was autumn. Already, along the top of the frieze, drooping boughs took shape, their leaves picked out in shades of golden brown and red to tone with Patrick's kitchen colour scheme. And caught in motion, trotting from left to right across the centre, was beginning to materialise the first of a family of wild boar. This one was a juvenile, its coat striped horizontally in tawny and cream. Her needle was threaded with a soft chestnut red as she layered in a fold of velvet ear.

Her immersion in the work was deep, and the noise of an engine invaded her consciousness only when it buzzed to a halt outside the kitchen window. Her first thought was of Monsieur Bouschet's small tractor, but its whine was too insistent and its arrival too abrupt. It sounded like a mobilette.

Callers being enough of a rarity at Les Fenils, Catherine had formed the habit of going to the door to greet any new arrival rather than waiting conventionally for the knock. She pulled open the door – which was still distended with damp and sticking in its frame, even after six weeks with very little rain. There on her terrace she met an incongruous sight. A small orange motor scooter ridden by a young man in a striped sweater of the kind favoured by cartoon burglars, above motorbike boots and a black skirt. Sticking out from the front of the handlebars he held what appeared to be a seven-foot lance.

She opened her mouth to hail him, found no suitable words and closed it again. The new arrival dismounted and lifted his spear free of the scooter. As he approached she saw that it wasn't a skirt he had on, nor an apron or sarong, but the cassock of a priest; above the crew neck of the sweater he was wearing a dog collar. And the lance, now slung over his shoulder at a jaunty angle, did not seem well adapted for battle. It ended not in a point but in an ornamental orb, and around the uppermost one-third of its length was furled some kind of cloth.

'Good day, Madame,' he said, taking off his helmet and holding it at his breast like her champion in the lists. 'I have come to beg your good offices.'

With equal gravity, she showed him inside.

'Monsieur.' Was that right? Or should it have been *mon père*, or *monseigneur*?

She made to usher her visitor straight through to the kitchen, but he stopped in the hallway and bent to unzip his boots. They were apparently rather tight; a one-legged struggle ensued, during which the flagpole (as she had decided it was) toppled from where he had leaned it and wedged itself across the passageway at a forty-five-degree angle, barricading her into a small space behind her front door. His apologies, as he hopped to extricate himself from the remaining boot, were as incoherent as they were profuse. It was only when they finally managed between them to unjam the pole and manoeuvre it though the kitchen door that he was able to stand upright and address her properly once more.

'Madame,' he said, straightening the front of his frock. 'Père Amyot, at your service. I am the *curé* of the parish church of St Julien the Hospitaller. In town – that is to say, in St Julien.'

She smiled and held out a hand, but he was still wearing motorbike gloves, so there was a short hiatus while he removed them.

'Catherine Parkstone,' she said. 'Can I offer you something to drink?'

The invitation was accepted with the usual protest about not wanting to put her to trouble. Catherine lit the gas for tea.

He did not take the chair she had pulled out for him but stood holding his pole aloft, the guardsman at attention.

'Please.' She still had cups to find and the sugar to fetch from the dresser, but sitting down herself seemed the only way to persuade him to follow suit. 'Now, what can I do for you?'

Normally, she would have avoided such a direct question, but it was clear this was no mere social call – nor a pastoral visit to a new member of the flock. There was the flagpole, after all, now leaning against her kitchen table. It was probably best to get to the point.

Père Amyot placed his gloves inside his helmet and laid it on the table. 'I am told you are a needlewoman.'

'Well, yes. I have a little business making cushions and curtains.'

Instead of responding to this, he turned to his wooden pole and slowly began to twist it round and round. As he did so, a length of damp-stained, heavy cream linen unwound itself into his other hand. Presently, a second length of wood emerged from the folds of cloth, then finally tasselled ropes worn to a smooth shine. Catherine watched in fascination as the priest rearranged the ropes, pulled and tugged and manoeuvred until the smaller rod fell into place horizontally, a few inches below the orb which topped the main pole. As it did so, the material dropped down and opened out so that she saw what it was the linen was backing, displayed in its full glory.

And glorious it was. Perhaps three feet wide by four feet deep, it was a tapestry banner of the kind she surmised might be used for processional purposes. It wasn't woven but worked in fine needlepoint, like her own tapestries, and like the tapestry at Bayeux. The colours were faded but still softly luminous – pale cornflower blues and dusty brick reds against a ground of greyish gold – and the stitching was finer than any work Catherine had ever attempted. You had to get really close before the individual stitches were apparent: tiny, tight flecks of colour applied to the canvas long ago.

'St Julien,' said Père Amyot, indicating a figure on the left of the tableau. 'Our holy patron.'

So absorbed had she been in the workmanship that Catherine had scarcely noticed the picture itself. It showed a mountain river, suspended in motion as it tumbled over rocks, and a small boat bearing across three cloaked figures. On the bank stood St Julien, one arm raised in salutation or blessing; behind him was some kind of rude wooden hut and next to it a chestnut tree. The saint himself was intact, and the scene behind him, but the figures in the boat were frayed and difficult to make out and where the river should flow into the foreground at the bottom of the banner, it ended in ragged gaps of bare canvas.

'Moths,' was Catherine's professional assessment.

The young priest lifted penitential eyes. 'My predecessor. Towards the end . . . he was old and sick, things slid a little. And once the damage was done it was hard to stop it getting worse.'

She nodded, peering at the loosening stitching nearest to one of the areas of damage. Applying an experimental finger, she found the threads clammy to the touch; soft – softer than they ought to have been.

'Damp, too?' Put as a question, it seemed less accusing.

'He was sick,' insisted Père Amyot with stubborn loyalty. 'Church vestries can be damp places.'

Catherine nodded.

'I didn't know what to do,' her visitor continued, 'about the deterioration. But then Monsieur Castagnol mentioned you.'

'Monsieur Castagnol?' Patrick, a churchgoer? It was difficult to envisage.

'Yes. He mentioned your name, as I say. So I wondered whether you could mend it.'

Mend it? He made it sound like running up a rip in a curtain lining.

'*Mon père*, I couldn't possibly repair this tapestry. It must be, what, three hundred years old at least.' The estimate was a conservative one, unless it was a copy; there was something almost medieval in the design. And the silk of the stitching was as fine and worn and faded as any museum exhibit. 'You need a specialist restorer – a historian of these things. Somebody who knows what she's doing.'

'*Ah, bon.*'

He sounded so crestfallen that she cast around for encouragement. 'But there must be museums, surely? If not at Alès, then Montpellier or Nîmes? A curator who undertakes this kind of work, or who can put you in touch with an expert who does?'

'I suppose so.'

'Or might not the church authorities be able to advise you, recommend where to send it?'

'Yes. They might.' He glanced down, diffident. 'The thing is, experts, museums . . . It would not be cheap.'

She laughed before she sould stop herself, and winced for his awkwardness as he realised what he had said. 'Madame, I didn't mean that you—'

'I know. It's quite true my services would come cheaper, but honestly, I wouldn't know how to begin. Even just matching the fibres, finding silk to marry with the original.' How to achieve those age-bleached hues? Vegetable dyes, undoubtedly; probably you would have to manufacture your own blends. Already she was starting to imagine how she would tackle the project – but this was no good. 'Really. You need a trained restorer. I might ruin it, and it's a piece of history. It's probably valuable.'

The idea of its value didn't seem to cheer him up at all. Perhaps it was the insurance.

'It's also beautiful,' she said, eyes lingering on the saint's narrow nose, his pale oval eyes.

He looked too, and she had a feeling he had spent time this way before, scrutinising the image of his patron. Then he seemed to relax a little, turned and offered her a smile. 'It is, isn't it?'

'Why the boat?' Catherine suddenly wondered. 'I thought he was St Julien the Hospitaller?'

'That's right. He set up a hostel – some say a hospice – close to a river. He took in poor travellers, and those who were destitute or sick. He also had a ferry boat, and rowed pilgrims across the stream for free.'

Catherine peered at the unravelling pilgrims; even before the ravages of moths and damp, their hoods would have cast their faces in shadow.

'The story has it that Julien gave up his own bed to an itinerant leper. The leper was really an angel, and told him he was absolved.'

'Absolved?' Why would a saint be in need of absolution?

'Ah, yes. When he was a young man, Julien killed both his parents.'

She stared at the priest. 'Oh my goodness. Why?'

Quietly matter of fact, he told her, 'Julien's wife had given them her bed for the night. Julien came home, found them there, and mistook them for his wife and another man.'

Making his deed, no doubt, to French minds, completely excusable.

'A double murderer,' she said. 'An unusual choice for canonisation, don't you think?'

'God loves to forgive sinners,' he replied simply. 'Think of the Magdalene.'

Catherine, for whom patricide and matricide hardly ranked on a par with relaxed sexual morals, said nothing for a while and went back to studying the tapestry. The chestnut tree behind St Julien caught her attention. The tree of bread; the tree of life.

'So, was he a local man? A home-grown cévenol saint?'

Following her gaze, Père Amyot touched the leaves of the tree and gave a soft laugh. 'We like to claim him as our own, yes, but so do many other regions, I believe. As so many of the legion of the saints, he has no date, no country, no tomb.'

She warmed to the young man; he was such a strange mixture of gravity and gaucherie. She remembered the tea, which must be more than brewed, and rose to fetch the sugar and the cups. She also found she had an urge to feed him. 'Have you ever had flapjack?' she asked, reaching into the larder cupboard for the tin.

When she had poured the tea and laid the plate on the table, he indicated the banner once more. 'St Julien is the patron saint of pilgrims and wayfarers,' he said. 'And of innkeepers and ferrymen.'

'And hospital workers?'

He returned her smile. 'Also of circus performers, though I have never been sure quite why.'

There followed a pause while he took a bite of her homemade ginger flapjack – which had perhaps gone chewier in the tin than she realised. She had moved aside her tapestry frame to make room for the teapot, folding in the loose material at the sides to cover the area on which she had been working. Père Amyot now picked up a corner of fabric. 'May I?'

She nodded, and watched him uncover the half-finished boar. He studied it in silence for some time. If she expected the conventional bland compliment, she was surprised. 'You know it was the symbol of the Camisards in this neighbourhood?' he said.

'What was?'

'The wild boar. It was taken as their badge by a cell of Camisard dissenters who lived in the mountains here, above St Julien.'

She hadn't known, and couldn't think what to say to him.

'I believe their idea was that the boar is by nature a peaceable animal but will fight fiercely if it is cornered.' He turned to her inquiringly. 'Am I to take it, therefore, that you harbour dissenting sympathies?'

'Well, I . . .' An occasional loose affiliation to the Church of England hardly made her a dangerous Huguenot heretic.

But his eyes were twinkling; she was being ribbed. Perhaps the flapjack had made him brave. 'Don't worry, Madame, I make no judgements. I have not seen you in church, that is all – and you are English.' (What else, she found herself wondering, had Patrick said about her?) 'But you are not alone, not by any means. There are still many Protestants living in Lozère.'

Catherine grinned. 'Still hiding out in the hills?'

'Indeed. But I assure you that we no longer hunt them down as we once did.' He nodded towards the flag of St Julien. 'You see how it is. I am even prepared to entrust the sacred patronal banner to a dissenter.'

It remained impossible, of course. It was quite beyond her expertise; it would be sacrilege even to attempt it. But when, ten minutes later, the priest puttered off down the mountain on his mobilette, he did so without his lance. After he was gone she went straight back indoors, called up the Amazon website and typed in 'tapestry' and 'restoration'.

Catherine was half asleep when, ten days later, Patrick Castagnol called round to see her unannounced. For some time she had not been sleeping well at night. There was a barn owl which frequented her terrace; no doubt it roosted somewhere in the rafters of one of her outhouses and at dusk it worked the yard methodically, keeping it free of vermin. In the early winter she had enjoyed watching its pale swoop in the fading light; she'd toyed with the notion of adopting it as her familiar, like a friendly ghost. But recently its screeching in the small hours had left her cursing the bird as she tossed and turned. Perhaps it sensed spring in the shortening spans of darkness, and was calling to some hoped-for mate – or perhaps some quickening in herself had made her more receptive to its cries. Either way, it had eaten into her sleep in the past week, leaving her unwontedly sluggish in the mornings and dreamily absent by the afternoons.

On this particular day she had sat down to her tapestry – Patrick's tapestry – after a good lunch; the February sunlight was striking her kitchen window and falling clean and pale upon her work. The individual stitches stood out, hard-edged and separate, like pixels on a screen when viewed from too close up; the colours refused to blend and coalesce and she grew dizzied, losing sight of the picture she was trying to build, and instead sat staring at nothing, her thoughts adrift. The outside door was open. She had taken to leaving it ajar on sunny afternoons in an attempt to dry out the swollen frame and sill. In her sleepy reverie she did not hear him, and was startled when she caught a movement and looked up to see him standing in the kitchen doorway.

'I'm sorry, Catherine. Did I surprise you?'

Stupid with sunshine and drowsiness, she couldn't at first find any words.

'I can see you were deep in concentration on your work,' he said, and she could hear the amusement in his tone. 'For breaking which, I must apologise most abjectly.'

She shook herself. 'Oh, no. It's all right. I was miles away, to be honest. Come in.'

He was already in, and examining over her shoulder the tapestry frieze. She had to repress a foolish schoolgirl urge to cover it with her arm, to issue disclaimers.

'What have we here?'

'It's the boar, from the woods. The family of boar.' The first young animal was finished now, and in front of it the great bony back of its mother was taking shape, dark and bristle-haired. 'It's for you, actually.' She glanced up at him, where he leaned close, and immediately felt the clumsiness of her offering. 'That is, if you wanted it. I was thinking of it for the back of your settle, but of course you may not want it upholstered, or you might have other ideas for a design.'

Whether he was looking at her, or still at the tapestry, she wasn't sure, and she didn't look round again to check; her neck felt hot. The pause lengthened painfully.

'Yes,' he said at last. 'I like it. I shall have the living woodland creatures in my kitchen, even when their cousins are in my stewpot.'

Then he laughed and the tension was broken, and she rushed on with her plans for the rest of the frieze: the two further striped juveniles running ahead of the sow, and the greenery for the borders – including acorns, she thought, as well as chestnuts, as being the staple foods of the boar.

'I will leave the details entirely to you,' he said as he took a seat beside her at the table, 'since you seem to have it perfectly in hand. I'm sure it will be a delight. But it was in fact another work of art that brought me here.'

'Oh?'

'Something created by another hand.'

Ah. 'You've been speaking to Père Amyot.'

He smiled. 'He mentioned that you had at least agreed to take a look at poor, tattered St Julien.'

'Well, yes, but I think it very unlikely that I'll be able to do anything personally. It needs a specialist in antiques – in restoration work. I only let him leave it with me so I could have a think, see if I had any ideas. I'm really not the person to do the work myself.'

He looked at her, one eyebrow slightly elevated. 'Have the methods of tapestry-making changed so much, then? I would have imagined it to be a highly traditional pursuit.'

'Y-yes.' She hesitated. 'The methods are pretty much the same as always, I suppose. It's fine needlepoint, in silk, rather than a woven tapestry, so it's similar to how I work. But matching original materials and dyes, halting the deterioration to the existing fabric requires specialist knowledge, as does re-creating what is missing from the original image.'

'But if you had advice? If you could find out about those things, get hold of suitable materials, might you then be able to undertake the task?'

'I suppose,' she began, and halted as suspicion formed in her mind. He had been talking to Père Amyot, after all. 'You as well,' she said with a grin. 'It's because I'm cheap, isn't it?'

To his credit, he didn't protest, but merely

smiled and turned his palms upwards in a gesture of *mea culpa*. 'The congregation of St Julien has limited means. There are not the resources to pay for the good saint to be restored to glory in some *musée des beaux arts*. But I understand the price could nevertheless be found to secure the services of a fine craftswoman.'

Brushing aside his gallantry, Catherine returned to her objections. 'I wouldn't know where to begin. I don't know much about old tapestries at all. I mean, of course I've seen them in châteaux and museums, and I can tell if they are woven or stitched, but I've never made any kind of study of them. I wouldn't even know how old this one is. Père Amyot seemed quite vague about it.'

Patrick didn't nod, but nor did he dissent from her protestations. He simply regarded her steadily, and then said, 'Have you visited the house of silk – the Éco-musée de la Soie at St-Hippolyte-du-Fort?'

She seemed to recall hearing about the place, or maybe seeing a leaflet in the tourist office in Mende. 'No, I haven't.'

'We should go. May I take you there? Perhaps one day next week?'

Catherine wanted to laugh. Something about his manner of asking made it sound as if he were offering her dinner and dancing.

'That would be very nice,' she said demurely. 'Do they have many tapestries there?'

'Certainly. They have some traditional handicrafts

183

on display: weaving, embroidery and especially tapestry work. And a wealth of information about the processes, too – about the yarns and how they were produced, the spinning and dyeing.'

It did sound fascinating, even if she remained dubious as to whether a museum visit would equip her any better for the renovation of St Julien and his ferry passengers.

'And beforehand I might buy you lunch. There is a very pleasant little restaurant in St-Hippolyte.'

'Oh, no, it's I who should be treating you. I owe you a meal – several meals, I'm sure. You are always cooking for me; let it be my chance to pay back some of your hospitality.'

His jaw hardened and she foresaw opposition to this proposal, so she followed it rapidly with another.

'Have you seen the banner, close to? Had a proper look, I mean. The damage is quite serious. Come and see.'

He rose willingly and she led him through to the hallway where the saint was leaning against the wall, next to where her fleece and scarf and waterproof hung on a row of hooks. The light wasn't good here for examining the tapestry, so she moved it further along the corridor to where there was a brighter bulb.

'Oh dear, yes.' He peered at the ragged moth holes, but he didn't sound deterred at all; if anything she thought she detected relish. 'I can see it is going to be quite a challenge.'

Suddenly exasperated, she said, 'For somebody, undoubtedly, but not for me.'

Still scrutinising the banner, he stood back a little. 'Julien's pilgrim visitors are certainly mysterious shades. Travelling incognito.'

'Maybe they were lepers,' she hazarded, 'come to seek sanctuary at the hospice.'

'Will you give them faces, do you think, or leave them to the anonymity of their hooded cloaks?'

'Whoever does the work,' she replied smoothly, 'would have to decide. Some glimpses of features, I think, under the shadows of their hoods.'

He nodded his approval. 'And the river, here, will take a good deal of work.'

'Fish,' it occurred to her all at once. 'Might there be leaping fish?'

'To symbolise St Julien's provision of nurture, perhaps?'

'Yes. To go with the chestnut tree.'

Side by side they continued to stare and imagine, until she found herself saying, 'Do you suppose she was a woman? The original maker, I mean.'

She wasn't sure why it mattered, or why she was asking Patrick. When he didn't respond immediately, she went on, 'With secular tapestries you always think of women sewing them, don't you? Like at Bayeux – the womenfolk stitching while their husbands went off to defeat Harold and occupy England.'

'Except that I believe they now think it was sewn by the good ladies of Kent.'

Impervious to the diversion, she pursued her thought. 'That's a secular tapestry. But what about religious ones?'

Women weren't centrally involved in church ceremonial in those days – not that she had a clear idea of when exactly 'those days' were in this case, but it was a safe bet. Would this have been something they could do?

Apparently he caught the drift of her ponderings. 'An act of devotion falling to the female part. A suitable job for a woman.'

Ignoring the goad, if such was intended, she focused on the other thing he had said. 'Devotion?' She gazed at the saint's long features and the soft, faded gold of his halo. 'Do you think they would have seen it that way?'

Stitching the image of an ordinary man, a man in a story – a sinner who became a hostel-keeper: it was hard to imagine it being conceived as worship. But if Patrick attended Père Amyot's church, then he must be a Roman Catholic; he must, she had to suppose, believe in saints.

'Isn't all art an act of devotion?' He said it quite simply, so that she found herself answering with more frankness than she would have expected.

'Well, I'm not exactly a spiritual person, so I'd never have put it in those terms myself. But yes, I think there is some special kind of immersion that comes with the creative process. A special kind of connectivity.'

What pretentious nonsense was she spouting? She felt herself flush, but he was nodding and giving her a slow, serious smile.

'My mother painted,' he said. The personal revelation – one of so very few from him – flustered her a little, so that it was a moment before she gathered her thoughts.

'That painting in your kitchen – the small landscape in oils, on the wall near the bookshelves.' Sombre hills, a threatening sky. 'Is that hers?'

His delight that she had noticed it was undisguised. 'I have others. Upstairs in my room, mostly. But that one is my favourite.'

She resolved to take a proper look the next time she visited. But there came into her head the voice of Monsieur Bouschet. *His father kept three hundred head of sheep at one time.* How common was it for a farmer's wife hereabouts to have painted in oils?

Leaving the banner where it stood, they returned along the corridor towards the door. Patrick had arranged to pick her up on Tuesday morning for their outing to the museum and lunch and she was thanking him when he stopped her with a hand on the arm. He was looking at the *Bête du Gévaudan*.

'The Black Beast,' he said, 'if I am not very much mistaken. Our local bogle, the icon of our bloodstained past.'

For a minute, man and wolf eyed each other

appraisingly in the dimly lit hallway. Then Patrick turned to Catherine, his face intent.

'It's wonderful,' he said. 'I should dearly like to have it. Is it for sale?'

CHAPTER 12

THE HOUSE OF SILK

The silk museum in St-Hippolyte-du-Fort was a building much like any other in the region. It crouched low against a hillside at the edge of the little town, and the blocks of grey-black granite from which it was constructed matched so exactly those of the stone walls supporting the banks of terraces which shelved above and below it, that it seemed as one with its landscape – a landscape so immemorial that it was hard to think of it as manmade at all.

The museum, it emerged, was open generally to the public only from Easter to All Saints. They were lucky, on the Tuesday of their visit, that a party of schoolchildren had booked a tour; apart from the gaggle of chattering, rucksacked nine-year-olds and their harassed teacher, Catherine and Patrick were the only visitors. For a while they hung on the fringes of the school group, taking advantage of the demonstrations and explanations offered to the children by the young women of the museum staff. But soon, by unspoken consent, they chose to linger behind, letting the primary-coloured crocodile pass ahead of them into other rooms and giving them space to absorb the displays at their leisure.

The place was well laid out. Scrubbed wooden floors and unadorned stone walls set off glass cases containing sprays of mulberry branches and, hidden amongst the foliage, silkworms at every stage of development, from fat, striped caterpillars to fleecy cocoons. The tapestries which Patrick had brought them to see were in a ground floor gallery. Religious as well as secular subjects were depicted here; the imagery was rich and the workmanship fine, and there were saints aplenty – but no other St Julien. Another room contained examples of the old machinery of production, from combing and spinning to the weaving of the finished cloth; the museum girls had things set in clattering motion for the instruction of their young audience. But what detained Catherine the longest, and Patrick by her side, were the signboards which ran the length of a long attic under the steep-pitched roof, telling in text and sketch and sepia print the story of silk in the Cévennes.

One photograph, in particular, arrested her attention: it showed a young girl in smock and clogs, standing grinning at a loom. She could not have been more than eight or nine, bringing to mind the images Catherine had seen of Manchester cotton spinners of the same period. But whereas she recalled the English factory urchins as always looking pale to the point of consumptive, this child was stout and dimple-elbowed; even in black and white there was no disguising the ruddiness of her cheeks. Her grin was lopsided, missing a front tooth, exactly the way Lexie's had been one summer at about the same age.

Patrick, she became aware, was no longer looking at the photograph but sideways at her.

'She's beautiful,' she said, laughing a little in embarrassment at her own irrelevant sentimentality. 'She looks, I don't know . . . so modern.' As if it had been taken just the other day; as if she was one of the children from the school party downstairs, dressed up in period costume.

'Eighteen sixty-two,' read Patrick. 'She must have been one of the last. So young, and soon to be out of a job.'

Within the timescale of man's cultivation of these hills, the flourishing of the silk industry had been but a brief episode. Though known briefly here as early as the thirteenth century, they learned that it took hold with wide prevalence only in 1709, after what the signboards termed '*la grande gelée des châtaigneraies*': the great freeze of the chestnut groves. A century and a half later it was dying. Quite literally so, in fact: in the 1850s, disease struck the silkworms, and within a decade the silk industry had gone.

After they had seen enough, they wandered back downstairs and out into the February sunshine. The school party had been issued with clipboards and lists of quiz questions, and had been let loose to roam the galleries in packs; out here, however, all was tranquillity.

'How long do mulberries live?' Catherine wondered aloud as she gazed down over the terraces of close-planted, pollarded trees.

'A long time, I believe. Fifty, eighty years? Why do you ask?'

'Oh, I don't know. I was just wondering whether the grounds had all been planted up again like this when they opened the museum.'

He looked at her curiously, so that her face grew a little hot. 'I know it's silly, but I was wishing it might always have stayed this way, when every-where else changed.'

It was the notion of continuity that appealed to her, the idea of unbroken cultivation – even if, when silk production ceased, the trees may have stood untended for a few generations.

'Strange,' he said, 'to think that so much of the landscape must once have looked like this. Every other hillside clothed with mulberries.'

'Yes.' She turned to him eagerly. 'It's so hard to imagine, isn't it? The way we see it now, it seems so permanent. It's funny to think that maybe it's not.' The chestnut woods, like those around La Grelaudière; the valley pastures which provided winter grazing for the sheep. It was impossible to think of it as transient or new. How could it not have been that way forever?

He was smiling at her, but his voice was serious. 'Nothing is wholly immune to change.'

They walked further on, past the end of the museum building and up some steps, to where a stone bench commanded a view down over the valley of St-Hippolyte. Here a crook of the hill provided shelter from the slight breeze, and a gap in the mulberries created a patch of unbroken sun, free from the fretwork of shadow cast elsewhere by the leafless branches. Catherine sat down at one end of the bench and turned her face up to the light.

'Mmm. Warm.'

'Mmm,' agreed Patrick, following suit. Then, to her surprise, he swivelled sideways, pulled his feet up on to the bench with knees bent, and lay back flat on the sun-warmed granite. The excellent lunch they'd had earlier at Patrick's 'very pleasant little restaurant' and the bottle of Châteauneuf du Pape they'd shared seemed to be catching up with them both. His head lay not five inches from her lap, and his eyes were closed. Up close, his hair looked softer and not as springy as she had thought, though the grey might be stiffer than the black. She had to resist the urge to touch it and find out.

He looked very peaceful. People were supposed to look younger in sleep, but in Patrick's case, sleep – if indeed he was asleep – had if anything the opposite effect. The flesh had slackened and lost its tautness, making him appear more worn but also somehow more comfortable; his face had lost the guarded look it always had when he was awake.

Legs stretched out before her, Catherine closed her own eyes to rest them for a second, and was surprised when, what felt like only moments later, she heard a quiet cough beside her.

'Madame?'

'*Oui? Pardon.*' The instinct to apology might be English, but it was the French language which now came first to mind.

The young museum curator was looking down at Patrick, still uncompromisingly asleep at Catherine's side.

'Madame, if you please, we'll be closing soon. Closing in ten minutes. You need to wake your husband.'

They spoke little on the journey back to La Grelaudière. Patrick drove at a leisurely pace – the only sensible way to take the winding roads, having chosen a route which scaled the hills, in preference to a longer and faster road round. He made smooth work of the hairpins, always seeming to select the line of least deviation, and he slowed the car with the gearbox on the downhill runs, instead of snatching at the brakes as she herself still had a tendency to do.

It was six o'clock and dusk was tumbling round about them when they crested the final ridge before the valley of St Julien. Without warning, Patrick slowed, pulled over on to the mixture of grass and gravel at the side of the road, and stopped. The sun was behind them, casting its glow of winter pink to chase away the golden remnants of the spring day, but Catherine felt no urge to turn. Together, with their backs to the sunset, they looked down silently on the little town and, above it, across to the woods of home.

The route they were on had been unfamiliar, but a thought now occurred to her. 'Is this the road that brings us down past the Besson farm? You know, Madame Besson – she's the cousin of Madame Peysasse in the grocery shop.'

He nodded. It had been getting dark when she was up here the last time, too, at Thanksgiving.

'Maybe I should plant some mulberry trees,' she said.

He raised a quizzical eyebrow.

'At Les Fenils, on the terraces. Some of the plum and cherry trees are really much too old, past their useful fruiting life. I could have a few mulberries instead, and cultivate my own silkworms.'

'And make your own silks for the tapestry of St Julien?'

He was laughing at her, she knew. She had no idea how many mulberry trees you would need to produce even one skein of tapestry silk, not to mention the equipment that would be needed. The machinery at the silk museum had filled a room.

And yet she had a feeling he wasn't patronising her when he said quietly, 'It is a pleasing notion, to be sure.' He narrowed his eyes and stared at the valley below them. 'To re-create something of that former landscape, even just a small part, would have an attraction.'

He let in the clutch and pulled back out on to the road. The past was the past, she thought, and things could alter their aspect with the passage of time. Nothing, as he had said, was wholly immune to change.

It was dark well before they reached the hamlet, a thorough-going darkness devoid of stars, for clouds had massed with the twilight, blacking out the sky like a tarpaulin. As they passed the twin gateposts of the Bouchets' farm, he slowed again, approaching at a crawl the hairpin turn which followed. It was where the track forked off – the one that led to his own house.

'Shall I drive you straight back,' he inquired, 'or can I persuade you to come and share a glass or two to round off the day?'

Catherine was tired, and actually a little queasy from swinging round so many corners; taking in snatches of scrolling view from the passenger seat was a different matter entirely from watching the road in her more accustomed position as driver. But he had been so kind to take her out, and she had lost the battle over the bill at lunch, and it seemed churlish to insist on being taken home when the hour was still so early.

In his kitchen he lit the lamps and fetched a bottle and glasses, and they settled companionably on either side of the long refectory table. Neither of them, it emerged, had any desire to eat again, for the lunch had been a substantial one in the old manner as well as very good, but Patrick produced little savoury biscuits and a few Niçoise olives, tiny, tart and blue as sloes. The bottle was a Sauterne – a strange choice, she thought, with the olives and salty biscuits, but one which, to her surprise, worked perfectly. Conversation was easy and comfortable. The kitchen was warm, the wine seductive and the night outside cold; the woods were dark and the way steep, and she had on shoes more appropriate to eating out and visiting museums than to tackling a mountain path.

Nevertheless. 'I really ought to be going.'

'You don't have to.' He said it quietly and almost completely without emphasis. It would be good to forget the walk home, to turn away from the night and the woods. It would be good to stay.

Like Bryony did, like Bryony did, like Bryony did.

'No.' She spoke with finality and she sensed his glance falling away. 'No, honestly. Thank you.'

But he had been so generous today with his companionship; they'd had a good time, he'd begun to unbend. She hated to end their day this way, in awkwardness. 'You can see me as far as the bridge, though, if you're willing. And, Patrick . . .'

'Yes?' He looked up again, half expectantly; she braved his eye and offered a smile.

'Do you think I might borrow a torch?'

CHAPTER 13

THE SEVENTH DAY

Towards the end of February, Bryony telephoned, around the time that Catherine had never lost the habit of thinking of as half term. They hadn't spoken in over a fortnight – not that that was in any way unusual – and Catherine was delighted to hear her voice.

'Bryony. How are you?'

'Knackered.'

That raised a grin. Bryony was always knackered; she wouldn't have known what to do if she hadn't been knackered.

'Things are busy at work, are they?'

'Busy isn't the half of it. Busy would be a breeze. I fantasise about being merely busy. January's often a quiet month – the post-Christmas lull, you know – but not this year. It was wall-to-wall, and piled high solidly in between. And February's been worse.'

'It'll calm down.' Though there never did seem to be any less frantic periods, if Bryony's account were to be believed.

'Oh, it's easy for you to say. Up that mountain of yours without a care in the world, and time to call your own. Keeping pigs. Have you got one yet, by the way?'

'Oh, shut up.'

The line crackled. 'God, I'm fed up with it, Cath.'

Catherine said nothing. This was new, the note of real weariness in her sister's voice. Usually she loved to moan; the moaning had always seemed as essential to her as the adrenalin of the job. But suddenly she sounded tired – she sounded her age.

'Seriously, I've had enough. I'm worn out with it, physically and mentally. It's a real effort to get myself out of bed and into the shower. And then at the other end, I bring files home but I have to force myself to open them. It used to be a pleasure.'

'Or a compulsion, more like.'

Her sister rode the jibe. She sounded too weary for anything but honesty. 'Not quite that, I hope. But it was compelling, I used to find it compelling. Recently, I don't.'

Catherine groped for reassurances but none came immediately to hand; that mergers and acquisitions could ever have the power to compel was beyond her imagination. She resorted to the tried and trusted.

'As you say, you're tired. Everyone gets tired, and being tired makes you jaded.'

'Tired,' repeated Bryony, and Catherine thought she said it oddly; distanced by the miles and by having no sight of her face, it was hard to gauge her mood.

'Maybe you need a holiday. Apart from those few days here with me at Thanksgiving – and, I sincerely hope, Christmas Day – you haven't had any proper time off in a year. Wasn't it last February you went to the Canaries?'

'Early February.'

There was a difficult pause. In a conversation with Bryony any pause was unusual enough to be difficult.

Then, 'You're right,' she said slowly. 'Up to a point, you are right. I do need some time off – I desperately do.'

Desperately? Desperation was not a state Catherine associated with her sister; and, actually, it wasn't desperation that edged her voice. It was something much more emphatic, like resolution.

Catherine fell back on the only thing she had available to offer. 'You could come here again. You know that. You're always welcome. We can . . .' We can what? Go for long walks? Visit the silk museum? '. . . go shopping in Alès. Montpellier, if you like. Maybe we could both have a couple of nights away, down at the coast. It would be fun. I haven't been anywhere since I arrived, not even for a night.'

She'd had, in fact, no desire to go anywhere at all; no curiosity, as yet, to explore any further afield than the valleys surrounding her own house. For now, there seemed to be enough for her here.

'I did think I might come down there,' said Bryony.

'Well, that's great! It'll be—'

'But not for a holiday.' Her sister's voice cut across her, sounding hasty, almost offhand. 'If I needed a holiday I'd go to Gran Canaria again, get some sun. Or if it was two weeks, Antigua. But I don't need a fortnight with the sun lotion and too many Bacardi and tonics. I need a proper break. A *proper break*.'

This last was repeated on a rising tone. A tone not to be gainsaid, thought Catherine, visited by the picture of Bryony the senior partner in negotiation mode. She said nothing, and waited.

'I've put in for a sabbatical.'

'For a . . . ?' Catherine stalled.

'A sabbatical. You know, "six days shalt thou labour", and all that. Except in our case it's fifteen years we have to put in, after qualification, before we're entitled to it – which in my case means I've been owed one for six years. My seventh day is long overdue.'

Sabbatical? Catherine had imagined those were just for people in universities, having time out from teaching to write their book. Did lawyers really have sabbaticals?

'What would you be doing? I mean, would they expect you to do something specific?' A book? Legal research? Bryony would surely do that in a library in London, not halfway up a mountain in France.

'Anything and nothing. There's no particular expectation, it's just time off, to do your own thing. They call it "self-development".'

It was exactly the sort of phrase at which Bryony normally scoffed, but she wasn't scoffing now.

'And what would you do?'

'Oh God, I don't know. Sleep for a week. Learn the saxophone. Read *War and Peace*.'

Bryony would hate *War and Peace*. 'How long do they give you, then?' she asked.

'Three months.'

'Three *months*?' Her sister couldn't have had more than two consecutive weeks away from work since the summer she graduated. And even at university her holidays had been filled with vacation placements, mini pupillages, legal internships. What would she do with three months entirely to herself?

'You don't mind, do you, if I come down there and invade your patch?'

'Of course not. Don't be silly. It would be great to have some proper time together.' Catherine meant it; absolutely, she meant it. But her pleasure at the prospect was mixed with some alarm. They hadn't spent that long together since they were kids at home.

'Maybe I could help you with the business. The strategic side. I bet you haven't even got a development plan, have you?'

Caught between a wince and a grin, Catherine fenced her off. 'Well, I will let you at my accounts, if you like. And the French tax forms are a nightmare. I wouldn't say no to some help there.'

Her sister's grin was almost audible. 'But look,

Cath, I don't want you to think I'm just going to land on you for three months. I shan't take over your life, don't worry. I wasn't thinking of staying with you the whole time.'

Disappointment was tinged with just a little relief. This was all a bit sudden, after all. Bryony was Bryony and three months was three months. 'Oh, then what? Go travelling as well? "Do" the south of France?'

'No, no. I didn't mean that. I just meant, I don't have to stay at Les Fenils if I'll be in the way.'

'Oh, I'm sure you wouldn't be,' said Catherine robustly. 'It's a big house; I rattle around here by myself. The company would be very welcome.'

'Come on.' Sometimes there was no hood-winking a sister. 'Anybody else, and it would be true. Any normal person would be going slowly insane, living on their own up there with only the trees to talk to. But admit it, you love it.'

Catherine opened her mouth to speak, but Bryony was still talking.

'I'm sure I can find a place OK. It won't be the season yet. I'm planning to come in early April, so I'll be gone before the schools break up. There are bound to be holiday cottages available.'

Holiday cottages. All of a sudden, Catherine felt conscious of her tongue, which seemed bigger than before, and too dry. Oh, dear Lord, was that what this was all really about?

'Patrick Castagnol, for example. He might have an empty place I can use.'

Bryony said the name casually, but neither of them was fooled. *He might have an empty place.* Did that mean they had talked – that they'd already discussed it? Which meant they had been in touch. Just once, or maybe more than that; maybe all the time, maybe ever since—

'But if it's all right, I'd hope to come to you first. Stay for a while until I can sort something out.'

Or maybe not. Maybe Bryony hadn't spoken to him at all and the whole venture was born of wishful thinking on her part: a blind punt, a volley in the darkness. Catherine wasn't sure which was worse – that they had been talking or that they hadn't.

'Patrick,' began Catherine, and then stopped, unsure how to go on.

'That's not why. It might be part of it, but it's not the only reason. I do need a break. I'm really all in, with work. And anyway, if it were the reason, would that be so bad?'

Would it? There were ten reasons why it might be, none of which Catherine felt able to voice or even articulate to herself.

'There's nothing wrong with finding out, is there?' continued Bryony. 'I want to know. I want to try. You've had Graeme, a family. All I've ever had is work.'

Patrick Castagnol wasn't Graeme; Patrick wasn't . . .

'Maybe I want to have something different for a change. Something real.'

'Bry,' she tried tentatively, 'there's nothing real or unreal about life here or life in London. People are just people; work is just work. You know that really. As you said to start with, you're tired, and you're jaded. You need a change, a break, I agree. But it doesn't mean you have to toss away what you have, or rubbish it. And it doesn't mean you have to rush at anything you'll regret.'

There, it was said. She had done the big sister thing that she had determined she wouldn't; she had sounded the warning.

If the temperature on the line was a degree or two frostier, it was only momentary. Then Bryony was back to familiar form. 'Well, if it doesn't work out then, hey, at least I'll have had a good time. Decent grub, rather too much fresh air, and a Frenchman to put down to experience. And you'll have had your tax return sorted out.'

After ringing off five minutes later, Catherine remained seated at the kitchen table with the telephone in her hand. Her eyes drifted across unseeingly to where her tapestry frame lay, and her needle, threaded with black silk and tucked neatly into the muddy cloven trotter of the final juvenile boar.

Bryony and Patrick. That Saturday night in November had been one thing; to that she had accustomed herself. But coming here, perhaps starting up something more . . .

Of course, it was none of her business.

It was perverse, really, since Bryony was coming;

Bryony was going to be here for three months. But for the first time she could recall since she arrived at Les Fenils, Catherine felt heavy upon her the consciousness of being alone.

She rose from the table, replaced the telephone on the dresser and went to fill the kettle. Some decent, strong coffee was what she needed. And then she had new bedroom curtains to make for Madame Volpilière.

PART II

CHAPTER 14

THE SPRING TRANSHUMANCE

This time Catherine was going the same way as the sheep.

In a surreal reversal of natural laws, the undulating stream was flowing uphill, bobbing ahead of her along the narrow track. It was hot. Accustomed as she was by now to climbing these hills, Catherine's T-shirt was nevertheless clinging damply to her back. Then there was the smell; warm wool, lanolin – and manure. Following two hundred sheep up a mountain meant she was walking in fresh droppings. There was something mesmeric about watching the column of animals ahead – the dozens of constantly receding rumps, docked tails flicking ineffectually at flies – so that she forgot to notice the routine, sharp beauty of the hills, away above and to the side, taking it in only in snatches like gulps of cold, clean air.

Presently three sheep detached themselves from the flow, breaking away sideways to where a group of rocks shaded a patch of darker, lusher grass, and stopped to nibble. Catherine moved towards the truants and stamped her feet on the ground but they continued to tug and tear at the sweet turf, merely rolling marble eyes towards her as their jaws pursued their rhythmic rotation.

She was considering the prod of a judicious boot to a woolly ribcage when a dog from on duty up ahead took note of the miscreants and came to her rescue. He was no collie from the Scottish borders, nor yet a spaniel like Monsieur Bouschet's Flambard, kept for hunting in the woods around La Grelaudière. He was a *berger lozérien*. She had seen many like him before, working with the herds in the valley pastures: shaggy and rugged, their grey coats hanging in rat's tails, and with the most peculiar tufted ears, which gave them a comical air. This one knew his stuff and efficiently dispatched the sheep to rejoin their comrades.

Above Catherine at the next bend of the track, Madame Mériel's sister-in-law halted for a moment and looked back, raising an arm briefly in greeting. Her dog came back to her heels and they walked on together. Catherine had volunteered to make the journey with the animals today not as a social exercise, for there was little chance of conversation. It was more a desire for involvement, not just to see and understand but to take part. She was very used to her own company. It was no hardship to her, and nor was walking or being out of doors, heat, flies and smell notwithstanding.

Madame Mériel's brother and his wife farmed

in the valley, some six kilometres further down from St Julien. Or rather, they farmed there in the winter months; from now and for the next four months they would split their activities between the home farm and the high grazing fields, up above the tree line on the shoulders of Mont Lozère. Their name was Vaillant.

They'd set off early this morning. The plan was to drive the sheep as far as La Grelaudière today, where they would overnight in the sloping, stone-walled paddocks beside the Mériels' house. Tomorrow they would complete the second leg of the trek. Joined by the Mériels' own few head of sheep, they would travel on together as far as the sweet upland pastures which were their destination for the summer. They weren't the only ones on the move today. As they had passed along the main street of St Julien and crossed the stone bridge, other flocks were being driven into the village from side lanes and field entrances at every turn, and out again, not all taking the same way as the Vaillants but always on some path that headed upwards. By nine o'clock a noisy conflu-ence of sheep had clogged the market square. It had seemed to Catherine quite impossible that farmers and sheep should somehow manage to re-emerge as separate flock, and all still heading in the right direction.

After St Julien it had been calmer. There was at least one other flock up in front of them, but they were some distance ahead. Their route, after leaving the road a kilometre or so above the village, took them at first through enclosed fields.

'These are traditional pathways,' explained Madame Vaillant, dropping back for a moment to hold a gate as the two dogs ushered the sheep through. 'The transhumance has passed this way from time immemorial.'

'Isn't that a nuisance for the landowners and their livestock?'

'Undoubtedly. But it's only twice a year. And the stock soon get used to it.'

Indeed, a dozen pale golden heifers which had raised their heads from grazing to watch the cavalcade were already chewing again, jaws rotating thoughtfully, and as Catherine struggled to close the gate, their noses went back down to the grass.

Now it was almost eleven and they had climbed beyond the fenced farmland and were in rougher terrain. Much of the land here was terraced into old orchards, some still bearing the signs of active husbandry, other patches overgrown and apparently abandoned, but all spilling with blossom and bees. Catherine breathed in deeply, imagining the sweetness, and inhaling only the aroma of sweating sheep. Higher still, and the fruit trees were first interspersed and then gradually superceded by chestnuts. The trees were evenly spaced and the ground still banked into terraces, so that it was evident this had once been a site of cultivation. Now, however, the walls supporting the terraces were invisible for the most part under a blanket of encroaching green, even collapsed in places where the tree roots had swollen and distorted them beyond the point where the moss could hold them together. Nobody, she thought, can have made a living from chestnuts for fifty years.

Presently the terracing petered out. The chestnuts began to grow more thickly and with other trees between – holm oak and fir and hornbeam. The path narrowed, so that the sheep fell into a narrower column just two or three abreast, and they found themselves in woodland. The shade was a welcome relief for the animals, no doubt, as much as for their minders, and by common consent the pace of the march slowed to a dawdle. The insects were just as bad here, though. The small, darting flies they had brought with them from the Vaillant farmyard were joined by a new kind, fatter and more sluggish, which refused to be driven off even when swished at with a hand.

It was where the small wood ended and they came out again into sunshine and an expanse of open meadow that it was decreed they should stop for lunch. This was always a serious business for French people, even when they were on a mountainside with a flock of sheep. There was wine, a flat rye loaf and the inevitable cheese and sausage, wrapped in damp tea towels to keep them cool. Catherine added her own *petits pains* and bag of early-season cherries to the spread. Madame Mériel crowned the shared feast by producing a homemade pie. The *tourte cévenole* was the local equivalent of a Cornish pasty, food to be carried in the fields. The stout shell of pastry encased a filling of potatoes and onions, flavoured with herbs and melting with soured cream. Both Frenchwomen had brought cutlery and tin camping mugs; the corkscrew had not been forgotten.

The picnic might be elaborate but the halt was certainly necessary. When Catherine crossed her legs to sit down she became aware how her calves ached from the stretch of the ascent. And if she was glad of the break, the same was probably true of the sheep. They scattered across the wide sweep of grassland to find grazing to their liking, mingling peaceably with the flock that had preceded them up the hill. The two women who accompanied the other flock had sat down to eat under a group of trees a few hundred yards ahead, where a small brook bubbled over rocks.

'Where is your husband today?' Catherine inquired of Madame Vaillant as she sipped red wine from the cap of her water bottle. 'Looking after the poultry?'

'No. He's at work.'

'At work?'

'Yes. Tuesdays and Thursdays he works at the post office, just mornings, as an assistant clerk.'

'Oh?' Catherine was surprised. Wasn't farming a full-time occupation?

Madame Vaillant tossed a toe of *saucisson* to the nearest dog, which snapped it up while the other looked on with reproachful eyes. 'And then on Wednesdays I help out at the kindergarten,' she said, 'down in Mende. It keeps me young – or so I used to say, before I got so old.' She rubbed her hands comfortably over well-covered fifty-something knees. 'Even with the subsidy, there's not much of a living in sheep.'

Catherine nodded her sympathy and let her eye drift to the view before her. Now that they were above the first belt of woods she could see clearly the hills on the other side of the main valley, where other flocks were moving: thin capillaries of white creeping up the green. It seemed so much a part of the landscape; could such a phenomenon really be fragile? Fragile, as the cévenol silk growers had also once proved. *Not much of a living in sheep.*

'Have you a family?' Catherine asked.

'No. God chose not to bless us that way.' Madame Vaillant tilted her head, smiling. 'And you?'

'Two, a girl and boy. Both grown up long since, of course.'

Madame Mériel handed them each a fat slice of pie, and asked Catherine, 'Where is your sister today? Would she not have liked to have come too?'

'Oh,' said Madame Vaillant. 'Do you have a sister staying with you then?'

'Not staying with me, exactly, She's here for a few months, so she's renting a *gîte* over Florac way. One of Patrick Castagnol's places.' In fact, although Bryony had nominally taken one of the cottages, she was at Patrick's house more often than she was not. 'She's not a great walker, my sister.' That much at least was true. 'She's gone to Florac today to the *fête de la transhumance*.' *They've* gone, was what she really meant: the two of them together.

'Ah, yes,' said Madame Mériel. 'It has become quite an event. People have always turned out in the villages round there to see the animals pass through – far more than we've ever bothered here.'

'It's not for the villagers, though, is it?' said her sister-in-law. 'Maybe they used to come out to wave the herdsmen off, but never lining the streets ten deep the way it is now. And not all the folderol that goes with it, either. That's for the benefit of the tourists. Processions and garlanded floats and children throwing sweets to the crowd. I can't imagine the flocks would have made three circuits of the town square before it became a spectacle, can you?'

Catherine remembered this morning's mêlée in St Julien and grinned, but Madame Mériel merely shrugged. 'What's the harm in it? I'm sure Madame Park-e-ston's sister is enjoying herself.'

Soon, it was time to gather the sheep together and be moving on. The dogs were dispatched to do the rounding up, and it wasn't long before their own procession was back in motion, heading on up over the grassland and towards the next swathe of woods. But to call the meadows through which they passed 'grassland' did not do them justice. Over the last few weeks, since perhaps the middle of April, Catherine had watched the mountain pastures explode with life. This was turf which had never known the application of a chemical, and although there were grasses here, they were no more than a canvas on which were splashed a profusion of other colours: purple scabious and yellow gentian and lungwort speckled blue and pink, and many other wild flowers which Catherine could not identify. And butterflies: the whole surface of the pasture in the afternoon sunshine danced and bobbed with butterflies, white and yellow and brown, and tiny ones of a startling blue. Catherine half closed her eyelids and saw it in silks.

But as before, the sheep commanded the greater part of her attention. It was hotter now than in the morning, and as her sweat increased so did the irritation of the flies. She had more frequent recourse to her water bottle as the day wore on; by four o'clock it was empty and she was glad when a second halt was decreed, by a stream where she could fill it up. Their stopping place was again well fitted for its purpose. The stream rose temporarily from its deep cut, widening out below a small waterfall where it fell to carve a basin. The pool was deep immediately below the chute but the edges shallowed out to a gravelly margin where the sheep could wade in to their knees and drink. Catherine would have expected butting and barging but they queued patiently for their turn at the water, drinking with calm unhurry before moving aside to make room for the animals behind.

It was shortly after five when they reached the road just below La Grelaudière, and ushered the sheep up the final stretch towards the Mériels' farm and rest. Monsieur Mériel was in the small orchard at the side of the farmhouse and raised a hand in salutation at their approach. Behind him near the corner of the orchard leapt a formidable wall of flame. A sheet of corrugated iron had been bent up at the edges to form a flattish boat shape. The makeshift barbecue was piled high with branches – last autumn's fruit prunings, perhaps, by the lively crackle they produced.

They drove the sheep towards the farmyard entrance; with the two dogs stationed as sentinels on either side, the animals funnelled through without mishap. Madame Mériel skirted round to open the gate to the nearest paddock, and within minutes the flock were all safely corralled and the gate pulled shut behind them.

'*La bouffe*,' said Madame Vaillant with satisfaction,

as the three women leaned up against the dry-stone wall, breasts resting on folded arms. When Catherine looked uncomprehending, Madame Vaillant nodded towards the sheep, all of which had uniformly lowered their heads and were helping themselves to the succulent grass. 'Supper.'

'And for us also, a little later,' said Madame Mériel, smiling. 'But first, perhaps, a wash and something to drink.'

Catherine had been planning to go home to freshen up before the promised al fresco meal, but once she was comfortably installed at the Mériel kitchen table with a glass of wine in front of her, she found the motivation to rise again and climb the remaining few hundred yards of hill-side to Les Fenils had evaporated completely. In truth, she would have been very happy never to have to walk uphill again. Her feet were sore, her ankles were sore, her knees were sore. She felt the ache of every one of her forty-eight years.

'How far did we come today?' she wondered out loud, unlacing her boots.

Madame Vaillant pushed out her lower lip. 'Eighteen, twenty kilometres.'

'Is that all?'

The Frenchwomen both laughed, and Catherine laughed with them. 'Feels more like a hundred.'

'It's further by road,' said Madame Vaillant. 'The drovers' tracks are more direct.'

'And steeper,' pointed out her sister-in-law, massaging her thighs with the heels of her palms.

'A seamstress and a cheese-maker,' said Madame Vaillant with a mocking grin. 'What can one expect? Neither one of you would make a shepherd. There'll be herdsmen this week walking their sheep a hundred kilometres.'

Mention of cheese made Catherine curious. 'What about the goats? Why is it only the sheep that get taken up the mountain for the summer?'

'In the old days the goats were moved,' said Madame Mériel. 'They were part of the transhumance, just as much as the sheep. Milk cows, too, when the farmers had any, though there were never so many of those round St Julien, not in my time.'

'So why did it stop?'

'Milking,' said Madame Mériel simply. 'The sheep aren't milked. Not these days, anyway – or not in the summer.'

'But before, when the goats were moved, how did the farmers manage to milk them?'

'The stockmen used to move up to Mont Lozère for the summer with their goats, live up there in huts or makeshift shelters. The animals would be milked on the mountainside, and the milk brought down to sell, on foot or by donkey. We never summered the goats on the mountain ourselves, not since I was married, but my husband talks of it from when he was a boy and his father ran the farm. They milked by hand, mind you, in those days, so there was no heavy machinery to transport. That's what's made the difference really.' Then she laughed. 'That and our ruling masters in Brussels.'

'Of course.' Catherine grinned. 'I can't see milking into grubby buckets on the open hillside being compliant with European regulations.'

After a wash and a second glass of wine, the women went to set up the long table in the orchard. Not so much a table, in fact, as a series of boards and an old door resting on hurdles, but once covered with three white damask tablecloths and laid with cutlery and glassware and heavy blue linen table napkins, it was fit for an emperor's feast. Or a wedding, thought Catherine, watching flecks of apple blossom drift down around the scene and thinking suddenly and painfully of Lexie.

Places were set for twelve. Everyone from the hamlet was traditionally invited to celebrate the exodus of the sheep and the official start of summer. The Bouschets arrived first, Madame Bouschet bearing a large tureen covered with a tea towel. With them came Madame Volpilière, leaning on Monsieur Bouschet's arm, though Catherine suspected it was more to allow him the pleasure of chivalry than out of any necessity.

'*Alors*, Madame,' he said as he came to take Catherine's hand. 'You have done a good day's droving work. Shall we make a farmer of you yet?'

Monsieur Mériel, having pronounced himself satisfied that the fire was in a condition to be left, drove down to fetch his mother-in-law. The elder Madame Vaillant, dowager sheep farmer and senior family member, was seated in the place of honour at the head of the table, with Madame Volpilière at her side. The two elderly women began a dissection of neighbourhood news while the younger guests gathered to stand and watch the fire. Even Guillaume was invited and came, though he stood a little back from proceedings and said little, merely accepting the proffered glass from his hostess with unsmiling thanks. He never sought Catherine's eye, nor anyone else's either, and she was content to leave him be. Last to arrive, full of elegant apology, was Patrick Castagnol – and he came alone.

Madame Mériel handed him a glass of wine, taking from him in exchange the two bottles he had brought. 'But where is Madame Park-e-ston's sister?' she asked.

'She sends her regrets,' he replied. 'A slight indisposition, a headache, nothing of concern. She was extremely sorry to miss this festive occasion.'

'What a shame,' said the younger Madame Vaillant. 'I would have liked to have met her,' while Madame Mériel telegraphed her sympathy to Catherine. But Catherine found she wasn't entirely sorry. It was easier to be with Bryony or

Patrick separately; there was less awkwardness than when the three of them were together.

'Bryony has always had headaches,' she threw out at random, for something to say.

'It'll be that city job of hers,' pronounced Madame Vaillant.

'Computer screens are the worst thing,' agreed her husband. 'That, and strip lighting. I quite often get a headache on Tuesdays and Thursdays. Too much time indoors.'

'Has she tried lime flower tea?' wondered Madame Bouschet solicitously, directing the question somewhere in between Catherine and Patrick.

The male guests were soon after pressed into service to assist with the setting up of the spit. This was a remarkable contraption of black-leaded iron which looked at first sight like some elaborate man-trap or instrument of torture, but which when manoeuvred into position could have graced a Tudor kitchen. The earlier flames had died low and the branches, though they still held their shape, were glowing a throbbing orange. Anywhere within a few feet, the heat was searing. Monsieur Mériel produced a side of lamb and hauled it into place on the spit.

They were called to table by the re-emergence from the kitchen of Madame Bouschet's tureen, now furled with fragrant steam. They took their places, and Catherine found Patrick at her left elbow.

223

The soup was delicious: a thick potato broth flavoured with something green. Catherine couldn't place the taste, which was hard-edged, savoury and astringent.

'*Herbe de Maggie*,' we call it,' said Madame Bouschet.

Catherine smiled. 'Like the stock cubes?'

'Exactly.'

'Lovage,' she said suddenly, inhaling with her face to her bowl. It had grown wild at the bottom of the garden in Long Hartslow; Lexie used to feed it to her guinea pig.

Then there was a salad, served on a flat, round dish the approximate size of a tractor wheel. Tiny baby turnips and carrots and beetroot and radishes, blanched and cooled, all of them cut with a tuft of leaves attached and served with a rich, yellow aïoli. Infanticide, it seemed like to Catherine, the slivers of vegetables uprooted at birth.

'Isn't it a waste,' she wanted to know, 'eating them so small?'

'Not at all,' said Monsieur Bouschet from across the table. 'It's a *salade de l'éclaircissage*. We always have it in the spring.'

Catherine frowned, trawling her vocabulary. *Eclaircir . . . ?*

'Thinning the seedlings – a salad of thinnings.' Patrick leaned a little towards her as he spoke. They had all been speaking French, of course, so now his English had a confidentiality about it.

'It's a feast,' said Monsieur Mériel. 'And if not for us, then for the goats.'

Patrick was still looking at her; although he switched back to French, his tone was teasing. 'But you must know all this, Madame the gardener. Seedlings, even in England, one assumes, need to be thinned out.'

Catherine grinned at him and recited, 'Two in every three must go, to give the others space to grow.' When he raised an eyebrow, she added, 'My grandmother. She had rhymes for everything.'

'And how does your garden grow?' he said, in English again.

'Oh, quite well, I hope,' she replied, surprised that he should know the line from an English nursery rhyme. 'I've had some early radishes already, and I've got most of the ground I'd prepared planted. A lot of it went in back in March or April, the onions and carrots and leeks, you know. But I haven't put in the beans yet. And I've got some little courgette plants that I bought at the market on Thursday. I was planning to bed them out this week.'

'Soon.' She had spoken in French, and Monsieur Bouschet leaned across his plate, wagging an admonitory crust of bread. 'Those beans need to go in very soon, if they're to have any kind of chance.'

Conversation widened to the table in general, ranging to and fro over the best seasons for sowing vegetables. Catherine felt all at once the weight of her tiredness. Sitting back in her chair and listening to the debate, the weight became a contented lethargy; this was how it felt to be among neighbours. And the lamb was starting to smell delicious.

Monsieur Mériel had thrown some fresh rosemary branches on the fire, which had stirred the glowing embers back briefly to a crackling flame, and the orchard air was thick with the barbecue smell of charring meat.

'Is it traditional,' she asked quietly of Patrick, 'eating lamb to celebrate the transhumance? Only it does seem a bit . . . well, cannibalistic.' Then she laughed at this flight of sentimentality, before he could. 'You know what I mean, though. Sheep farmers who've walked all day with their flock, keeping them safely on the path, then when they stop for the night, dining enjoyably on a nice piece of mutton. It's a little close to home, don't you think?'

He surveyed her with amusement dancing in his eyes. 'What else should a shepherd eat?'

'Yes, yes. Why do they keep the animals in the first place? I know. But during the transhumance, when they are actually on the move with the sheep, it still seems rather pointed.'

'During the transhumance, especially,' he said, with a lift of one shoulder. 'How else to arrange things, with three or four days on the march? What better than food that transports itself?'

Catherine shut her eyes. A simple fire of sticks

over stones. The flash of a skinning knife in the firelight. One lamb which all day had lagged too far behind the rest. Involuntarily, she shuddered.

Even so, it did smell delicious.

CHAPTER 15

A SWARM IN MAY

'Beautiful.' Catherine looked down at the small, screwed-up face in the picture in her hand and said the only thing it was ever possible to say in these circumstances. 'He's beautiful.'

The Bouschets had been her guests for Saturday lunch and now, with the table cleared and coffee at their elbows, the photographs of the new grandchild had come out. Catherine settled to it very comfortably. There was something universal about women sharing photographs; she could have been back in Long Hartslow, waiting in the infants' playground to pick up Tom or in the Five Horseshoes after a PTA meeting.

'He looks just like his father. Of course, you don't know Jean-Marc, but everybody says so. Look here.' Madame Bouschet leafed through the pictures she had brought. 'Here is Jean-Marc when he was a baby. He was a little older when it was taken, about a month, I think. But aren't they just like two halves of a broad bean?'

Catherine slid back her coffee cup and set down the two photos side by side. She was usually of the persuasion that all newborn babies look too much the same for any useful observation of inherited traits. But perhaps here there was a resemblance: something in the set of the mouth, or the shape of the chin. Then she superimposed a drooping, grey moustache on to the image of the newborn.

'And you, Monsieur,' she said, raising her eyes to the child's grandfather. 'I think he looks like you.'

The gratification this produced was tangible; there was actually a visible swelling of the chest.

'Of course,' agreed Madame Bouschet stoutly. 'He's a handsome boy, like all the Bouschet men. And he's named for my husband, too, you know. Augustin.'

'So that's five boys now, and still just the one girl? Your Cécile is going to be overrun with male cousins. She'll have to practise her football.'

'Oh, I think she'll manage to hold her own, all right.' Madame Bouschet was grinning, and Catherine joined her. She had been introduced to the little girl, along with her mother, Claudine, one market day in the winter. Four or five years old, ruddy and broad-stanced, she looked as though she could withstand a few firm tackles.

'When are you hoping to meet him?'

'Soon, soon.' The Frenchwoman took a peck at her coffee. 'I was there for the first few weeks with all the others, Claudine's and Isabelle's. But this is not so simple.'

'Paris?' Catherine remembered the objections: the long journey, the crowds, the daughter-in-law's cooking.

But this was dismissed with a swing of the blue-black bob. 'It's different with sons. *C'est pas évident.*'

Monsieur Bouschet looked at his wife, and Catherine thought she saw amusement quiver his moustache. 'She has her own mother there with her at the moment,' he explained.

'Ah. Yes. I see.'

Catherine had never shown her own pictures. In fact, she couldn't recall having had them out of the dresser drawer since dropping the tin in there on her arrival: the old shortbread tin with the photos of Lexie and Tom as children. So she fetched it out now, for her neighbours to exclaim over – how pretty, how healthy-looking, how well grown for only ten and eight – while she went through the Bouschet snaps: their own three and then the grandchildren, smiling by a Christmas tree, standing knee deep among chickens, playing with pebbles in the dust.

There was one she remembered taking of Tom after he'd accidentally sat down, paddling in a stream on holiday; there he stood, laughing and unrepentant, his short trousers wringing wet. Madame Bouschet, who had been examining it, turned it round for Catherine to see.

'Is this in the mountains?'

Catherine shook her head. 'Not in France, no.

And not what you would think of as mountains either. It was taken on Dartmoor. In Devon, in England.'

'You talked, though, of holidays here, too, I think?'

'Oh, yes. But that was longer ago. My sister and I, when we were small, came here with my parents. We stayed near Sainte Enimie two years running, and once down near Le Vigan. We never brought our two here. Graeme, my husband, liked to holiday in England. Devon mostly, and Cornwall. St Ives, where the painters go.'

Monsieur Bouschet took from his wife the photograph of Tom in the stream. 'Well, it looks to be a beautiful place.'

That made Catherine laugh: the surprise of it, and the note of consolation.

'England is beautiful. Parts of it, anyway, certainly – like anywhere, I suppose. We may not have mountains like the Alps or Pyrenees or even the Cévennes, but the Lake District is spectacular, and the Peaks and the Dales. And Scotland and Wales, of course, have some real mountain areas.'

'And what about where you lived?' Madame Bouschet wanted to know. 'Was that a pretty place?'

Beau was the word she used: that catch-all which in French covers everything from a new dress to the majesty of Mont Lozère in a winter's dawn. Catherine was unsure how to answer her.

'Pretty enough, yes. The village itself was nicely

kept, and with quite a few old houses. Thatched roofs, you know, that sort of thing. And the church was very fine, parts of it going back a thousand years. The countryside was pleasant, too – though rather full of cars and people, with being not far from London.'

'Do you miss it?'

A simple question – and the answer, she found, came simply too. 'No. No, I don't. Though I do miss my family.'

'Ah, well. Children.' Madame Bouschet picked up a picture of her new grandson. 'We can't keep them close by us for ever, can we, more's the pity.'

Catherine split the remaining contents of the cafetière between her two guests, and rose to take it to the sink and fetch from the larder cupboard the box of marzipan *calissons* that Patrick and Bryony had brought back from a jaunt to Aix-en-Provence. They were in Alès today, trying a new restaurant of which Patrick had heard great things.

When she returned to the table, Madame Bouschet had shifted her chair along and was examining the tapestry stretched over Catherine's frame.

'This is the one, isn't it? The banner of St Julien, from the church in town. Père Amyot mentioned that you were repairing it.'

'I'm having a go, yes.'

'I remember the little boat, from years ago when the banner used to be used. Those people are far too big for it, I used to think. It would capsize in a minute with those three big lumps standing there. And besides, there's no room for their legs. Look at it, it's just a shallow barque.'

Her husband, drawing his own chair near, nodded slowly. 'Unless they are kneeling. I always thought perhaps they were kneeling before the saint. Or praying for a safe crossing.'

'So you know the tapestry? You remember it being on display?'

'Oh, certainly,' said Madame Bouschet at once. 'And not just on display, either. It was in regular use thirty years ago, for the processional. And on the day of the patronal festival it used to be paraded right the way round town. We loved it as kids, dressing up and marching in line. It was as good as a carnival.'

Catherine caught the affectionate glance Monsieur Bouschet gave his wife; under the table he had taken hold of her hand.

'When did it stop – the parade, and using the banner in services? Père Amyot said it had been in storage. That's how the moths got to it.'

The French couple both shook their heads. 'Must be twenty years at least,' said Madame Bouschet. 'Maybe twenty-five.'

During the reign of the sick predecessor – or the predecessor's predecessor.

Monsieur Bouschet rubbed his moustache with a broad finger and thumb. 'The church was different in those days, like a lot of things. Nowadays it's a much leaner operation all round. Poor Père Amyot struggles just to keep things going.'

'That's why I was persuaded into attempting the restoration,' Catherine admitted. 'It's really a job for an expert – a textiles curator in a museum. But there's just no money to pay for it. The tapestry would probably end up having to be given to the museum to pay for its own repair – if they even wanted it. There seemed to be no other way.'

'What a blessing, then,' said Madame Bouschet sincerely, 'that the church has you to provide your skills for an affordable price.' For nothing, in fact, though Catherine wasn't about to say so.

Slightly embarrassed, she switched tack. Something else had been exercising her. 'Why do you suppose the church is so out of funds? Compared with the past, that is.'

Monsieur Bouschet gave a shrug. 'How can there be money in the coffers, when there is no congregation?'

'Are the numbers so small, then?' Catherine pressed down a twinge of guilt; she still hadn't got round to acting on her resolution of paying her respects at the church of St Julien the Hospitaller.

'People don't go to church any more,' said Madame Bouschet.

Her husband snorted scornfully. 'There aren't enough people left here. If there were more, maybe the church would be filled.'

'Augustin,' began his wife. But he was away.

'Twenty, thirty years ago, St Julien was a different place. It was a thriving town. The shops were busy, the church was packed. But how can a place survive when its population is bleeding away?'

An image came in Catherine's mind, one she had not considered properly before: the ruined house at the rocky promontory in the woods above Les Fenils. It wasn't the only one, either. Halfway down to St Julien was another clutch of ruins, what might once have been two or three farm-houses and a scatter of outbuildings – the best part of another hamlet.

'It's all the fault of the Parc National,' Monsieur Bouschet went on. 'There's nothing here for people, nothing they're permitted to do, so why should they stay? Who stays, of the young people? Who has stayed at La Grelaudière? Not Jean-Marc. Nor the girls – neither one of them has married a farmer. No one but Guillaume, that's who.'

'They still let us work on the land,' said Madame Bouschet with the mild, resigned air of one who knows the script by heart.

'Yes, but who wants to stay and work a farm when there's no community around it? Take away our industry and our commerce, take away the opportunities for our young people, and what is left? A vehicle without an engine. That's what it is. A rusting shell.'

He had said his piece. His wife let the dust settle

for a while, peering down at the fine stitching of St Julien's banner. Then she turned to Catherine. 'Is it very different? The way a tapestry like this was made back then, from how it's done these days?'

'Not really, as far as that goes. The actual method seems to have stayed pretty much unaltered for hundreds of years. Thousands of years even. It's more about the materials – getting the right yarns, and the right sorts of pigments for the dyeing.'

'So you mean you've had to dye your own thread?'

'No, luckily not. I'd been looking into it, finding out about the traditional vegetable dyes they used, but then I talked to a very helpful curator at the Musée des Beaux Arts et d'Archéologie in Montpellier. He's a restorer, costumes mostly, and furniture fabric, but he gave me some excellent advice. He put me in touch with the workshop which supplies his silks, and I've been able to buy what I need.'

'A man from the museum,' said Madame Bouschet in tones of respect. 'Well.'

'The staff at the silk museum in St-Hippolyte were helpful too when I rang and talked to them, telling me more about the way the yarns used to be made. I looked at some of their tapestries when I went there in February, and I've visited a lot of churches and châteaux, looking for other examples. Tapestries of the same period, you know.' Which according to the 'man from the museum' in Montpellier was most likely seventeenth century, or early eighteenth, though perhaps a copy of an earlier work or executed in the primitive style, an echo of medieval religious art.

'And I've found books, too, with dozens of illustrations. It's not just the method, you see, it's the images, too. The symbolism. These processional tapestries were rich in it – it's like a language all of its own.'

Catherine broke off, slightly embarrassed at her own rush of enthusiasm. It was really Patrick Castagnol she'd been waiting to talk to about all this. The chestnut tree, in particular, and what looked like a sprig of leaves in the saint's hand. Her research suggested it could be hyssop, a herb apparently believed to heal leprosy. Patrick might know – but somehow she hadn't had the moment to ask him.

'The thing is,' she continued, 'there's no record of exactly what the tapestry looked like before the damage. No photographs or anything – or at least the church doesn't seem to have any. Perhaps you two might remember.'

They both shook their heads slowly, staring down at the textile image. Catherine had worked over the hoods of the cloaked figures, picking out in greys and umbers the heavy folds of fustian, but their faces remained an eroded blank.

'The boat, yes,' said Madame Boushet, 'and the funny people with short legs. But I'm afraid it's no good asking me much more than that. I can't say I ever studied it that closely.'

'Me neither,' admitted her husband. 'It was just a banner. And it's a long time ago.'

'I think perhaps they are lepers.' Catherine leaned forward between her guests and traced the lowered edge of one hood with the tip of her finger. 'Shading their faces, don't you think, with their hoods pulled forward that way? Keeping themselves covered, to hide their sickness.'

'Yes,' said Monsieur Bouschet slowly. 'That would make sense. Lepers, travelling to the hospice of St Julien.'

'Funny, though. With the chestnut tree, it seems to be a local scene. Would there ever have been leprosy here in Lozère?'

A shrug from each side.

'Or maybe it's allegorical. The leprosy is simply sin: they're sinners coming to the saint for a cure.' Patrick would have an opinion on it, she was sure.

'Well, whatever the case, that's beautifully tidy stitching,' pronounced Madame Bouschet. 'You're making a very neat job of it, very neat indeed. As good as you did on my kitchen curtains.'

When, a short time later, Catherine had seen her neighbours over her threshold and into the sunlit yard, Monsieur Bouschet halted and turned.

'I almost forgot,' he said. 'We brought you something.'

He indicated it with his thumb: a round, lidded basket to the side of the step. She assumed it contained vegetables, and perhaps a few goose eggs like the ones Madame Bouschet had dropped by the previous week. But as she stepped towards it, she thought she could hear a faint whirr coming from it, like the drone of distant tree-felling.

'They're always very quiet when they first swarm,' said Monsieur Bouschet.

'When they swarm?'

'Docile.' He nodded reassuringly. 'They have a big feed before they fly, fill their bellies with honey. It makes them sleepy. Very easy to handle.'

Docile. Catherine swallowed hard. How long had it been there, the ominously humming basket? Three, three and a half hours, while they had lunch and talked?

'It's the first of the season,' chipped in Madame Bouschet, 'and early for up here in the mountains. A May swarm is a precious thing. Plenty of time to establish itself before the end of the season. It should build itself up nicely and give you a decent yield, come August.'

A swarm in May, recited the voice of Catherine's grandmother in her head. How did it go on? *A swarm in May is worth a load of hay*. She made a feeble effort at protest.

'I don't really—'

'We saw you weren't using them yet.' Monsieur Bouschet tilted his head towards Madame Sauzet's beehives, up beneath the chestnut trees at the end of the house. 'It might benefit from a good scrub-out, just to make sure there are no mice. Those hives can't have been used for a year or two. But the bees will do most of the spring-cleaning for you. They're good little housewives, are bees. They like a tidy home.' His face was straight but the light was lively in his eyes.

Pulling herself together, Catherine matched her smile to those of her departing guests. 'It's very kind of you. Really, very kind indeed. Thank you – thank you, both.'

'It's nothing,' they insisted. 'Thank you for an excellent lunch.'

As they walked away arm in arm across the terrace and out of view down the slope of the lane, she turned to go back inside the house, casting one glance back at the buzzing skep. Thank goodness for the internet, she thought. She needed to google 'bee-keeping'.

CHAPTER 16

THE EX FACTOR

'Talk to me, Mum. Talk to me about anything but cake.'

Catherine had been outside in her vegetable patch when the phone rang, hoeing around and between her wigwams of beans. It was almost a daily task; they'd had light rain most nights this week and hot sun toasting the soil every afternoon, and she sometimes felt as though the weeds were starting to sprout again before the hoe was back in the woodshed. But with the help of her DIY manual, and giving a cautiously wide berth to any of the existing and highly suspect electricals of Les Fenils, she had rigged up an outside bell for her telephone. When it stuttered to jangling life at just past six o'clock, she'd felt certain it was Lexie, and had run inside.

'Tell me what you've been up to, Mum. Tell me about tapestries, and goats. Regale me with stories of French plumbing, and greenfly on the broad beans. Or what about Aunty Bryony? She must have done something – I don't know – inappropriate. Tell me anything you like, just so long as it has absolutely nothing to do with cake.'

'Oh dear,' said Catherine, laughingly disobedient. 'Is it that bad?'

'Worse. If I never see another fondant fancy in my life again, it'll be too soon. When I shut my eyes at night I see three-tier rich iced fruit cakes. Leaves of sugar confetti float down like snowflakes, and an icing bride and groom do a slow smooch in the middle to the Dance of the Sugarplum Fairy. I swear they're going to be dancing on my grave – and it won't be long, either, at this rate. *Fondant Magazine* is going to kill me.'

'Oh, sweetheart!' It was impossible not to smile, though the frustration was obviously real. 'You were loving it so much at the beginning. What happened?'

'Nothing happened, exactly. It's just . . . well, it's just cake.'

'Right,' cued Catherine, and waited.

'Nothing but bloody cake. Icing. Ladies who make bunny rabbits out of it. Ladies who weave it to look like baskets. Ladies who've built complete replicas of their village church in marzipan and sugar. I've got icing coming out of my ears.'

It was understandable perhaps, but it had happened so quickly. At *Air Cargo Monthly* she'd lasted eighteen months or more before she'd reached this point.

'Is it the people?' Catherine thought of the pastel cardigans.

A hesitation. 'They're OK.'

'OK?'

'Oh, they're lovely. Really, very nice. The staff, and the people you meet at the sugarcraft exhibitions, the ladies you get to interview. All of them, lovely. I think that's the thing. It's all so unremittingly *nice.*'

'And the air freight people weren't nice?'

'Some of them were, some of them weren't. But at least they were serious.'

Catherine smothered a sigh. Men in suits. That had been the complaint last year, nothing but grey men in suits.

'Actually, that's not right, because cake people are serious too. Frighteningly serious, some of them. But at least the air cargo people were serious about something serious, if you see what I mean.'

Refrigerated containers, belly hold capacity. What was it Lexie had said in September? *At least icing is real.*

Very tentatively, she said, 'I suppose it gives people pleasure.'

She was surprised, at that, to hear her daughter laughing. 'Oh, it's all right, Mum. Don't worry. I'm not going to chuck it in, not just yet. I probably ought to give it a year. Doesn't look great if you've moved about every five minutes. But I might be on the lookout soon, in case something else comes along.'

Relieved, Catherine agreed. 'That sounds sensible. Look around, but don't rush at anything.'

'Maybe I should go freelance. Specialising in air container traffic and the art of sugar.'

'Well, whatever happens, writing about cake decorating was never going to be an entire career, was it? But it's all good experience.'

'Ha, easy for you to say. You didn't spend half of Friday talking to a woman from the Women's Institute who judges icing competitions. Twenty marks for the smoothness of the overall cover, twenty for colour and consistency. Twenty for design and twenty for accuracy of general execution. Which leaves, most importantly, twenty marks for that extra, elusive star quality she's always looking for. The X factor.'

They were both giggling freely now.

'I mean, *star quality*. It's a *cake*!'

'There were people like that in Long Hartslow. Don't you remember Mrs Chapman? WI cake competitions are no laughing matter.'

'I'm afraid Gram rather caught the brunt of it. This judge person lived out Chelmsford way, so I went on to Walton afterwards, and I don't think I talked about anything else. Apparently, she's only ever awarded a score over ninety the one time, and the icer went on to work at the Ritz.'

'How was she?'

'Same as usual. I'm actually not sure she knew what I was on about – which may have been a blessing.'

Both now sober again, Lexie asked Catherine about Bryony, and Catherine answered with evasive truths: places she'd been out to but not with whom. Then Lexie said something else, with an edge of such studied casualness that Catherine was on the alert at once.

'Have you heard about Dad?'

'Have I heard what?'

'About Dad and Suzannah.'

She knew immediately what was coming. She had imagined it often enough, over the last seven years; she had steeled herself. It was the one thing she knew had the power to hurt her – even here, and now, at all this distance. That he should prefer another woman in his bed, she had long since come to terms with; the wedding, which had been a quiet affair, had left her largely unscathed. But a baby. She'd always known, of course, that Suzannah would want a baby; and Graeme would hold it, and love and nurture it – a baby that wasn't Lexie or Tom.

'They've split up.'

Catherine said nothing. Her mind was a literal blank. She fed in the information but her brain seemed unable to process it. She waited for a response, and found none.

'Mum?'

'Is he OK?' she managed after another moment.

'I guess so. He didn't say much about it – how he felt about it, I mean – and I didn't ask. All he said was, it had been coming for a while and they'd both agreed it was the right thing.'

Graeme and Suzannah, over. She tested it again: still nothing.

'It's funny, because you'd never have thought it,

at Christmas. They were . . . well, they were the same as ever. Nothing to suggest this.'

'You can't always tell, I suppose.' Other relationships, from the outside, were always unfathomable, weren't they, in the end?

Lexie, unusually awkward, chose an unfortunate platitude. 'At least they didn't have kids.' Then, realising her error, 'Little kids, I mean. Mum, you know I didn't mean—'

'I know you didn't.'

'Well, look, I'd better go. I'm meant to be going out tonight. Nothing exciting, just the pub, with one of the photographers from work. Girl not boy, before you ask. Caro – she's actually quite good fun. But if she mentions cake I'm going to have to kill her.'

When her daughter had gone, Catherine laid down the receiver slowly and stood gazing down at her hands. For the first time she noticed she was still wearing her gardening gloves, her old ones, bought from the garden centre on the Wycombe road.

Graeme and Suzannah. She would have forgiven herself if she had felt some small stirring of triumph – or at least of relief. But she was unable to identify any very definite feeling about it at all.

Except, eventually, as she headed back out to her runner beans, one gradually crystallising thought. Poor bloody Graeme. *Again.*

★　★　★

246

The following Sunday afternoon Catherine came in from her regular walk to find Bryony in the kitchen. It was many months since she had ceased the habit of locking her door when she went out for anything less than a day trip to Alès. As she reached Les Fenils, her mind had been full of the rush of water: the colours and textures of the river she was re-creating in the foreground of the St Julien tapestry. She had still been wrapped up in her ideas as she entered the hall, kicking off the canvas shoes that were more comfortable than socks and boots for walking in the heat. The sound of scraping chair legs brought her up with a start.

'Hello?' she called out, apprehensive as she pushed open the kitchen door.

'Oh, hi, Cath.' Her sister glanced up briefly, and then down again, frowning, at the letter in her hand. 'Help me out here. What for the love of Nora is a "tampon"? Apart from the obvious, that is.'

Spread across the table in front of her was a scatter of notebooks and papers, and the blue document wallet marked INVOICES, ETC. in Catherine's tidy capitals. The dreaded tax return.

Catherine grinned. 'I gather it's a seal.'

'As in "arp, arp" – balancing beach balls, swallowing sardines?'

'As in signed, sealed and delivered.'

'And do you have one? I can't make head nor tail of this form, but it seems insistent that you

247

have to have this tampon thing, and affix it pretty much everywhere, before you can do anything at all.'

Torn between laughter and a sinking heart, Catherine went to the stove.

'Tea?' She couldn't face this without it.

'It's all very well,' grumbled Bryony, 'asking me to get your books straight for the tax man. I mean, I'm fine with the maths. Unlike you, I might say – you seem to have lost a decimal point somewhere on this page. But I need you for the incomprehensible language. We didn't learn a lot of accounting vocabulary at GCSE.'

The kettle set to boil, Catherine came and sat down next to her sister, eyeing with distaste the spill of paper. 'The thing is, I don't have a business seal. I suppose I shall have to find out about getting one. I did try phoning them at one point early on, saying that I didn't have one.'

'And?'

'They said that was fine, I just had to put it in writing to the URSSAF.'

'The who?'

'The Union de Recouvrement des Cotisations de Sécurité Sociale et d'Allocations Familiales. So I wrote, as instructed.'

'Then it's OK? You've got a dispensation?'

Catherine grimaced. 'Nothing so simple. They said they couldn't accept my letter because I hadn't affixed my business seal.'

Face in hands, Bryony groaned, but the groan

turned into a snigger and soon both of them were giggling like teenagers.

'Why do they have to be so bloody *French*?' said Bryony. 'Every other note on this form is about some sodding paragraph of the Napoleonic Code. Fill in a number wrong somewhere, and you're probably for the guillotine.'

She seemed to be making headway with it, though. Columns of figures had appeared on several pages of the fat, officious-looking booklet which Catherine had been sedulously ignoring since December. Very grateful for even this degree of progress, she rose to make the tea.

'You have to register your business too. With that lot you mentioned just now – the USSR, or whatever it was. You have done that, at least, have you? Only I couldn't find any documents. They should have issued you with an enterprise code – some kind of business registration number, I suppose. You need it before you can get anywhere.'

Catherine winced as she sat down with the mugs. 'I haven't got round to it yet – one of those things that you keep putting off, you know. It didn't seem to matter until it came to filing my returns at the end of the year.'

She didn't like the way Bryony was staring at her, and that slow, disbelieving shake of the head.

'Cath, you are completely useless, you know that? Like one of those helpless females whose husband has always done the finances. Jeez, you're meant to be a businesswoman. You shouldn't be allowed out without a nursemaid.' Then she sat back in her chair and grinned. 'Damn lucky you've got me.'

'Absolutely. A book-keeper who refers to the *sécu* as the "USSR". Very inspiring of confidence.' She riffled through some letters that were still in the document wallet. 'Here. This is the form they sent. It seems pretty simple, why don't we do it now?'

Her sister pulled it from her fingers and laid it on the table. '*Nom du responsable*. Name of the responsible person? I think we can manage that – though it's a blatant misdescription, in your case.'

'I remember reading it through,' said Catherine, 'and checking some of the notes. You can just put my name again where it says *nom d'entreprise*. I don't need a separate company name. It's just me, I'm the business as well.'

As instructed, Bryony wrote. Then she said, '*Siège social*. What the heck's a *siège social*?'

'Social seat,' Catherine translated helpfully. 'I looked it up, before. It basically seems to mean headquarters. Where my main business address is.'

'So, here then?'

'Where else?'

'I don't know. I thought maybe you had a registered head office in Zürich or Rio de Janeiro.'

Bryony wrote again, but then stopped and held up the pen, wagging it from side to side. 'And registered head office is exactly what it needs to be. You're not allowed to have a social seat until you've had it approved at the Mairie.'

'Oh dear, I must have missed that bit,' said Catherine. 'Is it me, or does this stuff send you round in circles? You can't file your tax return with the revenue authorities until you have a business registration number from the URSSAF, and you can't register with the URSSAF until you've had your address approved by the Mairie. All we need now is for them to tell me at the Mairie that I can't register my business address until I've filed my tax return.'

Bryony shook her head again but she was grinning. 'With, don't forget, your tampon duly affixed.'

'Look, let's leave it for now,' said Catherine. 'I'll go to the Mairie on Tuesday when it's open again, find out about registering my address. You've been a big help already. Really – thanks.'

Pushing this aside along with the nearest sheaf of papers, Bryony picked up her tea and took a swig.

'Oh, I almost forgot. Patrick said to give you these.'

Out from her bag, where it hung on the back of her chair, she pulled a pair of thick, white canvas gloves. Gauntlets, one might even have said; they appeared long enough to come most of the way up Catherine's forearm.

'Though God knows why you'd want them. I didn't like to ask. Unless you're planning on taking up falconry – or driving a nineteen twenty-six Hispano-Suiza.'

Catherine took them from her and turned them over in her hands, smiling. Inside the broad, stiff cuff was a cotton lining, gathered to a band of elastic designed to fit tightly at the wrist.

'They're bee-keeping gloves,' she said. 'He mentioned he had a spare pair.' She rubbed absently at a receding lump near her elbow. 'Bees do have a nasty habit of getting inside your sleeves.'

'Right.' Bryony looked nonplussed. 'And he also said to tell you that Sainte Enimie was a leper.'

'Really?'

'That's what he said. Believe me, I asked twice to make sure. It's not exactly the usual sort of neighbourly message, is it, like he's barbecuing on Saturday or could he borrow your hedge-trimmer?'

Or your bee-keeping gloves. Catherine's smile widened.

'So what's it all about?' Bryony wanted to know. 'Isn't Sainte Enimie that little town we went to on holiday when we were kids?'

'That's right. It's where she lived. She founded the monastery there, and the town's named after her.'

'And she was a leper?'

'Apparently. I never knew – and I suppose Patrick must have forgotten about her when we were talking about leprosy in Lozère, and then he remembered later. I must go and look her up. I'm not even sure when she lived – I mean, she'd be medieval, of course, but I don't know which century.'

'So that's the kind of thing you chat to Patrick about, is it? Lepers through the ages?'

Catherine scrutinised her sister for any sign of jealousy or pique and detected only bemusement. 'Amongst other things,' she said. What he and Bryony found to talk about she could not imagine – or did not choose to try.

For a moment she considered explaining about the shadowed faces in St Julien's ferry boat. But the attempt was likely to be fruitless, so she let it be. Instead, she stuck to a more conventional inquiry. 'Where is he today?'

'Gone to Montpellier.'

Catherine nodded and they sipped their tea.

'He goes every Sunday. Leaves after breakfast and doesn't come back until late afternoon.'

There was a pause, while Catherine wondered if this intelligence required some response from her.

'All he says is that it's "a regular lunch engagement".'

This time, something was clearly expected, so she tried, 'Have you asked him about it?'

'No.'

It was unlike Bryony, in Catherine's experience, to be reticent; but after all, what did she know about how her sister was with other people? *With Patrick.* The clipped negative, however, seemed to have brought the slightly awkward conversation to a full stop. Catherine was wondering whether to put the kettle back on for another cup when Bryony spoke again.

'I think he meets a woman.'

Catherine's hand closed more tightly round her teacup.

'Bryony,' she began, without any very clearly formed idea of what she would say. But then, unexpectedly, her sister was laughing – a stark, abrasive sound.

'D'you know what the irony is? It's his wife. He's seeing another woman and I think it's his bloody wife.'

'Sorry?'

'His ex-wife, is what I mean, of course. They were married eight years, he told me that much. Been divorced for some time, though he didn't say how long. But I'm sure it's her. I'm sure he's spending his Sundays with her.'

'What makes you think so?' That was probably wrong. She should have been refuting the very notion of another woman, not merely querying her identity. But she was too honest to dissemble by instinct, and now it was too late. 'Was it something he said?'

'No. No, he's always very discreet.' The bitterness was unconcealed. It was a short step, after all, from discreet to secretive – to high walls and closed doors.

'There's a picture.'

'Really?' Catherine had observed an absence of

254

personal photographs on Patrick's walls: his mother's landscape in oils, but no other pictures.

'In the bedroom.'

Ah.

'It's not a photograph. A drawing – just a pencil sketch. Maybe one of those you have done in the street for a few pounds. Like in Montmartre, only less tacky. Maybe some art student, paying the rent.'

She nodded; she knew the kind of thing.

'Maybe that's why he kept it there. Not quite like a photo, that you'd take down. Though you'd think she might have taken it with her when they divided things up. Unless it was a present. Maybe she had it done for him, for a birthday or Christmas – he wouldn't give back a present.'

Catherine looked on in compassionate silence as her sister worked the thing round and round, theorising and rationalising, as she might do a legal problem. Then she said quietly, 'But why do you think it's her he goes to meet?'

'She's very beautiful.' It wasn't clear whether this was an answer to her question or merely a continuation of Bryony's own train of thought. 'Chic, in that way Frenchwomen have. *Gamine*, you know. Like Audrey Hepburn in *Sabrina*.'

'Sabrina wasn't French.'

'Wasn't she? So why did she keep singing *La Vie en Rose*?'

'Because she'd been at school in Paris. An American can go to Paris.'

'But Audrey Hepburn was French, wasn't she?'

'Dutch, I think. Or maybe Belgian.'

'All right then, not Audrey Hepburn. Audrey Tatou. Either way, she's still bloody beautiful.'

Impatient of her own digression, Catherine returned to the issue. 'Why are you so sure he's with her?'

'It has to be a woman, doesn't it?'

'Why? Just because he's French, you mean? Because he's a man?' *Because it's Patrick.*

'Because if it was just some regular business meeting, his lawyer or his bank manager, he'd have told me about it.'

'Would he? Does he talk to you about his business?'

She suspected she knew the answer. Bryony shifted, fretting at her mug with one fingernail.

'I just know it's a woman. Why else would he leave me on a Sunday morning, when we're getting up late, and have only just made coffee.'

Sunday morning coffee in bed. With her mind fleeing from the image, Catherine conceded the point for argument's sake. 'All right, let's suppose it is a woman. But why the ex-wife? Why Audrey, just because he's left a sketch of her on his wall?'

This time there was a pause. Perhaps, thought Catherine, because it's easier to put a shape to our demons. Bryony picked up her cooling tea, touched it to her lips and put it down again.

'It was just something last week. Last Sunday, after he'd left and I was kicking about, wondering what

256

to do. I thought about sticking my nose out in the woods, and that man was there. The Frenchman from the hamlet, the old guy with the moustache.'

'Monsieur Bouschet.'

Bryony nodded. 'He was coming down the track with that ginger dog of his, and a gun and some dead things. He stopped to say hello – just to pass the time of day.' She raised her eyes to Catherine for a moment. 'He's a bit inscrutable, isn't he, that one?'

Grinning at the epithet, Catherine asked, 'What did he say?'

'Oh, well, I told him Patrick had gone to Montpellier, and he just said something about the past. You know my French, I didn't quite grasp it straight away, but I'm sure he mentioned the past. *Le passé*, right?'

'That's right.'

'*Les liens du passé*, is what I think it was. I'm a lawyer, remember – I don't need telling what a lien is.'

The ties of the past. 'His wife.'

'Has to be. Suddenly I find I'm the bloody Other Woman.'

Catherine wondered whether to put an arm round her sister, but it seemed too much like a confirmation of her fears, so she contented herself with a non-committal hand of sympathy on her wrist.

'She looks young,' said Bryony.

Her lips were pressed together in what was

almost a pout, and Catherine felt a terrible urge to disloyal amusement. 'She probably was. When were they married? It might have been drawn when she was twenty-five.'

Such logic was waved away. 'It's that look, the way those Audreys look. She'll be young and beautiful when she's sixty. I hate Frenchwomen.'

Later, when she was alone again and had tidied away the papers and invoices to make space for her tapestry, Catherine had leisure to examine the matter but found it hard to reach any conclusions. In fact, all she encountered was confusion.

The most insistent question – the one which Bryony had carefully not voiced – was the meaning of the drawing. Did a sketch on a wall mean Patrick was still in love?

On the heels of this conundrum pressed another, and that was Bryony's attitude. She seemed put out, certainly – upset, even – by his Sunday desertions, but rather more irked or offended than truly knocked from her stride. But Catherine hadn't been privy to the details of Bryony's liaisons since Jamie Coldridge in the lower sixth. Even then, she was far from sure she'd had the whole story. How was she to judge the state of her sister's feelings? Bryony liked to appear tough; she liked to treat her love life as a subject for light remark. But over Patrick she'd been conspicuously reticent; there hadn't been the usual throwaway comments. Was that for her benefit, Catherine wondered, because he was her friend? Or was it because this was different? That thing Bryony had said on the phone from England: *something real.* If so, why wasn't she more distraught?

Why, as well, had she not raised it with Patrick directly – Bryony, who was in general so forthright? Was she simply too proud to ask, to seem to be making a claim? Or was it that she didn't want to know the answer?

CHAPTER 17

ONE'S OWN CHERRY TREE

The French and their lunch break – Catherine ought to have been wise to it by now. But the Mairie in St Julien was scheduled to reopen at 14.30 – the perspex notice screwed to the door clearly announced the fact – and in her innocence she had believed it. Now, however, an additional piece of signage had appeared. In permanent marker on torn cardboard, it informed prospective inquirers, 'Back at 15.00.' It being now somewhat more than a quarter past three, Catherine tugged at the long brass door handle and was genuinely surprised to find it unyielding.

Madame Volpilière was more phlegmatic. Without even a shrug, she made straight for the wooden bench which stood against the wall of the Mairie and settled herself in the sun to wait.

'It's the youngest Cassini girl this afternoon,' she said. 'She'll not be back from driving to the dairy.'

Resolving to follow her example and be less British about it, Catherine took a seat beside her. There was a general grocery shop, once, where they'd stayed on holiday near Le Vigan. It was

called Huit à Huit, like the Eight Till Late conven-
ience stores in England, and it did indeed open
at 8 a.m. and close again at 8 p.m. – but in
between, its shutters came down between the
hours of twelve and three while the proprietor
went upstairs for his pork cutlet.

Here in the street, the afternoon heat was at the
peak of its strength; between the hard stone
surfaces it had an intensity it never seemed to
gather at Les Fenils. (In St Julien, remembered
Catherine, there was no problem with growing
tomatoes.) There was no tree or canopy, nothing
to provide shade for the bench. The full sun was
not unpleasant if you sat very still and closed your
eyes against the glare. The elderly, she seemed to
recall, were often sensitive to bright sunshine, but
Madame Volpilière had tilted her head back and
raised her papery cheeks to the light, so that
Catherine struggled to banish the mental picture
of a basking lizard.

'She's a good girl.'

'I'm sorry?' Catherine collected her scattered
thoughts.

'The little Cassini lass. She'll be here when she
can, I'm sure.'

'Right. Yes.'

A drink of water would be very welcome.
Catherine, conscious of the glass of wine she'd
had with lunch, thought with nostalgia of the water
coolers to be found in urban waiting rooms and
reception areas, with their stacks of disposable

plastic cups. The St Julien Mairie offered no such fripperies.

'Are you thirsty?' she inquired of her companion. Madame Peysasse reopened her shop door at three; she could nip along the street and buy a small bottle of Volvic.

Madame Volpilière pressed her thin lips more tightly together and shook her head. Such was her general appearance of desiccation that it was possible to imagine her surviving without water at all, as had formerly been believed of snakes. But Catherine remembered how at lunch in the restaurant in Mende, the old lady had mixed water from the carafe with the half-glass of wine she'd permitted the waiter to pour for her; like a child, Catherine had thought at the time, but now it seemed no more than common sense.

The day had begun productively enough. The morning, indeed, had brought quite a measure of satisfaction, as she had picked up Madame Volpilière and ferried her to an outpatient eye appointment at the small hospital in Mende, making use of the waiting time to visit the printers – the cousin of Maître Dujol – and talk about having a stamp made for her business. *Catherine Parkstone*, it was going to say, *tapissière artisanale*, and she was rather proud of the designation. Then, after making a few other necessary purchases, the two women had repaired to a quiet restaurant near the station. The place was chosen to suit the traditional tastes of Madame Volpilière, and she clucked her approval of the dim interior with its heavy linen tablecloths and heavier cutlery. The menu was traditional and heavy to match, a little too much so for Catherine's preference and for the weather, though the grilled trout was excellent in its way. Her luncheon guest did no more than pick at her *ris de veau*, but even if eating was a skill she no longer possessed, the pleasure she took in the ritual of the meal made Catherine glad to have brought her.

Even with the windows fully wound down, it had been hot in the car on the drive back to St Julien. The two cups of black coffee she had taken to counteract the alcohol only added to its dehydrating effect, and her tongue felt thick in her mouth. She wanted nothing now but to be finished with her errand at the Mairie and be free to head back up to the cool of the hills and La Grelaudière.

It was twenty-seven minutes past three when Mademoiselle Cassini appeared, waving penitently in the air a large bunch of keys.

'My apologies, Mesdames,' she called out as she trotted up, in shoes as unsuitable for running as they must surely have been for driving a cheese van. 'Am I a bit late?'

Catherine, for all her impatience, found that she was the one ready with the polite denial, while Madame Volpilière merely rose in silence and moved sedately towards the door.

Once inside, Catherine stood at the reception desk and waited while the youngest Cassini girl went round switching on lights – in spite of the bright afternoon sun which flooded in through the deeply recessed windows – along with computer, fax and photocopier, summoning them all into burring, beeping life. Behind her, Madame Volpilière moved to a row of metal chairs and sat down again.

'*Alors*, Madame,' said Mademoiselle Cassini at last, approaching her side of the desk and composing her outdoor, farm-girl features into an official smile. 'Now, how can I help you?'

'Well, I'm not sure if you can help or not,' began Catherine cautiously, 'but I was told it was the Mairie where I should inquire.'

'Oh?'

'It's about registering the *siège social* for my business.'

'Ah.'

'Yes. I understand – at least, it says here,' she fished from her bag the tax authority's leaflet, 'that I have to have the approval of the local Mairie for my business headquarters. My business address, you know.'

'Hmm.' *La petite* Cassini seemed to have a wide repertoire of non-committal vocalisations.

Handing her the leaflet seemed the best plan: let bureaucracy speak unto bureaucracy. The French girl read the paragraph to which Catherine had directed her and then looked up, the formal smile back in place.

'I see. Yes, I should be able to arrange that,

Madame. I just need to find the form. Wait just a moment, please.' And she retreated through a half-glazed door marked '*Privé*'.

'Quiet this afternoon,' remarked Madame Volpilière as Catherine joined her on the metal chairs to sit and wait. Evidently, this was a disappointment, a missed opportunity for the refreshment of neighbourhood connections.

Mademoiselle Cassini must be having some trouble locating the correct form. Eventually, however, she returned, clutching a fan of papers, and Catherine rose and returned to the counter. When a pen had been found – and then another, which worked – the young official asked, 'Name of applicant?'

'Catherine Parkstone,' said Catherine, proceeding to spell it helpfully before she was asked.

'Name of enterprise?'

All unrolled without difficulty until it came to the central question. 'Proposed address of *siège social*?'

'Les Fenils,' began Catherine.

The pen halted; Mademoiselle Cassini looked up. 'Ah,' she said. And then, 'Oh.'

'Is something the matter?'

'Of course, I'd forgotten.'

Catherine didn't at all like the rueful tone of her voice. 'Forgotten what?'

The young woman's eyes flicked towards Madame Volpilière and back again. 'You live up there. Les Fenils, you say – that'll be up at La Grelaudière.'

'Yes, that's right.'

'I'm afraid that's a zone designated as exclusively residential, Madame.'

Residential . . . The information refused to sink in; it defied logic. Monsieur Mériel's concrete milking parlour, his wife's cheese stall. Even the Bouschets with their retirement that wasn't.

'Are you sure?' she said cautiously. 'I mean, there are other businesses there.'

'Really?' For the first time, Mademoiselle Cassini looked almost sharp, and Catherine wondered if she should have kept quiet. Self-conscious, she found herself thinking, unaccountably, of Patrick's unlicensed still.

'Well, yes. Most people there are farmers.' It felt foolish to be stating the shiningly self-evident.

'Ah,' said the girl, 'agriculture.' She laid down her pen and straightened up, crossing her arms. 'Agriculture's different; it's special. There's an exception for agriculture and associated trades.'

Of course, there would be, wouldn't there? Maybe she should get that pig after all. Catherine Parkstone: pig farmer and *tapissière*. Silk grower, too, perhaps, into the bargain. Then a dark thought struck her.

'Is it because of the Parc National?'

'Partly that, yes. The hills, you know,' Mademoiselle Cassini unfolded an arm and swept it towards the windows, 'development, industry, it's all tightly controlled.'

Industry. Catherine pictured the tapestry frame

266

on her kitchen table, the armchair in her wood-shed waiting for new cushions. I'm very quiet, she considered saying. I won't make any noise or smoke, or pollute the stream with effluent.

Instead, she tried, 'Is there anything I can do? Someone I can contact? Some system of appeal?'

The girl regarded her doubtfully. 'You might try writing here,' she said, indicating the address on the bottom of an information sheet with little encouragement or conviction. 'They might be able to help.' Then the regulation smile returned. 'Is there any other way in which I can be of service, Madame?'

Catherine thanked her, took the forms and leaflets she was offered and turned to Madame Volpilière, who rose to her feet. They were at the door when at Mademoiselle Cassini's 'Oh' they looked round.

'I'm sorry, I forgot,' she said. 'There's just one more thing, Madame. If you're writing a letter about it, you won't forget to affix your seal, will you?'

Instead of heading straight home when they reached the car, the two women took a detour. It was at Madame Volpilière's request; instead of crossing the stone bridge and making for the turning to La Grelaudière, Catherine wound her way through a series of small, steep backstreets until she reached a stone wall and a pair of tall, wrought-iron gates. The cemetery of St Julien the

Hospitaller was not adjacent to the church, which stood on the tiny *place de l'église*, tucked behind the market square; rather, it lay apart, completely enclosed by a shoulder-high, grey-black granite wall. From above and at a distance, descending by road, the cemetery was easily visible, crowning the summit of the small rise in the valley floor on which St Julien was constructed. But from below you came upon it suddenly, the dark wall appearing at an unexpected right angle after the last turn of tightly grouped houses. There was just about room to park.

From the back seat where she had laid them earlier, Catherine lifted and handed Madame Volpilière her bunch of garden roses, their stalks bound together with baling twine.

'How often do you come?' asked Catherine as she pulled open the heavy gate to let her elderly neighbour pass through before her.

'Every two or three weeks, if I can. I don't like to be a burden.'

Leaving the widow to find her husband in privacy, Catherine lingered inside the gate. There on the wall was a fountain – or, rather, a small alcoved trough with a tap above it, topped by a roughly carved fan or seashell. *Eau potable*, proclaimed a sign: drinking water. The stone basin was lined with what looked suspiciously like lead. Catherine turned on the tap and released a trickle of water, tepid from standing in sun-warmed pipes – no doubt of lead as well. She cupped her hands and drank.

Frustration at the stupidity of it was the main thing she felt about her visit to the Mairie. Wretched Parc National, she thought, remembering Monsieur Bouschet and smiling. But there was a trickling sense of her own stupidity, too. How could she have come here and started work so blithely, without troubling to check these sorts of details? Bryony was quite right in her assessment – she was a shambling amateur, an original innocent abroad. And was it really a mere 'detail', a wrinkle to be ironed out, no doubt after the prescribed amount of penance, banging her head against administrative brick walls? What if it proved a more intransigent barrier? What if there were no way round it? If everything turned out to be a house of cards?

Putting the idea from her head, she ambled along the gravelled path towards where Madame Volpilière stood, her small figure further truncated by the summer grass which swathed her to mid-calf. Beyond her, over by the far wall of the cemetery, there was somebody else. Catherine recognised the long, black skirts of Père Amyot. The sleeves of his cassock were rolled to the elbow and he was rooting up rosebay willowherb by the armful and piling it in a wheelbarrow; on his head, pirate-style, was tied a spotted headscarf.

Neither widow nor priest seemed to notice Catherine. She moved to stand a discreet pace behind her neighbour's elbow, and looked down at the unremarkable grey headstone. *René Volpilière,* she read, born 21 March 1920, died 7 November 1991, and underneath, the single word *regretté*. Sorely missed – but that was eighteen years ago; was the loss still real, still sharp?

The roses were still in her neighbour's hands. In front of the headstone an old glass vase, dry of water, held a plume of something brittle and brown. Catherine gave a quiet cough.

'Would you like me to empty the vase, Madame, and put some water in it?' The 'Madame' came out unexpectedly, but didn't feel inappropriate.

'Thank you. Very kind.'

Madame Volpilière stooped and lifted the vase, and Catherine was surprised to see her bury her nose in the dead stalks. Looking more closely, she identified what had once been fennel fronds, and sprays of purple-flowering sage.

'He loved his herb garden, did my René. Sage was his favourite. He liked me to cook a loin of pork, when we had killed a pig, simmered slowly with sage and lemon and milk. The lemon sets the milk to curdle and thicken, until it's sweeter than cream.'

Past pleasures: Catherine wondered when her neighbour had last cooked a fillet of pork. Leaving her holding the dried herbs, she took the vase back to the fountain by the gate, and rinsed and filled it at the tap.

On her return, she ventured to ask, 'You've just got the one son, I think you said?' The old lady had never volunteered much about her family. A son, was all she'd said; moved away, a long while since.

'Yes. Roger. He's in Montréal. He went when he was twenty-four, married a local girl and settled. They've got two children. Three grandchildren now, too.'

A whole family, most of whom she'd presumably never met – while she spent her Christmases with a great-niece by marriage.

As if reading her thoughts, Madame Volpilière said, 'They've asked me to go out there.' It wasn't clear whether she meant a visit, or moving to be near them. Either way, the answer was plain. 'It's quite impossible, of course.'

They stood a little longer in silence, contemplating the grave, before at length Madame Volpilière spoke again. 'I never wanted to bury him here.'

'Didn't you?'

'No, not here, in town, in the cemetery. I wanted him at home with me.'

Catherine found no suitable response to this.

'Naturally, I know it's not how things are done. It's even the law. But I know he would prefer to have been at home, under the cherry tree with Loulou and Lissette. He loved those dogs.'

Understanding, Catherine nodded.

'It's not as if I have any religion.' Her glance strayed towards Père Amyot and his wheelbarrow, then back to Catherine. 'Have I shocked you? It isn't what's expected, is it, for a lady, and of my generation especially, to be without God. An old widow like me, she should be a good churchgoer, or at least a believer. Church and hearth: devoted and devout. Well, that's not me, at least not the church part. René believed, I think, in his own fashion. But I'm still certain he would rather have been under his own cherry tree. It's where he belonged.'

As they walked slowly back to the car, Madame Volpilière took Catherine's offered arm. For the first time all day, the old lady's movements began to suggest fatigue. *Where he belonged.* Catherine found herself thinking of her father – of smoke blowing away across the tidy lawns of Colchester crematorium – and of her mother in a high-backed chair in Walton-on-the Naze. Of Tom in St Andrew's and Lexie in London, of Graeme in High Wycombe without Suzannah, and of her sister, somewhere in the hills with Patrick Castagnol. And finally, tentatively, she thought of Les Fenils.

'Right, then,' she said as they reached the car and she opened the door for Madame Volpilière. 'Shall we go home?'

CHAPTER 18

LATE NIGHTS AND EARLY MORNINGS

By the third week in June the heat was oppressive. Ten days or more without a wisp of vapour to veil the sun had sent temperatures even at the altitude of Les Fenils spiralling too high for comfort. Up here in the mountains, indeed, where the air was emptier and the sky closer, the radiance seemed if anything more intense than down in St Julien.

During the day Catherine kept to the upper end of her terrace near the chestnut trees, where the hum from her beehive vibrated the air, the sound of insect activity lulling her to laziness. The rest of the yard was too exposed, and too often affected by a stale, encroaching odour from her septic tank. Perhaps she should have someone in to inspect it. It was very hot for sitting outside, in any case, after the first part of the morning. The glare was too intense to make working out of doors a possibility, even simple hand hemming, and if she occasionally took a drink and a novel out for an after-lunch siesta, she was beaten back indoors within ten minutes.

Above the house, the woods shimmered with evaporating moisture for the first few hours of daylight, presaging the heat to come. By eleven the lustre had gone; the trees seemed to lose their power to cool the air, their leaves as dusty and parched as the rock at their backs or the earth at their feet.

But the nights were the most striking thing as far as Catherine was concerned. The house, which felt cool in the daytime, its shady interior a contrast with the blaze outside, was transformed into an oven after dark. The thick stone walls, with their residual membrane of damp, placed by day a grateful metre's buffer between herself and the sun. As night fell, the process seemed to reverse itself; the walls ceased to be her cool armour and became instead a stifling blanket. For the first time she rued her bedroom beneath the eaves; the shingles of the roof, on which the sun had battered ferociously all day, gave off heat like a radiator.

Sleepless in the dark, Catherine lay and listened to the noises of the night. Every living creature, sluggish with the heat all day, seemed now to be awake and abroad, rustling and scuttling and scurrying. The sounds rang with clarity in the breathless air and straight in through her open window, so that the life outside seemed to be all around her bed. Her friend the barn owl struck easily and often, dealing audible death to small, nameless animals on the terrace below. And behind it all, a ceaseless backdrop, was the soft maraca rhythm of the cicadas.

On the hottest nights she gave up the uneven fight. Extracting herself from the clinging sheet, she would go downstairs and read or work – or simply stand at the window and stare up at the canopy of stars, her mind a leaping blank, or across and down into the teeming blackness of the gully. Catherine felt strangely clear-headed on these hot, solitary nights. She found she no longer needed the sleep she had when she was younger – the sleep she remembered craving when the children were babies, when she'd have bartered her future for one undisturbed early night. As she grew older, would she need it less and less? With the elderly it seemed to go either way – some slept all the time while others appeared to give it up altogether. If the insomnia of old age was to be like this, it seemed no terrible sentence.

It was different from the restless wakefulness of the early spring; her lack of sleep left her not exhausted by day but filled with a pleasant lassitude, while at night her mind and fingers were visited by a sharp focus and purposefulness such as she hardly remembered in years. Sometimes she rose and dressed at 4 or 5 a.m. and went out to work on her vegetable patch in the cool of the dawn. In the small hours she read every one of the complete works of Dickens she had brought with her from England, reviving forgotten acquaintances and forging new ones; this done, she set about Zola in the French. She finished the wild boar tapestry and began another, this time for herself alone.

The choice of subject was idiosyncratic, since she had no need of the created image, having the original constantly to hand. It was the view from her kitchen window, the view from the place at the table where she generally sat to work. She knew it so well now by all its lights and moods that she had no need to look up from her tapestry frame; on these quiet midnights she sat and worked from memory in front of the rectangle of black. In her emerging picture, it was morning: not first light but the soft luminosity of a break-fast time in spring, the sun breaking over the head of the valley to the left and outlining every leaf in gold. An edge of granite framed the scene as it did in life, the dark stone of sill and lintel echoing that of the cliffs which dominated the gully. Those features apart, the picture was nothing but trees: the tops of her own fruit trees in the foreground and, stacking up behind, the chestnuts and oaks and pines which filled the gully and cloaked the side of the ridge opposite. Somewhere behind those trees must be Patrick's house, but her tapestry showed no sign of it. The streaks of hanging vapour over the woods weren't chimney smoke but a remnant of morning mist, yet to be dispersed by the sun.

On this particular Sunday night, Catherine had gone to bed at an unusually early hour, perhaps ten or ten thirty. She had woken again shortly before midnight, her brain instantly alert and her eyes open but unseeing, full of the shapes and colours of her tapestry. Pulling an unnecessary cardigan over her nightdress, she padded downstairs on bare feet. (Was it imagination, or did the temperature fall between the top of the stairs and the bottom?) The worn flagstones of the kitchen floor were pleasantly cool. As she stood at the sink to fill the kettle, her toes found a shallow groove between the slabs and curled into it comfortably. After her short sleep, her mouth felt sticky and stale. Mint tea was what she needed.

She lit the gas and set the kettle to boil, then went out on to the starlit terrace, still barefoot, and across to her pots of herbs, arrayed along the woodshed wall. The stalk of green mint bled on to her fingers as she tore off a sprig, releasing its startling, antiseptic tang: hardly a vegetable smell at all, she always thought. Steam was rising from the kettle when she got back and, too impatient for a teapot, she poured hot water straight over the mint in a mug. She watched in fascination as it darkened and lost its shape, turning washy like seaweed in the water. The astringent fumes prickled her eyes.

A wave of dizziness overtook her. It wasn't tiredness, and she remembered that she hadn't eaten since some time in the morning – the previous morning, now. When Graeme had moved out and Tom had left for college – when she was first on her own – it had been an immutable point with her, that she still ate and slept regularly. The maintenance of the old routines of marriage and family was something to hold tight to in the new, uncharted life. Never was she still in her dressing-gown at noon; never were her meals eaten standing with a plate at the sink, but always at the table with a knife and fork and glass, and a jug of water. In those early weeks she'd had to force herself to cook, denying the voice which told her it wasn't worth it just for one. It was months before she was able to open a bottle of wine and pour herself a glass, alone, on a Friday evening.

How distant that time seemed now; how foreign, in some ways, that other Catherine. But regular habits had stuck; she had carried them to France with her – until this past week or so. It had been too hot, in the daytime, to think of eating, far too hot for lighting the gas. She'd made a big pot of soup three nights ago in the late evening, fat and chunky with things from her garden, and eaten it in the darkness of late nights and early mornings, with torn fistfuls of bread. In between she'd drunk water and homemade lemonade by the gallon, or grazed on wild strawberries by the roadside when she ventured for a walk, but had no urge for more.

The soup was gone now, and it was cool in the kitchen; perhaps she should make an omelette. Or perhaps later. Pulling her tapestry frame towards her, she picked up her needle, still threaded with silk of a purplish brown. It was funny: a composition consisting almost entirely of leaves, and she found herself so often stitching in every colour but green.

She worked with complete absorption for more than an hour, and was just straightening her back and thinking about the omelette again when she heard an approaching engine and, soon after, the scrunch of tyres on pebbles. Her watch told her it was after 1 a.m. Not a diesel, like a farm vehicle or the Bouschets' old Peugeot estate. A much smaller engine: the little hire car from the airport at Nîmes. Bryony.

Catherine was at the door before her sister, while her mind conjured horrors one by one. It must be Mum. Or Lexie. Or Tom. All of it was nonsense, though, she told herself, because she had a landline, didn't she, and so did Patrick. If anything had happened, Bryony would have rung. And her sister, climbing out of the car, looked very much as normal. She wasn't bleeding; she wasn't crying; the car looked undamaged.

'Hi,' said Bryony. 'Can I come in?'

Wordlessly, Catherine led the way through to the kitchen and waved at a chair. Refilling the kettle was an automatic gesture.

'You were up, then.' It wasn't a question, and Bryony didn't even sound surprised. She sounded pretty ordinary, in fact – maybe a little distant, but otherwise not far from her usual dry self.

'I was working,' said Catherine, then by way of explanation adding, 'It's been hot.'

Bryony nodded. 'Bloody hot.'

Catherine sat down across the table from her and wondered whether she should speak first. *Is everything OK?* But clearly not; at one in the morning this was unlikely to be a social call.

'Cath, I'm going home.'

Bryony's eyes were down on the table, giving away nothing. Painstakingly, Catherine breathed.

'I'd have been heading back in a few weeks in any case. I'm due back at work, in theory anyway, before the end of July. It was only ever meant to be a three-month sabbatical.'

Her voice was level and calm, but neither of them missed the significance of that 'in theory'.

'I've been over to the holiday cottage and packed up the rest of my things. It's all in the car now. I'm going straight off to the airport, but I thought I'd call round and say goodbye.'

Catherine regarded her evenly. 'It's one fifteen in the morning.'

When Bryony said nothing, she continued, 'There won't be any flights, not at night. And actually, from Nîmes, isn't the only flight to Stansted the one in the afternoon?' Even if it wasn't fully booked.

Still no reply; Bryony was staring determinedly at the edge of Catherine's tapestry frame. In this mood, she was quite capable of sleeping on a bench seat in departures and flying back via

Stuttgart – or driving through the night to the Channel tunnel.

'Coffee,' said Catherine, rising. 'You at least need coffee if you're going to drive at this time of night.' It was a naked delaying tactic, a means of inducing Bryony to stay long enough to get comfortable – or for tension to relax its grip and tiredness to kick in.

'I . . .' The first hesitation – that was surely a good sign. 'Maybe not coffee. Just some fresh air to clear my head. Let's go outside for a minute, and then I must be off.'

Catherine led the way back out to the terrace, where she could now make out the suitcase lying on the back seat of the hire car, and the carrier bag of shoes on the passenger seat. Such a small amount of baggage, after all. *Only ever a three-month sabbatical.*

Behind her, Bryony sat down on the stone step, and Catherine heard the rasp of a match. That explained the desire for 'fresh air'. But she hadn't known Bryony was smoking again.

'Just this one, and then I'm off. Can't smoke in the car – bloody Avis.'

With her back to her sister as she stared across the dark gorge, Catherine metered her voice to lightness. 'It's very late.'

There was stillness behind her. The heartbeat of the cicadas seemed to pulse louder in the silence. Then, taut and brittle, Bryony's voice. 'I want to get away from here.'

281

At once, Catherine was down on the doorstep at her sister's side. Very gently, she asked the question.

'What happened, Bry?'

'What happened is, I was an idiot.'

The Sunday lunch engagement, it had to be. 'Audrey?' she said softly.

There was a sound from Bryony's throat, difficult to decipher, somewhere between bitter and dismissive. She took a pull on her cigarette, though it didn't seem to give her any pleasure.

'You confronted him about it?'

'There was a receipt – for flowers. More than forty bloody euros, by the way. He didn't even bother to hide it, just left it lying on the table. Fancy florist in Montpellier, today's date. I wasn't going to ignore it, I'm not that spineless. He was practically shoving it in my face.'

'And he admitted it? About seeing Audrey, I mean?'

'Oh, yes.' The twist in Bryony's features was painful to see, like the contractions of cramp.

'And it is his wife, is it?' It felt like turning the knife, but it also felt necessary. 'He's still seeing his wife?'

The twist tightened, and Bryony screwed out the stub of her cigarette in the dust at their feet. For a moment, Catherine thought her sister was about to give way and cry, and she laid a hand on her arm. But it wasn't tears, it was something worse, something uglier: something closer to laughter.

282

'Oh no, she's not his wife. Nothing so banal. No, she's his daughter.'

'Audrey is Patrick's daughter?' repeated Catherine, floundering.

'Yes. She's doing a sandwich year at the university in Montpellier.'

'Well, then . . .' That was good, wasn't it? Patrick with a daughter – it was difficult to adjust to. So strange that he had never mentioned her, all the times she had chattered on about Lexie and Tom. Even after he met Tom at Christmas.

But this made it all right, didn't it? He wasn't seeing someone else; there was no other woman. No one but Bryony.

'It explains the sketch,' she said, feeling treacherously like laughter. 'Why he kept it on the wall, I mean. And why she looks twenty-five in it. She probably is twenty-five.'

'Twenty-one, in fact.'

'And he buys her lunch every Sunday, like the original doting papa.' Rather sweetly old-fashioned of them, she thought. 'And flowers.'

'It was her last weekend,' said Bryony. 'She's going back home. But you're missing the point.' Her evident impatience made Catherine regret her lapse into levity. 'She isn't Audrey. She's Megan. Her name is Megan.'

'OK.' She was still at a loss as to what she was being told.

'It's a sandwich course, I said. Megan is studying French law in Montpellier, just for the year. As

283

part of her law degree course at the University of Keele.'

'She's studying in England?'

Now Bryony was actually laughing, only quietly, but slightly too high in pitch. 'She is. Megan Castagnol is studying at an English university because she's English. Except that she doesn't use that surname, Patrick says. People in England can never cope with the spelling. That French *gn* sound – they always want to put a "y" in it. So Megan calls herself by her mother's surname. Which is Greenwood. Such a quintessentially English name, don't you think? Under the greenwood tree. Down by the greenwood side.'

'You mean, her mother – his wife . . .'

'Is English, yes. Jenny, apparently. Jennifer Greenwood. About as English as you can get, I'd say.'

Patrick with an English wife, an English daughter. It made no sense at all – and yet, immediately, it did. The Penguin paperbacks in his kitchen. The easy, idiomatic usage. *How does your garden grow?*

She reeled in her spinning thoughts and tried to focus on Bryony. 'But does it matter? If he isn't seeing her. If it's just his daughter he has lunch with. If this Jennifer is safely back in England, she can't hurt you, can she?'

The ugly laughter again, making Catherine wince and tighten her fingers on her sister's arm.

She felt gooseflesh there, although it was far from cold.

'Oh yes, she's back in England. Still lives in their old flat in Islington, I gather.'

'*Their* old flat?'

'Yes. That's the other little thing. Patrick wasn't just married to an Englishwoman, he lived there as well. Thirteen years altogether, including eight married to Jenny.'

Patrick in London – Patrick living in London for thirteen years. What was it he'd said? *University, city life. I came back.* And Madame Bouschet: *He came home for a month when his mother died. He's a good boy.* Through her own dislocated reflections, she heard Bryony, still speaking.

'He worked in London, too. As an international investment banker, as it happens. In the Square Mile. Crédit Belge on the corner of Leadenhall Street. Just near that Thai restaurant I like.'

'Well, that's . . .' Coincidental? Something to talk about, something in common? Of course it was none of those things. It was disorientating; it was incomprehensible; it was all wrong.

Bryony's denunciation appeared to have run its course. They sat together unspeaking, letting Catherine's uncompleted sentence settle about them. There was no sound out here on the terrace now but the cicadas. The human presence on the doorstep seemed to deter the nocturnal scuttlers and scamperers; the barn owl was nowhere in evidence. For a moment it was almost peaceful, so that Bryony's renewed onslaught gave Catherine a start.

'Just round the fucking corner! For years we worked in offices less than twenty yards apart, for God's sake. I must have passed him in the street, bumped into him at the tube station or in the pub at lunchtime. And he's never said a bloody word about it.'

'I suppose it's a while ago.' Though what relevance that might have, she had no idea.

'He's been laughing at me, Cath. All this time, he's been fucking well laughing at me. Taking me for a fool.'

'I'm sure he—' Catherine stopped. Defending him would be no comfort to Bryony in her present state, and she found in any case that she had no stomach for it. In truth she was sure of very little right now, as far as Patrick was concerned. Had he indeed been laughing at Bryony – laughing at herself, too? She fought off the picture of his mocking eyes. Or was it merely a habit of defensive secrecy, the maintenance of impregnable private walls? Either way, he'd apparently been happy enough to draw her sister in as far as his bed, but no further.

'He's just been playing games, acting the French country squire, the son of the cévenol soil, pretending to be something he's not. Making me fall for an image of something, and it never bloody existed.' Bryony stabbed a trainered toe at the butt of her cigarette. 'I honestly thought he was different, if you can believe it. Different from all the men in London with their city suits and their city cynicism. Out for a fast buck at work and a fast fuck afterwards. I thought he was something else – something solid. How can I have been so pathetically naïve?'

Something solid. Patrick chopping wood, Patrick stripping ivy from the outhouse wall. The imagined reality of him – the gentleman peasant, as substantial as the rock of Mont Lozère – she had known it was to be mistrusted when Bryony had said it back in February. That treacherous 'something real'.

'No,' said Catherine stoutly, pulling her sister's arm up and inside her own. 'Not naïve. It can't be naïve to trust people . . .'

'Ha.' Bryony's unspoken scepticism was eloquent – but it wasn't what Catherine had meant to say. Her sentence had tailed away without its ending. People we're sleeping with? People we love?

Then Bryony turned to face her. 'You never said anything either.' Almost at once she tempered the accusation. 'You never knew either.' But the blame was still quite clearly there.

No, Catherine told the silence. *No, I never knew.*

'Why the hell would he pretend like that? What the hell trip was he on, playing us both for idiots?' But Catherine had no answer to give her sister.

The venting of anger seemed finally to have drained Bryony of her earlier impatience; her arm was no longer rigid against Catherine's side but merely inert. Catherine tugged it closer. Bry had always had those bony elbows, right from being a small child. Self-conscious at thirteen, fourteen, she'd covered them with long-sleeved tops, even on the beach.

'Let me make up the spare bed.'

It was a risk; it might rekindle the urge to flight. There was a pause – but no resistance. Tiredness washed from Bryony in waves.

'Come on. You can help me with the duvet cover. Double ones are always easier with two. It might be cooler up there by now, and the shutters have been closed all day in that room anyway.' When there was still no answer she added, with what she hoped was decisiveness, 'Sleep.'

Unprotesting, Bryony allowed herself to be pulled to her feet, and Catherine led the way indoors.

Waking later than of recent mornings, Catherine was surprised to find she had slept, and slept well. Whether the same could be said of her sister was doubtful. Bryony was downstairs and eating a length of baguette, spliced and slathered with apricot jam. That she was eating seemed on the whole to be a good sign; much less encouraging was the fact she was already dressed – or perhaps still dressed – in yesterday's jeans and T-shirt. The suitcase was still on the back seat of the car.

'You know you can have a shower if you like,'

said Catherine. 'The pressure's not great, but the water's good and hot.'

Impatience, however, had reclaimed her sister. 'Thanks,' she muttered through a mouthful of bread. 'But I'll be home by tonight. I can have a proper bath. First time in two months. What is it with the French? I couldn't live without a bath.'

Catherine – who remembered thinking the same thing at various points last autumn, even cruising the web for costings on bathroom suites – said nothing. Showers now seemed so much the obvious thing; she hadn't thought about a bath in months.

'It's all very well for you,' Bryony grumbled on. 'You've evidently gone native. But some of us need our home comforts, we're not cut out for life in the wilderness with a stack of firewood and a bottle of homemade grog. I miss London. Somewhere you can buy a morning paper on the way to work, or a pint of milk without an hour's round trip.'

All for the best, then. If that's what Bryony wanted to think, wanted Catherine to think, it seemed foolish to fight it. 'And fresh baguette for breakfast, ironically enough, instead of the day before yesterday's. Sorry about that.'

Bryony swallowed and put down the end of her bread. 'A bit chewy, it's true.'

'It's better toasted. Let me cut you another piece and put it under the grill. And have you had coffee?'

'No.' Her sister stood up. 'No thanks, really. I

never eat breakfast at home. Another strange foreign habit I've picked up, but it can't be good for you.'

It was a relief to see her grinning, at least. 'But coffee.' Bryony never went anywhere without coffee.

'I want to get on the road.'

Catherine raised an eyebrow and cast a glance out towards the empty hills. 'Before it gets busy?'

But Bryony was undeterred. 'Don't want to get stuck behind some bloody combine harvester all the way.'

'I'll make some to take with you.' Turning to the hob covered Catherine's smile. It was June, and the nearest wheat field must be thirty miles away. 'You can have my thermos. I'll get another one – they have them in the ironmongers in St Julien. We do have some newfangled things up here, you know.'

Bryony relented. She sat down again and began prising flakes of crust from her abandoned baguette. Her eyes were too bright, her cheeks too flushed. The last thing she really needed was caffeine, but still Catherine heaped in a double measure, just hoping she wouldn't take the hairpins like a rally driver.

'I could drive you,' she found herself saying, without premeditation.

Her sister looked at her as if she were mad. 'And do what with the hire car? Push it into the gorge?'

'Drive you in the hire car, I mean.'

'And walk back?'

She was right, it was a crazy idea. 'There must be buses,' Catherine temporised. 'At least some of the way. And then a taxi.'

'Right, of course. Or you could hitch-hike, maybe catch a lift with a passing ox cart. Look, you're very sweet, Cath, but I'm a big girl. I don't know what you imagine, but I'm not sick or suicidal or dying of a broken heart. I think I can drive myself to the airport all right. I've had my sabbatical, and now I'm going home.'

Catherine stared at the steam which was starting to curl from the spout of the camping kettle. Bryony's last words had a sort of finality, and there seemed to be nothing more to be said – or nothing it was possible to say just now. *I'm sorry.* Those were the words that filled her head as she gazed into the rising steam. She felt that somehow she should be apologising to Bryony, or Bryony to her, though she couldn't precisely say for what, on either side. And yet she couldn't help feeling that there was a rift to be healed here; this morning there was something present between them, some awkwardness, some skirting round, some unquantifiable distance.

A curse on Patrick Castagnol.

Catherine made the coffee and poured it into the thermos. There was no further pretext for delay. Bryony waved away attempts to press upon her cherries, or a jar of jam, or chocolate for the journey, and ten minutes later Catherine was alone. The hunger of twenty-four hours was suddenly insistent, but there was no more bread in the house; she must make a trip to St Julien. Picking up Bryony's rejected breakfast, she took a large bite from the untouched end. Too much jam, she thought, as she chewed. Bryony always liked too much jam and not enough butter.

There was work to do, once she had washed the cafetière. Curtains to line for a neighbour of Monsieur Fraissenet, down in the rue des Quais; a pair of velvet cushions to finish for her market stall on Thursday; the kitchen window tapestry. Or perhaps it would be better to take a walk before she settled to work, before the heat began to build. But not up through the woods to the wooden bridge – not towards Patrick's house.

Patrick. Sitting down in Bryony's empty chair, Catherine drained the last dregs of the coffee into a cup. It was thick and sludgy, making her wince at the bitter taste even before it touched her tongue. Patrick married to an Englishwoman and living in a flat in Islington; Patrick working at a City bank, two minutes from Bryony. Patrick commuting on the tube and reading the *Evening Standard*, maybe watching Arsenal play at the weekend. Yet when she tested it, she was surprised by how little any of it surprised her. She had always known it about Patrick: that, as with an iceberg, the greater portion was unrevealed. It was only the specifics that were new.

He had no dog, it unexpectedly occurred to her.

They all had dogs, all the men here, even Guillaume. Especially Guillaume. Patrick went shooting but he went alone. She should have known there was something not quite right about a woodsman without a dog; something unreliable, something impermanent. He ought to have had a dog.

There were coffee grouts in her mouth, sticking to her teeth; the surface in her cup, she saw, was flecked with black. If the ironmongers couldn't get her a new filter for her old cafetière, would she have to order one direct from John Lewis on the web? Though, come to think of it, wasn't it actually made in France?

And he was a parent, too – an English parent. Patrick had watched his daughter's nativity play at a London primary school. He'd sat down with her, perhaps, on an odd day off, to watch *Blue Peter*. At bedtime, he'd read her the same picture books that Catherine read to Lexie and Tom. *The Very Hungry Caterpillar. Each Peach Pear Plum.*

Pushing away with a slop her undrinkable coffee, Catherine was smacked by a wave of anger. Bryony's question from last night was still without a proper answer: why the hell would Patrick pretend? She was furious with him for his stupid game-playing, if that's what it had been; furious for the stupid, pathological defensiveness of his concealment. She was furious at what he had done to Bryony. And she was angry with her sister, who never shared things either. She blamed her for her blindness – for chasing a chimera, for swallowing some empty fiction of the rural idyll, with Patrick in the leading role. But she blamed her also for her lack of tears – for apparently feeling little, in the end, beyond the pique of injured pride. She was angry with herself, too, though she couldn't have said for what. It was all a mess. It was all a pointless, horrible mess.

It didn't last long. Anger was a useless, self-destructive thing and by the time the cup and cafetière were washed and the crumbs wiped from the table, she had reclaimed her equanimity. A walk down the hill and back to clear her head, and she'd be ready to get on with those cushions. She had practically promised them for Thursday to a niece of Monsieur Folcher's.

All that week Catherine found reasons for not walking in the woods in the direction of Patrick Castagnol. She would not have acknowledged any positive evasion; he was her neighbour, after all, and sooner or later they must run into each other. But if a little time should be allowed to pass before she was required to compose herself to speak to him, it seemed to her no bad thing. There must, at the very least, be embarrassment on both sides. A few days' respite before the inevitable meeting might do something to reduce its sting.

Instead of the encounter occurring on Patrick's side of the gully, therefore, it took place on hers. It was Sunday morning, six days after Bryony's departure, and Catherine had been up since five.

294

The weather continued unbroken and the heat in the daytime was relentless. By the time Patrick appeared at just after seven o'clock, she had almost two hours' work behind her in the vegetable patch. She had weeded round her carrots and onions and lettuces; she had soaked the thirsty earth with spring water from the hose, shifting it along every ten minutes or so; she had harvested a fresh crop of garden strawberries, combing the fuzzy undersides of the leaves with her fingers to feel for the cool fruits, as many of which ended up in her mouth as in the basin. It was possible that Patrick had been up and about for just as long. He carried no gun today but, instead, a fishing rod and over his shoulder a leather bag, broad and flat like an old school satchel. He didn't arrive the way she would have expected, down past the beehives at the top end of the house; he came up the road from the direction of La Grelaudière. Kneeling among the strawberry plants, she didn't hear his footsteps until he was almost beside her – or, rather, above her, standing on the terrace some four feet above the bed where she worked. She had to sit back on her heels to look up at him. There was a crick in her neck as she raised her head.

'Good morning.'

'Hello, Patrick.' Say something else, she told herself; say something quickly, before this becomes uncomfortable. Say something about the weather, or his being out early, or the lack of slugs on the strawberries compared with back home in England. But no, not England.

'It's a beautiful day.' It was he who said it, but not at all as if he felt the need for inconsequentialities. He sounded – as he always did – ironic.

'Yes. Looks like being hot again.'

He signalled his assent with a brief jerk of the chin. Should she be grateful for his unselfconsciousness, or merely irritated by it?

'That's why I'm working now, while it's still cool. There's too much heat for me, later on.' *It's because I'm English*, she omitted to add. *I'm not used to it.*

'I've been fishing.'

'Right.' She couldn't think what else to say; the rod made any expression of surprise somewhat redundant, as did the rubber waders which clad his legs to the thigh.

'Brown trout.' He opened the leather bag and pulled out by the tail a fat slippery fish, not brown at all but spotted silver and black with a streak of yellow ochre along its side. 'They're in glut at the moment. I know the perfect place, a little basin below the rapids, just down from the hamlet. It's thick with new fish, I was practically treading on them.'

Was he going to offer to take her there? she wondered. Show her the place, lend her a rod – or else tease her for her squeamishness? But instead he dropped the fish back in his satchel and looked down at her in silence. The oblique morning sun was behind and above him and she couldn't see to read his face.

'I took only four – I have no need of more. Two small ones will make me a good breakfast. But that leaves the two beauties for tonight, and I cannot hope to do them justice on my own. They demand a guest.'

Demand. She clenched her teeth and examined the toes of his waders. But then he dropped his voice to a different tone and asked simply, 'Will you come, Catherine?'

Perhaps he wanted to apologise, wanted to explain himself – though she wasn't at all sure she was ready to listen to it. More likely it was an attempt to restore some semblance of normality, a gesture towards bridging over the chasm that had opened between them. If so, it was an exercise she was unconvinced was either possible or desirable. She should not go; she would not go. And yet, to her frustration, she could call to mind no plausible ground on which, without rudeness, she might refuse the invitation.

'I'll bring some strawberries,' she said.

CHAPTER 19

THE THINGS WE THINK WE WANT

'Dad seems fine.'

The words, as Tom spoke them, dealt Catherine a buffet of guilt, for Graeme hadn't entered her head in a week. She put it down to the heat, which locked everything in an intensity of here and now, and sapped energy for thought beyond the moment. England – the old life – seemed at times, these recent days, quite dizzyingly remote.

'He's getting on with things, you know. Pretty much his normal self.'

'Really? He's doing OK on his own?' Not that there should be cause for guilt; an ex-wife could scarcely be held accountable for the state of her husband's heart on splitting from another woman – but he was her children's father and his pain was their pain. And actually, hers, too, if only this heat would release her for the effort of empathy.

She became aware of Tom's silent laughter. 'What?'

'On his own, you say. You're where you are, doing what you're doing, and you're wondering if Dad is doing OK on his own?'

Catherine smiled. 'Your dad and I are not the same. He needs . . .' Graeme no doubt still needed what he had always needed, far more than she ever had: somebody to reflect back his ideas; external validation. '. . . people.'

'Well, he's got people. He might not have Suzannah, but he's still got work and he's still got his friends. He was off to play squash with one of them this afternoon. Practically threw me out.'

'He can't cook, though, can he? What will he be eating?' She was laughing at herself now, laughing at the cliché. 'He's never been able to grill a sausage without burning it. You remember how you and Lexie used to moan whenever I went out and Dad had to make your tea?'

'Oh, we just did that to keep you happy. Actually it was great, he used to send out for pizza and not tell you.'

'What did he give you for lunch today, then?'

'Sunday roast, actually. Pork with crackling, apple sauce, all the trimmings. It was great.'

'Really?' He was ribbing her, he had to be.

'Absolutely. They have a really good carvery at the Six Bells.'

Grinning, Catherine asked, 'How was the conference?'

'Not bad. There was a decent audience for my paper, even though it was Saturday afternoon and a lot of people were heading home by then. A few good questions, especially from this one professor, a bloke from Bristol. I had a chat with him afterwards and he gave me some really useful pointers. And we sat in on some interesting sessions on Thursday and Friday too.'

'We?'

'Me and Mo. She was giving a paper too. On Friday.'

'And you took her to Dad's?' Catherine tried, without complete success, to dismiss a pang of envy.

'Actually, no. She had to get back to St Andrew's last night – stuff to do today in the lab.' On a Sunday? Or was Tom just being cautious Tom?

'She'd never been to Oxford before. So we skived off during some of the boring bits and went to have a look at the colleges, except we ended up in Blackwell's instead. Mo and books, honestly, it's an addiction. If I ever can't find her, I just try the bookshops. Like trawling the pubs for a drunk.'

What does she read? Catherine wanted to ask. Does she love Jane Austen, like all young women her age? Or do her tastes run more to suit her name and ancestry: *Waverley*, or *Kidnapped* and *Catriona*? The question she chose was a safer one. 'So, she's a biochemist too?'

The brief burst of sharing was over, however, it seemed; taciturnity returned. 'Same lab, different group.' Then, with barely a pause, 'I saw Gram.'

'Oh, when was that?'

'Wednesday, before the conference. It was just as easy to get a train down the east coast line, then across to London afterwards and out to Oxford that way.'

Catherine left unchallenged this evident nonsense, hugging her gratitude close. 'How was she?'

It was the question she always put to Lexie, and Bryony, too, although there was no answer to be had, except the one he gave. 'Oh, you know. Pretty much as ever.'

'Well, thank you, love.'

'I'd hoped I might meet up with Lex as well while I was down south. But you know what she's like.'

'Work?' hazarded Catherine.

'So she reckoned. Some big assignment or other.' He snorted. 'A scoop, a major cake decoration story, about to break. Maybe she'll make the nationals. You'll be reading all about it tomorrow, even down there.'

'Tom.' But the reproval was for form's sake only; his amusement was more affectionate than derisive.

'Then I tried Aunty Bryony. I hadn't seen her in aeons.' Catherine's stomach took an uncomfortable lurch. 'She's usually good value, is Bryony. It's not everyone has an aunt who can drink him under the table and insist on paying for every round.'

Usually . . . 'Right. And, er, how was she?' The same thing she'd asked about Mum.

'Oh, OK.'

'But?' she prompted, without being at all certain she wanted to hear the 'but'.

The reluctance was unmistakable; but when she waited, finally he said, 'What on earth did you manage to do to her over there?'

'Why? What do you mean?'

'Have you two fallen out or something?' He sounded only half serious, but she was still glad to be able to answer with the truth.

'No, of course not.' Then, again, when he volunteered nothing further, 'Why?'

'Oh, nothing, really. Only that she seems to have fallen out of love with France in a big way, that's all.'

God, it was hot here in the kitchen, so hot and airless, making her labour for breath. At the other end, though, Tom seemed to have found his.

'She was so sold on the place after her last visit, back before Christmas. So Lexie said, anyway. She saw her in January and she said Aunty Bryony was like a bad travel brochure, proclaiming the virtues of the place. And then this sabbatical, which was meant to be such a big deal. Getting back in touch with nature or whatever. The simple things, the important things – the meaning of life. I had her waxing lyrical on the phone before she left. But I suppose it was always a bit unlikely for someone like her.'

So hot; suffocating. 'And now?' she managed to say.

'Now she's barely got a thing to say about it. We spent two hours in the pub on Wednesday night before I got the late train to Oxford, and I doubt if she mentioned France more than once. Work, clients, the state of the nation, the price of beer. It's like she'd never heard of the Cévennes.'

'She didn't say anything?'

'Like I say, hardly a word.' His reply gave her her answer, and she wasn't sorry he had missed her meaning.

A muffled announcement in the background caught her attention, recalling her to practicalities. 'You're on the train.'

'Yes, sorry, bit of a cliché, I know. I'm just on my way back.'

'I mean, you're on your mobile. The call – it'll be costing you the earth.'

'I'm a big boy now, Mum. I know post-doc scientists don't get the biggest salaries in the world, but it covers a couple of phone calls.'

She laughed with him. 'All right. I'm sorry.'

'OK, look, I'd better go, anyway. There has to be a buffet car, doesn't there, on the Edinburgh train? I didn't have coffee in the pub at lunchtime – it was that Cona muck.'

'Well, thanks for ringing,' said Catherine. 'And I'm glad your paper went well. You will send me an offprint, won't you, if they publish the proceedings.'

'Course I will.'

It was a joke between them, the copies of his articles which he always sent her and she couldn't read. But it also wasn't a joke; they were on her shelf and she wanted the full set.

'And listen, don't worry, Mum. It'll be all right,

honestly. It'll just take a bit of time for things to settle down.'

'Yes – thanks, you're right. She'll be so busy with work, I dare say, after her break, she won't have time for anything else.'

As soon as she'd spoken, she realised her mistake.

'She? D'you mean Aunty Bryony? I was talking about Dad. I just meant Dad was going to be OK.'

The trout were delicious. Sweet as the water from which they'd come, they brought to mind dark, dappled places and the sudden flash of sunlight.

By the time they were eaten and the bones picked clean, Catherine was finding she could almost relax – could almost pretend things were as they used to be between the two of them.

'It's all a question of "rural professions",' she told Patrick as he refilled her wine glass. '*Métiers ruraux* is the phrase. I have to show that mine is one of those.'

He attended to his own glass, then returned his scrutiny to Catherine. 'Indeed.'

'It's either that or *agri-tourisme* – like your *gîtes*, I suppose.'

The designation was acknowledged with a slight inclination of the head, though it could hardly be his primary source of income, she imagined, after twenty years in international banking.

'I've been reading through all the literature put

out by the Parc National. It seems that if I'm to obtain permission to operate my business from an address within the boundaries of the park, I have to demonstrate that what I do is a rural profession. It's a pretty vague phrase, but I did find a definition of sorts. *L'agriculture et les activités annexes.* My business has to be somehow subsidiary to agriculture.'

'And isn't it?'

The direction of his question wrong-footed her. 'Well, it's hard to see how, exactly. I imagined it meant things specifically linked to farming. Supplying animal feed or fertilisers, I don't know . . . Vets and farriers, maybe. Fencing, drystone walling, that kind of thing.'

He took a contemplative sip of wine. 'Your customers are farmers.'

'Some of them, yes.' Most of them, in fact, were in agriculture in some form, or had been before they retired – though she'd also supplied cushions to a *pâtissier* and the wife of a public notary.

'You live in a farming community, you supply your community. Farmers, one must presume, need soft furnishings as much as anybody else.'

'I suppose so.' If Patrick wasn't precisely smiling, the eyes that held hers across the table were certainly merry; she couldn't help but respond. 'Purveyor of tapestries and curtains to the neighbourhood herdsmen, growers and assorted smallholders.'

'And,' he added solemnly, 'official upholsterer to the agricultural trade.'

A giggle rose, unbidden, along with an image of the Mériels' goat-shed, the open sides hung with sprigged cotton drapes and the food troughs quilted to match. It might be the wine, not his usual red but a smoky white Burgundy that tingled the tongue and sent fumes up the back of her nose. The heat of the evening, and her discomfort when she first arrived had made her attack it more thirstily than was circumspect, and he'd been topping up her glass before it was empty, making it hard to keep tally. But she didn't much care; laughter felt good.

'The silly thing is, if I made some kind of tourist knick-knacks, I'd probably be all right. Madame Volpilière has a relative by marriage who lives over Génolhac way, inside the Parc National; she makes finger puppets out of local sheepskin, to sell in the village shop. That seems to count as *agri-tourisme*.' Fluffy lambs with dangling feet of wood on strips of leather. 'But curtains and armchairs aren't tourism – much too useful.'

'Farmhouse crafts.' Patrick turned the phrase over thoughtfully. 'It's certainly another argument. Aren't you using locally produced materials?'

She wrinkled her nose. 'Some of the wools for my tapestry work, I suppose. But I can't possibly source everything I need from round here. Nobody makes velvet in the Cévennes, do they, or zippers or lining material?' Another sip of wine, and she was laughing again. 'They can't, can they? There are no factories – because of the Parc National.'

He was smiling openly back at her now. 'As you so rightly say.'

'Anyhow, they're sending someone out to inspect me next month, an officer from the park authority. So I'll just have to do my best to look as agricultural as possible.'

There was no reply to this, only his eyes playing over her face, which felt hotter than it should. A confessional urge seized hold of her.

'Of course, I should have sorted all this out right at the beginning – nine months ago, not now. If I'd done my research properly I'd have looked into it before I even came here, instead of getting in up to my neck and only then realising there's a problem. I'm such a fool – I dare say you think me very stupid.'

His answer came slowly, the words weighed with care. 'I think you are a woman of common sense. As such, naturally you expect sound reason to prevail. You did not anticipate such vain bureaucratic impediments. Why would you?'

'Why? Because I was taking an important step. I'm meant to be a professional—'

But he waved her to silence with his wine glass. 'This is the nation of Napoleon, the nation of Colbert – we love to have our rules. But we are also a race of uncompromising individualists, of *petits anarchistes*. We take pleasure in the rules, but equal pleasure in ways to bend and break them. I think you need not fear for your business, Madame l'Anglaise. A means will surely be found.'

Catherine remembered her strawberries, which were in a basket by the sink. She fetched them over and placed them on the table between them just as they were: unhulled and still dusty with the earth's heat. Patrick poured them both a glass of water from the jug; he helped himself to a strawberry and immersed it briefly, shaking off the excess droplets.

'Good,' he pronounced simply, through a mouthful of fruit. 'You are happy in your situation at Les Fenils. Here I am surrounded too much by woodland to have success with strawberries. It's the same with courgettes, and anything ground-fruiting. All would be eaten by the slugs.'

She accepted the compliment with an absent smile, but her mind was still on the Parc National.

'Has it killed this place?' she wanted to know. 'The Parc National. Has it really killed the community?'

When he looked at her in surprise, she hurried on to explain. 'It's what Monsieur Bouschet claims, that's all. He says that by stifling development, it has depleted the population and driven the young people away. Bled the area dry.' What was the phrase he'd used? *A vehicle without an engine.*

'He says so, does he?'

'Yes. And the population has shrunk, hasn't it? It must have. There are abandoned houses everywhere.' The ruins at the promontory; the ruins on the way to St Julien.

He nodded, reached for another strawberry. 'And these old shells of houses, are they recently abandoned, would you say?'

'I don't know.' It was hard to tell, when buildings had doubtless been constructed the same way here for centuries, perhaps even a millennium or more. But the ruin at the rocky promontory had an almost ancient air, like the Roman remains in Orange or Avignon, or something sacked by Langlade in the name of King and Pope. 'Probably not,' she admitted. 'No.'

'The Parc National has been with us less than forty years, but Lozère has been suffering the ravages of fortune for a hundred more. Think of the silkworm disease.'

'Oh yes, of course.'

'Without it, you would have had no shortage of home-grown cévenol silks for your tapestries. Disease struck the chestnut trees soon after, too, and destroyed that source of livelihood. Then came the floods of nineteen hundred and ninety seven: the autumn rains burst the banks of many rivers, destroying whole villages and driving people from their homes and farms. The Great War took men away to fight and, of those who were not killed, many chose not to return. No, this place was decaying long before the Parc National began to do its work.'

Catherine gazed at him helplessly. *Decaying* . . . An image came to her of timber, strong and sturdy to look at but its core reduced to dust. She must

309

have looked aghast, because he smiled and reached to lay his hand on her forearm.

'Don't be too afraid. I dare say this place will survive as long as it has people to take care of it.'

'The Mériels,' she said, voicing her thoughts aloud. 'The Bouschets, who can never quite bring themselves to retire; the Vaillants and Mademoiselle Cassini and all those like them, with jobs in the village alongside the farm; even Père Amyot . . .'

'*Et toi aussi, peut-être, Catherine?*'

It wasn't so much the switch to his native tongue which caught her breath, nor the slight shift of his forefinger on the skin of her wrist, but her own name, spoken in the French way: Cat-rine.

'Me?' she managed to say. He was mocking her; he must be.

'Why not? You have a garden. You grow strawberries.' He took one from the basket and held it up, as if in evidence. Her arm prickled cold where his fingers had been. 'Are you not tending your small portion of the land?'

'And my bees,' she said, deciding to play along. 'I may not have my pig yet, nor my silkworms, but let's not forget the bees.'

'Ah, yes. Will you have much honey this year, do you think?'

'I don't know really, not at the moment. They seem to be going great guns, filling up the brood chamber. But I've only just put the first super on the top, last week, for them to start making honey for me. I thought I'd let the colony build itself up a bit first.'

He nodded. 'Do the gloves help?'

'Oh, yes, I forgot to say – thank you very much for those. It does make things easier, not to be having to watch all the time what's crawling up your sleeves.'

'No more stings, then?' He was looking at her wrists, and she pulled them back a little way towards her.

'No. It's been fine.'

'I think you become accustomed to them – to handling them, I mean – and they in turn become accustomed to you. It's anxiety and nervousness which results in being stung. If you are confident, the bees will have confidence too.'

'It's true. At the beginning, the first couple of times, they flew up and all around me like angry things. But now I seem to be able to brush them off the frames I'm looking at, and it doesn't irritate them at all. They just drop away in dollops, like treacle.' Like something she could never have described, nor previously begun to imagine: strange, living, dry, crunchy treacle.

'But you know the most amazing thing of all? It was that very first evening, when I had to transfer them into the hive from the skep they came in. I had no idea how to go about it, so I looked it up on the internet.' It had sounded the purest homespun nonsense, an old wives' tale if ever there was one: that a swarm of bees, if tipped out at twilight on to the bottom of a slope of white, would always run uphill.

'I felt such a fool standing there, with the heap of bees at my feet. I thought nothing would happen, or they'd all just fly off and leave me with nothing. But then one of them made a move up the board, and then a couple more set off, and suddenly all of them were crawling upwards, and under the lip of the hive and home. You'll think me very fanciful, I expect, but it really felt magical, like my own little miracle.'

He smiled at her pleasure. 'The first time you see it, it is a miracle.'

'It makes me wonder about all the other stories they tell about bees. Finding their way home from farflung places, for instance. Is that one true, do you think?'

'So I believe, yes. A friend of mine who lives in the plain near Arles tells me that when he buys a swarm he drives in circles on the way back to confuse the bees, to make them believe the distance too great to fly home. But here in the mountains I don't think we'd need to do that.'

Catherine laughed. 'I can't imagine bees, even with nature's built-in satnav, managing to retain their sense of direction round all those hairpins.'

'But come,' said Patrick, rising. 'We have nothing to drink with your excellent fruit.'

The bottle of Burgundy, she now noticed, had

been drained. From the shelf he fetched two more glasses and a fresh bottle, slimmer and unlabelled – perhaps another product of his still.

'Peach wine,' he told her, pouring them both a long measure. 'The young leaves of the peach tree are steeped in alcohol and sugar, and then the liquor is drained off and mixed with a light muscat. My grandmother used to make it when I was a boy.'

If she'd given this stuff to a child to drink, reflected Catherine as she took a sip, she ought to have been locked up; it was smooth and sweet as caramel but it kicked like Stevenson's Modestine.

'My grandmother kept bees. And she believed, as many peasants do, that the bees must always be told of a death. Whenever some old soul in the village had passed away, out she would go to the hives to share the tidings.'

Catherine buried her nose in her glass and inhaled. Was this, she wondered idly, what nectar smelt like to a honeybee?

'And secrets,' continued Patrick. 'If you want to ensure that your secrets are kept safe, you must tell them to your bees.'

'I don't have any,' she said.

There was a silence as her words, spoken without thought, spread out into the room, and consciousness settled on them both. The more the silence lengthened, the more the echo of her words began to assume the shape of an accusation.

When at length Patrick spoke, his voice was quietly resolute. 'I never lied to your sister.'

Another man might have said it pleadingly, or self-justifyingly; he seemed, rather, to be stating a simple fact. Except that it wasn't a fact, was it? Or not in any but the most distorted sense of what truth meant. Anger surged up in her, anger and hurt. Her throat felt tight, and her tongue was too big for her mouth. She thought of all the times when he'd deceived by saying nothing – by never mentioning his English past, his English family.

'There are lies of omission.' Her voice sounded cool and calm, far removed from herself.

But Patrick flapped this away, dismissing with a negligent gesture the concealment of many months. 'Not about the past. I mean about the future. I never lied to her about the future.'

Your sister; her. Couldn't he use her name?

'Bryony . . .'

'She wanted something, that is all. She wanted something and I gave it to her.'

Wordless still, she stared at him. The arrogance – the easy, unquestioning arrogance of it – quite robbed her of breath. Even so, if he had shown the slightest sign of self-doubt, she might have forgiven him, for, after all, said a voice in her head, wasn't he speaking the truth?

He picked up his wine glass again, though he didn't take a drink, and she thought she saw a tremor in his hand. Then he placed it down again, and reached to lay his hand over hers. She didn't pull away but stared down at their mingled fingers; it was as if they belonged to two other people.

'The things we think we want,' he said softly, 'sometimes it turns out they're not what we really want at all.'

'No.' It was all she could manage, a simple acknowledgement, though it might just as well be taken as denial.

His thumb rubbed queryingly at her knuckles; she knew he was seeking her eye, but she continued to evade him.

'I'm sorry if I hurt her,' he said. 'I'm sorry if I hurt Bryony.'

The air which had blocked her chest ebbed away, leaving her empty and spent.

'I don't think she's really hurt,' she said flatly. 'Not very much, anyway.'

It's we who are hurt. You and me – us.

Her hand still lay passive under his; still she frowned down at it with no sense of belonging.

'I ought to go home,' she said. But the idea of moving at all exhausted her, let alone of standing up and getting together her things, saying a remotely functional goodbye, and making her way back to her house, over the wooden footbridge and down through the dark woods. Fresh air would be a relief, might clear her head of all these phantoms, but the night which soaked in through the open kitchen window was sultry and hot; the very air, airless.

'Stay.' The word was almost a whisper.

She raised her eyes to his, finally, and met something truthful there, something naked and

315

unguarded at last. *A woman of common sense*, she thought. But maybe she didn't want to be that woman, maybe she was tired of being that woman. Maybe this time, for once, she wanted to throw common sense aside and be someone else. Someone more like Bryony perhaps.

But it was too late; all of it, too late.

'Keep the rest of the strawberries,' she said. 'You can bring back the basket another time.'

She pulled back her hand from his and stood up. As an afterthought, she picked up her glass and drained the rest of the peach wine, then waited for the punch to the back of her skull that would make this easier.

'I'm sorry, Patrick. Truly, I'm very sorry. But I really think I have to go.'

Catherine's order book, in the days that followed, was mercifully full. It kept her hands and surface mind busy during those hours when the heat subsided sufficiently to allow for work, and left no time for her to contemplate the view from her kitchen window – either in reality or as depicted on her tapestry, which lay neglected on the dresser. It meant she had no leisure, either, to contemplate the occupant of the house that lay across there behind the trees.

In the hours between, she fled from the sunlight into cool places. She found a corner at the back of her hallway, close to the north wall which ran beneath the cliff, where the temperature remained steady all day; she moved a small armchair there and dozed over *Legends and Folklore of the Auvergne*. Or, when the lack of moving air began to stifle her, she took to walking a short way up into the woods, to a place where the slope shelved shallowly enough to allow her to scramble down as far as the stream. There was a small pool there – scarcely a pool, in fact, just a slight widening, deepening and slowing of the water's rush, above a lip of rock which formed a natural dam. To one side and slightly above the pool was a large, flat stone which fell entirely in the shade for most of the day.

From here, Catherine could cool her feet – or rather, immerse them for a few seconds before she pulled them out again and waited for the shock of cold to hit her, retrospectively, like a cudgel.

There was a place a few yards upstream where the water ran shallower among low stones, and which was visited by Tom's little bird, the dipper. If she was sitting very still – as she almost always was – it would stay and bob for insects, sometimes for half an hour or more, in spite of her presence not twenty feet away. Once, it took a bath. Moving to a submerged stone, it opened its wings to a broken-looking angle and ducked its upper body, twice, three times, before closing them again and restoring itself with a vigorous shake, and then repeating the manoeuvre. She wondered if its feet didn't feel the cold, standing knee-deep like that in the stream. Moments later, twirling slowly round as it came, she watched a small brown feather drift down towards her and into her pool. Its weight was barely sufficient to dent the surface as it circled past, and she was curious to see that its downy tendrils looked almost completely dry.

More and more, Catherine found herself thinking of nothing at these times. Or she found that her mind could be absorbed completely by some tiny detail of observation or memory. There were times when she wondered whether she might be going just a little mad – whether she was spending too much time by herself. Perhaps the sun was addling her brain. These extremes of detachment could not be normal, surely. And yet it didn't feel like detachment, but rather like a closer form of engagement. It was like looking at a painting or a tapestry and abandoning yourself to the detail of colour and shape. Maybe she wasn't losing touch with the world at all; in fact, maybe she was more properly in touch with it than she had been before.

It was Sunday again, a week after she had dined on Patrick's trout, and she had taken a book down to the stream. It was just an old paperback from the shelf in her bedroom; she had no real intention of reading it again, only of dipping into it at random to snatch a few words here or a phrase there. Her eyes were half closed, watching the black silk fold of water where it furrowed through a gap between two rocks, wondering how something in motion could seem to stand so still, when her attention was caught by a movement higher up the gully. It was close to the place frequented by the dipper, except that the movement this time wasn't down on the rocks of the stream bed but higher up, among the trees which clung to the steep gradient of the bank. She looked up. Nothing.

Just as her glance moved away, the flicker was there again, more distinct this time, a glimpse of brown between the low-growing branches. *Wolf* was the idea that came first to her mind, setting her heart thudding in her ears – though no wolves had inhabited these hills for a hundred years. Hadn't the young Stevenson looked out for them in vain, even back then, disappointed that a man might walk the woods 'and not meet with an adventure worth the name'? But still the idea was hard to shake off. The shadow moved again. In fact the colour was closer to black than brown. The Black Beast of Gévaudan, she thought, trying to laugh at herself. And then she caught the flash of stripes above and behind: a family of boar.

Catherine held her breath as they gathered one by one at the stream to drink. First the sow and then her young – five, six, seven of them – jostled forward and lowered their snouts to the water. The mother was a hefty size, much bigger than Catherine had imagined; three feet tall to the shoulder and maybe five feet long, she must weigh in at fourteen or fifteen stone. It was astonishing that something of that bulk could move so un-obtrusively through the tangle of the wooded bank. It made her wonder whether the animals had often been there, moving just beyond the range of her vision, when she had walked in the forest and looked for them – whether they had watched her many times from the safety of their cover. The piglets were small; she guessed they could be no more than a few weeks old. They were a light chestnut that was close to orange, streaked with creamy white, and both the colours and the pattern of their dots and dashes were familiar to her, just as she'd depicted them with her silks. Their short, pipe-cleaner tails flicked in pleasure as they drank.

She was spellbound. For the time that they stayed there at the stream – perhaps two or three minutes in all – she did not move or breathe, or so it seemed to her, but simply drank in the sight as greedily as the boar supped the water. All too soon, the sow raised her head, ears quivering and small berry eyes blankly watchful, and then turned to trot back up into the bushes, nudging her offspring out of her way and leaving them to follow at her heels.

After all these months, she had finally seen the boar. She must tell somebody.

But of course there was no one to tell. Perhaps Tom; she might telephone him later, and he would be mildly, distantly pleased. But she couldn't tell the person she most wanted to tell, the person she would have run all the way to tell if she had seen the boar back in the autumn, or even in the winter, before Bryony came. She couldn't tell Patrick.

She couldn't tell him, she now saw with clarity as crystal cold as the water of the pool, because she was determined not to see him, or no more than in the casual, public way they were bound to do as neighbours. There would be no more intimate dinners, no more cosy-seeming confidences about bees and boars and lepers and saints. She would not expose herself to it; she knew it could only bring her pain.

All at once, her mind was flooded with the picture of her sister as she came through the kitchen doorway that morning at Thanksgiving, with Patrick's fingers at her waist and her eyes alight, full of excitement at seeing the wild boar. Catherine laid her palms flat at her sides on the cool of the rock, as if trying to ground herself, to earth herself against the spinning whirl of rage which took her in its grip. Why had things had to happen the way they did? It was all so bloody stupid. Why did Bryony, who was so disdainful of her rural life here and who mocked her at every turn – about her garden, about the pig – why did she have to come here and seize at some figment of a pastoral ideal, to grab at Patrick and take him for herself with both hands grasping and both eyes closed? Why did she have to come here at all? Bloody Bryony. *Why did she have to come here and spoil everything?*

★   ★   ★

It was three, maybe four days later when the phone rang and Catherine picked it up.

'*Allo?*'

'Hello? Catherine, is that you?'

The voice was English, faintly hesitant, disorientatingly familiar.

'Graeme?' It seemed like years since they had spoken, though it had been just after Christmas.

'You sounded very French just then.'

Something about the way he said it made her want to laugh – the first time she'd felt like it in a while.

'Oh, yes. I've gone almost completely native.'

There was a short pause on the line, and then he said, 'That's rather what we were worried about. Or something like it, anyway.'

'Sorry?'

'Lexie was anxious about you. She says she's been ringing and ringing and you haven't been answering your phone. She wondered if something was wrong. She'd even got as far as trying to call the phone company to check if there was a fault on the line – and you can imagine what that was like, with Lexie's French.'

It had not exactly been her strong point, at school.

'So in the end she rang me, and I said I'd have a go at getting through.'

'The phone's fine.'

Graeme was dry. 'Evidently.'

'I mean, it's been fine. No fault or anything. It's

just that I've been . . . well, I've been a bit nocturnal of late, actually. It's been very hot weather for several weeks now, and it's hard to work in the daytime. And too hot to stay in the house, even. I've been spending quite a bit of time up in the woods.'

'In the woods?'

'Yes. I like to find a cool place to read, or just sit.'

Another pause. 'And you're really OK?'

She supposed it did sound odd, to someone who wasn't here, someone who didn't know the place. She tried to explain. 'There's a stream. And a spot where it forms a sort of natural basin – a pool.'

'You swim?' There was amusement, now, mixed with the concern in his voice. Catherine had always loved swimming, had always gone in with the kids when they were small, something Graeme had never been able to fathom.

'No, actually, I haven't been in.' It surprised her, now he mentioned it, that she hadn't felt the urge. 'The water's freezing.'

'That never used to stop you.'

He was right. 'I . . . Sometimes I take a book.'

'Sounds like the life,' he said. 'One long holiday, reading novels by the pool.' But she could tell he wasn't entirely satisfied.

'How is she, anyway?' Catherine asked, seeking to deflect. 'How's Lexie?'

'Oh, fine. Her usual self. Full of how appalling her job is, though, just at the moment. The terrible people, the monstrosities of cakes. But I'm never quite sure how serious she is about it. Her send-ups are hilarious – I wonder if she's secretly enjoying herself.'

Catherine smiled. Lexie's tales of *Fondant Magazine* were certainly very funny, and largely affectionate. But it didn't mean she wouldn't suddenly ditch the post and walk out.

'I hope she doesn't do anything silly,' she said.

Graeme's shrug was practically visible to her. 'Would it be so silly, if she's fed up of the place? She'd soon find something else. Lexie will be OK.'

'Yes.' He was right again. Lexie was resourceful; she had talent and energy. There would be ups and downs – great lurches, sometimes – but she would always do all right in the end. 'I just wish she would find the next job before she chucks in this one, that's all.'

'Of course you do. But she doesn't seem to have inherited all of your common sense.'

There it was again, from Graeme, too. *A woman of common sense.*

'And I gather you saw Tom the other weekend.'

'That's right. He was down for a conference in Oxford and he came over on the Sunday, before he travelled back. He seemed in good form.'

'Yes. He told me his paper had gone quite well.'

'He was typically Tom-ish, though. Didn't really say a lot, except bits and pieces about his research. He always keeps his cards very close to his chest.'

'Yes.' So, did that mean he hadn't mentioned Morag?

'Nothing about women,' Graeme went on. 'There's never anything about women. I was hoping he might have a few confidences to impart, man to man, you know. But he's a dark horse.'

'Yes,' she said again, knowing she shouldn't be indulging a private smile.

The children: it was always the most natural and immediate subject between them, a matter of the closest common concern. It was also safe ground – safer than talking too much about themselves. But she should say something; she must say something.

'And what about you? I was sorry to hear about you and Suzannah.'

'I know. Yes. Thanks.'

That being all either of them could think to say on the subject of Graeme and Suzannah, conversation moved on to other things: Graeme's work, Catherine's order book, the comparatively cool temperatures in England. It might not be entirely easy talking to her ex-husband but between the difficult areas were well-trodden grooves which could still feel very comfortable.

'Look,' he said at length, 'I'd better go. But I can tell Lexie you're all right?'

It was unmistakably still a question, not a statement.

'Of course. I'll give her a ring tonight myself. It's just very hot, and maybe I've had a bit too much of my own company, that's all. It has been rather quiet round here.'

A rumble of laughter. *'Quiet?'*

She joined in as she saw the absurdity of it. And, perversely, their laughter made it easier to be serious for a moment, before she said goodbye.

'I'm fine, Graeme. Honestly, absolutely fine.'

Only after he was gone did she wish she had told him about the wild boar.

CHAPTER 20

STORM CLOUDS

The weather broke with the turn of the month. June blazed on to its last breath, but as it sank over the valley in the west, clouds were already banking behind the hills in the east, blue and angry. By midnight, as July crept in, the rain had begun. It pounded with insistent force on the roof above Catherine's bed. After the heat she had expected thunder, but there was none, only the concussive torrent of water. It was rain such as she had rarely seen here: not the slow, tenacious, soaking rain of the autumn, nor the flurrying showers of the spring but something more startling. Sudden, dense and powerful, it lasted only three hours at most, buffeting the darkness. But as the dawn rose, the outside world was revealed transformed, like a scene from a rainforest, all gleaming gloss greens and slowly rising vapour.

The air, which during the night had been bumped and chopped about like a small boat, had settled to a breezeless calm, the temperature blessedly cool. Barefoot in her nightdress, Catherine walked down the stairs and straight out on to her terrace, tasting on her lips the sweet morning humidity. She stooped and ran her hands along the line of her potted herbs, brushing the moisture from the fragrant, wet foliage. It felt almost cold; it felt delicious.

For once, she was in the mood for café au lait and a proper breakfast, and after it was eaten and cleared away she showered, dressed and sat down to run up some bolsters to cover for her market stall.

It was still early – far too early for the post van; early even for neighbourly calls – when there was a knock at the door. Besides, it couldn't possibly be the postman, whatever the hour, because she had heard no engine.

Patrick, she tried not to think, as she made her way to the door.

It wasn't him. The man who was standing there was so wholly unexpected that it was all she could do not to take a step back into her hallway. Tall and slightly stooping, his thin shoulders hunched beneath the same lumpy coat she had rarely seen him without, there on her threshold stood Guillaume.

'The telephone,' he said.

He was not swaying today but standing rock still, his eyes focused somewhere slightly behind her and to the left.

'Your telephone. It's not working.'

At his heel, planted four square, was a dog. Not the fawning yellow hound, which would now come right to the gate when Catherine's walks took her

328

through the hamlet; this animal was larger, a more densely muscled version of the *berger lozérien*. Its lips were drawn back in silent threat from amber teeth.

'The ducting,' continued its master. 'When it rains like last night, the ducting floods. The lines go dead. *Kaput.*'

He cleared his throat, a rough, guttural sound; it occurred to her he might be about to spit.

'Um, thank you,' she said, uncertain quite why he was telling her this, or what was expected of her. 'Ought I to—?'

But he cut her off with a peremptory shrug. 'It will dry out by tomorrow.'

Then why . . . ?

'Will you come?' he said. 'Madame Bouschet sent me to say, please will you come.'

He was still looking not quite at her, but now she could read something of his expression and it contained an anxiety that was more than mere social unease.

'OK. I'll get my raincoat.'

She picked up her handbag, too, and began to lace her boots, thankful that she hadn't begun work in her nightdress this morning as she often did. Something about Guillaume's presence made her reach for the heavy iron key she never used, though she felt a faint pang of guilt as she locked the door behind them. She made to head towards the downhill track but instead of following he forestalled her.

'No. The car.'

She turned back towards him, surprised.

'My van is off the road,' he said. 'The gearbox.'

'Kaput?' She proffered a smile, but the anxiety was back about him, so she hid it in her bag as she rummaged for the car keys.

'Right, then.' She opened the driver's door and climbed in, leaving him to go round to the other side. The dog, she noticed, made no move to join them and Guillaume paid it no attention; as she nosed the car round and set off down the hill, she watched it in her mirror, falling in behind them at an expressionless trot.

Nothing was said on either side during the short journey. Guillaume sat motionless and stared out of the side window; tension breathed from him along with a stale odour of sweat and dog and unaired bedding. In Catherine's stomach a knot was forming which tightened and twisted as she drove.

At the stone gateposts she slowed, and swung into the cobbled yard; behind them, the dog hesitated no more than a moment before loping on past, in the direction of home. *Escaping*, she thought disconnectedly.

The Bouschets' farmhouse door stood slightly ajar. Guillaume, having brought her so far, hung back, and it was Catherine who pushed at the heavy oak, calling out an uncertain hello. It was not the lady of the house who came to greet her but Madame Volpilière, moving with awkward haste, her face paper pale in the gloom of the kitchen.

'It's Augustin,' she said. Catherine's eyes adjusted to the light and she saw the two figures by the stove: the one propped at a drunken angle in the armchair, the other bending over him.

'What is it?' she asked, moving across to the couple. 'What's happened? What's wrong?'

Madame Bouschet's face was taut, her eyes almost wild. 'Heart attack,' she whispered.

He was conscious, but barely. His face was drained of all colour and flesh seemed to have receded from his cheeks and jaw, so that the lines stood out in deeper relief. His eyes were closed, while beneath his moustache his mouth hung slack and half open, the lower lip purplish-blue like a bruise. Only his breathing, painfully thick and laboured, gave any indication of life.

'Is the ambulance on its way?' asked Catherine, turning her concern towards Madame Bouschet – and with some guilty relief away from her husband.

'No time,' came the hurried reply. 'It would take them more than an hour to get out here from the hospital at Mende, and then the same to get back. That's why . . .' The Frenchwoman seized Catherine's wrist. 'Please, if you could drive us . . .'

'The Mériels are away, you see,' Madame Volpilière joined in. 'They went off early to the cheese market at Alès.'

'Of course.' Catherine threw off her daze of

331

inhibition and became a model of efficiency. 'My car is right outside. Can we move him? Is he in pain?' Then, remembering herself, she made herself turn back to Monsieur Bouschet. 'Are you in pain?'

His wife was gripping one of his hands; Catherine took hold of the other, feeling the drag of its lifeless weight. The fingers were very cold. His eyelids flinched, but he didn't speak.

'Can we lift him between us?'

Could they carry him, the three of them, and what was the best way to go about it? A blanket, perhaps, might help. She had forgotten about Guillaume – had assumed that he had followed his dog and gone home – but now he stepped forward from out of the shadows by the kitchen door. He pushed back the sleeves of his coat, slipped an arm under Monsieur Bouschet and hoisted him chest high with apparent ease, his knotted wrists revealing a deceptive, wiry strength. Wordlessly, he carried his burden to the door and out into the yard, followed by Catherine with her car keys and finally, clutching each other for support, the two Frenchwomen.

Catherine opened the back door wide, then leaned into the front to release the catch and slide forward the passenger seat as far as it would go. Guillaume stepped up to the car, lurching a little, leaned down and deposited the inert form of Monsieur Bouschet on the back seat. His wife picked up his feet – naked below the hems of his working trousers – and folded his legs up into the footwell.

Madame Bouschet went round to the other side and climbed in beside her husband, taking hold of his hand once more, and Catherine expected Madame Volpilière to take the passenger seat, but the old lady didn't move.

'The geese,' she said. 'They'll need feeding.'

'Thank you, Clémence,' said Madame Bouschet from the back seat.

Her neighbour nodded. 'I'll be by the telephone. Once it's dried out.' And with that she turned and walked towards the house.

Catherine pulled the car round on the cobbles. 'Mende,' she said. 'I'm going to the little hospital by the river, is that right?' The one where she had taken Madame Volpilière to see the opthalmologist; she couldn't imagine it had much of a cardiac unit, but pushed the thought from her mind.

'That's right. If you please.'

In the rear-view mirror she saw Guillaume watching their departure, motionless between the two gateposts like a third standing stone.

Taking hairpin bends at any speed was impossible. By hurrying all she was able, Catherine probably succeeded in shaving no more than a minute or so off the time it took to reach St Julien, at the expense of a churning stomach, palms which felt slippery on the wheel, and a rougher ride for her sick passenger.

Once on the main road, things were a little

easier, though it still twisted and turned, and there were few places where she could get up into top gear for much more than a hundred yards. And if the road was straighter, it was also more frequented; twice she was caught up behind a farm vehicle and twice she overtook where there wasn't quite room to see. It was difficult, too, driving with one eye on the slumped figure in the mirror. A little colour was returning, she thought, though his skin still had the sheen of wet putty; his eyes were open now but dull and glaucous.

'Aspirin,' she suddenly remembered. Isn't that what they should have done, straight away? There was something, wasn't there, about thinning the blood or breaking the clot? 'There's some in my purse, I think. In my bag – here.' She indicated the passenger seat with a stab of the elbow as she took the car round a steep left-hander.

Obediently, Madame Bouschet reached through between the seats to take the bag. As soon as she hit a straight stretch of road, Catherine leaned across to the glove compartment and felt for the small bottle of mineral water which permanently lodged there. She passed it back, just as her neighbour was taking out the aspirins in their strip of foil.

'I don't have any kind of cup, I'm afraid, so I don't see how we can dissolve them.'

It was a major handicap; they worked quicker in solution, she was pretty sure, and besides, would Monsieur Bouschet be able to swallow an undissolved tablet? His jaw, in the driving mirror, still hung loose, the lips flaccid.

Don't watch, she resolved, fixing her eyes on the curve of the road ahead, the black and white chevrons of crash barrier, the approaching snakes of white line. When she looked back, Madame Bouschet had a tissue in her hand and was wiping a runnel of spilled water from the side of her husband's chin. His eyes were closed once more.

He seemed to drift into sleep or unconsciousness then, and the two women rode on in silence, each looking out through her own patch of glass and keeping to her own thoughts. Catherine's mind, in fact, was a studious blank; she was shutting out a connection she didn't want to make, something stirred by the slackness of the face in the mirror. An image of her mother.

She hadn't looked at her watch when they set off – not at all, in fact, from the time when Guillaume knocked at her door. That, she estimated, must have been around seven thirty, and she was surprised to see that it was not much after nine o'clock as they drew into the outskirts of Mende. She must have succeeded in driving much faster than she realised. It meant that they ran up against the tail end of the rush-hour traffic – not much of a rush hour by the standards of the south-east of England, but enough to set Catherine back on edge at the wheel, and her feet fidgeting from accelerator to brake.

Every traffic light seemed to be against them; at every junction, it seemed, the next vehicle in front chose to turn left, boxing them in behind while it waited for a gap in the oncoming traffic. By 9.10 they were crossing the main town square; by 9.15 they were scarcely further on. It was some time since Catherine had dared to glance in her mirror, for fear of facing the accusation of the caved in, bloodless face. No noise came from Madame Bouschet, but nevertheless Catherine knew that she was crying; without turning round, she could sense the slow, silent tears.

Finally, at 9.22 a.m. they were turning in at the gates of the little hospital, and following signs marked '*salle d'urgence*', whilst steadfastly ignoring others insisting '*passage interdit – sauf véhicules de secours*'. There had to be some advantages to being English, Catherine decided grimly.

She pulled up right outside the double swing doors, on a piece of tarmac cross-hatched in yellow. She jumped out and went round to the back door. Monsieur Bouschet was lying back heavily in his seat; without Guillaume's assistance, she wasn't sure that they could lift him.

'Wait here,' she told Madame Bouschet, and ran towards the swing doors. But before she reached them she was met by two men in medical over-alls coming the other way, their eyes already behind her, on the car and its slumped passenger.

'His heart,' she said, in a voice which sounded far calmer than she felt. 'We think he's had a heart attack.'

★　★　★

336

There was little resemblance between a French hospital café and its English counterpart. Catherine had never been to an English hospital snack bar where the menu offered a choice of calves' sweetbreads or rabbit casserole. Starbucks this was not.

Neither woman had appetite for much of a meal, though it was well past noon and they'd had a long morning. From the car, Monsieur Bouschet had been manoeuvred on to a trolley bed and whisked away along a corridor and into a room with a curtained door where they were not permitted to follow. They had found a bench outside in the sun, where Catherine had kept up for some minutes a pretence at the hopeful chatter which was supposed to cheer anxious relatives in these situations, before lapsing into sympathetic silence – rather, she suspected, to the relief of them both. It was soon after eleven when they were allowed in to see the patient, though Catherine had glimpsed him only from the door, his face still submerged beneath the oxygen mask they had applied to him on the trolley, and tubes extending from both his arms. When his wife emerged, pale and unspeaking an hour or so later, it seemed expedient to go in search of the café. Somewhere less medical, somewhere more human where talk might be possible.

'The salads look nice,' Catherine commented encouragingly, lifting on to the tray an artwork of greenery and *fruits de mer* for which she had no real desire at all. 'Why don't you try one? Or maybe some melon and Bayonne ham?'

Playing along like a trouper, Madame Bouschet did not plead her lack of hunger, but agreed politely, even exclaiming over the beautiful *charcuterie*, before helping herself to a peach and a small portion of Camembert.

There were half-bottles of wine – not the screw-top variety sometimes found on trains and aeroplanes, but proper producer-bottled wines with corks – and Catherine toyed with taking one and pouring them both a glass, before deciding against it. British habits, in this respect, died hard, and it would have felt either too frivolous or too desperate.

'Was he awake?' she asked, once they had moved to a corner table and sat down. It seemed a safer opening, somehow, than *How was he?*

'At first. When I left he was asleep again. But it seemed like proper sleep, you know. Not like . . .'

Not like in the car: the groggy semi-consciousness, sunk beneath the blanket of pain.

'That's good.' Catherine turned over the two glasses on the tray – proper glasses, not plastic – and filled them both with mineral water from the bottle she had bought. 'Have they given him something?'

'To make him sleep, you mean? Yes, I believe so. And something to thin his blood down, too, the nurse said, and a painkiller – although maybe that's the same as the one to make him sleep. That's what all those tubes were about. And they are moni-toring him: his heart, his blood pressure – that's the wires. And then the oxygen, to help his breathing.'

The words tumbled out in a rush, after her previous silence. Catherine said nothing, merely nodded and pushed a glass of water towards her companion, who took it, sipped and set it down again.

'It seems such a lot of things,' she said.

Catherine thought she understood. So much complication; so much medicine and hospital hardware, fencing him off from her.

'Yes. Hospitals are horrible. Everything feels strange.'

She made an effort to eat some of her salad. It was surprisingly good, in fact, though that didn't help matters, only adding guilt to the rest of her inadequacies. Of course she could enjoy her food – it wasn't her husband. Trying to focus on Monsieur Bouschet, she thought of him the way he had been on that first morning after her arrival at Les Fenils. His few words; the hidden smile which twitched his moustache; the solemnity with which he had accepted the glass of water she gave him. And also the way he had forked down a trailer-load of hay without breaking sweat or even needing to remove his jacket.

'He must have been very fit,' she said – before rethinking. 'What I mean is, he must be very fit, with all the farm work, his active life. I'm certain it has to help, doesn't it? Give him a head start, when it comes to his recovery.'

Madame Bouschet glanced across at her, looking very much as if she'd like to believe her.

'He's strong,' she agreed. '*Fort comme un boeuf*, as we say in France.'

Catherine smiled. 'Strong as an ox.'

'And he's always outside in the fresh air. I like to joke about it, how he'd rather be out in the yard tinkering or up in the woods with Flambard than indoors with me. If it weren't for the fact the sun goes down at night, I sometimes think I'd never see him at all.'

'It seems so unfair,' began Catherine, and then hesitated, unsure if it was the right thing to say. But Madame Bouschet was nodding at her plate as she sliced her uneaten Camembert to slivers with a knife.

'It does, though it might not be a nice thing to say. All those men who sit about in offices all day and never do a day's turn with their hands, who've never got up at dawn to see to the stock the way my Augustin has done all his life. I can't help thinking, why should it be him and not them? Is that so very wicked?'

'Not at all,' said Catherine stoutly.

'Mind you,' Madame Bouschet's raven bob gave a swing as she looked up sideways like a bird, 'he does like plenty of butter on his potatoes. Noodles, too. He thinks nothing of them if I haven't stirred in a knob of butter.'

There seemed no useful reply to this, except the offer of a smile.

'Maybe after this he'll have to mend his ways. I'll have to get one of those cookery books that tell you about health foods. All rice, and poached fish in milk, and plain boiled chicken.'

Catherine relished this cévenol notion of healthy eating.

'And those menthol throat lozenges he's been sucking ever since he gave up his pipe, ten years ago – I told him, they're meant for laryngitis, but of course he won't listen. All those sweets, they can't be good for him.'

For his teeth, perhaps not, thought Catherine, but they were hardly to blame for a coronary.

'He'll have to slow down a bit, too, around the place. Can't be carrying on with all the heavy jobs, the way he's been used to, not for a good long while.'

'Could you get someone in to help?' Catherine pictured Guillaume, standing in the gateway as they'd left, 'One of your sons-in-law, maybe? Or, well, not that I'd be much use at all, but you know if there's anything I can do . . .'

'Oh, I expect I can manage most things by myself, for a time at least. It's only the pig and the few goats we have left, and the poultry. Besides,' she leaned forward, conspiratorial, 'maybe now finally I'll persuade him to retire. Properly retire, I mean. Maybe we can take a nice long holiday for his health, stay with Jean-Marc in Paris, or even in a

341

hotel. Or go down to Agde or Narbonne-Plage and stay at the seaside. Augustin loves the sea, and we haven't been, not since Isabelle was a baby. We hired a caravan down there that summer, two whole weeks, while Augustin's old uncle Gaston minded the farm. You should have seen him – Augustin, not the uncle – with his trousers rolled up to the knee, digging holes in the sand. Jean-Marc wanted him to dig a hole as deep as the well at home, and he was at it a whole morning. I said to him, when the children were in bed, I said, it's typical of you. Supposed to be on holiday, and here you are, digging like it's time to lift the potatoes.'

It was a long speech. It seemed to exhaust her energy, and she lapsed into silence, back into memory, perhaps, thought Catherine. But after a few moments she began again.

'It was our fortieth wedding anniversary last year, in April. We didn't do anything to celebrate it, not really. I just cooked him a roast duck, which is his favourite, and the girls came over with the grandchildren in the afternoon and brought flowers and cards. But we didn't have a party. We decided we'd wait for our fiftieth and then have a proper, big family supper, with all the cousins and friends, too, out in the orchard, and get that brother-in-law of Monsieur Folcher's who has the swing trio, and light lanterns, and put down some boards for dancing.'

'It sounds lovely,' said Catherine. 'I'm sure it will be lovely.'

The attempt at deflection was unsuccessful. 'Why did we put it off? We should have had the party last year for our fortieth. But we were busy, and it would have been a bit of work, and we thought fifty might be more of an event. You expect sunny weather to last forever, don't you, somehow? You never expect storm clouds. You think there will always be time.'

Catherine could think of nothing to say to this, and shortly she could not have done so, anyway, for her hand was seized in Madame Bouschet's. The fingers were hot and pressed her tightly. 'You should never put things off,' the Frenchwoman urged her. 'Never wait for another time.'

Soon afterwards, Catherine abandoned what was left of her seafood salad and decided that they needed coffee. There was a machine, worked by tokens to be purchased at the till; but it was good for do-it-yourself coffee, piping hot and with a convincing roasted smell.

'Will you be able to stay here overnight with him?' she asked, as she sat down again with the two steaming cups. 'Do they have facilities for relatives to sleep here, I mean?'

'Oh, of course. Sorry, you want to be getting back—'

'No!' Catherine was horrified. 'No, no, that isn't what I meant at all. I can stay as long as you like. It's not as if I've got anyone at home waiting to be fed, not even any geese or chickens, and I've no work that can't wait a few days. No, I just wondered, if he's going to be in here for a day or two' – longer, no doubt, if he needed surgery, but she wasn't about to say so – 'what you would do. But you know that if you can't sleep here, I'm very happy to drive you over again, as often as you need me to. It's not much more than an hour.'

To Catherine's surprise, she saw the older woman's eyes film with tears, for the first time since the car. 'Thank you,' she said simply. 'I really don't know yet what they'll say. But that would be very kind.'

Embarrassed, Catherine made to brush off any thanks, but found her hand taken hold of again across the table. 'I expect you think it very foolish. I can drive the car all right, down to St Julien to the shops, but I'm just not used to driving so far on my own. And I've never really worked out my way round Mende. Augustin always gets lost here too, when we come for any reason. It's the one-way system in the town centre – and the signposts seem all cockeyed, somehow. They never mention the places you want to be.'

'Oh, no, that would make it far too easy. It's always just *"autres directions"*, isn't it?' Catherine returned Madame Bouschet's squeeze of the hand. 'And there's so much waiting about in hospitals, too, isn't there? All the times when he's sleeping. Maybe if I'm here I can take your mind off things. Or if you don't want me, I can always take myself off into town and do some shopping.'

'Thank you,' said Madame Bouschet again.

They sipped their coffee, and Catherine left her companion to her own thoughts, which presently she spoke aloud.

'I wonder if Jean-Marc might come home for a while, to help with the farm, once Augustin is out of hospital. If he can get the time off work, that is. But I'm sure he'll try to come if I ask him. He's a good boy.'

A good boy. Catherine's stomach kicked; she was surprised to find it was the first time all day she had thought of Patrick.

'Of course, I must ring Jean-Marc and the girls soon. But I thought I'd wait until there's something more definite to tell them. Just until I've spoken to the doctor, you know. The nurse says he'll be round in the afternoon, around three, and should be able to give me some idea of how things stand.'

How things stand: the stoical euphemism reminded Catherine just how much was still at stake. Prognosis, exploratory tests, by-pass procedures.

'Do they allow mobiles in here?' They often didn't in hospitals.

'Oh, we don't have one of those things. It would be no use to us. We don't get any reception at La Grelaudière.'

'You can borrow mine, then, if they'll let you use it.'

'Thanks. Later on. That would be kind.'

Madame Bouschet had drunk scarcely a quarter-inch of her coffee; her peach was untouched. She

345

lapsed into silence for a little while, and then at length she said, 'He's a good man.'

Made awkward by this confidence – for it seemed genuinely to be so, and not a mere formula – Catherine said nothing.

'A good man, and a hard worker. I know I've been very lucky – that I am very lucky.' Something flickered across her face, which might have been pain or possibly even the ghost of a smile. 'But he does like butter on his potatoes.'

CHAPTER 21

THE FIRST HARVEST

'Dust down your red carpet, Mum. Put your best fizz on ice. Hang up the bunting, dig out your dancing shoes. I'm finally going to get my arse in gear and come and see you.'

Catherine tucked her tapestry needle away tidily into a bare patch of canvas and sat back in her chair, a foolish grin breaking over her face.

'I know I've been slack. Dreadful, really. Ten months and I haven't made it over there in all that time. OK, so I've been busy with my cakes – up to the neck in flipping fondant icing – but it's no excuse, and now I intend to put things right.'

'Sweetheart. That will be lovely. When are you thinking of coming?'

'Soon as possible, as far as I'm concerned. August seems like a good idea, if they'll give me the time off work. Or even if they won't, come to that. They can stuff their holiday entitlements. I need to get out of here before I go nuts.'

'Lexie—'

'I mean, listen to me. "Nuts", I said. Not crazy or bonkers, you note, but flaky toasted almonds.

Chopped mixed bloody nuts. See how I've got cake toppings on the brain? I'm going to turn into a cake before too long, I swear I am.'

'Look, love, you're welcome here any time. You know that. But you won't do anything rash, will you?'

'What, like tell them to stick their job in the sugar boiler and just walk out? I'm sorely tempted sometimes, I can tell you.'

'But don't you think that if you waited—'

'Oh, don't worry, Mum. I'm not walking out, not right now. I expect they'll let me have the time off. They damn well ought to. I've only had about half an hour's holiday since I started with them. Well, maybe a week. But hardly anything. And I've put in heaps of overtime – not that they count it as overtime, it's just what's expected of you – but I've still slaved through evenings and weekends often enough to keep them off my case if I say I want a week in the mountains with my aged mother.'

Catherine grin widened, affection laced with some relief. 'Aged, is it now? And you said I was going to need my dancing shoes. I thought you were taking me clubbing.'

'Yeah, right. Where's your nearest nightclub, d'you reckon?'

'Good point. Avignon, quite possibly.'

'Anyway, take my mind off it. Speak to me on non cake-related subjects. You're always great for that. How's that neighbour of yours, the old chap down the road who was in hospital?'

'Out now, and back home,' said Catherine. Following exhaustive monitorning by ECG and chest X-ray, Monsieur Bouschet had been pronounced stabilised and transferred for observation to a sunny private room, where he had shown himself surprisingly partial to lazy days of farming magazines and attentive female company. His lack of impatience with the arrangement, Madame Bouschet was sure, was an indication of just how sick he had been.

'They finally discharged him on Monday. They decided he was fit enough to recuperate at home, but he's still confined to bed. His wife says he's a devil to keep from getting up, though. The very first morning he was back, she found him outside talking to his dog.'

'Why doesn't he just have the dog in the bedroom with him?' was Lexie's logical question.

'I don't think it's that sort of dog.' Catherine smiled. Madame Bouschet wasn't that sort of wife, either.

'So what else is new? What have you been up to?'

'Well, I'm reasonably busy with orders. I've had quite a number of chairs to cover in the past couple of weeks, and several new orders for curtains. And the market stall has been doing really well. We get a few trippers coming out, now it's getting to the summer holidays. Honestly, just at the moment I think I could sell cushions and bolsters quicker than I have time to make them.'

'That's great. Way to go, Mum.'

349

Yes, great. But Catherine's conscience smote her; her stomach executed a small somersault.

'There's only one problem.'

'Oh, yes?'

'Well, it may not prove to be a problem. I'm very much hoping it won't turn out to be one at all. It's about registering my business, which I know I ought to have done months ago, but somehow I kept putting it off. And about the national park.'

'The *what?*'

Catherine's heart sank another inch. Had she never mentioned the park to Lexie? It suggested denial on a major scale.

'The Parc National des Cévennes. I live in a national park here, you see, and there are restrictions on development and the kinds of businesses you can open.'

'Blimey. And they think you're going to open an enormous, filthy great textiles factory, churning out black smoke and frightening the local wildlife?'

In spite of herself, Catherine raised a giggle; the image was so close to the one with which she had almost reproached the youngest Mademoiselle Cassini.

'Something like that, perhaps. I have to demonstrate that mine is a rural profession.'

'Well, you're doing it up a mountain. Seems pretty rural to me.'

'Hmm.' But she could equally well be doing the same thing in Mende, couldn't she – or Lyon or

Paris, come to that? 'Anyway, they sent someone round last week. Someone from the Parc National.'

'Like a park ranger, you mean?' Down the line, Lexie was giggling now too. 'Did he have a nice uniform? And a gun, in case of bears?'

'This is Lozère, not the Yellowstone. He had jeans – and a clipboard.'

'Well? What did he say? Do you qualify as rural?'

'That's the thing, I still don't know. Bureaucratic wheels round here all seem to grind so terribly slowly. He took a good look round the place, he asked me lots of questions and wrote down lots of notes, and then he went away.' It was all her own fault, for waiting so long before she began the process; now she was being made to pay, by having to wait some more.

'He said they'd write to me with a decision. It might take a couple of weeks, he said. Which in France probably means a month.' And then it would be August and everything would shut down anyway, which meant it might be September before she heard anything. And by September she'd have been here a whole year; she really needed to file her accounts with the tax authorities before then, and with the URSSAF, neither of which she could do without a registered *siège social*. The thing seemed to go round in circles – and they were beginning to close in on her like a noose.

Lexie's voice, six hundred miles away, was breezily confident. 'I expect it will turn out all right.'

'Oh yes, I expect so.' Catherine winced. 'But, come on. If you don't want to talk cake, then tell me what might be next. Have you begun looking around for another job yet?'

'Vaguely, I suppose. But there's nothing going. Or nothing I remotely fancy, anyway. I don't know, I just can't seem to get excited about another trade mag. Container transport, cake decorating, what's the next thing I'm going to spend my life becoming a world expert on that I care about less than squat? There was an opening the other week at *Model Tank Collector*. Can you imagine?'

'Not really,' admitted Catherine.

'I mean, of course I know it's just meant to be experience, fodder for the CV and all that. Writing, the interview practice, maybe a bit of subbing. So that in the end I'll have got all the points I need to collect the big prize. I'll magically have what it takes and land the fantasy plum job, editing or doing major feature pieces for some big national. But it's never going to happen, is it? All I'm qualifying myself for is to be editor of *Claims Adjustment Monthly* by the time I'm forty. Or the *Ferret Fancier's Journal*. Is that really what I want from my life?'

Catherine glanced down at the captured colours of her tapestry and then across into the brilliance of the reality beyond the window. 'Well, maybe not. But what other ways are there, to get on in magazine journalism?'

'Dunno. No. You're right.' But Lexie never

remained deflated for long. 'Maybe I should do something different. I always wanted to write, that's why I went into this business in the first place. So why don't I do that? Why don't I write?'

'You do write,' said Catherine, aware she was missing the point. Not that she was entirely sure what the point was – but no doubt she was about to find out.

'No, but I mean *write*. Really write, write something worthwhile, not just copy for other people, five hundred words here and three-fifty there, to fill column inches or a space on a page.'

'What would you write?' She hoped her daughter wouldn't think she was humouring her; she really wanted to know.

'Oh, I don't know. Longer articles, freelance stuff, stuff on subjects I'm actually interested in.' There was a fractional pause, then the trace of a waver, unusual in Lexie. Casually, she tossed out the thought: 'Maybe a book.'

'A book? What kind of book?'

'Well, I did think about one of those anthologies, some witty collection of ephemera on a random subject, like people keep by the loo. *The Little Book of Air Freight.*' She was giggling again. '*The Cakespotter's Guide.*'

Catherine knew to wait.

'But, no. I suppose I meant a novel.'

'Goodness. Do you have some ideas for one?'

'Well, you know. Some. Just sketchy stuff. Trouble is, with this job I never have a chance to sit down to it properly. I've got a bit of an outline in my head, and little snippets of scenes. But I haven't had time to get it down on paper.'

Was this the moment to point out that writing a novel was no substitute for a job? That it wasn't going to pay the rent? 'How exciting. I don't suppose you're going to tell me what it's about?'

'You don't suppose dead right. It would just sound stupid if I said it out loud. Besides, it's still at the development stage.'

'Absolutely. Keep it under wraps.'

'Maybe when I come to see you I might bring my laptop. It could be just the place for a spot of writing. Middle of nowhere, no one to talk to, nothing else to do.'

'Cheers very much,' said Catherine, smiling.

'Oh, shut up, you know exactly what I mean – no external distractions. It's ideal, alone at the top of a French mountain. It could be my very own writing retreat.'

'Absolutely,' she said again.

'You can do your tapestry or sewing or whatever it is and I can sit and write my novel. Then at seven o'clock we'll open a bottle of wine and see who's done the most. I can read you my best bits while you cook dinner. It'll be wonderful, Mum. I just wish I could come for the whole summer and not just a measly week.'

Catherine laughed. 'It will be wonderful. And you know you are welcome to come and stay for as long as you like – for as long as they'll let you have. There's only one thing – please don't say the word "sabbatical".'

The following day Catherine had promised herself a pleasurable task, though she was far from sure how easy it would be to accomplish. She was going to take the honey from her beehive.

Every jar of jam or pâté she had emptied over the past two months had been carefully washed out and kept. She had only accumulated six or eight jars, but her expectations were modest for this, her first harvest. After consulting websites, as well as the black and white illustrations in an old book borrowed from the mobile library which called in St Julien once a month, she had recognised the battered aluminium drum which stood in the back corner of the woodshed. Once she had hauled it out on to the terrace, wiped it free of the layers of grime and peered inside, the identification was positive. It was Madame Sauzet's honey extractor.

It consisted of an aluminium cylinder some three feet in height and one foot in diameter, with a hinged semi-circular lid, a tap arrangement at the bottom and, sticking out near the top, a crank handle like something from a pre-war Austin Seven.

Removing the flat, wooden super with the hoped-for honey proved trickier than anticipated. It had slotted on top of the main hive easily enough last month, but now when she tried to lift it off it was stuck fast. Her bees seemed to have mistaken the metal grille of the queen excluder which divided the super from the brood chamber for a wax base frame and had covered it with a lumpy superstructure of honey-filled comb which gummed everything together. Evidently they had not read the books as she had. This was also her first encounter with propolis, an evil brown substance with the texture of pitch, produced by the bees, apparently, with the sole purpose of making the beekeeper's life as difficult as possible. It was everywhere it shouldn't be, sticking things to other things and getting all over her hands, clothes and hair.

The super, once she succeeded in getting it off and into the kitchen – trailed by only a modest cohort of scandalised bees – was not as full as she'd hoped. The colony seemed to have concentrated its comb-building operations more upon the queen excluder and round the exterior walls of the wooden box than on the hanging parallel frames within that were provided for the purpose. The frames held only uneven patches of raised honeycomb, each hexagonal cell neatly capped with a seal of wax. Probably she should have put it all back, left it another month or two before embarking on her first extraction. But she was too eager to see and taste the honey.

The extractor worked on a simple centrifugal principle. Four of the frames were slotted into a wire rack within the drum to form a square; then the handle was turned to spin the rack, sending the honey flying from the wax frames. It ran down the walls of the drum and through a filter in the base before being tapped off and into jars.

First it was necessary to scrape the wax film carefully from the top of the cells, exposing the honey for release without damaging the comb. She had found a long-toothed steel comb for the purpose, conveniently left inside the extractor by Madame Sauzet.

When the first four frames were in place, she began to turn the handle. The trick was to know exactly when to stop. If the frames weren't spun for long enough, honey would be left in the cells of comb and go to waste; but rotate too long and the force of the centrifuge would damage the combs and result in honey containing unwanted gobbets of wax. By the time she had finished all twelve frames, her right arm was aching, but the extractor felt satisfyingly heavier than when she had begun. The extra weight of her glorious honey.

She placed a jar underneath the tap, opened it up and waited. Nothing happened at first, but then, with creeping slowness, a bubble began to form in the mouth of the nozzle. It wasn't the anonymous pale gold of shop-bought honey but a rich mahogany brown, translucent, smooth and thick as caramel. The bubble fattened and swelled until she thought it would separate itself into a single round globule but, when the tension finally broke, it did not wholly detach but drew with it as it fell a thin tail of honey, a fine thread which gradually strengthened into a drizzle.

Catherine put a finger under the stream and watched it coat her skin, then pulled away and sucked her finger, closing her eyes and letting the honey dissolve on her tongue. It tasted of woodland. Rather than the light, high, floral notes of meadow or garden honey, it rang with the pungent baritone of chestnut and hazel and pine: resinous, oaky, aromatic. The flavour of the forest; the flavour of Les Fenils.

The process was not to be hurried. The filament of falling honey was as slender as silk yarn; the rise of the level in the jar was indiscernible unless she forced herself to look away, to walk round the kitchen and shuffle jam pots and lids. To fill seven jars took more than an hour.

Held up to the light, the honey had a pleasing glow about it, like good antique furniture. It was not completely clear, and each jar was topped with a film of whitish foam, flecked with tiny particles of detritus: wax, she supposed, and in at least one case a bee's leg which had made it through the filter. Perhaps she ought to skim it off, but the honesty of it appealed to her; she took the lids and screwed them firmly down.

The very first jar she had filled was a wide, squat one that had once contained cornichons. She wiped it free of stickiness with a damp dishcloth and polished it dry on a tea towel. This one was to be a gift.

Coals to Newcastle, of course, she supposed as she set off down the track towards La Grelaudière. The Bouschets had half a dozen hives in their orchard and could have no possible need of more honey. But she wanted to give it to Monsieur Bouschet nonetheless. She wanted to show him the first fruits of the swarm he had given her; she wanted to watch him dip his finger in and taste it and pronounce it good. Beside which, honey wasn't bad for the heart, was it? It contained no cholesterol or free radicals or saturated fats, nothing to which Madame Bouschet could possibly find objection, and wasn't it reputed to have all kinds of mysterious healing properties besides?

Heat was gathering again, though the skies lately had been overcast; even walking downhill, Catherine's skin was soon prickling with sweat. Perhaps she should have waited until after dinner. But she didn't like to intrude at a late hour; Madame Bouschet had the convalescent so cocooned and swaddled about with care that he was probably sent to sleep before nine.

The house was quiet and the door closed. The geese were nowhere in evidence and set up no cackling alarm at her approach; no doubt they were at the back in the apple orchard, gorging on early fallers. Flambard didn't bark. More used, these recent days, to calling out a greeting and pushing open the door, something about the silence of the yard discountenanced Catherine. She hesitated, then knocked.

There was no reply, which seemed strange.

'Hello?' Catherine called, and lifted the latch of the farmhouse door.

Madame Bouschet was standing at the sink, a dishcloth in her hand. There was a motionlessness about her, a rootedness, which killed Catherine's cheery inquiry about the invalid. Madame Bouschet gave no acknowledgement of Catherine's entrance, but awareness tingled in the air.

'He's gone,' she said.

Catherine wanted to move but found herself unable. The Frenchwoman still didn't turn.

'Last night, in his sleep. Another attack, the doctor said. I woke up, and there he was.'

All this time, thought Catherine, while she'd been extracting the honey from the swarm he had brought her, and she had not known.

'I should have stayed awake for him,' continued Madame Bouschet.

The age old reproach. *Could you not watch one hour with me?*

'Don't—'

'It must mean it happened quickly. Peacefully – in his sleep. He would have woken me otherwise, wouldn't he?'

'I'm sure he would. Yes.'

'Père Amyot came. The doctor told him.'

'That's good.'

A short silence fell, both of them still unmoving.

'I'm sorry,' said Madame Bouschet. 'I should have come and told you, let you know.'

360

'No, no – why should you?'

'You've been so kind . . .'

She turned then, finally, and looked at Catherine with dry, bruised eyes. Catherine's feet found movement and she crossed swiftly to the other woman and laid a hand on her arm.

'I'm sorry, so sorry.' How uselessly inadequate; how derisorily, crassly inadequate. 'Madame, if there's is anything I can do, anything at all . . .' She tailed off helplessly.

'Marie-Josèphe. My name. Please, if you would. It's Marie-Josèphe.'

A tightness gripped Catherine's throat, making it difficult to speak.

'Catherine.'

Back in her kitchen, Catherine set down the jar of honey with the line of others on the table. The air felt subtly different from before, and she threw open the window to let in the early evening breeze. There were a dozen bees buzzing and bumping desultorily against the glass and she wondered whether others would be drawn to the lingering, honey-sweet smell which hung about the room. In fact it was too sweet, of a sudden, too cloying; it clogged her lungs, almost turned her stomach. She needed air.

Leaving the doors open wide behind her, she fled for the outdoors. It was starting to cool; she could almost imagine the spit of damp on her skin, like dewfall or the beginning of rain. But the afternoon's stored heat still radiated from the hard surface of the terrace, driving her up towards the shade of the chestnut trees, towards the cluster of empty beehives and the one that was occupied.

There she dropped to her knees in the grass. For some long minutes she watched, half mesmerised, the slow procession of bees as they returned from the last of the day's forays and crawled up the entrance board and into the hive.

'He is dead,' she told them out loud in the quiet of the evening. 'Beloved husband; proud father and grandfather; a kind and generous neighbour. Augustin Bouschet.'

CHAPTER 22

A WOMAN ON HER OWN

The funeral was held a week later. The little church of St Julien the Hospitaller filled up to chequered capacity with friends and cousins and neighbours for a simple ceremony, without music and with no flowers upon the coffin but a single homemade wreath. Père Amyot delivered a quiet eulogy about friendship and duty which was no less moving for being matter-of-fact, like the man himself. Catherine was not ashamed of her tears.

It was a blazing July day. The stone walls and high roof of the church had kept down the interior temperature, but as the congregation filed back along the aisle and out of the arched north door, the outside air which struck them was hot and thick as soup. Six men bore the coffin shoulder high as it set off for the short, steep walk to the hilltop cemetery: the two sons-in-law and Jean-Marc in his dark, Parisian suit; Monsieur Mériel; a scrubbed and sober Guillaume – and Patrick Castagnol.

There had been no need to greet or acknowledge him earlier, in the church, and nor did the issue arise now, for Catherine was not going to the graveside for the interment but heading straight back to the farmhouse with Madame Volpilière to uncover salads and set out plates.

It was a cold spread, uncomplicated but plentiful in the French style. Of the daughters, Isabelle had boiled a ham and Claudine an ox tongue, while Madame Mériel had baked a *tourte cévenole* as wide as a cartwheel. Monsieur Folcher had brought the bread up personally in his van in the morning, along with half a dozen fruit tarts, and Catherine had made three loaves of Irish tea brack to her mother's recipe; sliced and buttered and laid out in fans, the Celtic fare was passed off as 'something English'. Jean-Marc and his wife contributed an enormous box of shop-bought petits fours, with which they had battled in train and taxi, along with the baby and all his paraphernalia.

Avoiding Patrick still posed no great difficulty. The men congregated in the cool of the orchard, while the women gathered in the kitchen. The segregation, Catherine supposed, must be a traditional one, to allow the women to cry at ease, unobserved by the menfolk – though it might just as well be the reverse, to judge by the brisk bustle and chatter round the kitchen sink. The grandchildren ran in and out between the two camps, playing tag beneath the apple trees until the heat drove them back inside to beg for lemonade or water. Young Cécile's face was as red as the boys', her knees just as green, but nobody bothered to scold.

The daughter-in-law, whose name was Aurélie, was delighted to hand her son over to his grand-mother when he needed his bottle, and Madame Bouschet – Marie-Josèphe – was settled peacefully in a corner with the infant in her arms. Catherine brought her a glass of lime flower tea and knelt for a while at the side of her chair, admiring the timeless concentration on the puckered face of the baby as he sucked at the teat, and the curl and uncurl of his hands, grasping at nothing.

Neither woman spoke, for there seemed no need. But when Aurélie came to stand by them, Catherine offered the expected congratulations and compliments upon her child.

'How did he manage on the journey?' she asked. 'Was he very unsettled?'

'Oh, not too bad. We were able to book centre seats on the TGV – with a table, you know, and rather more space. He mostly slept in his carry-seat. Thank goodness for air conditioning on those trains.' She fanned herself with a plastic baby's bib.

'But the métro,' said her mother-in-law, 'it must have been a crush.'

A shrug. 'We are used to it. I take him shop-ping with me, you know.'

'He's certainly happy enough now,' said Catherine, watching his flannelled feet begin to kick gently as he drained the last of his milk.

'So, are you the English lady who's moved in?' Aurélie asked. 'You speak good French.'

Catherine smiled in amusement. It was the first time anyone had remarked on her French; to her neighbours at La Grelaudière, speaking the language was apparently only to be expected.

'Thank you.'

The Parisienne returned her smile. 'Also – I don't know – you don't look English, somehow.'

No tweed skirt, no Paisley blouse? No shorts and peeling sunburn?

'No, not at all, if you don't mind my saying so. I would have taken you for a Cévenole.'

By four o'clock, people had begun to drift away, the men appearing in ones and twos at the kitchen doorway, to collect their wives and pay their respects a final time to the widow before making their departure. It was almost five when Patrick came. Catherine was at the table, scooping tomato salad from three half-empty bowls into one for the fridge, and Marie-Josèphe was just the other side of her, stacking clean plates back in a cupboard.

'Are you going too, Patrick? I can't persuade you to stay and take an aperitif? I have a bottle of pastis; you could take it out into the orchard with a jug of water and some glasses. The men might all like to have a glass, perhaps.'

'Thank you. I will take the bottle outside, but as for myself, I really should be going.'

'So soon?'

How many times, after lunching here, Catherine wondered, had he shared a pastis with Monsieur Bouschet before walking home?

Gravely, he inclined his head. 'I'm afraid I must go. But thank you for your generous hospitality.'

She smiled sadly, and nodded, taking his extended hand.

'I'm so sorry, Madame, so very sorry. You know, I'm sure, that if there is anything I can do for you at any time, you have only to ask.'

As he turned to leave with the bottle and tray, his glance and Catherine's fleetingly crossed. His eyes were questioning, and regretful; she couldn't help feeling that he had been speaking to her, too.

Jean-Marc, Aurélie and the baby went back to Paris shortly afterwards, and of necessity the daughters, too, returned the large part of their attention to their children, husbands and jobs. In the days that followed, Catherine vacillated between wanting to be available, should Marie-Josèphe need someone to talk to or simply another living body in the house, and giving her space on her own to grieve. By way of compromise, she dropped in daily with random gifts – an old gardening magazine, some home-pickled shallots – and either stayed or came away again according to judgement. More and more often, she stayed.

Today it was a basin of chicken casserole she had with her, covered with foil. The scent, as she crossed the farmyard towards the door, stirred the chestnut spaniel, Flambard, briefly to animation. These past two weeks he had not greeted her approach; now the basin had him on his feet with muzzle tilted for just a moment, before he sank back down again to resume his silent vigil, all hope extinguished from his eyes.

'Good day,' she called out as she entered the kitchen, but the room was empty. She placed the casserole in the fridge and glanced out of the window towards the orchard. 'Anyone in?'

'Up here,' came the reply, muffled by the heavy oak of the ceiling.

Catherine had been in the bedroom before, but not since the master's death. Imagination or not, it seemed to her that a subtle shift had occurred in the balance of the room. The beams were still as massive, the furniture – with the exception of Jean-Marc's frivolous dressing-mirror – just as heavy and plain. The curtains and bolster cover Catherine had made were still there, in the hunting print chosen to suit Monsieur Bouschet. But a sprigged satin shawl lay across the bed, no doubt abandoned after a daytime nap, and the air was perceptibly softer, sweetened by the wide open window and the spray of late dog roses in a jug on the sill.

'He hated fresh air. I dare say he had enough of it during the day to last him the night as well. But anyway, he never wanted the shutters open in the bedroom.'

'I brought stew. It was a whole chicken, and you know how it's always too much for one.'

Stupid. The first thing she'd said and straight away the wrong one. But Marie-Josèphe turned from the window, smiling.

'That's very kind of you, Catherine. Very thoughtful. I haven't the energy for cooking at the moment. My daughters tell me I should be keeping busy to take my mind off things. But I don't want to.' In her hands she held a grey woollen sweater that Catherine had seen her husband wearing. 'I don't want my mind taken off it. Not yet.'

'No.'

'Claudine says I should clear his things out, pack them up and get rid of them. As if she thinks I shouldn't want the reminder. Or that somehow it will do me good. What's that word they use these days? "Therapeutic". But there's no need, is there? No hurry about it.'

'Of course not.' So different from a divorce, in this respect. Graeme's jumpers, sorted out from hers, to be taken away and worn.

'I've been wearing this one. Last night when I shut the chickens up. It wasn't really cool enough for a pullover, but I'd been indoors and I thought I'd feel the difference when I went out. It's what he always did. Always put on a pullover.'

Slowly, she ran the lambswool between her fingers, then lifted it against her face. 'It smells of him.' Another woman might have said it wistfully, but Marie-Josèphe was matter-of-fact. 'I shan't wear it too much, not when I'm working, or I'd have to wash it.'

And wash away his scent, this lingering physical trace of him. Catherine nodded her understanding. Then, diffidently, she asked, 'Might Jean-Marc like something?'

The widow laughed. 'Oh, I don't expect so, do you? Not in Paris. I can't imagine my daughter-in-law would like to see him in Augustin's old things.'

Catherine joined in the laughter.

'He's not as broad as his father, either. Mind you, Augustin was slimmer at Jean-Marc's age. He cut quite a figure, back then.'

'I'm sure he did.'

But that's not what I meant, she wished she could say. Not a sweater for Jean-Marc to wear but just to keep, for the smell, for the memory, the way you are doing. And the girls as well – they should have a sweater of their father's too. Instead she said, 'Shall I go down and make us a hot drink?'

'Let's both go. I only came up here to put this away.' She opened a deep drawer in a hefty oak chest beside the bed and laid the grey sweater inside; Catherine saw how she smoothed it flat with a lingering palm before she pushed shut the drawer.

In the kitchen, it was the lady of the house who filled the kettle, while Catherine drifted to the table. As always, half its surface was submerged beneath the daily impedimenta of house and farm. So many things that were his: the heavy canvas work gloves, far too big for Marie-Josèphe to use; the gunbelt and shooting magazines; the packet of menthol lozenges. The near end of the table, the end which was normally kept free for eating, and which had been cleared for bowls and stacks of plates at the funeral, was falling victim to the encroaching tide. Marie-Josèphe had apparently been shelling peas but had abandoned the colander and pile of pods in the middle of her task. There was a duster and a tin of polish, also abandoned, and even two unwashed cups. Catherine began idly to wrap the pea pods in the sheet of newspaper on which they lay and discovered underneath a scatter of unopened envelopes.

'The post,' said Marie-Josèphe, facing Catherine as she leaned her backside on the warmth of the range. 'All those letters of condolence. I haven't been able to face them yet.'

But it wasn't the handwritten envelopes that lay untouched; most were brown and typed and official. One near the top bore the logo of Crédit Lyonnais.

'There's just so much to sort out.' Abandoning pretence, Marie-Josèphe moved over and sat down at the table. 'Changing names on accounts, dealing with pensions and social security and heaven knows what.'

'Couldn't Claudine or Isabelle help you with it? Or could I?' Although her own dealings with French officialdom were not conspicuous for their efficiency.

There was no reply. Marie-Josèphe sat staring at the cluster of letters, shuffling them blindly back and forth. 'He always dealt with these things. The bank, the insurance, the farm accounts. I'm not much good with numbers, to be honest, never have been. I don't even know where he kept everything.' She waved a hand towards the other end of the table, where paper and large brown envelopes lay with seed trays and bags of goat feed supplement. 'I'm not sure what to do.'

'One of your daughters will help you sort through it all, won't they? Or Monsieur Mériel – might he not understand the farm accounts?'

'Oh, yes, everyone is very kind. But I didn't just mean the paperwork. I meant I'm not sure what I'll do.'

She rose again and went back to the range, where the kettle was beginning to sing. With a tea towel folded round her hand, she gripped the high, curved handle; one smooth wing of hair fell to hide her face, which was turned into the steam.

'This is no place for a woman on her own.'

She poured the water over tea bags in the glasses, and brought them over, taking the chair next to Catherine.

'It's different for you,' she said. 'You're young, you have your business. But what is there here for me now?'

'Madame Volpilière—'

'I know. She's been here on her own for eighteen years, with only her rabbits for company. But her

generation . . . it's different. I'm not like her. I
need people. I'm no farmer now, I'm too old for
that life. I'm a grandmother, that's what I am.
Perhaps a little house in town, near my girls. I
could be useful there, help mind the children.'

'But wouldn't you miss this place?'

'Miss La Grelaudière? My neighbours? Yes, of
course.' She smiled and laid a hand on Catherine's.
'You are all so kind.'

'But the place, I mean.'

'The mountains?'

Catherine nodded, feeling slightly foolish, but the
Frenchwoman gave the question serious thought.

'Of course I would. The spring, especially, and
early mornings in summer. It can be lovely here.'
Then she grinned. 'But I wouldn't miss the
autumn, and all that wretched rain.'

C'est triste, remembered Catherine, meeting her
smile. Sad, the autumn weather. But still, she was
reeling; she wanted to shout out in protest.
Madame Bouschet belonged here; like her
husband, her roots were surely deeply anchored
in the soil of Mont Lozère. A little house in St
Julien? It was unthinkable, a shift in the foundation of things. Madame Bouschet couldn't be
talking of leaving.

'Mind you, I'm not sure who would have this
place. There's nobody in the family wanting to
farm up here, no cousin or nephew, and I can't
think who would want to buy it, not these days.
It's not really what young people want, is it?'

Could she really sell up, just like that? 'Has the farm been in the family long?'

'It came from Augustin's side. His father, and before that a great-uncle. Further back, I'm not sure.' The slightest of sighs. 'But if nobody wants to take it on . . .'

They drank their tea thoughtfully for a moment. Catherine was more accustomed now to drinking it with the tea bag in, but the tannin still set her teeth on edge.

'While I'm here, I wonder if I might ask a favour?' she asked.

Marie-Josèphe brightened appreciably. 'Anything.'

'The trailer. I wonder if I might make use of your trailer? I have a commission to re-cover a small divan for a friend of Madame Peysasse, who lives in a farm on the Alès road.'

She had been over to measure it, and it was certainly too long to fit in her car, even with the back seat down.

'Well, yes, with pleasure, of course. But did you not say the trailer was too heavy for your car?'

'That's right, yes. I was thinking of the tractor.' Catherine had several times, this summer, seen Marie-Josèphe hauling hay up to the yard from the meadows below the house. 'I thought that maybe, if it's not too much trouble, you might drive the tractor for me.'

'Oh, no. I only drive the tractor just round the fields here, to help Augustin sometimes. I've

374

hardly ever been out on the road, and never further than the Mériels. Really, I couldn't.'

It was more or less the reaction Catherine had anticipated. She smothered a grin.

'But you have insurance? To drive on the road?'

'Oh, yes, I expect so.' Her eyes flicked to the muddle of papers at the other end of the table.

'Well, then. It really isn't far, this lady's house. Just the other side of St Julien, on the turning to Alès. You might even know it. Her name is Méjan.'

'Ah, yes. Madame Méjan. She's some distant cousin of my son-in-law, I believe – Claudine's husband. They keep goats.'

'That's right. There would be no difficulty, I'm sure. We'd go together, and I could see you in through the gateway when we arrive.'

Marie-Josèphe's brow lightened by a degree or two. 'They do have a good wide turning there, as I recall. A cattle grid, and no gates.'

'That's right,' said Catherine again. 'Plenty of room to swing in with a trailer.'

'Well . . .'

'I know you must have such a lot to do here. The paperwork and everything. But if you could possibly help me, I would be so very grateful. I'm really not sure, otherwise, what I will do.'

This final plea clinched it. 'Well then, let's try.' The Frenchwoman smiled sadly. 'We must do something, mustn't we? Now that you no longer have your driver.'

Catherine's mouth felt dry, suddenly, and it

wasn't just the tea. She couldn't have spoken, even if she could have thought of anything to say. But her neighbour was still smiling as she laid a gentle hand on Catherine's arm.

'Without him, I'm not sure what any of us will do.'

When August arrived it did not bring the unbroken sunshine of remembered childhood holidays, but a more fragmented gold. There had been more rainstorms in the last days of July, flooding out the telephones again and battering almost to the earth the apple-laden branches in Catherine's terraced orchard. The temperature rose again but the rain had left behind a haze of humid cloud, diffusing the sunlight into pale, shimmering layers. From the window of the small side bedroom, the view of distant hills was blurred to a monochromatic pallet. The raked mountain ridges and the banks of cloud behind were all but indistinguishable, lit in ascending shades of butter yellow. The light was no less intense for being dispersed; in fact, rather the opposite. There seemed to be no south any more, no source that could be pinpointed, but everywhere, instead, the same dazzling luminosity. Catherine felt she had a permanent squint when she was out of doors.

She followed the example of her downhill neighbour and threw open both shutters and window, letting in the soft, gilded air. Perhaps she should bring in some wild flowers too, or a few branches of rosemary and lavender to freshen the room. Lexie was coming. She would be here in just over a week. Nobody had slept in the room since Tom, at Christmas – and Bryony, on top of the covers, that one night before she went home. The bed could no doubt do with an airing. Catherine peeled back the sheet with which she kept it covered and hauled the duvet off and over to the window, where she draped it across the sill, sending a startled green lizard scuttling for the nearest crevice.

If Lexie could really stay the full two weeks she was talking about, she would need somewhere to hang her clothes – if, that is, she brought anything with her besides jeans. And if she was really going to write, she would need a desk. There was a small gateleg table in Catherine's room, which she never used herself. It would do nicely in here, beside the window; Lexie could look up from her page and drink in the view for inspiration. And some velvet cushions would look cheerful, scattered at the head of the bed.

There was so much Catherine wanted them to do together. While she minded her stall, Lexie might enjoy the market in St Julien. She would surely like a day's shopping in Montpellier. Perhaps she wasn't such a keen walker or nature-lover as Tom, but she was no Bryony, either. Catherine could show her the bees, and the woods, and the little pool in the stream where she'd seen the boar. If it was hot they might have a swim together, like when Lexie was a kid. And Marie-Josèphe was going to come to dinner, at least once while Lexie was here; she'd promised when they'd driven over together in the tractor to pick up Madame Méjan's divan. Catherine thought she might do an English steak and kidney, a proper steamed one in a basin, with suet pastry, and some of her own green beans. Lexie had always loved steak and kidney pudding.

Absently, Catherine plumped the duvet where it lay over the sill. Dust rose, as it always did from any soft surface in a house with walls of unrendered stone, and with it a distillation of cotton, warm bodies and hot, stale air. From higher up the window frame another lizard fled.

A car horn made itself felt, an impact in the still summer air rather than a sound. A double claxon, ricocheting from rock faces lower down the gorge. And then at the next turn of the road it was properly audible, *tootle-toot*, and beneath it the hum of an engine. The postman.

As was the habit of all her neighbours, Catherine went downstairs and out to meet him. He was whistling as he stepped out of the yellow van and strode towards her, boots gleaming in defiance of dusty August farmyards.

'Good day,' he greeted her, flashing his boyish grin, before adding in purest lower East Side, 'How'ya doin', lady?'

'Very well, thank you. And you?' replied Catherine primly in French. It was an exchange they repeated almost daily.

'Three, today,' he observed, handing over the envelopes.

'Thank you. Not too hot yet this morning.'

With a nod of the head he turned on his polished heels. She always wondered whether one day he might actually salute her.

When he was gone, the van horn echoing back down the gully, she retired inside to open her mail at the kitchen table. The first envelope was long, white and hand-addressed. When she slit it open, a cheque fell out: payment for Maître Dujol's new office curtains. As she lifted the second letter – small, slim, again handwritten – her eye fell on the one underneath.

Her heart tripped. She had put it out of her mind, assuming that nothing would happen now until after the August lull. But there it was: the stamp in red franking-machine ink. Le Parc National des Cévennes – Nature, Espace de Vie.

There was really no need, was there, for her fingers to be shaking as she ripped open the envelope? Or for the way her eyes danced and refused to focus as she unfolded the single A4 sheet? The words splashed in colour across the top of the letterhead arrested her first, daunting and distant even in translation – biosphere, patrimony – so that it was a moment before her glance slid down to the text of the typewritten letter.

Chère Madame Parkstone, she read, *j'ai le regret de vous informer—*

It was as far as she got; the words shifted and

blurred into confusion. Her brain baulked at the extraction of meaning, but at the same time it was racing ahead, throwing up possible, impossible futures.

What in the name of heaven was going to happen now? She'd been a blind, impractical idiot right from the start – a romantic fool. She had put things off, had shut out unpalatable bureaucratic realities. She'd stuck her head down in the sand and pressed ahead with this fantasy life of hers; it was nothing but play-acting, a stupid daydream, a *château en Espagne* as the French would say, and the whole edifice was about to come crashing down around her.

Maître Dujol's cheque, Madame Méjan's divan, the unfinished bolster covers for her stall on Thursday – what use was any of it if she was running an illegal, unlicensed business? Her swelling order book, the steady trickle of cash flowing into her French bank account, building up a nice little credit balance to supplement the nest egg from the sale of the house in Long Hartslow – it was all an empty mockery. She couldn't submit her accounts, she couldn't register for tax or social security, she couldn't do anything, because she didn't qualify as a '*métier rural*'. She forced herself to read the letter.

Having considered the nature and circumstances of your business proposal, we are of the opinion that it does not operate sufficiently within the sphere of agricultural and subsidiary activities and is therefore not within the definition of 'rural profession' as required by article 6.1.b of the National Park Regulations, issued under law number 2006–436 of 14 April 2006 . . .

It was so final, staring at her in black and white – and made all the more so by the formal business French and the litter of legal citations. But could this really be the end? Of course not, argued the resourceful part of her, the optimistic Catherine. There must be some means of appeal against the finding. This must be only the first stage; there must be further channels to try, higher layers of decision-making which she could pursue. Without intending it, she found herself recalling what Patrick Castagnol had said. *We take pleasure in the rules, but equal pleasure in ways to bend and break them.* A means, as he said, would surely be found.

Of course it would be found; it had to be. Otherwise, what the hell was she going to do?

CHAPTER 23

THE SCENT OF JASMINE

A few mornings later, Catherine was in her terraced vegetable patch picking caterpillars from her lettuces. She had no truck with chemical sprays, but nor had she ever acquired the hardened organic gardener's habit of dealing casual death by pinching or squashing or crushing underfoot. She was fastidiously placing the plump, furry larvae on top of the low stone wall which bounded the terrace on its uphill side. From there they were picked off by a thrush which followed after her at a polite distance of three feet. She and the bright-eyed executioner had first formed their partnership in the late spring, when every shower of rain had brought out regiments of snails. Catherine had placed the snails on a large flat rock beneath the cherry trees and the thrush had bashed them to pieces on it.

There was bare soil visible in places now where she'd been harvesting her summer salad crops, and up by the house she had trays of leek and cauliflower seedlings waiting to be planted out for the winter and early spring. Perhaps she would put some in this evening, after the heat subsided;

the warm soil and cooler, humid air would provide ideal conditions. She could prepare the ground now: breach the baked crust and turn over the friable earth beneath, digging in spadefuls of the Mériels' goat manure from the heap at the bottom of the orchard. The leeks would be ready by November or December and would last right through to spring with no problem. The cauliflowers were more of a risk, if they had sharp night frosts again this year; Monsieur Bouschet had grown them successfully last winter but his plot was more sheltered, and even the few dozen feet of extra altitude at Les Fenils might make a difference. *C'est pas evident*, as he himself might have said. She wished she'd thought to ask him about it.

Autumn, winter, spring. Yesterday morning, the future had appeared so certain, her own future (though she paid it no heed beyond her anticipation of Lexie's visit) as predictable as the succeeding seasons of the mountains. But now, after her letter from the Parc National, nothing seemed solid at all. Now everything was up in the air: her income, her livelihood, her place here in this community. But time would roll on regardless. The days would shorten and the soil temperature would fall; Lexie would come and the leeks would grow, and in the orchard the apples and Mirabelles would ripen and need picking, or else they would fall and rot – and all of this would happen whether her business was registered or not. She found in it a perverse reassurance.

It was after eleven o'clock when Catherine straightened from her weeding. Two vertebrae in her lower back seemed to have fused while she was bending to her task, so that she rose at an uncomfortable angle. Gingerly she rotated her hips in counterpoint to her shoulders, waiting for the blessed click of release. She had not meant to work for quite so long, but the sky was overcast and the heat had risen only slowly – though she was sweating profusely now.

She was dreaming of cold water when she heard footsteps approaching above. They were coming from the direction of the woods and not up the track from La Grelaudière. Nobody ever arrived that way, except Patrick, and Patrick did not come by any more. And it was not the tread of a single pair of feet but two or three or four.

'Hello?' she called.

There was no immediate answering voice but the footsteps came to a ragged halt, and after a pause a single pair of boots crunched towards her across the gravel. A face, bespectacled and benign, peered down at her.

'Ah, hello. I am very sorry to disturb you, Madame. I wonder, might I possibly trouble you for a bucket of water?'

The request, so absurdly unexpected, produced a spurt of laughter which Catherine turned into a cough.

'Certainly,' she said, and began to move towards the worn granite steps.

'It's not for me, you understand. Or not exactly. It's for my donkey.'

Delighted, she smothered more laughter. At last, a Stevensonian pilgrim, and in her own front yard. What had been Patrick's description? *Elementary school teachers from the Paris suburbs, with earnest wives and pale, freckled children.* The man holding the halter rope was thirty or thirty-five; he could well have been a teacher, by his serious, slightly harassed look, but his wife had the freckles and there were no children.

'It is rather warm today,' the husband explained, 'and we couldn't get down near the stream for her to have a drink. The banks are very steep.'

'They are,' agreed Catherine.

'It looked as if it might have been dangerous. We prefer to keep to the paths.'

'Very sensible, I'm sure.'

At the other end of the rope stood Modestine, or her contemporary counterpart, heavy-headed and droop-lidded. Her short, knock-kneed legs did indeed look unsuited to scrambling into ravines in pursuit of water, even had they not had to support her barrel of a body and the couple's bulging pack. She certainly looked in need of a drink.

'Let me go and fetch that bucket.'

She found one under the sink which was moderately clean, and filled it from the tap. Then she came back out on to the terrace and placed it down in

385

front of the donkey, which lowered its head and began to suck noisily.

'I have hay, too,' it suddenly occurred to her. 'Just there in the cattle byre.'

'That's terribly kind of you,' said the wife, 'but no, thank you. The hire people in Le Monastier said to feed her twice a day, morning and evening. And we don't want to do anything wrong.'

'Actually,' said her husband, 'I think we may have slightly lost our way. Is the *grande randonnée* near here? We were supposed to follow it as far as Le Pont de Montvert.'

'You've come a distance from it, I'm afraid. You need to be on the other side of the gully. Go back up the way you came, and cross over at the wooden footbridge.' That might be interesting with the donkey – but they must have come down that way. 'Then, a short distance up the other side you'll come to a sort of T-junction, and there you turn left. That's the *grande randonnée*. It's marked on the trees in red and white.'

'I see. Thank you. So, how long do you think—'

The telephone rang, jangling Catherine's outside bell and bringing the donkey's head up with a jerk, almost upending the bucket.

'Excuse me for a moment, would you, please?' she said, and went inside.

'Hello. Is that Mrs Parkstone?'

Mrs Aldridge's voice sounded much as it always did, except that she rarely addressed Catherine that way.

'Speaking.'

'It's your mother, dear.'

She knew at once. It could have been something else, of course – some angry outburst, a financial query, another minor stroke. But there was no need for Mrs Aldridge to say anything else, to speak the ineradicable words. Catherine knew.

'When?' was the first question, the one which seemed most important. 'When did it happen?'

'This morning, about nine. We found her in her chair, sitting upright, and very peaceful.'

Nine o'clock English time, ten o'clock here. She would have been pricking out her leeks. Though why on earth should it suddenly matter so much, where she had been and what she had been doing, when she hadn't spoken to Mum since before the weekend, and then only for a few minutes? When she hadn't been back to see her, not once in eleven months.

'The doctor has been, and signed the certificate. Another stroke, he said. It would have been very quick.'

Eleven months. It would have been the easiest thing in the world to drive to Nîmes or Rodez and hop on a plane. She couldn't pretend she had somehow been too busy, or claim any other excuse. If she'd wanted to go, she would have gone.

'I don't know if you have an undertaker in mind – of course, you will want to think about it, talk to your sister, and the family. But there is one we deal with regularly, Mr McCorquodale. He's very reliable, very accommodating. If you wanted me to contact him for you, I'd be very happy, you have only to let me know.'

She could tell herself there was no point, that Mum wouldn't have remembered, might not even have known her. It was a long way to go, not to be recognised. But in the end, she hadn't gone because she couldn't face it. Her own mother.

'I did try your sister first, what with her being here in England, but I couldn't get hold of her. They said she was in a meeting. But now, of course, you'll want to tell her yourself.'

Catherine roused herself. 'Yes. Thank you, Mrs Aldridge. Thanks very much. For – well, you know – for everything you've done . . .'

'She was a wonderful lady.'

'Thank you,' said Catherine again, and put down the phone.

Through the window, it was almost a shock to see the young tourist couple still out there on the terrace as before. The donkey still had its nose in the bucket: the old red plastic one, the one that came from Mum as a little extra present when she got married because you can never have too many buckets. Catherine stared out at the little tableau and her mind crowded with a rush of disjointed images. Mary and Joseph on their way to Bethlehem. A school nativity play when the kids were small. Tom in his pyjamas with a white velour dog for a lamb, and Mum there at the side of the stage with her camera. The photo was here, in the shortbread tin in the dresser drawer. Pictures of Mum, too. Pictures of a younger Mum, of Mum from before.

What would she do? Orphaned, adrift, what would she do without her mother?

She did what an Englishwoman always does. Somehow she made her way to the door and out on to the step.

'Tea,' she said.

The teacher and his wife stared at her. Even the donkey lifted its great grey head, chin dribbling, and gazed at her with mild, stupid eyes. Catherine's tongue felt bloated, her mouth dry; she licked her lips and was surprised to taste wet salt at the corner of her mouth.

With some difficulty, she swallowed. 'Would you like . . . That is, may I offer you a cup of tea?'

She turned and went back inside, and the young woman followed her while her husband hitched the halter rope to a ring set into the outhouse wall, probably for just such a purpose. Catherine had no doubt that they thought her demeanour slightly odd and she summoned an effort at normality.

'Sit down, won't you? I expect you're parched. I know I am, from working in the garden. What time did you set off this morning?'

'About eight. We like to make an early start when we can, get some kilometres under out belts while it's still cool.'

Catherine nodded. 'Is a tisane all right for you?'

But her fingers wouldn't seem to grip the lid of the jar in which she kept Marie-Josèphe's lime flower tea, and then her hands were shaking so much that she had to put it down on the table, and her concerned guest spooned the brittle green flowerheads into the old Denby teapot.

The young man appeared in the kitchen doorway and hovered there, unwilling, perhaps, to take a seat until invited.

'Make yourself at home,' said Catherine with a weak smile.

Please stay, she willed them. Drink my tea, tell me about your expedition – though she had no strength to question them about it. She wanted them to stay because when they were gone – when this whimsical interlude was over – reality, which for the moment was held in temporary suspension, would have to be faced. She would have to ring Bryony, and Lexie, and Tom, and apply her mind to flights and funeral arrangements. It would be true. Her mother would really be dead.

In the end, though, it was she who grew impatient and had to put an end to it.

'It should take us another six days, I think,' the woman was saying, 'which is two days less than Stevenson took for this leg of the journey. But the tracks are better nowadays, of course.'

'Yes. Look,' Catherine stood up, straightening with some effort her uncooperative knees, 'I'm really sorry. Do please finish your tea. And there are biscuits in the tin there, if you'd like one. Or take some with you if you want. Don't mind me. I just need—'

They were both staring openly now, their puzzlement undisguised. Catherine took hold of the table with one hand and managed to steady her swaying legs.

'I need to go and start packing.'

That night Catherine went to bed dry-eyed, but she woke with a wet pillow. She had been dreaming of learning to swim in a mountain pool near Le Vigan – except that in the dream she was not alone in the river. Her mother was there, walking slowly backwards away from her, arms outstretched but always a finger's length away, while Catherine's lungs burned and her neck strained with the effort of keeping her mouth clear of the water. When she surfaced from the dream her throat was clogged with sobs.

Unable to recapture sleep, she rose and went downstairs in her nightdress, as she had been used to doing in June. Now, though, the night temperature was less oppressive, falling with the earlier dusk to an ambient softness; in fact, her unslippered feet were almost chilly. For once, she lacked the energy to put on the kettle, normally so much a reflex on her nocturnal wanderings. She picked up her tapestry frame and laid it down again, then walked to the window.

How do you remember a mother? Someone who

has always been there, from time before memory: a given, a constant presence, once more real than self. How can you think about her the way you would another person? When Catherine closed her eyes, no images came at all but only a warm, cocooning scent, and the comfort of arms she would never feel again. And yet when she grasped for it, the scent evaded her, evaporating in the stone and oak and herbs of the kitchen. What was her mother's smell? She tried to reconstruct it – well-washed wool and soap and that jasmine perfume she wore – but it was gone.

She was a wonderful lady, Mrs Aldridge had said. But how did she know? Mum had been a shell of herself these past four years in Walton-on-the-Naze, and for maybe a year before that. *You didn't know her,* she ought to have said, *you never knew my mother.* In the home, she hadn't even smelled of herself. The wrong fabric freshener in the laundry; the institutional soap. And when was the last time that Catherine or Lexie or Bryony had brought her a bottle of her perfume? It was a French brand, the jasmine scent; Catherine could easily have bought her some in Mende or Alès and sent it in the post.

Woodenly, Catherine walked to the dresser and opened the drawer. The cloth-bound exercise book was where it always was, and she lifted it out and carried it to the table. On the cover, in felt-tip, the word RECIPES was written in her own 21-year-old hand. Inside, the cuttings snipped from the Sunday colour supplements were dull and yellowed; in places, the glue showed through, blotching the paper to the same grey as the type. In between the recipes she had cut out and kept were what she was looking for: here and there, the scribbled instructions her mother had copied down for her.

All the family favourites were here. Not only Irish tea brack but coconut cherry cake and butterfly buns – not that she had made those since the children were small; they were a thing to do together, just as Mum had made them with her and Bryony. And Christmas cake, Mum's own patent recipe, with glacé pineapple and chrystallised ginger. Nobody made Christmas cake quite like Mum's, though Catherine had imitated it herself every year since she left home, until this one. She could have made one and sent it, couldn't she? Mum could have had a slice after her Christmas dinner.

They always chose what to have for tea when it was their birthdays. She had continued the tradition herself, later, with Tom and Lexie, but they had often preferred to go out, to Pizza Express or the Tex-Mex place in High Wycombe, with a crowd of friends, and the cinema or bowling beforehand. But at home it had always been family birthday tea, and Mum had cooked to their command. Bryony had generally chosen something exotic: Caribbean chicken with peppers and banana, or spicy stir-fried prawns, which she insisted they all eat with chopsticks. For Catherine it was toad-in-the-hole or lasagne, or a picnic pie her mother used to make with potato, cheese and onion – oddly similar, it now occurred to her, to a *tourte cévenole*.

Over the page was another old favourite, Boston-style roast pork with beans. Catherine had tried to make it for Mum and Bryony one Sunday lunchtime when she was newly married, and had misread the instructions, adding a tablespoonful of ground cloves instead of a teaspoonful. Graeme had tasted it and almost choked, and she had sat down on the floor and wept like a child while he rinsed off as much of the sauce as he could and added another tin of tomatoes, being very good about not laughing. Looking closely now, Mum's handwritten 'tsp' was very much like her 'tbsp'. Pulling the open book up against her chest and hugging it there, Catherine found that she was crying.

In the morning, if not rested then at least super-ficially refreshed by a shower and the application of a rare smudge of powder, she walked down the hill to speak to Marie-Josèphe. On the doorstep of the farmhouse she felt a reluctance to be bringing the reminder of death to a house of mourning. But she was welcomed in, and given coffee, and her paleness commented upon in spite of the powder, so that it was less difficult than she'd feared to impart the news.

'My mother has died.' It sounded more

theatrical in French, but also more formal, somehow more containable than yesterday, telling Bry and Lexie and Tom.

'Sacred Jesus.' Marie-Josèphe crossed herself before taking Catherine's hand in both hers. 'You poor little thing.' Forty-nine years old, and that was exactly how Catherine felt. Tears filled her eyes once more.

'I shall have to go home for a while. For the funeral, of course, and then there will be a lot to sort out. She still has a house – rented out, you know, but I expect we'll give the tenants notice now and put it on the market. And all her things to be gone through.'

The task sounded distant and unreal, as if she were talking about another mother, another daughter. At the same time, the idea of it exhausted her.

'We did clear out a lot of things when she went into the nursing home, but there's still her furniture – it's let as a furnished house – and the attic is full to bursting.'

Marie-Josèphe nodded. 'And your sister. She is there?'

Catherine had forgotten that her neighbours knew Bryony, . . . though in truth they had scarcely met her while she was here.

'Yes. She'll help of course. She hopes to have some time off work, or otherwise it will be week-ends. I don't want to decide on my own about what to keep and what to sell or throw away.'

'No. Quite.'

'And there's Lexie. I'm sure she'll come and help, too.'

'Ah yes, your daughter, the journalist. So now her visit here will be postponed. And I was so looking forward to meeting her. Perhaps she will come back with you, or visit later, in the autumn.'

Later, the autumn: Catherine's mind refused to move that far ahead. 'Perhaps.'

There was a pause, and then the Frenchwoman set down her coffee cup. 'She had been ill, I think you said, your mother?'

'Y-yes.' Ill – it was so completely the wrong word. As if Mum had gone down with a bout of flu or been in bed with chickenpox. 'Alzheimer's, and then a stroke. She – well, she hadn't been herself for a long time.'

A hand on her arm; another short silence.

'You know, if there's anything that needs doing up there while you are away, I should be very glad to see to it.'

'No. It's very kind of you, but there's nothing to do.' It wasn't a mere polite demur, she realised; it was the truth. 'I really don't think there's anything to take care of at all.'

After the first visit, the other two were easier. Madame Volpilière, an intimate with loss, fetched a dusty bottle and poured her a stoical Benedictine, although it was barely ten o'clock. At the Mériels she stayed longer and was offered a glass of sweet homemade liqueur, which she resolved not to touch but in the end drank without noticing, and had to fight off a refill. Aware of the time and that she was taking them from their work, she declined their pleas that she stay for lunch and walked back up the hill, feeling leaden-footed and very slightly queasy.

Back at Les Fenils, she stood at the sink and drank three mugs of water straight down. It must be crying that had dehydrated her; she felt there would never be an end to her thirst. She knew she should eat, though she had no appetite for it, and forced her way through half a piece of bread and cheese, finding swallowing painful.

She had phoned yesterday to book her air ticket from the small airport at Rodez: an open-ended return. The flight out wasn't until tomorrow afternoon at two, which left twenty-four hours to fill. The time seemed interminably long and any occupation to which she might have turned her hand, vain and purposeless. She should clear the fridge, take any spare milk and other perishables down to Marie-Josèphe, but that was a job for the morning. She should pick the runner beans – but what was the point when next week they would be rotting or turning to wood on the vine? Her clients, she had already rung yesterday: Madame Méjan, to tell her there would be a delay with the upholstering of her divan; old Monsieur Martinet, to say that his kitchen curtains would take a little longer. She had warned Madame Volpilière that she'd need an alternative lift to the bank next Friday. Her bag stood packed in the bedroom, all but her toothbrush. There was nothing left to do.

Except for one thing, she remembered. The bees: she had not yet told the bees. Outside, it was hot, with the heavy, dragging heat of the middle of the day, a time when Catherine usually stayed indoors. *Mad dogs*, she thought, but couldn't raise a smile.

Instead of heading straight up the yard in the direction of the hives, her steps were drawn towards the edge of the terrace, where it shelved down to her vegetable plots and orchard. There, the smell of the rosemary bushes which lined the upper rim of the terrace towards its eastern end hung thick in the heated air. Madame Sauzet, like most French country people of her generation, had had no time for decorative gardening in the English style. Fruit and vegetables, herbs for the stewpot, and at most a few tubs of geraniums for a splash of colour by the house were all that most of them deemed necessary. Here, however, beyond the rosemaries, was a small area of trees and shrubs which served no culinary purpose. A forsythia had given a dash of brilliance to the upper terrace in April; a cluster of old rose bushes stood in front, their fine upper stems brought low by the weight of overblown flower heads. And right at the end was another sweet-scented shrub, a sojourner from north Africa or the Far East, its waxy white flowers open flat as hands in the midday heat. Catherine drew near, closed her eyes and breathed in deeply, no longer fighting the exhaustion of the past day and a half but letting it rise up and claim her. Her chest swelled with her mother's scent. The scent of jasmine.

CHAPTER 24

PATRICK

It was early the same evening that he came. When she heard his rap at the door, Catherine assumed it must be Marie-Josèphe, come with the excuse of some small offer or gift, or perhaps Madame Mériel – though it was unusual for either of them to knock. She had been crying again, and when she opened the door, he appeared through a residual blur of tears.

'Patrick.'

'Catherine.'

By his tone, there was no doubt why he had come, and no need for him to utter the polite formula of condolence. She turned in silence and led him through to the kitchen.

'Do sit down,' she said in someone else's voice, formal and detached.

Obediently, he sat, while she walked over to the window, her back to him. A thought occurred to her.

'Did Bryony ring you?'

But it was nonsense; there was no earthly reason why it should have been her.

'No.' He sounded diffident, unexpected for him;

400

almost meek. 'I ran into Monsieur Mériel in the woods, on the way back down from seeing to his sheep. He told me.'

She nodded slowly, then turned and approached the table. When she was near enough for him to speak softly, he said, 'I'm so sorry, Catherine.'

Then with a half grin that was a return of his usual self, he produced from his canvas shooting bag a slim, unlabelled bottle.

'I thought perhaps . . .'

Catherine fetched the glasses.

If he had wanted to explain, to apologise or justify himself, she would have had no strength for it, but he made no attempt to do so. It seemed he had come only to sit at her table, to share his *eau de vie* and listen to stories about her mother, and she was thankful for it. He had come to be the friend he had once been.

Like a friend, he knew the right questions to ask.

'What made her laugh?' he said, as he poured their second drink.

'Oh, so many things. She laughed easily, before she was ill. Silly stories in the newspaper, bad adverts on TV, anything absurd. When we were in the car, as kids, she used to keep us entertained by doing funny voices for all the people in the street. It drove poor Dad crazy.'

She gazed down into her glass. 'She missed my father. I mean, that's stupid, of course she missed him – how could she not? But what I'm saying is,

I think she missed him far more than she ever admitted, even to herself. She wasn't made for living alone.

'Especially when she first began forgetting things, when the dementia first began to take hold. Then it was tough. She didn't rage and rail against it, as it must have been tempting to do, but dug in quietly to fight it all the way. Writing everything down; making lists; checking everything twice and three times.

'I had her to stay quite often, when she was first ill. But it wasn't easy. We were both so used to our own space, our own routines. Having our kitchens to ourselves. It was fine for a while, and then we'd start to get on each other's nerves, and she'd go home.'

'Very natural.' Patrick smiled at her from across the table. She looked up, dazed; she had almost forgotten he was there. 'Independence,' he said. 'It's a hard thing to relinquish.'

But she'd had to in the end, hadn't she? Mum had had to relinquish her autonomy, not so much to Catherine or even to the nursing home, but to the encroaching disease which, resist as she might, was in the end too much for even her iron will, and drove her back to reliance on other people, to the infant dependence she had struggled so hard against. That was the worst. That was the hardest thing to see, the thing Catherine most hated about visits to Walton-on-the-Naze: to see her mother no longer putting up a fight.

Maybe that was why she hadn't gone, the reason she hadn't got on a plane in eleven months, when she ought to have done. *Oh, Mum, I'm sorry. I ought to have come . . .*

She made no attempt to hide her tears from him. He was round the table in a moment and kneeling beside her chair. Only the smallest movement was required: a slight tilt forward brought her forehead to rest on the shoulder nearest to her, her nose butting the cotton twill of his shirt. *A shoulder to cry on*, she thought, and the sound in her throat was a sob that was almost laughter.

He didn't kiss her at first. His arms came round her and he stroked her back, over and over, running his palms down the knots of her spine. He might have been caressing a cat or soothing a sleepless child. His lips when they found hers were rough on the outside, more abrasive than she remembered Graeme's being, but inside they were satin. Their tongues were peppery hot with *eau de vie.*

She was too numb for shyness, and when he took her by the hand and led her to the stairs, her feet moved easily enough, although she was glad of his supporting arm. Her window and shutters were wide open to the fragrant evening air, but it must only be in imagination that she could smell jasmine. The duvet, abandoned in early May, lay folded in the wardrobe; her bed looked strangely naked in nothing but a sheet. When he helped her off with her shirt and they lay down, the linen was cool against her exposed skin. She shivered. He felt it, and murmured in reassurance. *Cat-rine. Chérie.*

His weight as he moved above her had a welcome solidity and her hands found their own way to a place below his shoulder blades, taking tight hold. Her knees came up and slackened. Eight years was a long time but Patrick was watchful and there was very little discomfort, and that little very quickly overtaken. But as they rocked together, the escalation of sensation took him away from her and she from him, so that when she cried out, and he soon after, the sounds drifted to her ears as cries more of isolation than of fusion.

Afterwards, however, as she drifted towards sleep, she felt the dusting of tender fingertips across her arms and shoulders and breasts. There was closeness and comfort in it, and she was grateful.

Catherine woke first, to a residual drugged warmth, quickly displaced by the returning stab of loss. Patrick lay on his back, as men will, one arm flung expansively across both pillows; his chest, above the furrowed sheet, was peppered in springing black and grey. His face had loosened its taut lines, the way it had on the bench beneath the mulberry trees at St-Hippolyte; at these close quarters, he looked almost vulnerable. It wasn't difficult to slide away from his arm without waking him, pull a T-shirt over her nakedness and slip down to the kitchen.

The two glasses and the half-empty bottle of *eau de vie* were still on the table, her chair drawn drunkenly back, but there was no guilt or reproach; even as she straightened the chair, it was like looking at a scene from a film – sweet and sad and quite removed from herself.

She corked the bottle and carried the glasses to the sink, then filled the kettle and opened the fridge. Really, she ought to start to empty it, and parcel up the eggs and leftover *saucisson* to take to Marie-Josèphe. But Patrick would want breakfast – they had eaten nothing last night – or a café au lait at least, so the butter and milk she would leave for now. She wondered if his habit was to sleep late when he wasn't shooting or fishing, and was invaded by a fleeting impatience at his presence, when she should be thinking about packing up and getting to the airport, and about Mum.

She wanted nothing herself except a small black coffee; she might have a sandwich later, at the airport or on the plane, if only to kill time. But the rye loaf in the bread bin was passably fresh, and there was an open jar of her honey: the sluggish half-jar from the bottom of the extractor, when the trickle finally ran out. She found the small enamel tray which she hadn't used since Tom had stayed, and spread over it a checked table napkin. Three slices of bread, the honey jar and a square of butter on a saucer; the sugar bowl and her own Denby mug for his coffee. The ensemble gave her quiet satisfaction. Whatever else – and she was far too tired to contemplate the 'else' – Patrick had been very kind to her last night. And he was, after all, a guest in her house.

Guest. A curious epithet in the circumstances, but it felt right, nevertheless; certainly more so than 'lover'.

Back in the bedroom, he was stirring. When she'd found a place to lay down the tray and turned towards the bed, he was fully awake and subjecting her to an unswerving scrutiny. The mixture of appreciation and amusement and query in his eyes forced hers to drop away. When he made space, she sat down on the bed but did not look at him, self-conscious in her old T-shirt. He was close enough for her to smell again the tang of last night, and it was tempting, just for a moment, to lie down again, to wrap herself in his morning warmth and pretend everything was all right. That this was real; that the journey ahead of her, and what lay at the end of it, were not.

'I brought you coffee,' she said, when the silence became awkward.

But he wasn't helping her at all. 'I saw.'

'And bread and honey. I don't know whether you like to eat breakfast.'

'Oh, certainly. Thank you very much.'

She rose again and brought the tray over, giving both of them something to look at and do with their hands, as she passed him the mug and sugar bowl. Gravely, he measured in two spoonfuls and thanked her again.

'My flight is at two o'clock.'

Immediately, she winced. How pusillanimous it sounded, how dismissive: the coward's exit route.

'Of course. You have to pack.'

His gaze drifted to the bedroom door, where her bag had stood since yesterday morning. She felt her cheeks grow hot, but also a shot of irritation that he should be the cause. What had she to blush about? She did have things to do; she did have to leave; her mother was dead.

It seemed simplest to leave him alone to his breakfast and go back down to sort out the fridge and turn it off, and give her seedlings a last watering before the sun was too high. There were all the shutters to close and latch, and the outhouses to lock. And the bees: she should look in on the bees. In fact, she ought to boil some sugar syrup and set it out for them; she had the extra bags of sugar stored ready in the top of the larder cupboard. The books said they would need a feed before the autumn, and who knows how long she would be away?

As she her heavy preserving pan on the gas to boil, a thought occurred to her and she went to the kitchen doorway, calling out, 'If you want a shower—'

But he was already at the foot of the stairs, fully clothed and quite unrumpled, not at all as if he were wearing yesterday's shirt.

'I should leave you. You have a lot to do.'

'Yes.' Then she could think of nothing to add, because what she wanted to say – *thank you* – was clearly out of the question.

He was holding the breakfast tray, so she moved forward and took it from him. 'The gas is on,' she said, rather desperately. 'I'd better—'

'Of course.' They were still standing with the tray between them, but he took hold of her shoulders and pulled her into a cluttered half-hug.

'*Bon courage,*' he murmured. Then he released her, turned and was gone, pulling shut behind him the heavy oak door.

She stood in the empty hall and stared at the closed door. Contrarily, having wanted him gone, she now wished he had offered to drive her to the airport; his presence, paradoxically, had freed her from thinking about things – and that included himself as well as Mum. She blamed him for asking no questions of her, nor making any kind of declaration, although she was ill prepared to deal with either.

Turning to take the tray back to the kitchen, she managed somehow to overbalance it and sent the jar of honey toppling to the stone flags with a dull smack. She put down the tray and knelt beside it on the cold granite. The top half of the jar was intact, the lid still affixed, but the lower half was distorted, wider and foreshortened; a network of small lines spread across it like a bruise. As she watched, honey began to bleed slowly from one of the cracks, until the image melted and was lost in tears.

CHAPTER 25

HOME TRUTHS

Stansted Airport was a shock to the system. It was one of those places, in any event, which seemed to have grown exponentially every time you went there, and it stood in especially stark contrast to the tiny terminal at Rodez, which was little more than a clubhouse for the local flying school and a few businessmen with private light aircraft, until invaded once every twenty-four hours by the passengers and staff of Ryan Air. The daily flight from London Stansted landed and emptied, filled up and took off again; twenty minutes later, Catherine imagined, the bartenders would be back to the unnecessary polishing of gleaming glasses or contemplation of the cows which grazed placidly beside the runway. Not so at Stansted.

Her flight had taken off on time, but there was some problem or other over landing slots, and they seemed to go round and round for ever, tilting and flattening again, the earth disappearing and appearing at the left-hand windows, until she was thoroughly queasy. Then there was an endless wait at the baggage carousel among harassed parents and their fractious, sunburned children. It would have been more sensible not to check in a bag, but with an open-ended stay before her, it had not seemed possible to travel quite that light. She adjusted on her shoulder the small rucksack she had brought as cabin luggage. From under the top flap protruded the rolled length of her unfinished tapestry: the view from the kitchen window at Les Fenils. That it was foolish to have brought it, she was well aware. She had drawn the line at paying the extra to check in the frame and, without that, and the carpet bag with all her silks, she was hardly likely to do any work on it. But it was something. A reminder, a souvenir – or maybe a talisman of her return.

Eventually, her bag appeared up the ramp and trundled towards her. She took it, negotiated the short queue at customs, and then headed out in search of the bus that would take her to her hire car. Outside, the unrecirculated air was a relief, though it had been raining and there were residual, cold flecks in the wind. Diesel exhaust fumes, you would imagine, and wet pavements and queuing holidaymakers would smell pretty much the same the world over, but they didn't: everything smelled indescribably English.

The Avis car park seemed to be approximately five miles from the terminal building, unless they were taking the kind of route designed to deter homing swarms of bees. She was far from certain that she knew what a Nissan Murano looked like – nor what colour was meant by 'Saharan stone' – and it took some time to locate her car among the waiting rows. She slung her bag in the back and adjusted the driver's seat; the previous occupant appeared to have been an oversized basketball player.

When she turned the key in the ignition, the radio came to life, in the voice of James Alexander Gordon. Catherine had almost forgotten, in the confusion of the last few days, that today was Saturday. '. . . Derby County 1, Ipswich Town 0 . . .' Not that she had ever listened to them since Dad was alive, but there was something so soothingly British about the classified football results. A universality of culture, she conjectured, as she clicked it off and struggled to find reverse: this crowded island, unified by rain and roadworks and the storylines of *EastEnders*. It ought to feel a world away but now that she was back here and pulling away on the proper side of the road, it was completely familiar and immediate and ordinary, just as if she'd never been away.

Bryony's choice of bed and breakfast was an idiosyncratic one, for a woman of her taste and means. Catherine located it, from the rudimentary map on the back of the card her sister had scanned and emailed to her, in a quiet street of 1930s bungalows at the side of town furthest from the sea. But, after all, it was deep in the school holidays; no doubt the smarter places and those on

412

the seafront were all fully booked, and Catherine was not sorry.

It was strange to be arriving in Walton-on-the-Naze and not heading straight for the nursing home, but Lilac Lodge was even stranger, with its low bay window, net curtains and complete absence of lilacs. Perhaps there had been a tree once, but at some point in the last decade or so the small front garden had been dug up and relaid in all-over red brick to provide hard standing for guests' cars. Catherine's was the only one apart from an old silver Nova. Bryony was late.

The doorbell sounded a silky double chime, and the proprietor came to the door in a waft of lavender and an ensemble of fine mauve wool to match the name of her establishment. 'Seaside landlady' was not a phrase that Catherine could fit to her at all.

'Miss Beale?'

'Actually, I'm Mrs Parkstone. My sister will be here later.'

'Well, do come in. I'm Mrs Edwardstone. Have you any more bags?'

'No. This is it.'

'Let me show you to your room, then.'

It was clean and airy, comfortable enough in a chintzy way, with a handbasin and lilac towels.

'Welcome to Lilac Lodge, and I do hope you'll have an enjoyable stay,' said Mrs Edwardstone.

'Thank you.'

Bryony, evidently, had not told her of the reason

for their being there – and indeed why would she? – and Catherine was relieved not to have to accept the woman's polite condolences.

There was a kettle in the room and a single floral cup and saucer, laid carefully upside down, and downstairs the small television lounge she had been shown on the way through, but Catherine felt a sudden need for noise and people.

Having ascertained from Mrs Edwardstone that the Golden Hind on the main road offered an extensive and varied menu, and that of course Miss Beale, when she arrived, would be informed of her whereabouts, she headed out. Not that she had any appetite for a meal, but Bryony might want to eat, and she would most certainly want to drink.

It was still early, but it was Saturday and the place was filling up. Catherine armed herself with an orange juice and found a table in a small side bar. There was a private feel to it, surrounded by shoulder-high wooden partitions topped with brass rails; she put her drink on a dog-eared beer mat. Crisps, she thought as she surveyed her surroundings, perhaps she should have bought crisps.

When Bryony appeared an hour later in a flurry of raincoat and briefcase, Catherine was on her third Britvic.

'Hi, Cath. Sorry. Have you been here ages? The trains were a nightmare, even on a bloody weekend. I had to go to the office today, didn't have any

414

choice, and I knew you weren't coming until tonight, but things ran on, you know how it is.'

They ought to have been crying and hugging, thought Catherine as Bryony pecked her on the cheek, but her sister was holding a vodka and tonic in one hand and her briefcase in the other.

'Client documents,' she said, following Catherine's glance. 'Laptop. Confidential stuff, shouldn't really leave it in a hotel room.'

'Right. No.' Catherine could almost smile; Lilac Lodge was an unlikely setting for commercial espionage.

'D'you want another?' Bryony inquired, though she was already sitting down on the seat opposite and laying her raincoat next to her, folded with the lining out.

'I'm fine, thanks.'

'Good journey?'

'Not too bad.'

'And you've got someone to feed the pig while you're away?'

That made everything slightly less abnormal and stilted, and Catherine laughed and let the tears come to her eyes.

'Something like that, yes. So,' she swallowed, 'how far have you got with things?'

'Well, I came down yesterday morning – which is why I really had to go into work today – and met this McCorquodale man, the undertaker. Mrs Aldridge put us in her office. He's booking the crem for Thursday morning.'

Catherine nodded. Colchester crematorium, the same place as their father. She remembered Madame Volpilière standing by her husband's grave. *Under the cherry tree.*

'I've fixed us another appointment with him for Monday. He's just here in Walton, in the High Street.'

'Great. Thanks.'

'He was asking about readings.' Bryony sipped her vodka, eyes narrowed to a squint. 'Whether there was anything special Mum liked. A poem or whatever. I was thinking about some Donne. She was very fond of Donne. Only it's a bit of a cliché, isn't it? And it'll have everyone wailing. *All other things to their destruction draw; only our love hath no decay* . . . Donne's so irredeemably miserable.' She grinned at the irony. 'Mum liked a laugh. How about a bit of Wendy Cope?'

Catherine stared down at her empty glass, turning it slowly round on its mat. 'I wondered about day lilies.' Orange ones, like Mum had chosen for Dad's coffin.

'Yes.' There was a rare crack in her sister's voice. 'Or I thought maybe jasmine.'

There was silence for a while, but there was intimacy in it, and solidarity.

Then Bryony spoke. 'The crem can provide someone to do the service if you want, or you can have your own person. Mr McCorquodale asked if we knew a priest. I told him we didn't.'

Catherine thought fleetingly of Père Amyot.

'No,' she said. 'But can't we just do it ourselves? It would be more personal.'

'Apparently they're not keen on that. I suppose they think you might struggle, when it came to it.' Another grin, darkly amused. 'I think they want someone there who's in control of their faculties, to make sure we get through the service on time, and don't hold up the queue. It gets pretty busy there, I gather.'

'Finally – there you are!'

They both looked up with a start to see Lexie, who had appeared round the end of the wooden partition.

'Honestly, Mum, it's been a nightmare tracking you down. I had to go to the nursing home first, and Mrs Aldridge put me on to the fragrant Mrs Lilac, who sent me round here. Why on earth don't you have your mobile switched on – or ever check your voicemail? Hi, Aunty Bryony.'

Half in and half out of her chair, Catherine was engulfed in a big, messy hug. She pulled her daughter close, smoothing her dishevelled hair with one hand, then held her out at arm's length to survey her face: eyes unashamedly red and swollen, nose blotchy the way it always looked when she'd been crying, since she was about three.

'Sweetheart,' she said, and her own eyes filled again.

'But, really. Why don't you have your mobile on? How's a girl supposed to get hold of her mum when she needs her?'

Catherine gave a watery grin. 'Sorry, love. I'm out of the habit, I suppose. There's not much network coverage in the mountains, so I hardly ever think of it. I should have charged it up to bring with me, but I honestly forgot. I was . . .' She kept her eyes carefully away from Bryony. 'It was all such a rush, coming away.'

Bryony went to the bar to fetch her niece a glass of white wine ('Just one, I'm in the car') while Lexie installed herself in the chair next to Catherine's.

'You know, there's not a hotel room to be had anywhere in Walton. Every guest house, every B and B, all chock full. Mrs Lilac was just letting her other room to an old couple from Stoke Newington. I'm having to stay in flipping Frinton-on-Sea – rang and booked it just now. "Don't arrive too late," the woman said. She sounded about ninety. Probably puts the cat out at half past nine and goes to bed.' She giggled. 'And I bet she reads *Fondant Magazine*.'

'Maybe you could share my room instead. It's not a twin, it's double. I can't see that Mrs Edwardstone would mind us sharing, if you don't mind.' They hadn't shared a double bed since Lexie was twelve: in a Travelodge near Liverpool when they'd had that girls-only trip to the Grand National, while Graeme took Tom to the railway museum in York.

'As long as you don't mind the snoring.'

'And kicking me in the night.' Catherine

narrowed her eyes in mock admonition. 'You've always been a jiffly sleeper.'

When Bryony returned with the drinks, and Lexie had rung the Frinton landlady to cancel her room, Catherine said, 'It's wonderful to see you, sweetheart. But what are you doing here? I thought you were working this weekend, somewhere down west.'

'Newquay – the North Cornwall Baking Festival.' She snorted. 'I was supposed to be there all weekend. But last night and this morning were quite enough. I've bunked off. You're over from France, of course I want to see you. Especially now,' her voice thickened, 'now that I won't be coming out to see you over there after all. What I mean is, you're over here, so of course I want to see you here, don't I?'

Lexie's ardour outran her coherence. Catherine took hold of her hand and squeezed.

'And besides, I'd like to be involved in things. Planning Gram's funeral, I mean. The music, and what gets said about her, and everything. If that's OK with you as well, Aunty Bryony?'

Bryony nodded wryly. 'The more the merrier.'

They were all able to laugh, then, and it was easy to laugh some more as they talked about Mum and her maverick musical tastes, which ranged from Mozart to Barry Manilow but with unaccountable detours into thrash metal and Gregorian chant.

'Perhaps we could walk in to a nice bit of

plainsong,' suggested Lexie, 'and she could go out to Metallica.'

Then, because she didn't have to drive after all, Lexie went to the bar for another white wine and another vodka and tonic for Bryony. Catherine succumbed and had a Benedictine, thinking of Madame Volpilière. It tasted of herbal shampoo.

'What did you mean, though,' she asked her daughter, 'about this weekend? Bunking off, you said. It is going to be all right, isn't it? You won't be in trouble?'

'Bit late for that, actually, Mum.' Lexie's chin was at a dangerous angle; Catherine's stomach sank, the way it always had in the face of that jutting chin.

'Why?'

'Well, I was thinking, I have to get away from here. First I wondered if I might phone my boss and ask for compassionate leave or something – or else bring forward the time off I'd got booked to come and see you. But then I thought, what's the worst they can do to me? So, they fire me, I thought, just means more time to help you with Gram's things and clearing the house and stuff. And then I thought, why not save them the bother?'

'Jeez,' said Bryony. 'You mean you've actually resigned?'

'Yup. Done the deed. Texted my boss at lunchtime and told him I'm off. They owe me heaps of holiday and I can take it in lieu of notice.'

'Oh, Lexie. You're sure you're not doing something hasty?' *You're upset about Gram*, she wanted to say, but it was too trite, too self-evident.

'Honestly, Mum, it's fine. In fact, I feel great about it. I was out of there the minute I got the chance in any case. I really was at the end of my tether with that job.'

Catherine sighed and gave her daughter's hand another squeeze. 'I know you were. And I'm sure something else will come along. You'll have more time, now, to look around properly.'

But Lexie twirled the stem of her wine glass. 'I don't know. It's like I was telling you, I just can't work up any enthusiasm for the other jobs that are available. All these specialist publications, in-house company mags, hobbyist stuff – it's just more stupid niche journalism. I really am fed up of it, Mum, all of it. I want to write something that matters.'

Oh, dear. 'The novel, you mean?'

'Really, you're writing a novel?'

If Catherine had thought to count on Bryony as an ally, the spark in her sister's voice quickly disabused her.

'Not writing it exactly,' said Lexie, 'or not very much yet. But I really want to spend some time on it. Give it a proper go, see if I can do it, you know.'

Bryony – the career woman, the workaholic – nodded traitorously. 'Great. Why not?'

There were so many reasons why not. Money

and security and having a direction, but also, more than anything, not wanting to see Lexie disappointed. Instead, Catherine said, 'What about finding some freelance work, using the contacts you've made? I think you mentioned once that might be a possibility. Then you could work on the novel in your spare time.'

'God, did I really ever say that? Individual feature articles about air freight and cake. What a life.' It looked for a moment as if she might cry, so despondent was she at the prospect, but suddenly she was giggling instead. Irrepressible, unputdownable Lexie. 'Air freight and cake. Cake and air freight. Fuck it all – if you'll excuse my French, Mum.'

'Quite right,' said Bryony stoutly.

'Oh, sweetheart,' said Catherine, laughing. 'I'm sure whatever you do will work out for the best. I can't see you not falling on your feet one way or another, somehow. And whatever you decide, you know I'll help in any way I can, don't you? Not just money, but anything at all.'

'I know, Mum. Thanks.' Lexie patted her arm, then pushed back her chair and stood up. 'Now, are we going to order some food, or what? It's gone nine o'clock and I'm starving.'

The remaining days leading up to the funeral passed like a series of unconnected dreamlike sequences, interspersed with bouts of crying whenever Catherine was alone. The loss of her

422

mother seemed to have fuelled a desire to recreate not her own childhood but Lexie's, and the two of them spent late nights cross-legged on Mrs Edwardstone's mauve chintz bedspread, playing whist and rummy and giggling at nothing. It could have been twenty years ago, were it not for the contraband whisky they shared from the bone china tooth mug. Following the meeting with the under-taker, Bryony went back to London but she kept her room at Lilac Lodge and was back again almost every evening, and on Lexie's mobile in between. On the Tuesday, Tom arrived and with him Mo, who was dark and diminutive and forthrightly Scots and with whom Catherine instantly fell in love. The elderly weekend couple returned to Stoke Newington and Tom and Mo moved into Mrs Edwardstone's third bedroom and the whole family was together.

It was curious, though, how an occasion like this, so bound up with the past, made the party seem incomplete without Graeme. He decided to come over the night before the funeral, on the Wednesday, to save himself an early start and, as he told Catherine, to take the rare opportunity of seeing Lexie and Tom together in one place. He managed to find a hotel room on the seafront; Bryony got away from work in good time for once, and the six of them went out together for an evening meal.

They hadn't booked, but they found a pub with a large empty table, and a rather more congenial atmosphere than the Golden Hind. The food was not of the battered, deep-frozen and microwaved variety but home-cooked to order; while they waited, Catherine and Graeme went back to the bar to fetch a second round of drinks. There was time to perch on a pair of bar stools for a while before they rejoined the others.

'How are you doing?' he asked, with a hand on her arm; she could tell he really wanted to know so she tried to answer him honestly.

'Oh, you now. All right. I'd already adjusted to the idea of being without her.' She must have done, up to a point, mustn't she, if she hadn't been back to see her in nearly a year? 'At least, I thought I had. But actually, it seems you never do, not really, not until it happens. It's still a shock.'

He nodded, eyes on her face.

'I don't mean it was a surprise, because it wasn't. I didn't feel surprised, in my mind. What caught me unawares wasn't the fact of her dying but the force of it. The physical impact, if that makes any sense.'

Like standing ankle deep in the surf and knowing full well a cold wave is going to hit you, but the knowledge doesn't lessen the brunt of its strike.

'I think so,' he said, frowning, then added, 'She was great. Back then, before . . .' But he ran out of words, and finished inadequately, 'She was great.'

'Thanks.' Catherine laid her hand on top of his,

where it still rested on her arm. 'And how about you? How are you doing?'

Without Suzannah. She also genuinely wanted to know, and she knew he knew it.

'Not too bad. I guess I saw that coming too, but it didn't make it any easier.'

Is this what remained, eight years after a marriage? This residual loyal watchfulness; this fearfulness for each other's hurts.

'There've also been a few little differences, to be frank, about money and her equity in the house. I'm buying out her share, and you know how it is, when solicitors get involved.'

'Messy,' she agreed. 'Poor you.' The uncoupling of their own material affairs, however painful, had been conducted with dignity on both sides, and she remained grateful for it.

His confession about Suzannah seemed to call for the sharing of some home truths of her own, so when he inquired about France and how things were going there, she didn't reply with a platitude.

'I'm honestly not sure. I think I might have backed myself into a corner with the business. Or rather, I was always in a corner and I'm only just realising it.'

'Really? How come?'

'Oh, it's complicated. But basically, it's to do with development control, because I live in the national park. They won't let me register to trade. I'm not sure of the way out of it – whether I'll be able to carry on at all.'

'Seriously?' He stared at her in dismay. 'But that's awful. Look, I don't know anything about France or national parks, but my French is OK. If you want me to look over anything for you, documents or whatever, see if I can help . . .'

He broke off, as he caught the expression on her face. When they were married she'd been in the habit of leaving things to Graeme, tax and insurance policies and investments and the like. But that was a long time ago.

'I've somehow got by for eight years without a man to read things over for me,' she pointed out. But she was grinning; they both were. 'Thanks, anyway.'

'You know, Cath . . .' They hadn't touched their drinks, but now Graeme selected his pint from next to Tom's on the bar and took a swig, foaming his upper lip. 'I wasn't intending to say anything, because you seemed to have something good going there and I didn't want to confuse matters. But if you're not certain any more . . .'

Wary, she picked up her own glass, took a sip of characterless pub wine. 'Confuse matters how?'

He laid his pint down again and sat back on his stool. 'You know my squash partner, Phil? I'm not sure if you remember him.'

She did remember; she nodded.

'Well, his wife has opened a shop.'

'Carol?'

'No, they split up. This is a new wife, Tasha. Anyway, she's a potter, makes arty pots. Not just artefacts, actually bowls and mugs and things you can use, but very "designer", if you know what I mean. I've seen her stuff and it's rather good.'

Tasha. *Younger, is she?* But that would be a cheap shot.

'The thing is, the floor space is larger than she really needs for her own stock, and she's looking for a partner or a sub-tenant, someone to go in with her on the lease and share the premises. And ideally, it wouldn't be another potter, Tasha says; she'd rather find someone who works in a different medium. But not a painter. She's thinking of craft stuff, but useful as well as decorative. To fit in with a homewares theme. She actually mentioned fabrics. Oh, and the shop's in Aylesbury, by the way.'

Aylesbury? Catherine found it impossible to react to what he was telling her. It sounded ideal – in another life. She couldn't seem to relate it to herself.

'But I live in France,' was all she could find to say.

He laughed aloud. 'I know you do. That's why I wasn't going to mention it. But then, just now, you seemed to be saying it was all up in the air, that you might not be staying there after all.'

Not staying? Had she said that? And if she hadn't said it, was it what she was thinking? Was it really a possibility, that she might not go back?

When she tried to imagine her life there – now, here, sitting on the bar stool and staring at Graeme

427

– it proved elusive. The terrace, her beehives, the chestnut woods: they all seemed very far away. But so did Aylesbury, and Tasha the designer potter. She was nowhere; she was floating, unanchored, between two existences, and for a moment she felt pure panic.

'It's OK.' Graeme's smile now hovered somewhere between amusement and concern. 'I just thought – selfishly I suppose – that it would be nice to have you back. But it was only an idea.'

'Yes. I know, of course. Thank you for thinking of it.'

'And even if you did come back and do this, or something like it, it wouldn't mean you'd have to sell up in France, would it?'

'N-no.' Not now, it was true. Not with Mum's house to be sold. There would be enough money from her share for a flat or a small house in England.

'You could still keep your place in the Cévennes, and use it for holidays. For you and the kids.'

Somewhere for Lexie to write her book, perhaps. But Les Fenils, just a holiday home? Powerfully, she was overtaken by the memory of Monsieur Bouschet: the tone of his voice when he spoke of tourism, his lament for a community without a heart.

'I don't think I could do that.' She gazed down at her wine. 'I think I'd have to choose.'

'Well, look, it's something to think about, that's all. I've got Phil and Tasha's number if you do decide to look into it.'

'Where have those drinks got to?' Lexie's voice came from behind her, making Catherine spin round. 'There are people starting to sicken from thirst back there, you know.'

Graeme clapped his daughter on the shoulder. 'Right, you'd better give us a hand with them, then.'

'What were you two thick as thieves about, anyhow?' Lexie asked Catherine as they wound their way back to the table.

'I'm not exactly sure.' She shook her head and smiled. 'But I think your dad just offered me a job.'

There was no time for Lexie to do more than raise an inquiring eyebrow before they were sitting down again, and conversation was halted by the appearance of the waitress bearing plates. The fish pie was more than passable, and Catherine discovered she was properly hungry for the first time in days.

Mo, sitting to her left, had chosen the same thing and jabbed appreciatively at the air above it with her fork. 'Goo',' she said, with a mouth full of mashed potato. Then she swallowed and passed judgement more intelligibly. 'It's nearly as good as my grandma's, and she makes the best fish pie in Invergordon.'

'Don't take any notice of her,' said Tom from the other side of his girlfriend. 'This bonny wee Highlander thing is all an act. One of her grandmas, I know for a fact, lives in a flat in Morningside. The other's from Birmingham.'

'Oh, shut up. Grandma Cargill did live in Invergordon. She only moved to Edinburgh when Gramps died.' Then she realised what she'd said; pink crept up towards her curly dark fringe. 'Sorry. Tact – never my strongest suit.'

Catherine restrained the urge to hug her. 'Where did you and Tom disappear off to this afternoon?' she asked her, by way of deflection.

'Oh, just around the town. We had a walk on the clifftops to take a look at the Martello tower, and then had a mooch round the shops.'

'Shop, she means,' said Tom, 'in the singular. She found a second-hand bookshop, and that was it for the day.'

For this, he received a toss of the dark curls.

'Find anything good?' asked Lexie from across the table.

'One or two.'

'Or twelve or fifteen,' said Tom. 'Luckily, we have a paperbacks only rule when we're on our travels. And she has to carry them all herself – no sneaking any into my rucksack when I'm not looking. Trouble is, there's a knock-on. I usually end up lugging the tent and camping stove and both sleeping bags. The other weekend I got back, unpacked and found I'd been carrying a pair of electric hair straighteners.'

Mo, trying to look injured, succeeded only in dissolving into giggles. 'Well, better that than what I'd look like in the morning without. You should try having my hair.' The offending ringlets danced.

'In a *tent*?' Lexie's scepticism was spiced with grudging admiration.

'Battery-operated,' explained Mo.

'Do you two go camping a lot, then?' Catherine wanted to know.

'Oh, yes, all the time.' Mo leaned forward eagerly. 'Ever since the weather became decent, at the start of the summer. We go somewhere almost every weekend. Just pack the tent and hop on a train and see where we end up.'

'Mo loves camping, but she's got something against campsites. So where we end up is usually in a bog, or at the top of a mountain. Sometimes both.'

'Ach, who needs showers and washbasins when there are mountain streams?'

'And battery-powered hair straighteners, obviously,' put in Lexie.

Graeme grinned at his son. 'And a man to carry them for you.'

'Actually, we've got the tent here with us now,' said Tom. 'It was our back-up in case we couldn't find a hotel. But also, we're not due back in the lab till Monday, and we thought about having a night up on the Suffolk coast. Mo wants to go to Minsmere and see the avocets.'

Mo turned to Catherine. 'Tom tells me you have a dipper.'

She laughed. 'Well, it's not my personal dipper, you understand. In fact, I rather tend to think of it as Tom's. But, yes, there are dippers. And wild boar.'

'Not quite so camper-friendly, those,' was Bryony's observation.

But Mo was wide-eyed with delight. 'Really? How wonderful! Oh, I'd love to see wild boar. Tom, we must go. We have to go and stay with Catherine, as soon as we have some more time off. Shall we?' Then to Catherine. 'May we, please?'

Catherine let her smile speak for her.

'Why don't we fix it now?' said Tom. 'Lexie, aren't you meant to be going soon too? Why don't we try to coincide, make a family trip of it?'

His sister nodded, but brandished a provisory fork. 'Just so long as I'm not required to sleep in a tent.'

Dates began to be discussed, and Catherine was already planning menus and excursions in her head when she caught Graeme looking at her. *Holidays. For you and the kids.*

'When are you likely to be going back, Mum?' Tom was asking her. 'It would be nice to come soon, before the weather gets too cold.'

'It rains in September,' said Catherine slowly. 'September and October, there's a lot of rain.'

They were all looking at her. 'So, when?' insisted Lexie. 'Let's make it firm. When are you going back?'

Tentatively, trying out the words, Catherine said, 'I don't know.'

There was no harm, was there, here amongst her family, in seeing how it sounded? 'I'm really not sure when I'll be going back. Or even if I'm going back at all.'

Outside, it was raining again. This was English rain, distinct from any of the many, varied rains that swelled the skies of Mont Lozère; itself colourless, it haloed the street lights in fuzzy amber and glazed the pavement with a reflected orange sheen. Or maybe it was the street lights which were English and not the rain. The scatter of lamps in the centre of St Julien were furnished with plain, domestic bulbs – and besides, it was months since she had been out at night beyond the unlit environs of La Grelaudière.

They said goodbye to Graeme and, voting down Bryony's suggestion of a cab, walked together the quarter-mile back to Lilac Lodge. Catherine was glad of the cool, damp air and the chance to stretch her limbs, though the short walk would scarcely have counted as such to her French neighbours. Bryony and the youngsters opted to sit up in the small guest lounge and watch the late film but Catherine, suddenly exhausted by the evening's conversation, decided to turn in.

When she had cleaned her teeth, though, and changed into Tom's old pyjamas, she felt unready for sleep. Tomorrow's funeral was casting its shadow – and what was the point in going to bed now anyway, when Lexie was sure to wake her when she crept in later? Lying down on top of the bedspread, she tried for a few pages and then rejected her French library book, followed by Lexie's paperback thriller. But maybe Mum had some books. She may not have been able to read for two years, maybe more, but Catherine recollected books still standing on the shelf above her bed.

Mum's things, packed up discreetly by Mrs Aldridge before their arrival at the nursing home to save them that melancholy task, were in her old tartan suitcase and an assortment of cardboard boxes. There were just five boxes, along with the suitcase; they were hardly in the way at all, stacked there in the corner of the room. So little space taken up – so little to show for the end of a person, the four last years of a life.

They had all been putting off opening the boxes until now. The worst, because the most intimate, would no doubt be the suitcase, containing the nightdress she had changed out of on the morning of her death, her hairbrush and other small personal items. Mrs Aldridge would have laundered any clothes that had been worn, and folded them; she was a thoughtful woman, and a stickler for detail. Books – which box were the books most likely to be in? Catherine chose a flat one at the bottom of the pile which she seemed to remember, when they carried them in from the hire car, having been heavy. She pulled it out on to a clear space on the carpet. She slid her fingers under the cardboard flaps, which were not taped but simply tucked one inside another, and lifted them apart.

Underneath lay another layer of what appeared to be wrapping – some heavy fabric wrapping – and then familiarity registered with a jolt. It was hers – her own work. The tapestry she had sent Mum for Christmas.

Had Mum ever really looked at it, the boulder-strewn mountainside, the bubble of water over rock, and if so, had she been able to make the leap of connection to her absent daughter? Had she thought of Catherine at all?

Examining it now, she could recall sitting over it and sewing, but none of the energy of creation. The vision she'd had for the scene was lost; the canvas lay across her lap, flat and lifeless under the pale wall lighting, reduced to a patchwork of unconnected stitches. She couldn't even place, as she stared down, the precise location she'd been trying to depict. It must be somewhere up on Mont Lozère, certainly; somewhere beyond Patrick's house on the other side of the gully, up past where the trees ended and the grasslands began, where the Vaillants and the Mériels grazed their sheep. But where, exactly? And where were the sheep? Why was the pasture in the tapestry deserted, when its colours were of summer grass?

That landscape – the real one, not the silk image – seemed not merely far away from her but completely beyond reach, even in imagination; less like a place forgotten and more like somewhere she had never been or which had never existed. This was where she was now, this guesthouse bedroom, sitting in her son's pyjamas and waiting for her mother's funeral. Tonight it had felt seductively homely, with the whole family together in the pub. But at the same time she knew it couldn't last. Tom and Mo would be off back to Scotland and Bryony to London; Lexie had her own future to sort out. There was Graeme, and he had been kind – but Graeme was the past.

The other tapestry – the one she had brought with her, the one of Les Fenils – was untouched since her arrival. Still tightly rolled, it lay by the skirting at her side of the bed, half hidden behind her rucksack. Tomorrow, perhaps, when the funeral was over, she should do some work on it. There must be a craft shop in Walton or Frinton where she could buy silks to supplement the few skeins she'd tucked inside the tapestry. Or perhaps she might have a walk round Colchester, after their funeral lunch, and find a shop there. Mo would probably come with her, if she asked her; there was always the chance of a bookshop.

This time there was no need to unfurl the tapestry to see it clearly in her mind. It was there in every detail when she closed her eyes. But could she do justice to the work without being there in the sunshine by her kitchen window? Would the light come alive for her? Would the colours be true? Yet how could she leave it like that, rolled up in a corner, abandoned and incomplete? *Unfinished* – like her life there.

That's when she knew that, whatever she might

decide in the long term, she had to go back. There were too many loose ends just to be left hanging. There was Madame Méjan's divan, for one thing, covered with a sheet in her woodshed. There was the renovated banner of St Julien the Hospitaller, almost ready for return to the safekeeping of Père Amyot. There were her winter leek and cauliflower seedlings, and the fruit in the orchard that would soon be ripe. There was Marie-Josèphe Bouschet, who would be wondering how she was getting on, and Madame Volpilière who'd be missing her company tomorrow on market day. There was the Parc National. There were her bees.

And there was Patrick Castagnol.

CHAPTER 26

IN THE ATTIC

The funeral was horrible. Funerals, she had always been told, were meant to help the bereaved; to bring – she shuddered at the word – closure. If so, thought Catherine grimly, it was the same kind of closure brought by amputation of a diseased limb without the benefit of anaesthetic. The planning of the funeral had felt, at times, like an act of love. She and Bryony and Lexie and Tom had laughed and cried over the things Mum would have wanted; it had brought them close, to her and to one another. But the service itself was not, for her, remotely beautiful or uplifting or cathartic. The pain of loss was racking and raw; she got through it by gripping tight to Lexie's hand to her left and Tom's to her right, and concentrating hard on anything but Mum.

The lunch, afterwards, was another ordeal. The modern hotel, on the outskirts of Colchester, provided an anonymous room and anonymous sandwiches and Catherine stood beside Bryony and heard over and over what a wonderful person her mother had been, from friends and neighbours

438

who hadn't visited her in four years. Mr McCorquodale attended to make sure things ran smoothly, and Mrs Aldridge came and stayed to the end. There were tears in her eyes as she said goodbye over the muzak in the foyer.

'What a kind woman she is,' said Catherine to Lexie, when she was gone. 'Really genuine.'

'Yes.' Lexie nodded slowly. 'Gram was lucky.'

'Y-yes,' said Catherine, and tried to believe it was true.

The next morning, Bryony caught the 8:04 train to the office. On Saturday Tom and Mo set out for Suffolk with their tent and binoculars, and on Sunday afternoon Lexie hugged her mum with a final tearful squeeze and headed back to Stockwell and her flat.

'I've got stuff that needs doing,' she said for the fifth time as she wiped her nose by the station ticket barrier. 'There's no choice. I've still got my desk to clear at *Fondant Magazine*.'

'I know, love.'

'And I think I may have left a salmon steak in the fridge. I'll need breathing apparatus to dispose of it. But I'll be back soon, I promise. I want to come and help you with the house.'

The tenants had been given two months' notice, but they found a new place within the fortnight and Catherine agreed to remit the final month's rent before Bryony could object. They put the house straight on the market. It was Catherine who met the estate agent with the keys one Tuesday morning. It was the first of September, but the sun, which had scarcely been in evidence since her arrival in England, had decided to fight a rear-guard action and shone sharp and unhazed as if it were June. Probably she should have accompanied the agent round the rooms, pointing out conveniences and marketable features, but she lacked the heart. Since the tenants had moved out, the kitchen was Mum's kitchen again, and the sitting room was their sitting room, the one where they had watched *Blue Peter* and sat on the floor as a family to play Monopoly on winter Sunday afternoons; her bedroom was again her bedroom, and she had no appetite for extolling its south-west aspect and the size of its built-in cupboards. Leaving Mr Burgess of Notley and Burgess alone with his clipboard, she opened the back door and wandered out into the garden.

The tenants had been dutiful, but no more. They had kept the lawn cut using Dad's old motor mower from the shed, and some of the shrubs had been pruned back, if not this spring then probably last autumn. The borders, though, which had once been Mum's endeavour and delight, were an overgrown riot of late summer flowers and waist-high nettles. The old swing, ropes green with algae, hung idle from the ash tree.

The sensation of loss rose up from nowhere to engulf her, compressing her lungs and knocking her off balance with the power of its assault. She had to put out a hand and take hold of an ash branch to steady herself, and to concentrate on breathing, in and out. *Mum*, she said, not even certain whether she spoke aloud or not. The ache was as physical as hunger. She ached for Mum, and for family. It was almost overwhelming, the sudden sense of impotent, nostalgic craving: for childhood – her own, and Tom and Lexie's – and time beyond recapture. And not just time either, but place as well. But as she clutched the branch and strove for equilibrium, the scene on which her longing fixed was not this old familiar garden, nor the shady lawn at Long Hartslow, but a fresher vision, a wilder landscape. She yearned quite tangibly for Les Fenils.

With the house empty, there was no reason to remain in Walton-on-the-Naze. For a day or two, while she arranged the valuation and for dealers to come and view the furniture, she retained the room at Lilac Lodge, grateful for Mrs Edwardstone's occasional conversation, a refuge from being quite alone. But alone is what she had grown used to being for more than eight years now, and as the days interposed themselves between herself and the funeral, more and more she desired the space and leisure of her own company. Weary of pub food and seafront take-aways, she wanted to cook her own meals.

Her own bedroom was the smallest, but the natural place to sleep. It was no longer her bed; the old singles she and Bryony had slept in as children had been replaced with three-quarter size beds when they rented out the house. They'd had a firm in to redecorate, too, painting over the frieze of flower stencils she'd created at fourteen during an ill-advised Laura Ashley phase, and which Mum had never got rid of. But it was still her room, still with the floorboard by the door which creaked when you went to the loo in the night, and the window which framed a corner of the poplars next door when you lay in bed. There were still rooks in the top branches.

Strangely, it was here in her old room that Catherine thought of Patrick. Perhaps there had been too much else crowding him out, until now. The experience of her night with him, even at the time peculiarly distant, had been pushed back, submerged beneath her grief for her mother. Even now, it wasn't that she thought about him in any conscious way; rather, that images from that night surged back at unexpected moments, catching her by surprise, sharp and vivid and sweet. Mostly, she pushed them quickly back down again. But once or twice, lying in the half-darkness with the curtains open, she allowed herself to feel, and the feeling that came was a deep yearning, as strong as the yearning she had felt in the garden the day the agent came. And not merely as strong as that, but actually indistinguishable from it. Her sense of Patrick, the pull he exerted, was the same as the pull of the rocks and the gully and the chestnut woods. Patrick and the place: it was all one.

When she went back . . . if she went back . . .

it would be an act of blind faith, like taking a hairpin bend at night. The moment of plunging uncertainty, with the headlights pointing in one direction and the road veering vertiginously in the other; the hesitation, then the spin of the wheel into total darkness.

The one thing Catherine had not been able to face was clearing out the attic. This she left until a weekend, two or three weeks after the funeral, when Bryony could be there. In the end, Lexie came too, and the three women embarked on the task together.

'*How* many books?' Lexie sat back on her heels, almost bumping her head on the slanting rafter. She had just opened another cardboard box – something like the tenth – and was waggling at them a yellowing paperback. 'She must have about half a ton of them up here. It's a miracle the floor hasn't given way.'

The boards which rested between the joists were indeed haphazardly arranged, and the boxes, balanced across them, were sagging with age and the weight of their contents.

'Moving them is going to be interesting, certainly,' agreed Catherine.

'Oh, Jeez.' Bryony shuffled over on her knees and peered in distaste at the contents of the latest box. 'We should have thrown them out years ago. What was the point of moving them all up here when Mum left? They should have gone straight to the tip.'

'Or Oxfam,' said Catherine. They had a skip arriving on Monday, and she was perfectly prepared to be ruthless about some things – the sheer scale of it left them no choice – but books were books, and hard to throw away.

'I don't know, Mum.' Lexie fanned open the pages of the paperback in her hands, wrinkling her nose. 'They smell a bit musty to me. And the pages are all spotted. D'you reckon they'll want them?'

'Jumble sale, then. There must be someone who'd like to read them.' Mum had such wonderful bookshelves, eclectic and extravagant.

They were both looking at her, though, Bryony with scepticism, Lexie with pity.

'I know,' said Lexie. 'Mo. Maybe she'd like some of them. Just a boxful. We could have a look through and sort some out for her.'

Catherine smiled her gratitude. 'I might take a few too.'

Though how she'd get them to France on Ryan Air was another matter. That was if . . .

'Let's shift them to the end there for carrying down, anyway,' said Lexie. 'We can't sort through them up here.' She tugged at the side of the box closest to her, which didn't shift but formed an ominous bulge.

'Carefully,' said Bryony.

One by one, lifting them with both arms underneath, they moved the boxes of books, restacking them in the pool of light beneath the single bulb near the hatch.

From back at the gloomy end of the attic, Lexie gave a squeal. 'Oh, fabulous! Look at these.'

Her mother and aunt crawled along the boards to join her. The box she had opened was spilling folds of satiny fabric. Catherine took hold of a handful and lifted. Old clothes – but she never remembered Mum in these. Shot silk in two shades of grey, a tailored cocktail dress with tight, cap sleeves. An ankle-skimming party frock in rich, deep burgundy.

Lexie was stroking the material and purring. 'Just gorgeous. Pure retro. Weren't the fifties great? Do you think she had shoes to match, and little clutch handbags?'

'Good grief, can you imagine?' said Bryony. 'I had no idea she had this stuff.'

'I thought I knew all her dresses. These surely weren't in her wardrobe, were they, when we were kids? Or we'd have been stealing them for dressing up.'

'Course you would,' said Lexie. 'And so would I, if I'd known Gram had them up here. In fact, I fancy them for dressing up now.' She giggled and held the grey silk up against her. Then she pulled a face. 'She was a bit flipping skinny then, though, wasn't she?'

Catherine gazed at her daughter in the shadow, seeing her mother instead, and feeling the telescoping of time. 'It must have been before we were born,' she said.

'Maybe I could let it out.' Lexie looked wistful,

then grinned. 'By which, of course, I mean maybe you could let it out for me, Mum. It would be nice to have something of Gram's.'

'Of course it would.' Catherine thought of Marie-Josèphe in her husband's grey wool sweater. 'We should all take something to keep.'

'And Mo, too,' said Lexie. 'I know she didn't meet Gram, but I really think she'd like something. She'd look fabulous in this burgundy, with her dark hair.'

Nodding, Catherine fingered the dress. 'It would need taking up, though. Mo is tiny.'

'When you two are quite finished with the fashion retrospective,' said Bryony, 'perhaps we can shift this clutter to the hatch. At least it'll be lighter than bloody books.' But she paused to admire a stole, in creamy imitation mink, before smoothing it lovingly with her palm and folding it back into the box.

Lexie climbed down the stepladder and Catherine and Bryony passed her the boxes one at a time, ready for taking downstairs. The piles on the landing were slowly mounting and the attic was emptying correspondingly.

'Right,' said Lexie's head from the square of the hatch. 'Time for a cup of tea. I'm parched. Feels like my throat is solid dust.'

When she was gone, Catherine sat back on her heels and brushed the hair from her eyes. It was hot up here under the bituminous black felt.

'It's going to more than fill the skip,' said Bryony.

446

'Hmm. Perhaps we can put some of it into storage.'

Cross-legged, Bryony was rubbing the tops of her feet, which were reddened where she'd been kneeling on them. 'But it's just rubbish, most of it.'

'Even so.' It was something she'd been thinking, but she hadn't found the moment to broach the subject. 'I'm not sure we should sell all the furniture.'

Bryony stared at her. 'But we've had it valued.'

'I know, yes. And of course we should sell the bulk of it, we can't store a whole houseful of furniture. But perhaps a few of the better things. The dining table and chairs, I thought, and the antique chest from the landing, and the kitchen dresser. Things that are special or hard to replace.' Mum's bedside dressing-table with the three-way mirror, which they used to pull round to the perpendicular when they were kids and see repeated images of themselves, shrinking away to infinity.

'What for?'

'Well, you never know. None of us needs it right now, I agree. But Lexie and Tom – they won't be in rented places for ever, will they?'

Bryony grinned. 'Lexie might, if she wants to be a novelist.'

'OK.' Catherine threw back a smile. 'But Tom, then. He and Mo seem quite serious. They might want their own place before too long, and it seems a pity to have to start from scratch when they could have a few of Mum's things to get them going. And also . . . well, actually, I might want some of it myself.'

'Have you got room? I thought you even sold some of the furniture from Long Hartslow when you moved?'

'I did. No, there wouldn't be room for much else at Les Fenils. But I'm not quite sure what I'm going to be doing.'

'How do you mean?'

She swallowed. 'Graeme mentioned a job, in Aylesbury. A shop, where I could sell my tapestry work, and home furnishings. Like I'm doing in France, but from permanent premises.'

There was no response, so she plunged on. 'It doesn't mean I'd have to sell up in France. I could keep Les Fenils for holidays, is what Graeme suggested. But I'd need a flat in England, and I'd need to furnish it.'

Bryony, still staring, looked very much as if she might say something, but didn't.

'Not that I've made up my mind yet. Not at all. It's all just possibilities at this stage, you know. But I suppose I'd like to keep my options open. It'd be a pity to sell everything and then regret it.'

'Right.' Bryony sounded distinctly doubtful.

'I would pay the storage costs, of course. And if I do end up taking anything, or Tom or Lexie, then of course we'd buy it from you, your half of it, I mean—.'

'Shut up, Cath. I may be a tight-ass lawyer, but I don't begrudge you a few old chairs.' She uncrossed her legs and swung on to her knees. 'Now come on, less talk and more action. We've still got more boxes to go through.'

The final two boxes, right in the far corner of the attic, contained photographs. They dragged them closer to the light to take a look. One of them contained a wedding album, bound in silvery white and with feathery tissue paper between the pages. Mum and Dad smiled out, looking shockingly young and awkwardly overdressed and quite unmindfully happy.

'That's the one they had framed in the sitting room,' said Catherine, touching the page. But the rest she had never seen before and it was strange to see the familiar image from other angles and perspectives, with less perfect smiles and more natural slants of the chin, as if the day had somehow come alive.

'She was beautiful.' Bryony sounded croaky.

'You have it,' said Catherine.

The second box contained their school photographs: the annual formal portraits in immaculate uniforms and with hair freshly combed, alone and then together, with Catherine's arm round Bryony's shoulder. Beneath the cardboard frames were holidays snaps, going back year by year, filed in the yellow Kodak envelopes in which they'd arrived from the developer. Catherine opened one at random and was met by a view of mountains. A vivid foreground of rosebay willowherb and, behind, ridge after ridge of hazy blue, scaling away towards an indistinct horizon. These were her mountains; this was unmistakably the Cévennes.

As she began to go through the pictures, jigsawing together the landscape around Le Vigan, she became aware of Bryony looking over her shoulder.

'Oh, look.' Catherine held one up. 'Remember this wood? We had a picnic there and you wouldn't sit down because there were ants.'

'The size of small armoured tanks, as I recall.'

'And this one, with the waterfall. Mum's written on the back. St-Laurent-le-Minier. I wanted to paddle and she said it was too steep.'

'She had a point. You'd have broken your neck.'

'I don't remember this one. Looks like somewhere higher up. Maybe on Mont Aigoual.'

Presently, her sister stopped commenting, and the two of them studied the photographs in silence, each keeping to her own memories. When Bryony broke the silence, therefore, it was all the more of a shock.

'I googled Patrick Castagnol.'

'What?'

'Patrick. I googled him – checked him out.'

'Why?'

Patrick. It was the first time his name had been spoken between them since Bryony left France. Even on the telephone, back in the summer, specific mention had been avoided.

'I suppose I was curious. More than that, I needed to know. About Crédit Belge and his career in London. What he did here and whether anyone had run across him.'

Typical of Bryony; the need to have him pinned down, pegged, pigeon-holed – edged, perhaps, with just a little spice of revenge, after all his elaborate secrecy. But she didn't seem vengeful. She seemed subdued; if anything, slightly self-conscious.

'A first, I couldn't find him. I almost began to wonder whether he'd made it all up. Another masquerade, another fantasy. There was nothing on the internet at all.'

Catherine frowned down at a photo of a hillside, bisected by a drystone wall. 'Oh?'

'So then I started asking questions – very discreetly, of course – at work. And nobody knew anything. But I have a friend in the Serious Fraud Office, Mitchell, and I took him for a drink and pumped him for information.'

'Fraud?' Catherine's stomach plummeted. 'Patrick?'

To her surprise, Bryony laughed; dry, ironic laughter.

'Oh, no. Not Patrick. Quite the opposite, in fact.'

'What do you mean?' All this talk about googling and London and the SFO, it seemed so remote from her, from France and from the Patrick she knew – or thought she knew. But she was tight with impatience, nevertheless, to hear what Bryony had to say.

'It seems he didn't just retire or resign when he

left the City. He was bundled out and back to France in a hurry, and his tracks rubbed out. He was sent home whence he came for his own protection, believe it or not. Patrick was a whistle-blower.'

'How? What happened? Tell me.'

'Mitch was vague about the details. Some insider trading scandal, but it was big stuff. Major players, careers destroyed, millions lost. You remember the whole drama over Schoerings Bank? Well, it was connected with that, only some of it was hushed up.'

'And Patrick?'

'He found out what was happening, at Schoerings and another couple of places, partners of Crédit Belge. He went to the authorities. They could have protected him, of course, made sure he kept his job, but there were some nasty people involved, Mitch said. Personal threats were made. So Patrick preferred to get out, somewhere right away. And where further from everything and everyone than up a mountain in Lozère?'

It did ring true; somehow, it fitted. But it still felt oddly remote, a story unconnected with herself. 'Why are you telling me this?'

Bryony pursed her lips, as she always did when trying to be patient. 'Isn't it obvious? It explains everything. It explains why he lied to us – or at least why he concealed the truth. There he is, supposed to be safely away from all contact with England, with London. First you turn up on his

452

doorstep, and then me, a bloody City solicitor, of all things, from slap in the middle of his old stamping ground.'

She leaned forward, clutched Catherine's arm. 'I mean, good grief, Cath, there were actually partners from my firm involved in the Schoerings mess, representing some of the directors who were charged. Who can blame Patrick if he didn't fancy any awkward questions, if he just decided to avoid the issue? The poor bugger thought he was well out of it, and it followed him right to his own front door.'

'I suppose,' began Catherine, and then halted. It might explain Bryony, his secrecy with Bryony, but why with her? Was simply being English enough to justify the barriers he had raised?

That night in June, on the pulsing terrace, Bryony's denunciation of his guilt had been too dramatic, too black and white – and now the exculpation was just too tidy. Patrick was Patrick, whatever the details of his English past. He was cautious and self-protective and satirical and aloof, and this tale of whistle-blowing and escape, for all she could see, made little difference to any of that. He was what he was.

'You can see exactly how it would happen,' continued Bryony. 'He'd be careful at first, not mention anything, just in case, just instinctively. Because it wouldn't matter, would it, when he first met someone, whether he told the truth or not? And then, after a while, when maybe it ought to matter, it was too late. He'd started off on a path of not saying, and he had to keep it up.'

Why was she saying all this? Why did it still matter to her what Patrick's motives were? Why did she still care?

'So you can't blame him so much for any of it, can you?'

Catherine surveyed her sister. Bryony had not been there between herself and Patrick the night before she flew back for the funeral – not in the kitchen when he came round the table to take her in his arms, nor later in the bedroom. Certainly not for herself and, conviction told her, not for Patrick, either. But since she had been in England, Patrick had been a recurrent, awkward presence between the two of them, between Bryony and herself. Perhaps it was time to clear the air.

'Bryony—'

'Look, Cath—'

They spoke at once, both stopped at once. It was Bryony who pressed ahead.

'You're the one he cares about, you know. You've always been the one.'

A wedge of something solid blocked Catherine's lungs. The blood swished loud in her ears.

'Did he tell you that?'

'No.'

Bryony still had her hand on Catherine's arm. She was staring down at her fingers, head bent. 'He didn't have to. I worked it out.' Then she laughed, a bitter, rueful, sardonic Bryony laugh. 'In the end.'

And then she did something she'd almost never done, even when they were girls, at home. She looked straight up at her sister and said, 'I'm sorry, Cath.'

'Tea,' came Lexie's voice, drifting up through the hatch from the landing below. 'Are you two coming down or am I coming up?'

PART III

CHAPTER 27

RETURN

When Catherine came back, the autumn transhumance was over. The herds that had grazed the breezy heights of Mont Lozère throughout the summer months were safely penned in lowland paddock, barn and byre, feeding on tired, October grass and the first of the winter's hay.

The rains had begun. From the airport at Rodez, having picked up her car at alarming expense from the small passenger car park, she took not the main road via Mende but the more direct, cross-country route: the route she had taken with Patrick Castagnol on their way back from the silk museum in St-Hippolyte-du-Fort. She crossed the first corniche in tolerable visibility; on the treeless tops, the rain streaked diagonally in a stiff breeze but the wipers, set to their fastest speed, kept the windscreen clear enough to reveal good stretches of the road ahead. It was when she was in the next valley, the one before St Julien, that the wind dropped and the cloud descended, so that as she began to climb again, zigzagging up the wooded hillside, the rain no longer simply fell from above but seemed to saturate the air from every direction at once. It closed in from the sides and in front, blotting out trees and crash barrier and tarmac until there was nothing but impenetrable grey. Catherine flicked on the head-lamps; all this achieved was to light up two furrows of blind, yellow rain, so she switched them off again.

At her enforced snail's pace, the bends came more infrequently but still contrived to take her by surprise; distances were distorted, and more than once she thought she must be at the final right-hand turn, the one that straightened out towards the ridge, only to find, a hundred yards later, that the road doubled back the other way. By the time she finally reached the col, it made sense to pull over and wait to see if the weather would clear. The road on the downhill side, winding towards the Besson farm, was steeper and narrower than on the uphill, its drops more precip-itate. It would be nice to be able to see where she was going.

This must be more or less exactly the spot, she realised as she drew up on the loose stones at the side of the road, where Patrick had stopped that day in the spring; where, with the sunset behind them, they had looked down together on the Valvert. She remembered vaguely having babbled about mulberry trees. This afternoon, she could have been looking at any valley – or indeed at sky, or sea. She knew that somewhere below lay the town of St Julien, with its old, stone market square, and the space at the end towards the bridge which marked her own pitch. The church belfry must be there, and the little walled cemetery on the top of the hill. She knew it from context, the way you know the airport runway lies beneath you on a descent through cloud; but she knew it from memory, too, close and familiar in every detail.

Then, as she stared into the enveloping blank, she became aware of movement. The grey was shifting, beginning to swirl and lift; its flat monochrome acquired texture and perspective, separating into individual patches of mist, the rain itself materialising from the blur into hard, descending lines. And there was light: light behind the cloud above the crags behind her. The closest pine trees loomed into view beside the car, and beyond them a clump of dripping chestnuts. And then, as she peered down into the gloom, a patch of the valley floor was suddenly revealed – one field and a farmhouse – sunlit in miniature, further away than she had imagined.

She drove on. Soon she was passing Madame Besson's place and, soon after, entering the main street of St Julien. The shutters were down on Madame Peysasse's shop – Monday, half day closing – but she had, in any case, no desire to stop. There was a cellophaned sandwich from the aircraft in her bag, and an apple from England, and besides, she was impatient to be back at Les Fenils.

The road from St Julien onwards she could have driven in the densest fog. Her hands on the wheel anticipated every corner, and knew just what angle to take on every bend. Here was the straight stretch where she might get up into third gear, before sliding down to second again for the sharp left-hander. Here was the stream which crossed beneath the road and overflowed across it after heavy rain; here the turn where the ruined houses lay off to the right, invisible today in the gloom.

La Grelaudière was just as she had left it, only damper. Smoke wreathed all four chimneys, massing low beneath the weight of rain, and choking the air so that she breathed the scent of wet charcoal even through her closed car windows. There was a light in Marie-Josèphe's kitchen window, although it was barely five o'clock. Catherine had spoken to her on the phone, to tell her she was coming back; she ought to call in and say hello, but not now. Tomorrow would do.

Leaving the hamlet behind and rounding the next bend, she applied the brakes so sharply that she almost skidded on the loose gravel. In the middle of the road stood a figure in a shapeless coat, and at his heels two rain-soaked dogs. Hatless, his hair was plastered down about his thin face. Catherine wound down the window and leaned out, blinking, into the wet.

'Guillaume.'

'Madame Park-e-ston.'

'Can I give you a lift home?' she asked, avoiding the gaze of the larger dog, which was eyeing her with bristling suspicion.

Guillaume did not answer, but swayed closer, clutching at the frame of the car window and clearing his throat.

'I'm sorry,' he said with a slow frown. 'About your mother.'

A few minutes later she was pulling on to the terrace at Les Fenils. In this weather, the granite walls were blacker even than usual, giving the house a sombre aspect. The oak door, when she turned the key and pulled at the iron handle, was already swollen with damp – or perhaps it was gummed fast from being out of use – so that she had to jerk with all her force to free it from sill and frame. But when she pressed the switch she was pleased to find she had electricity, and her hallway sprang into light. Her walking boots were there – the sturdy ones she hadn't bothered to take to England with her – and next to them the old roasting tin, still sticky with the residue of the sugar syrup she had left out for the bees on the morning of her departure. That was odd: she had no recollection of bringing it back inside.

Perhaps it was the dash in from the rain, and the sticking door, followed by the crowd of visual images, but it was only then that something else registered upon her notice. The smell. Above the background must of damp stone and unchanged air lay a warmer, sharper fragrance. Something which was always there, but which ought not to have been today: the ubiquitous scent of Les Fenils in winter. The scent of woodsmoke.

The note lay on the table in the kitchen, close to Catherine's empty tapestry frame. It began without any salutation, and was written in the careful, looped copperplate taught universally in French schools in the 1950s.

> *I've lit the woodburner – it's been so wet and sad this week. There's a navarin of lamb in the larder cupboard.*
> *Marie-Josèphe Bouschet*

'We've missed you.' Marie-Josèphe spoke with her back to Catherine the next morning, busying herself with coffee pot and cups.

'Thanks. Me, too.' Wanting to say more but unsure quite how, Catherine asked instead, 'How have things been?'

'Not so bad. Madame Volpilière had a bit of a chill. She kept to her bed for a week or so, but she's back on her feet now. Madame Mériel got the sheep safely back down, and the Vaillants, too. They were lucky the weather held off, because the rain began early this year. Almost as soon as the flocks were in – such miserable weather for you to come back to.'

Catherine nodded as she took the cup she was handed. 'And what about you?'

464

'Oh, keeping busy, you know. Seeing to the goats and the pig and the birds, it's work enough for one pair of hands, so I can't say I'm idle. And the girls have been up here nearly every day, with the grandchildren. I'm having my little Cécile this afternoon, in fact, while Claudine goes over to Mende to the chiropodist. She's been having a bit of trouble with her arches. Too much time on her feet, she says, chasing round after those terrors of hers. I'm picking Cécé up at four, from the *maternelle*. The boys are going to a friend's house, luckily, to play football.'

'It must be her last year there.'

'At the *maternelle*, yes. She goes to big school with her brothers next September. She tells me so nearly every time I see her.'

'I bet she does.' Just like Tom, the year before he left playgroup to go to the infants with Lexie. He was longing for a proper uniform, with thick grey knee socks like the older boys.

'She's not too old to be chasing the chickens, though, all round the yard if I didn't stop her. Heaven knows how they ever lay again after that child has been here. But she does love it up here at the farm.'

Ideas of selling up and moving to the valley appeared to have receded.

'And Jean-Marc?'

'He has plenty of work, he says, which he's glad of, though it meant he couldn't come to stay this year for the Assumption, as he usually does. And little Augustin is teething, the poor mite. They say his chin is red raw.' The grandmother rubbed her own chin, as if in sympathy. 'But what about your daughter? Will she come now, for that visit she had planned?'

'I'm hoping she might come soon – and my son and his girlfriend, too. They haven't fixed a date yet, but they talked about coming to stay all together, some time this autumn.'

'Even though the weather is so sad at this time of year?'

Catherine smiled. 'Even so.'

They sipped their coffee in companionable silence for a moment, before Marie-Josèphe volunteered, 'I bumped into Madame Méjan last week. On market day.'

'Oh dear, yes.' Something cold clawed at her insides. 'I still have her divan in the woodshed. It's been there since the end of July.'

And now it was October. That meant it was more than a year since her first invoice, her first receipt – for the work she did in Patrick's kitchen. More than a year, with no accounts filed, nor even a formal business registration. She would have to give back the divan. What she was doing must assuredly be illegal by now.

'I told her I was waiting to bring it back, in the trailer, when it's done. I told her we are partners, you and I.'

Partners. It was the same thing her husband had said to her, here in this kitchen, back at the tail end of last year. Catherine smiled gratefully, even while she shook her head. 'I don't know. There are problems, you see. I'm not certain I'll be carrying on with the work.'

'The divan, you mean? Or with furniture in general?'

'All of it. The sewing, the market stall. My business – everything.'

Marie-Josèphe set down her coffee cup with a startled clink and stared at Catherine. 'But why?'

She blew out her cheeks and let them slowly deflate – something she was aware of doing only when in France. 'It's the Parc National,' she said. 'Your husband seems to have been right about the park. They won't let me trade from Les Fenils. They want to stop me working here.'

The smooth, black bob tossed back emphatically. 'Then we shan't let them.'

'Well . . .' Catherine smiled wanly at her neighbour. 'I don't really see what I can do about it. I can't operate without a *siège social*, and they won't let me register up here as a seamstress, because it's not a rural profession.'

'What nonsense,' said Marie-Josèphe.

'Yes, but in order to file my accounts with the tax authorities—'

'Farming,' interrupted the Frenchwoman with a flourish of her small, brown hand. 'Farming is a rural profession.'

'Yes, but—'

'I am a farmer. I am registered here, to farm

the land. This is my *siège social*. I have Augustin's business seal, right there in the cashbox.' She indicated a cardboard shoe box at the end of the table, half hidden beneath a woollen scarf and a packet of pig vitamins.

Catherine simply sat and gazed.

'We can say that you work from here, too. You and I can be in business together – my animals, and your needlework. I am already your driver, am I not? The trailer is parked here, and the tractor. I could even store furniture for you sometimes, in one of the outhouses. Why should it not arrange itself this way, if we are partners?'

There were so many reasons why the idea was crazy, and why it would never work. Why no bureaucracy would ever swallow such a fabulously unlikely version of affairs. Except, perhaps, in France. Opening her mouth to protest, Catherine found instead that she was laughing; very soon her neighbour was laughing with her and holding on to her hand, and the two women both laughed until they were wiping tears from their eyes.

Then, coughing and swallowing, Marie-Josèphe said, 'But all this is only on one condition.'

Catherine looked across at her. 'Oh, yes? And what condition is that?'

'That you're the one who deals with the accounts.'

Lexie rang the following afternoon. It was only three days since they had spoken, and Catherine hadn't expected to hear from her quite so soon; since Mum's death, however, it seemed they neither of them liked to leave it so long between calls.

'Guess what, Mum?'

Catherine couldn't suppress a smile. The bounce was back, her daughter's joyful bounce.

'Tell me.'

'I've got a job. A new job, starting on Monday.'

'Oh, really?' It was not at all what she'd been expecting – or not so soon. So much for the novel.

'Yes, and it's going to be completely brilliant. Not that it's something I know anything about, at least not yet. It'll be another steep learning curve as far as the subject matter goes. But I've met the people, the editor and the chief features woman and one of the researchers I'll be working with, and they're totally committed, couldn't be more so. Really serious – but not too serious, if you know what I mean. They can have a laugh as well.'

'Well, that's wonderful, love.' Serious about what, this time? she wondered. Committed to what? Breeding Border terriers? The manufacture of soap? Bringing industry updates to the actuarial profession?

'The post's a flexible one, too: features and interviews, primarily, but news-gathering and bits of research as well, and a chance to have an input in layout. They seem to work very collaboratively, so everyone gets some say in editorial direction. Honestly, I'm so excited about it.'

'I can tell.' Grinning, Catherine decided she didn't much care what the publication turned out to be. So what if its glitter might fade in six months' time, or nine months or a year? For now she was content to savour the delight of hearing Lexie so happy.

'Only thing is, I have to start at once.'

'You said, yes. On Monday.'

'But what I mean is, they need me straight away, they've been really short-staffed, so I won't be able to get any holiday for a while. Not before Christmas, most likely. I'm really sorry, Mum, but it means I won't be able to come and see you just yet.'

'Oh, goodness, sweetheart, don't worry about that. I'm just so pleased you've found a job you're keen on. You can come and visit any time – Christmas, next year, whenever suits you. It doesn't matter at all. You know that.'

'I suppose so.' She sounded unconvinced.

'I'm not going anywhere,' said Catherine, realising the truth of it as she spoke the words. 'Whenever you want to come and stay, I'll always be here.'

'But I really wanted to come over with Tom and Mo. We were going to have such a great time. We'd got it all worked out. We were going to take you out and pamper you and have a proper family holiday. Now they'll come on their own and I'll miss all the fun.'

'It's a shame, I agree.'

'And without my gentle refining influence they'll probably have you crawling all round the woods looking for lesser spotted worzel warblers. And Mo will play the bagpipes at dawn and frighten all the neighbours.'

Catherine giggled. 'It is a pity,' she repeated, and meant it.

After Lexie had asked after things in France, and was preparing to ring off, Catherine asked her, 'So, what is it, actually, this magazine you're going to be working for? You haven't said.'

'Oh, didn't I mention it?' said Lexie innocently. 'Well, actually, it's something you'd be interested in, according to what Aunty Bryony says. In fact, I might even buy you a subscription for Christmas.'

A dark suspicion took hold of Catherine, but she was grinning, nonetheless. 'Go on.'

'I'm going to be working at *Pig Farming Today*.'

On her fourth day back at Les Fenils, when Patrick had still not called on her, she determined to go and see him.

There had been distant thunder in the night, sounding from somewhere the other side of Mont Lozère, over behind the head of the gorge. The rain had thundered, too, on the shingles over Catherine's head, merging with the noise of the storm and allowing her only fitful sleep. By dawn it had eased and by ten o'clock, after she had worked at her tapestry for an hour and drunk her third cup of coffee, the cloud had risen sufficiently to let in a watery sunlight, which gleamed faintly on wet rock and dripping leaves. It would have changed again in an hour, no doubt. She must go now.

She laced up her walking boots and donned her raincoat, taking with her a warm scarf and, as an afterthought, a jar of honey from the row on the shelf. He had his own supplies, of course, but she was versed enough now to be aware of the subtle variations produced in honey by flora and terrain. From the creamy paleness of *miel toutes fleurs* to the deep, sap-laden brown of chestnut honey, the palette ranged rich and diverse. Who could say how different her own product would be from that of the other side of the valley? And she knew he liked it for breakfast.

The air was fresh and sweet in spite of the damp, and the path gave softly underfoot. Walking was exhilarating and she lengthened her stride; her limbs felt warm and stretched well before she reached the wooden footbridge.

Her spell away from here – England, and the loss of her mother – had given her perspective. She was no longer prepared to let things coast along the way they'd been with Patrick, unspoken and unresolved. She'd had her fill of shadow boxing. Of course she was aware that confrontation might bring pain. But she needed things to be straight and open between them; for good or ill, she decided, the time had come for honesty.

He wasn't outside in his orchard or vegetable garden, nor at the woodpile. But when she pushed at the house door, calling his name, he appeared in a moment and took her hand in both of his. The brief pressure he applied was no more than expected of friendship, and his face was unreadable in the shadowy corridor room.

'Catherine,' was all he said, and led her through into the kitchen.

They stood with the table between them.

'So you're back.'

The first sliding untruth. She raised her chin and faced it down. 'You didn't know?'

Smiling, he bowed his head in concession, but he held her eye. 'I met Gaston Mériel, out on Wednesday morning with his gun. He told me you had come back.'

'But you didn't come to see me.'

He contemplated her levelly for a moment. 'I wasn't sure how welcome I would be.'

She had wanted honesty, but in the face of his directness, her resolution failed her. 'I-I've brought you some honey,' she said. 'It's part of my very first batch, that I took off in July, before . . . before I went away.'

She placed it down on the table, intending to pass it across to him, but instead he came round to her side and took it from her hand. He held it to the light and narrowed his eyes assessingly.

'A good colour,' was the verdict. 'Dark and woody. Forest honey.'

'It's thicker than it was when it went in.' For a moment she forgot herself as she peered with him into its tawny depths. 'Thicker and more opaque. I think maybe it's starting to chrystallise.'

His eyes flicked from the honey to her face. 'It will change, certainly. Honey does change after it's in the jar.'

They were standing close together, and it made her uncomfortable, made it more difficult to say the things she had come to say. She turned away and moved to take hold of a chair, pulling it out from under the table. It was a prop, something to do with her hands and body.

'Would you like some coffee?' he said, and she flushed because it looked as if she had been making to sit down, and because he was grinning at her – the old, teasing grin.

She'd already had too much caffeine this morning; it was making her even jumpier than she needed to be. But on the other hand, it might be simpler to talk with a cup in front of her.

'Thank you. Yes.'

While he spooned coffee into the percolator, she took off her raincoat and scarf and laid them over a chair, then sat down and looked about the room. There were her family of boar, on the back of the wooden settle; there, framed now and mounted on the wall, was the Black Beast of Gévaudan. Neither Patrick nor Catherine spoke, and the longer the silence continued, the more impossible it became to broach again the subject she had cut off. She sensed the first hot tightening of a headache; more coffee would only make it worse. She should leave now; she should go before it rained again; she should never have come.

'Tell me about the funeral.'

His words, as he set down the coffee between them, surprised her from her own thoughts, so that her answer came without consideration, without self-consciousness.

'Bloody unpleasant. If you mean the funeral itself, it was just something to be survived. For all our care and planning, it didn't feel as if it had much to do with Mum at all. Those places are so cold.' As if in demonstration, she gave a shiver now.

'And the family? Your children?'

And Bryony, and Bryony.

'It was wonderful to see them – or would have been, in other circumstances.' She frowned down at her cup. 'No, actually, it *was* wonderful, whatever the reason. My son's girlfriend was there – I hadn't met her before – and we all talked and talked.'

'Are they serious, do you think, your son and the girl?'

'Yes,' she said slowly. 'I think they are. I hope so. You know, it's funny,' she chewed her lip, still staring at her coffee, 'a family death, it ought to have been awkward for her, coming in as an outsider like that. But somehow because of Mum we were all rather . . . I don't know, open maybe, vulnerable or accessible or something. Why ever it was, we all seemed to talk more than I remember us doing in years.'

'And now you miss them?' He spoke gently.

'Yes,' she said at once; then, after consideration, 'Yes and no. They have their own lives, and I have mine. My daughter has a new job, in fact. She rang to tell me the other day.' Raising her eyes at last, she offered him a tentative smile. 'Writing for a pig farming magazine.'

He smiled back, but seemed in two minds about something. Having picked up his coffee cup, he put it down again.

'My daughter has no job yet.' He was looking at her, watching, perhaps, for a reaction. 'My daughter, Megan. She's in her final year now, at Keele – she finished her sandwich year in Montpellier this summer. Most of her friends have things lined up already for after they graduate, but not Megan.'

It was an olive branch, even if not a direct apology. Catherine swallowed; her mouth felt dry. Definitely too much caffeine.

'What is it she wants to do?'

'Her degree is in law with a languages component, and we always assumed she would be a solicitor. Recently, though, she seems to be having

476

second thoughts. Her mother – my wife, my ex-wife, that is – would still like her to apply for a training contract, join a firm in the City.'

They were skating dangerously close to Bryony again.

'And you? What do you think?'

A shrug. 'I think Meg must make up her own mind.'

She nodded, and they both sipped their coffee. It was hot and black and very strong, searing Catherine's throat and gunning straight for the seat of her headache. She must speak soon, or else go home; go home to be somewhere cool and quiet and alone.

Before she could change her mind, she began.

'Bryony said—'

But that was already no good. It was hard – too hard. This had to be not about Bryony, only about the two of them. About Patrick and herself.

He regarded her steadily, searching her eyes. 'What did Bryony say?'

Having begun in the wrong place, she could find no way on with it, and sat wretchedly in silence, avoiding his gaze. So instead it was Patrick who stepped across the gulf between them.

'You and Bryony are very different people.'

She dared not look up, and nor was she sure how to help him forward on this path, so he was obliged to try again, from a different angle.

'I'm no saint.'

'No.' *I don't need you to be,* she wanted to say. I don't need you to be a saint, or anything you are not. I just need you to be honest with me.

'I slept with Bryony because she wanted me to.'

Don't say it, she willed him. Don't say that it meant nothing.

'And – I cannot deny it – because I wanted to, as well. As I have told you, I am no saint.'

The coffee, bitter and swirling, settled uncomfortably in her stomach.

'You are different,' he continued. 'You are not Bryony. You are Catherine.' There was a pause, laden, expectant. 'I could never have taken you to bed for a little easy pleasure.'

Shocked into glancing up for a moment, she could almost have laughed at the intensity of his expression. Only a Frenchman could talk that way, surely, in all high-minded seriousness?

'With you, it could only ever be something . . . something more . . .' His hand grasped at nothing in the air.

It must be the caffeine, mustn't it, making her pulse race like this? Because he had taken her to bed, hadn't he – or she had taken him. And what had it been, this 'something', this 'something more'? What had it meant, for him?

'It has always been you, Cat-rine.' The close echo of her sister's words threw her off balance, so that the rest of what he had to say came through to her only slowly. '. . . ever since the autumn, when you strayed into in my kitchen like some rare wild creature from the forest. When you ate my wild boar with such delicious reluctance. I fell at once. I have been quite enslaved.'

Her face heated; her eyes pricked with tears. She stared at his hands, which had dropped to the table. This talk of enslavement was grandiloquent nonsense. It was not to be trusted; she was sure it was not.

'Well then, why . . .'

Why had he kept her at a distance, and teased her, and held back his past? Why had he said nothing?

He had no answer for her. That's why he was silent – or that was what she thought. How could there be any answer to her question?

She watched in curiosity as he moved his hand forward and took hold of her fingers, turning them over, before sliding his hand into hers, palm against palm. The pressure was warm and frank and human.

'I was daunted,' he said simply. She risked a glance up, and met no pretension in his face, no glint of mockery, of himself or of her, no lavish apology, but only a quiet bid for understanding. 'You were so self-contained, and I was daunted by it.'

It was such an inversion of her own experience of things that at first she was uncomprehending. She, the self-contained one, the forbidding one? He, the uncertain; he, the afraid? And yet as he continued silently to hold her hand and his words found meaning, she could begin to recognise the spark of truth in them.

Very gently, she laid her other hand over their two linked ones, and rubbed at the skin of his knuckles with her thumb.

'It's hard,' she began, battling to put words to what she felt. 'It's hard for both of us, to be open to another person. We're not twenty years old. We've been married, had children. Have children, I should say.'

They'd had loves; they'd had losses. Who knows how he'd been hurt, or by whom – and perhaps she would never know, and had no need to know. But you could be sure that he had been hurt, as had she, as had anyone of their age who had led a life.

'If that means we seem self-contained or self-sufficient or defensive – if we actually are that way, at times – then I'm afraid that's the way it is.'

She was looking at him steadily now, and it was he who glanced up, stricken, and then down again.

'But that doesn't mean . . .' She was struggling now. 'It doesn't mean we can't . . .'

In the end it was Patrick who helped her out, with a return of his infectious grin.

'Two self-contained, apparently immovable objects, and an irresistible force. At least, as far as I'm concerned it appears to have become irresistible. What do the laws of physics tell us? That the self-containment will have to crack.'

She managed to grin back, though it felt a little

wobbly. 'But what if the cracking is painful? Too painful, I mean, for one of us, or both?'

Patrick's shrug was quintessentially French.

'Shall we try the experiment and see?'

CHAPTER 28

REDEDICATION

The feast day of St Julien the Hospitaller falls on 12 February. This year, the morning of the festival dawned a transparent blue. At high altitudes, frost picked out the lines of crag and tree with almost unnatural clarity, and brushed the winter grass with silver.

The little town of St Julien de Valvert, sheltered from frost in the crook of its valley, came to life early, as it always did. Madame Peysasse folded back the metal shutters of her grocery shop front with a clatter and clang, startling a tortoiseshell cat which had been washing its paws in the middle of the main street. Propping her door wide, the shop-keeper began to carry out trays of onions and leeks and Spanish oranges and purple winter kale, and to set them out on the pavement trestles. Just along the street, Monsieur Folcher had been open for half an hour; the scent of warm vanilla announced the readiness of his first batch of morning brioches.

Already, at this early hour, the town appeared *en fête*. The strings of multicoloured bunting – stored in the back room of the Mairie and taken out twice a year, for St Julien's day and 14 July

482

– already hung across the street in zigzags and round the perimeter of the market square, looped from shop to shop. At the Mairie itself, the flags were out, not just the tricolour which hung there every day, but to its left the circling stars of the European Union and to its right the flag of the Lozère *département*, the fleurs-de-lys of France halved with the vertical bars of the Bishop of Mende in proud scarlet and gold.

By ten o'clock, a small wooden stage had been erected in the *place de l'église*. It was a simple affair, not much more than a sturdy adapted table with a set of steps behind. Père Amyot, wearing a leather flying jacket over his cassock and surplice, was busy testing the sound system for his makeshift pulpit, checking the wires which connected the microphone to the single box amplifier and thence to the old Peugeot car battery. Everything seemed to be in order.

A small crowd soon congregated. There were no tourists here; no outsiders at all, in fact, only the inhabitants of the town and its surrounding farms and hamlets, taking a morning's break from their work in field and yard and dairy to enjoy the promised spectacle. There hadn't been a procession for the patronal festival in years. Quite how many years the older members of the gathering debated in gaggles. Twenty-five, was it, or thirty? Marie-Josèphe Bouschet, remembering processions of the past, smuggled away a tear; Catherine, at her side, saw it and gave her arm a squeeze.

This year, the practice was to be revived for a reason, and that reason was leaning now against the church wall, over behind the wooden staging. The processional banner of St Julien the Hospitaller, restored to the full glory of its former days, was to be rededicated by Père Amyot at noon in a simple open-air service, after first being paraded through the streets of the town, following the route it used to take and escorted by the gathered townspeople.

Everybody was here. The Mériels and the Vaillants had left their goats and sheep and come to witness the festivities, accompanied by assorted dogs. Guillaume was looking uncomfortable in a stiff-collared shirt. Old Madame Volpilière was leaning on a cane to one side and the arm of Monsieur Mériel to the other. The schoolchildren and their teachers had the dispensation of a half day's holiday, and the Bouschet grandchildren were there with their classmates, chasing and tagging between the knots of adults. At the last minute, Madame Peysasse, Monsieur Folcher and the other *commerçants* locked their doors and joined the throng, together with Maître Dujol in his notary's suit and the youngest Mademoiselle Cassini from the Mairie, clutching her bunch of keys.

Over by the church wall, Père Amyot had taken off his leather jacket and slung it over the protruding corbel of a nearby buttress. Grasping the banner by its heavy oak pole, he began to turn it slowly, unwinding the stout fabric until the whole banner fell free. A few adjustments and a pull on the tasselled ropes brought the wooden crosspiece up into position and stretched the tapestry into view. Catherine could make out, across the few yards' distance, the detail of her own handiwork: the trees and rocks and the tumbling water; the saint with his arm upraised; and in the boat the hooded travellers, come to seek cure and renewal, or absolution, or simply a place to rest.

She let her eye roam round at the faces of her neighbours and, behind them, the old church and the other buildings of the square, venerable and solid in their grey-black granite; and above the shale roofs, mounting away beyond, the familiar backdrop of the hills, where walled green pastures led up to rockier steeps and the chestnut woods of home.

Everybody was here – except one. But as she scanned the faces again, suddenly there he was, weaving through the crowd towards her, looking straight at her and smiling.

1	21	41	61	81	101	121	141	161	181
2	22	42	62	82	102	122	142	162	182
3	23	43	63	83	103	123	143	163	183
4	24	44	64	84	104	124	144	164	184
5	25	45	65	85	105	125	145	165	185
6	26	46	66	86	106	126	146	166	186
7	27	47	67	87	107	127	147	167	187
8	28	48	68	88	108	128	148	168	188
9	29	49	69	89	109	129	149	169	189
10	30	50	70	90	110	130	150	170	190
11	31	51	71	91	111	131	151	171	191
12	32	52	72	92	112	132	152	172	192
13	33	53	73	93	113	133	153	173	193
14	34	54	74	94	114	134	154	174	194
15	35	55	75	95	115	135	155	175	195
16	36	56	76	96	116	136	156	176	196
17	37	57	77	97	117	137	157	177	197
18	38	58	78	98	118	138	158	178	198
19	39	59	79	99	119	139	159	179	199
20	40	60	80	100	120	140	160	180	200

201	216	231	246	261	276	291	306	321	336
202	217	232	247	262	277	292	307	322	337
203	218	233	248	263	278	(293)	308	323	338
204	219	234	249	264	279	294	309	324	339
205	220	235	250	265	280	295	310	325	340
206	221	236	251	266	281	296	311	326	341
207	222	237	252	267	282	297	312	327	342
208	223	238	253	268	283	298	313	328	343
209	224	239	254	269	284	299	314	329	344
210	225	240	255	270	285	300	315	330	345
211	226	241	256	271	286	301	316	331	346
212	227	242	257	272	287	302	317	332	347
213	228	243	258	273	288	303	318	333	348
214	229	244	259	274	289	304	319	334	349
215	230	245	260	275	290	305	320	335	350